LADY FOR
A SEASON

MELISSA ADDEY

For my father, a foundling who built his own loving family.

Have you read my other historical fiction series?
Download two prequel novellas FREE from my website

www.MelissaAddey.com

and join my Readers' Group, to be notified about new releases.

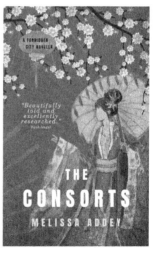

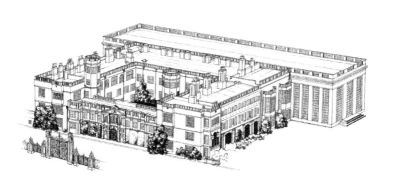

Atherton Park,
Buckinghamshire

England, 1813

CHAPTER 1
The Third Room

"You're wanted, Maggie."

Maggie rocked the baby girl she was holding. Number 18,723 was asleep, unaware that her weeping ragged mother had just left the room, probably never to see her again. She would go back out into the cold January streets of London, childless, with an endless absence in her heart, and her daughter would be raised by strangers.

The Foundling Hospital staff around Maggie were busy with other babies of varying ages, from a newborn up to a confused toddler who could only just walk, turning his face in all directions, searching for his mother.

Maggie laid the baby down in a basket. The nurse by her side was briskly completing the paperwork for the new child, noting her stated age of three months and the name her mother had given her, Mary. The name would be changed at once, of course, giving the child a fresh start in life, but her file would include these details, along with a description of her current clothing and any distinguishing marks. Noted and filed, too, would be the small scrap of lilac ribbon the mother had left, a token she could refer to if it were ever in her power to reclaim the child. Judging by her clothing, Maggie doubted this would ever be possible. The lilac ribbon would never be seen by the child. She would shortly be christened Betsey and given the surname of Guildford, one of the roads surrounding the Hospital. Betsey would be sent to a foster family in the countryside to be raised until her sixth birthday, after which she would be returned to the Hospital, there to live until she was fourteen, when she would be sent out into the world as a servant, while a boy child of the same age might be apprenticed to learn a trade.

"You're *wanted,* Maggie. Matron's in the parlour with a visitor." The girl sent with the message hovered anxiously in the doorway.

Maggie touched the sleeping baby's cheek. "God bless you, Mary," she whispered, knowing hers would be the last lips to speak the name the child's poor mother had given her. She wondered, as she always did, what her own true name had been, what token her mother had left for her, hoping against hope to one day be reunited. She had never dared look for her file, not even in the six years she had worked in the receiving rooms at the Hospital since turning fourteen herself. While most girls left the Hospital at fourteen, the Matron at the time had approved of Maggie's calm demeanour with the younger children and kept her as a member of staff.

The parlour was a small, neat room, with stiffly uncomfortable chairs, where Matron held weekly meetings with the chaplain or sometimes received visitors such as parents asking to reclaim their children. Possible benefactors or other visitors of greater importance would not be shown in here; they would be taken to the grandly painted and gilded 'court' room which

Maggie had only ever half-glimpsed through an open door, where the governors held their meetings.

Today Matron was accompanied by a smartly dressed man, perhaps forty years old.

"Come forward, Maggie," she said. "This is Doctor Morrison."

Maggie bobbed a curtsey.

The doctor inspected her. "She might do. I cannot take one of your younger girls, you understand, I need a steady hand, as we discussed. How old are you?" he asked.

"Twenty, sir," said Maggie.

"She is not particularly pretty," said the doctor to Matron approvingly.

Maggie did not feel hurt by this. It was her opinion also, having seen herself occasionally in a looking glass. Her plain brown hair and eyes, her pale skin, were unlike those girls at the Hospital who had rosy cheeks or sparkling blue eyes, ready with smiles for the lady visitors who sometimes gave out treats, favouring the children who were better looking than the rest. She knew she was plain, but as the sins of pride and vanity were frequently railed against by the chaplain during prayers, it was probably for the best.

"The girls of the Hospital are clean and neat and that is all that is required of them in the way of looks, sir," said Matron.

He nodded. "Indeed. And you will understand, of course, Matron, that good looks would only be a possible temptation which is to be avoided."

Matron's eyes narrowed. "Is the gentleman inclined to interfere –"

"Oh no, no, let me reassure you there has been no such trouble, he has never… I only meant to say that I would not wish to hire a girl with excessive charms. One does not wish to unnecessarily excite… but no matter, I can see that Maggie is a very likely sort of girl for the position I have in mind. Is she calm where others are excitable? Whilst the gentleman in my care is mostly very amenable, there can be moments when one must be firm to secure tranquillity and obedience."

"She is not a flighty girl by any means," Matron reassured him.

"Then I believe she will do very well."

Matron nodded. "She will be ready for you tomorrow morning as agreed."

The doctor rose and gave Matron a brisk bow. "You have been most helpful," he said. "Until tomorrow." Without any further word to Maggie, he left the room.

"Well, now, Maggie," said Matron. "You may sit down."

Maggie sat down on the hard chair, mindful to maintain a straight back, for Matron disliked slovenly posture. "Am I to assist the doctor in some way tomorrow morning, Matron?"

"Doctor Morrison came to me to help him find a most particular servant. As a physician, he specialises in the care of lunatics and those who are afflicted with such nervous excitement or melancholy as renders them unfit for usual and proper society. These poor souls are generally cared for in institutions such as Bedlam here in London, for those of the lower orders, or Ticehurst House, in East Sussex, for the gentry. But there are a few whose families have requested that they be housed privately, and such a one is a young man named Edward, who is in Doctor Morrison's care." She nodded meaningfully at Maggie, who gazed back, still uncertain of what was happening.

"You will join the household in which he lives. Your chief duty will be as a companion to him, to keep his spirits high but not recklessly so, and to give what domestic and attentive comforts may be appropriate when he is afflicted."

"I am to be his servant?"

"You will be a superior kind of servant," explained Matron, seemingly well pleased. "There is already a cook and a maid of all work there, as well as a local man from the village who will take care of any heavy work, so you are more in the way of a personal attendant. A gentleman would usually have a man-servant or valet, but it seems Edward does not respond well to men. He does better with women about him and so the good doctor has decided it would be best to humour him in this."

Maggie's head was full of questions but one above all was now on her lips. "I am to leave the Hospital?"

"Yes."

"For good?" Out into the world, all alone… a little flutter of fear ran through her.

Matron gave a small smile. "I know you have grown fond of the Hospital. It is all you can remember and all you have known. You have stayed with us beyond the usual time when you would have been sent out into the world. But this is a very great opportunity for you, Maggie, to be placed under the employ of a physician who ministers to the gentry and care for one of his private patients. I will be sorry to see you go, but I could not have asked for a better position for you."

"Who is the patient? You said he is a gentleman?"

"It is all I know of him and all you will know of him, Maggie. Discretion is vital to the doctor in his line of work. You are not to gossip with the maids or villagers or speculate on who his family might be. You need only care for him and be grateful for your good fortune."

"Yes, Matron." She clenched her hands together, nerves rising.

"There will not be time to make you clothes, as we did not know you would be leaving so soon. But Tabitha has already sewn herself two dresses for when she joins the milliner to whom she has been apprenticed and she is close to your size. You can take hers and she can start again."

"Where is the house where I will be working?"

"It is in a village named Harbury. In Warwickshire, to the north-west of London. It is more than eleven hours' travel, so with the short days it will take a day and a half. The doctor has his own carriage. He will collect you tomorrow morning and take you there."

Maggie tried not to gape. She had thought the doctor's patient would be somewhere in London. Instead, she was to travel away from everything she knew to another county, one she knew nothing of.

Maggie followed Matron to the sewing room, where Tabitha was informed of what was planned.

"You will help Maggie pack," said Matron. "I will send one of the boys to the dormitory with a trunk."

"Yes, Matron," said Tabitha.

"I'm sorry to be taking the dresses you made for yourself," said Maggie when they were alone. "There is no time to make my own."

Tabitha shook her head. "I have another two weeks before I begin at the milliner's, I can make more." She pulled out the two dresses she had made, identical grey wool, with long sleeves and high necks. "They're very plain, but Matron said they are serviceable and that I should not seek to draw attention to myself." She made a face.

"Perhaps when we are out in the world, we will be able to make dresses like the ones the benefactor ladies wear," said Maggie, knowing full well that such elegance would always be beyond their means as servants and apprentices.

Tabitha giggled. "Imagine, all silks and lace, with flowers and ribbons on our bonnets."

Between them they rapidly filled the small wooden trunk provided with Maggie's meagre possessions: one of the dresses, a petticoat, two shifts, three day caps, two night caps, two bibs and aprons, and a pair of stockings.

On her bed Maggie laid out the clothes she would wear on the morrow: the other dress, a shift, a petticoat, stockings, and a cap.

Matron reappeared in the doorway. "These are also for you, Maggie." She handed over a Bible and a folded letter on thick paper. "Keep them in your trunk and turn to them should you need guidance in the world."

"Yes, Matron," said Maggie.

"Ooh it's the letter everyone's given when they leave the Hospital," said Tabitha excitedly when Matron had gone. "Let's read it. I wanted to see Mary-Anne's, but she wouldn't let me."

They sat, heads together, and read the letter.

You are placed out as a servant by the Governors of this Hospital. You were taken into it very young, quite helpless, forsaken, poor and deserted. Out of Charity you have been fed, clothed and instructed; which many have wanted.

You have been taught to fear God; to love him, to be honest, careful, laborious and diligent. As you hope for Success in this World and Happiness in the next, you are to be mindful of what has been taught you. You are to behave honestly, justly, soberly and carefully, in every thing to every body, and especially towards your Master and his Family and to execute all lawful commands with Industry, Cheerfulness and good Manners.

You may find many temptations to do wickedly, when you are in the world; but by all means fly from them. Always speak the Truth. Though you may have done a wrong thing, you will, by sincere Confession, more easily obtain Forgiveness, than if by an obstinate Lie you make the fault the greater, and thereby deserve a far greater Punishment. Lying is the beginning of everything that is bad; and a Person used to it is never believed, esteemed or trusted.

Be not ashamed that you were bred in this Hospital. Own it; and say, that it was through the good Providence of Almighty God, that you were taken Care of. Bless Him for it.

Be constant in your Prayers and going to Church; and avoid Gaming, Swearing and all evil Discourses. By this means the Blessing of God will follow your honest Labours, and you may be happy; otherwise you will bring upon yourself Misery, Shame and Want.

It did not make for cheerful reading, the dire warnings making Maggie more nervous rather than less, and even Tabitha looked dispirited.

"Are you afraid?" she asked Maggie. "I know there was one girl, apprenticed out to a milliner like I'm to be, and she got beaten something awful. The governors had to intervene; it was that bad."

Maggie swallowed. "The Hospital do their best to provide good homes and occupations for us all," she said, trying to sound brave. "I will pray for you to be happy," she added, hoping to offer further reassurance both to herself and Tabitha.

"And I you," said Tabitha, giving her a fierce embrace.

Maggie was still anxious when it came time for bed, but she reminded herself that Matron had been well pleased with her prospects, and that was a thought worth clinging onto. She took off her brown and red uniform for the last time, slipped on her nightgown and got into the cold bed that had been hers for the past fourteen years. She lay in the dormitory, listening to the growing sounds of sleep around her, wondering in what kind of bed she would next lay down her head.

In the grey light of dawn, Maggie stood shivering, less from the cold than from shock. She wore the long, plain grey woollen dress Tabitha had sewn and a coat over it of brown drugget. The dress felt odd to her, for it had no waist like the Hospital uniform, gathered instead just below her breasts, though not tightly, for Tabitha had been more generously bosomed than Maggie. She had tied her hair in the two plaits she had always worn at the Hospital and pulled on a small woollen bonnet in the same brown drugget, tied on with a strip of the grey fabric that had made her dress. The same laced-up ankle-height boots she had worn for the past two years, worn but well polished, completed her outfit. Behind her were the gates of the Foundling Hospital. In front of her, the wide fields that surrounded it, where the children were brought out to take healthful exercise. Beyond the fields, a few scattered buildings, growing denser as she looked outwards, to the centre of London, around which a faint mist of the smoke from morning fires rose, grey against the yellow dawn.

The last time she had been outside the precincts of the Hospital she had been but six years old, returning from her foster home, which she now could barely recall, only a jumble of faces and names. Maggie had not been poorly treated, but there had been a briskness to her foster mother when young Maggie had craved affection, and she was frequently reminded that one day she would be returned "to the 'orspital," so there was never any doubt in her mind that as a foundling, she belonged entirely to the Hospital. The girls with whom she had grown up had gone into service long ago, but Maggie had been sheltered within the walls for an additional six years, and now the world outside the Hospital was large and frightening. There was a road coming up towards the Hospital from London and it was this that she watched, supposing that Doctor Morrison would arrive from that direction. It would have been some small comfort if Matron had stayed with her a longer, but the farewell had been quick and without emotion.

"Know your place and work hard, Maggie, and all will be well."

"Yes, Matron."

And she was gone.

A neat black carriage with two brown horses was approaching at a brisk trot along the road from London. Maggie took a deep breath. What if she should be snatched away by an unscrupulous man and taken… somewhere? Maggie was unsure where that would be exactly, but dire warnings were often issued by matrons making veiled threats about how cruel the outside world could be, how men might "take advantage" and be the "ruination" of an unwitting and too trusting girl. They never gave much in the way of particulars, all that Maggie had gathered from them was that men, in the outside world, were not to be trusted by girls who wished to remain godly and content. And yet here she was, standing outside the Hospital, about to get into a carriage with a man whom she had only met for a few moments, and become his employee.

The carriage pulled in close, and Maggie stepped back. It had rained heavily the night before and she did not want her clean new dress spattered with mud. The door swung open and there was Doctor Morrison. He nodded to her to step in, while the driver dismounted, pulled down the steps, then lifted her trunk onto the back, settling it on top of a far larger trunk already strapped in place.

Maggie climbed inside the carriage, which was impressively smart, lined with a dark grey wool and with seats which had been padded, so that they were softer than Matron's parlour chairs. There were even curtains for the windows, all made from the same fabric, with a narrow braid trim in a similar shade.

Doctor Morrison nodded to her. "Good morning, Maggie. I am glad to find you punctual."

"Yes, sir. Good morning, sir." She had been so intent on

the carriage she had barely looked at the doctor sitting opposite her.

The driver closed up the stairs and the carriage door, then resumed his seat. Doctor Morrison rapped on the roof of the carriage with his cane. The carriage moved forwards at once, jolting Maggie. She grabbed the edge of her seat to steady herself.

"Have you never travelled in a carriage before?"

"No, sir." She had been in a cart once, fourteen years ago now, but never since.

"You will be used to it by the time we reach Harbury. We will drive all of today and arrive there late tomorrow morning. We will stay at a coaching inn along the way."

"Yes, sir."

The carriage rocked along the road. Maggie dearly wanted to press her face to the window and look out, to observe the streets from this place of safety, but Doctor Morrison was speaking, and she had to pay attention.

"My practice is based in Leamington Priors in Warwickshire. It is known for its healthful spa waters and has long been a place for invalids to recuperate from their maladies. A fine Pump House and Baths will be opened there in the next few months, as demand has grown from people wishing to take the waters. Harbury is a village outside of the town, half an hour away by carriage from Leamington Priors."

Maggie nodded. She had never heard of Leamington Priors, nor of Harbury. Doctor Morrison might as well have been telling her he was taking her to the Americas.

"My patient, the young gentleman I spoke of, resides in Harbury, in a cottage which I procured for his convalescence. He has a delicate nature, prone to melancholy and occasional fits of fear or rambling, which his family felt were unsuited to his position in society. He was placed under my care some eight years back, leaving the school which he had until then attended."

"How old is he, sir?"

"Two and twenty years, which means he is now of age, of course, but his family feel he is safe and comfortable in my care, so he remains there."

Only two years older than herself. "Who are his family?"

The doctor frowned. "Discretion does not allow me to tell you that, Maggie. And I hope that you will not prove to be a gossiping sort of girl, who seeks out information of this kind. All you need to know is that he is of a good family who wish the best for him and that, due to his affliction, I consider it best for him to live as simply as possible. No airs and graces, nor formality. He lives a wholesome life, well provided for but with simple comforts. The servants are encouraged to treat him as they might a family member."

"What should I call him?"

"You will call him Edward."

That response was odd, implying that the doctor had re-named his patient, much as the foundlings were re-named as soon as they came into the Hospital. "Is that his real name, sir? Does he respond to it?"

"It is his Christian name. As I said, you will treat him as a loving sister or cousin might treat an afflicted brother or cousin. You will not use formalities with him, he has not responded well to them in the past. I believe they stir up too many memories of his previous distresses and confusions. Thus, you will call him Edward and he will address you as Maggie. There will be a sense of kindness and kin between you, which will help him to remain settled. I have studied many of the great practitioners in this field and they agree with me that the patient should be removed from all objects that act forcibly on the nerves and excite too lively a response. The insane do best when removed from their houses and friends and confined at some distance from home, preferably in the country, which is better for both privacy and opportunities for healthy exercise. Ivy Cottage is blessed with a large private garden. Part of your care of Edward will include daily walks within its confines. Maniacs respond well to kindness and tenderness, hence your position as his companion."

"Does he receive treatments, sir?"

"Most certainly. Aside from your attentive domestic comforts and healthful exercise, I myself regularly administer such treatments as bleeding, purging, vomiting and bathing. All of these are known antimaniacal remedies and have done him good. There is also a delivery of spa waters once a week, which enable him to take the waters in complete privacy. And there are other remedies, should he require them." He looked her over. "You may wonder at his manner of dress, which is very simple. But it is beneficial for my patients to be dressed warmly and comfortably but without overt elegance or reference to their prior station in life." He regarded Maggie seriously, making sure he had her full attention before continuing. "I ask furthermore that you do not inquire after his family name, his previous circumstances or any other such matters from his past, as they are only likely to cause him further distress. You will confine your conversation to his present life, for example the weather, the natural world around you, and so on. He likes to read. You need not concern yourself when he does so. The books I have provided are those I deem suitable for his current state of mind, inviting interest without excitement."

Maggie nodded and asked no further questions, gazing instead out of the window as they passed buildings and people going about their business, and the wider open spaces as they left the city's outskirts behind them.

For the most part, Doctor Morrison dozed. There were regular stops at coaching inns, large, noisy places where they could relieve themselves if necessary. They ate both their midday meal and dinner in one, Doctor Morrison in the main dining room, Maggie sent to a room where servants ate bread and cheese or ham with weak ale, rowdy rooms that she was glad to leave. They slept in the inn where they took their dinner, Doctor Morrison presumably in a private bedroom, Maggie dispatched to sleep with the maids of the inn. It was a cold chamber with four beds, though she was accustomed to both cold and dormitories, so it was not a hardship and the bed, at least, was relatively clean, without any sign of fleas. It was noisy, however, with snoring and boisterous singing from the inn downstairs late at night, as well as coaches and carriages coming and going. The second day of their journey, Maggie joined the doctor in dozing as they travelled through the countryside, occasionally waking to see farmland and tiny villages go by, one very much like another. Maggie was glad of her woollen dress and coat, which kept her warm enough.

In the late morning, the doctor sat up and showed more interest in their surroundings.

"We are close to Harbury," he declared. "I will introduce you to Edward as well as the rest of the household, then leave you for a few weeks, as I have business to attend to in Leamington Priors. I will return every two months to administer Edward's treatments."

Maggie straightened up and peered through the window. The countryside was undulating, with green fields, dotted with sheep

"The earth here is poor," said the doctor. "Farming yields smaller crops here than parts of the country with richer land. Of late there has been quarrying for limestone, which has employed many of the men from the village."

They came to the outskirts of a small village, in the centre of which stood a red brick windmill, three times the height of the two-storey buildings surrounding it.

"The new mill," said the doctor. "It brings more work into the village, for those who still raise grain crops."

Maggie nodded.

"That is All Saints' Church." The doctor pointed at a crenelated tower rising behind a grey stone wall. "The vicar will visit each week to pray with you both, as Edward cannot leave the grounds to attend church. Too many people around him might unnecessarily alarm or confuse him. The cook and maid, of course, may attend church on their own account."

The carriage pulled up outside a large cottage and the door opened at once, as though the occupants had been looking out for them. A stout older one emerged, wiping her hands on her apron, followed by a younger one with fair hair, adjusting her cap, no doubt to look neat for her employer.

"And this is Ivy Cottage. Good morning, Eliza, Agnes," said the doctor. "This is Maggie, Edward's new companion."

"Morning, sir," they chorused, bobbing curtseys. They

nodded pleasantly at Maggie, who nodded back, relieved that they appeared friendly.

"Eliza is the cook, Agnes the maid of all work," said Doctor Morrison. "Eliza, I hope you have a good meal for me. I've had nothing decent since we left London."

"Oh yes, sir," said the stout woman. "I've a rabbit pie and a good ham ready for you, baked bread just this morning."

"Good girl," said the doctor. To the driver he said, "I'll be ready in an hour or so."

Doctor Morrison followed Eliza into the house, leaving Maggie with Agnes and the driver.

"I'll fetch you a plate," said Agnes to the driver, simpering, for he was not a bad-looking man. She hurried back into the house.

"D'ye need a hand with this?" asked the driver as he lifted down Maggie's trunk.

She shook her head. "I can manage." It was not heavy, and it gave her something practical to do, since she felt uncertain. Should she walk into the house or wait to be lead there? The Doctor had simply gone in. She took a couple of steps forwards but Agnes was back before Maggie had even stepped over the threshold, carrying a plate with two thick slices of bread with ham and a tankard of ale.

"There's my girl," said the driver, winking at her, which made Agnes blush. "You'd better lead her inside," he added, pointing at Maggie. Agnes appeared disappointed to be so easily dismissed, but smiled again when he added, "When she's settled, you'll have time to keep me company while I get this down me, eh?"

Agnes lifted one side of the trunk and Maggie grabbed

the other. "Why, it don't weigh much," she said. "You ain't got much in the world, have you?"

"No," said Maggie. Almost everything in the trunk were things she had not had two days ago. To her it had seemed a sudden largesse of possessions.

"My, but you're plainly dressed," continued Agnes. "Are you one of them Quaker girls?"

"No," said Maggie. Although Agnes' own dress was a simple one, Maggie could see that more care had been put into making it look fetching, being made in a bold blue with puffed sleeves at the shoulder which only served to make Maggie's dress look even more plain than it had when she had first seen it.

Once inside, Agnes pointed right and left. "That's the kitchen, that on the other side's the parlour. There's an outhouse out the back. And a pump. We don't have to go to the village pump, got our own," she added proudly. "There's a big garden out the back, goes right down to the stream. We need to lug this upstairs."

They made their way awkwardly up the creaking stairs, into a corridor with three doors.

"This is ours," said Agnes, opening the first one to show a plain room with three single beds neatly lined up. There was a small wooden table with a jug and a basin for washing, and a chamber pot in the corner of the room. Two of the beds had a chest at the end, the third, closest to the door, did not.

"That's your bed. So you can go to him easily in the night," Agnes added.

They placed Maggie's trunk at the foot of her bed and left the room.

"That's Edward's room," said Agnes pointing at the next

door. "He'll come down when he's called for. Anyway, you must be half starved. Shall I make you a plate an' all?"

Maggie nodded gratefully. She wondered what was behind the third door but did not want to seem nosy.

Back downstairs, Maggie caught a glimpse of the doctor in the parlour, sitting down to a good spread, attended by Eliza, who was answering his questions about provisions and firewood supplies. Maggie followed Agnes into the kitchen, where the maid put together a plate like the one she had given the driver.

"I'll just see how Will's getting on," she said, sidling towards the door, no doubt keen to make every moment count with the driver.

Maggie sat at the table and ate. The bread and ham were both good quality and she had been given a large portion. The water was fresh and cold, and there was ale, too, but she drank only a little, unused to the taste.

She had just finished eating when she heard the doctor calling her name and presented herself in the parlour. It was a good-sized room, with two armchairs and a fireplace, a shelf with a few books, a small pianoforte, a table and two wooden chairs in the corner, where the doctor was sitting, Eliza standing to one side.

"Ah Maggie," he said. "Be so good as to fetch Edward for me. I would like to see him before I go, and I need to introduce you. He will be in his bedroom."

Maggie made her way back up the stairs and paused outside Edward's room before knocking.

"Come in."

The young man seated by the window was bent over a large book. The light streaming through the window illuminated his unfashionably long shoulder-length fair wavy hair, turning it golden and bringing something ethereal to his figure. She could tell by his long legs that he was tall, but there was in his posture a desire to stay small. His shoulders were hunched, his arms close to his side, his neck bent downwards. His clothing was neat and clean but by his dress Maggie would have thought him a servant. He wore a brown woollen suit with a baggy jacket and breeches, a waistcoat in a lighter brown, thick woollen stockings and sturdy shoes, like her own. His shirt was a cream colour, but he did not wear a high collar as the governors of the Hospital had done.

"I'm Maggie, I'm to be your new... companion."

He looked up, startled at the unfamiliar voice, then unfurled to his full height, even taller than Maggie would have guessed. His head came up last, so that Maggie could see his face. His skin was very pale, and he was overly thin for such a tall man, but his eyes, when they met Maggie's, were a rich deep blue. They reminded her of a ring she had once seen on a visiting lady's hand and for a moment she forgot her manners and stared.

The man bowed, a slow graceful movement, not the sharp half-dips that most men gave. "Maggie. My name is Edward." His voice came out deeper than Maggie had expected from a man of such slight build.

She bobbed a curtsey. "Edward." It felt odd to call him by his first name, as though he were one of the children at the Hospital in her care, but, she reminded herself, he *was* to be in her care, and perhaps thinking of him as a child was best.

"Doctor Morrison is in the parlour and would like to see you."

He blinked at the name, not quite a flinch, but there was something fearful about it, there and gone in an instant.

Maggie stepped back onto the landing and he followed her down the stairs, ducking his head under a low beam before they entered the parlour.

"Ah, Edward," said Doctor Morrison, standing up to greet them as they entered. "You have met Maggie I see. She will be your new companion. And are you well, in yourself?"

"Yes, sir."

The doctor looked him up and down, having to lift his chin to do so, since Edward was a head taller than him. "Yes, yes, you seem well enough, I am glad to see."

Maggie thought it an odd assessment, for Edward was pale and too thin for his height, but perhaps he had been worse in the past; the doctor must know his business.

"Well, now," continued the doctor. "I must make hasten to Leamington, for I have been gone more than two weeks. Edward, I will return in a month's time for your treatments. Maggie, Eliza and Agnes can answer any questions about the household that you may have." He came to the door, where Eliza stood waiting with his hat. "Eliza, I commend you for a good meal. Good day to you both."

"Good day, sir," they replied in unison.

He strode out through the front door which Eliza was holding open. Maggie caught a glimpse of Agnes hastily snatching the plate and tankard back from the driver and bobbing a curtsey to the doctor as he climbed into the carriage, as though she had only been there to fulfil her housework duties. The driver winked at her, cracked the whip and the carriage drove away.

Now that the doctor was gone Maggie felt at a loss. She was

to be a companion; she was to keep Edward contented and well in himself. At the Hospital there would have been the daily routine of the children being woken, washing, eating, being taught their lessons, attending prayers and so on. What should she do here? What sort of routine was Edward accustomed to? Perhaps she should see what the garden had to offer. The doctor had spoken of healthful exercise, after all, and walking in the garden must form a part of this. She returned to the parlour, where Edward was sitting in one of the armchairs close to the small pianoforte which sat in an alcove of the room, once again holding a book.

"Shall we walk in the garden? It is a fine day."

He rose at once without speaking and headed out into the hall. Maggie followed, glad that he was so easily compliant with her first suggestion, but at the back door he opened it and stepped back, still holding it, and stood still. Was he refusing to go out? She looked up at him, confused, but he made a small gesture with his other hand, indicating that she should go out before him, that he was holding the door open for her.

Maggie had never had someone hold a door open for her. She had seen the governors do so for lady visitors, or the servants and staff do so for the governors. She had held many doors open herself for her superiors, but now Edward was treating her as though she were his superior, or a lady. She hesitated, but ducked her head in awkward thanks and stepped out into the garden. Perhaps he meant to get rid of her, would shut the door behind her and leave her standing outside like a fool, but he did not. Instead, he followed her.

"Thank you," she murmured, oddly touched that this silent man should show such courtesy to one who was, after all, his servant.

The garden was very large, stretching out ahead of them. It was enclosed on both sides with high hedges, presumably for the privacy the doctor was so insistent on, but Maggie could not see to the end of it. It began with a lawn and a few bare rose bushes, but sloped downwards further along. Glancing at Edward, Maggie walked forwards and he, still silent, kept pace alongside her.

"Do you walk here every day?" she asked after a few steps.

"Yes."

"And about the village? Or further afield?"

"I am not permitted to leave the garden."

They walked on a little further. The ground sloped downwards, towards a row of trees and low bushes, before rising steeply beyond, up a forested hill.

"What is at the bottom?" she asked.

"A stream," he said.

"Will you show it to me?"

Silently, he walked with her to the bottom of the slope, to where bushes and trees rose up and now Maggie could hear the gurgling of a stream, which they shortly came to. It could only be knee deep, might dry up in summers, but for now it wound its way between the bushes, forming tiny pools here and there.

"It's very pretty," she said. "Are there animals?"

He had been looking at her, but when she turned towards him his eyes slid away, as though her gaze was too much for him. He ducked his head but did not reply.

Maggie knelt at the side of the stream and let the cold clear water wash over her hands, then stood, drying them on her apron.

"Frogs." His voice was low, a murmur.

"I'm sorry?"

"I see frogs, in springtime. A fox most evenings. Deer in the summer, they come to drink when there's not much water about." He was looking beyond her, up at the woodland, as though seeing the animals in his mind and for a moment she wondered whether he was seeing things that were not there, but he seemed to know what she was thinking, for he added, "Not now, they come when they think no-one is near."

"Do you hide so they can't see you and be scared?"

He nodded.

"I've never seen deer nor a frog," she said. "I saw a fox once, a long time ago. I should like to see more animals. There were none at the Hospital."

"Hospital?" He sounded scared. Had he been kept in somewhere like Bedlam? Everyone in London was afraid of the likes of people that were kept there and indeed of the gaolers, who were said to be cruel.

"The Foundling Hospital," she said. "I was a foundling and raised there. When I was fourteen I became part of the staff there, before I came here to you."

"A foundling."

"Yes."

"Your mother gave you away."

Maggie hesitated. Having seen so many women bring their children to the Hospital, she could not think harshly of them. They came weeping, they came with bruises or dressed in rags, they came out of desperation, and they left pathetic tokens of their intentions to one day return for their children, however unlikely that might be. "Yes. She gave me into the care of the Hospital, that I might be raised well and not suffer hardship."

He gazed at her for a moment before his eyes slid away again. "My mother sent me here."

"To make you well again," she said gently, meaning to comfort him.

"So that I would not embarrass her," he corrected, and Maggie heard the misery under it, the grief of being unwanted.

"How long have you been here?

"Several years now."

"Always with Eliza and Agnes?"

"Yes."

"And any other people?"

He looked down. "There was a man when I first came. Then a woman. Before you. Bridget."

Maggie thought it better not to ask more questions. He seemed unwilling to give much detail and she was mindful of Doctor Morrison's instructions not to inquire overmuch into her patient's history.

"How did you manage to see the animals?"

"I sat quiet for over an hour each time."

That was reassuring. If her patient's idea of passing the time involved sitting in silence out of doors watching wild animals, he did not sound dangerous.

"Shall we try now?" she asked.

He glanced at her, as though surprised. "To watch for the animals?"

"Yes."

He nodded and settled himself on the bank. Maggie watched him and sat in a similar position, knees up, arms wrapped about her legs, making herself small and still.

Perhaps an hour slipped by in the cold January sunlight. Edward's fingers and toes were growing numb with cold, but he did not want to move. Not because of the animals, for twilight would have been a better time to wait for them than broad daylight, but because of her. Maggie. He had been expecting, dreading, another Bridget, a hard-faced, hard-voiced woman who had barely tolerated his presence, who had seen it as her task to strip from him any of his small pleasures in life. And here instead was a young woman of his own age, with bright eyes and a gentle voice, who was prepared to sit with him in the cold for the hope of seeing a glimpse of a wild animal. He wondered how long she would stay after she had seen what the role would entail, whether she would be frightened away by his strangeness, his wrongness. Everyone had always told him he was wrong and different, so it must be true. Would she be able to bear life at Ivy Cottage? He hoped so, but he did not want her to suffer for his strangeness.

"We should go back in," he said. "It is too cold to stay out long."

She turned her head and smiled at him. "My nose is cold," she said. "But I would like to try again one day."

Slowly they got to their feet and made their way back up the steep bank. At the top, Edward slipped. He flung out his arms to help himself balance and Maggie grabbed his hand, steadying him.

"Thank you," he said.

She laughed. "I cannot have you fall into the stream in this weather," she said. "You would die of a chill and Doctor Morrison would say I was a poor companion."

He managed a smile as they reached the safer ground of the garden and once again he held the door open for her, which she appeared both awkwardly pleased by and grateful for. But when she went into the kitchen to speak to Agnes and Eliza, he stood in the hallway, looking down at his own hand, trying to hold onto the feeling of how she had held it. Her cold fingers tightly clasping his, helping him find his feet in that moment of unsteadiness. It had felt like care, and he had forgotten what being cared for felt like.

On their return to the house, they went into the parlour. Agnes was pumping water and Eliza was cooking. It was clear that, while pleasant women, they had their own work to do and saw Edward as entirely belonging to Maggie. So far, she had seen little of the lunatic about him, but she supposed that would reveal itself in due course. He was currently choosing a book, after which he settled himself into an armchair.

"What do you do, most days?" she asked him.

"Read."

"All day?"

"There is not much else to do. The vicar, Mr Robertson, brings me new books when he can."

Maggie perused the books on the shelves. There was a large handsome Bible, a leather-bound Atlas so heavy that Maggie's wrists felt weak when she lifted it, as well as works by Shakespeare and Milton, along with books that had evidently been used to educate Edward: *The history of England, from the earliest times to the reign of George II.* by Dr. Goldsmith; *The British Youth's Instructor: Or, A New and Easy Guide to Practical Arithmetic*; A *Short Introduction to English Grammar: with Critical Notes*; *A Tour Thro' the Whole Island of Great Britain. Divided into Circuits or Journies* by Daniel Defoe, and others of a similar nature. Clearly his education had continued, even though he was not at school.

"What do you like to read?"

"I prefer books on the natural world," said Edward. "Botany, or animals, geography."

They ate a simple supper of pease soup with bread and butter, hot and filling, served to Edward and Maggie in the parlour, while Eliza and Agnes ate in the kitchen, though the food was the same. Darkness had already fallen and shortly after supper they retired to the bedrooms.

"Leave a candle burning," said Eliza to Maggie. She offered her a lamp made of metal, which surrounded the thick candle within, allowing light to emerge only through many tiny holes, thus avoiding the risk of fire. "You may need it if you have to go to him in the night."

"Does he wake often?"

Eliza nodded without offering further information, busy divesting herself of her clothing and changing hurriedly into a nightgown against the cold. Carefully, Maggie placed the candle in its holder on top of her trunk, where it glowed softly.

The room was chilly, but the blankets on the bed were thick and after all the new experiences and lack of sleep the previous night, Maggie fell asleep.

"HELP!"

Maggie awoke with a start in the darkness, unsure of where she was. The Hospital? No, she had left there… the inn? No, no, she was in Ivy Cottage, and the shouting she had just heard was a man's voice, it –

"PLEASE!"

Eliza sighed. "He's having a nightmare. You must go to him."

Fumbling in the unaccustomed space, Maggie grabbed at the lamp and made her way along the corridor into Edward's room.

"PLEASE NO! DON'T!"

"Edward!" she whispered, scared by the fear in his voice. "Edward, it's me, Maggie."

"NO!"

It was hard to make out much in the dim light, but Maggie crept forward until a flailing arm caught her about the waist. She grabbed hold of it, felt for his hand, clasped it. "Edward. Edward, be calm. All is well."

He did not shout again, only gasped, panting for breath. His eyes opened and he stared wildly about the room.

"Edward? Are you awake?"

"Yes." His voice was tiny after the shouting and her shoulders relaxed, relieved that the crisis had passed.

"All is well, I think you must have had a nightmare."

"Yes. I am sorry to have troubled you." He sounded fearful.

Maggie knelt by his bed and touched his cheek, which was wet with sweat. She used the sheet to wipe his face, still clasping his hand. "What did you dream of?"

"I do not recall."

She did not believe him, his shouts had been too intense for that to be true, but she did not ask further questions, only stroked his hand for a few moments.

"Are you well now?" she whispered.

"Yes," he murmured, and she left the room and returned to her bed.

Eliza and Agnes were asleep again; evidently they were accustomed to Edward's nightmares, but Maggie was shaken by how frightened he had sounded, caught up in some dark horror in his mind. What fears plagued him, what had happened in his young life to lead to such shouts of terror in his dreams? She lay tensely for some time, wondering if he might scream again, but there was no further sound from him and at last she fell asleep, to unsettling dreams of her own, in which hands reached out to her in the darkness and yet she could not see whose hands they were.

In the morning, she washed and dressed and came down to the kitchen, where Eliza was chopping vegetables.

"He's already up. He wakes early," she said, nodding towards the parlour. "Agnes'll bring your breakfast."

"Does he have nightmares often?" Maggie asked.

Eliza nodded. "Most nights."

"*Most* nights? Why?"

Eliza shrugged. "He is a lunatic," she said, matter-of-factly. "It's part of his affliction. I'll send in breakfast directly."

Maggie found Edward buried in a book again and wondered if this had been his life, a silent solitary world of books, perhaps taking him through their pages into other worlds and places, providing companionship and something to occupy his mind during the day, dark nightmares haunting him at night.

"Good morning, Edward."

"Good morning, Maggie. I am sorry to have frightened you last night." He swallowed. "I do not sleep well."

She gave him a bright smile. "You did not frighten me, but I am sorry you do not sleep well. We must try to remedy that."

He stared down at his book again, as though what she was saying was not possible, but he did not wish to argue the point with her.

Agnes brought a tray of sliced bread, a toasting fork, butter, preserves and a pot of tea. Maggie poured tea for them both and sat before the fire to toast the bread. It was good bread, and the preserves were well made, but Edward ate only a single slice of unbuttered toast before returning to his book. She resolved to keep him better occupied than he had been so far. That might tire him out for the nights.

"Shall we go into the garden?"

He followed her to the back door, holding it open again for her. They stood for a moment in the cold morning air, the frosted grass before them.

"We should build a bench so we can watch the animals without sitting on the cold ground," she said.

He stared at her as though she had suggested something very odd.

Maggie had seen an old, rotted tree trunk lying half in the stream the day before and headed there at once. "Help me pull this up," she called and soon they were struggling up the bank with it.

"We can borrow a few logs from the woodpile," she said, and set off back towards the house at a brisk stride. Edward, with his longer legs, quickly caught up with her.

Arms filled with logs, they returned and built a lopsided structure that bore a passing resemblance to a bench. Once on a wet day at the Hospital they had used such logs for a walkway across a courtyard, though they had been scolded for it and made to take the muddy logs back to the woodpile where they belonged, but here there was no-one to scold.

This seat became part of their morning routine in the following days. Wrapped in their coats and carrying hot tea, they spent hours each day perched on the bench, sometimes speaking of something, such as parts of the stream icing over, sometimes in silence. Many days passed before they were rewarded by a flash of orange as a fox passed. The next day, they marvelled at the careful cautious approach of a group of deer, come to drink at the stream. Once, as the sky grew dark, they caught sight of a badger, waddling through the undergrowth, and Maggie, eyes alight with excitement, nudged Edward to look. Her wide smile brought a smile to his face. Her excitement was contagious.

The nightmares still came every night without fail, so punctually that Maggie would sometimes wake a moment before Edward cried out. She accepted them as part of her life here, even though she hoped over time they might lessen, if Edward were to be better distracted.

Each Sunday, the vicar, Mr Robertson, visited and insisted on reading them the entire day's sermon, then praying with them. He was a kindly man, but treated Edward as though he were a child, going so far as to pat him on the head when leaving. Then again, he had known him since he was fourteen, so perhaps in his aging mind Edward was still only a boy. He made up for it by bringing books with him, which Edward devoured and shared with Maggie.

They took turns reading to one another, poring over books together. Their favourites were those on botany and agriculture. The illustrations were beautiful, and they tried to identify everything in the garden and patch of woodland over the stream, sometimes carrying the books with them to their bench and reading them there until they were called for meals.

Eliza was a good cook. Maggie, for the first time in her life, knew what it was to be full at every meal. The Hospital had not starved the children, but there had never been second portions, and the food had been tediously monotonous and often watery. Breakfast and supper had mostly been bread and butter or gruel. In the middle of the day, dinner was generally cheap cuts of meat such as stewed shins of beef with root vegetables, or boiled mutton. At Ivy Cottage porridge was common at breakfast, but it was thick and usually served with cream and honey. Dinner was often a stew, with rabbit, beef or mutton, potatoes and greens, but thicker and better flavoured than any Maggie had previously known. For supper they might have bread and cheese with a hot broth and there might be a treat such as pound cake or biscuits during the day, for both Eliza and Agnes had a sweet tooth.

"The doctor don't stint us," Eliza said to Maggie, when Maggie expressed surprise at being offered cream and honey in her porridge. "He ain't stingy, says we must eat good wholesome food and dress warm in the winter."

Maggie and Edward ate together in the parlour, while the other two women ate in the kitchen, preferring to chatter together, for they regarded Edward as a patient and treated him as such. They were kindly enough but treated him with a pitying air.

"'Tis a shame he's a lunatic," Eliza said, one day after Maggie had been there two weeks. "He's handsome enough, if he had a little meat on him, but he can't help being afflicted, I s'pose. Poor lad."

"Has he got better or worse since you've known him?"

"Quieter," was Eliza's considered response. "More docile-like. When he were a little boy he'd try and run off, but the doctor weren't happy about that, gave him a whipping and more treatments till he calmed down. You'd hear him crying when he were first brought here of a night, made your heart hurt to hear him, but he wouldn't take comfort from anyone. These days, he's quiet enough, apart from his nightmares. Watches his animals down the garden, reads his books, eats and sleeps and lets Doctor Morrison treat him without fighting back. So I suppose you could say he's improved."

Maggie soon found out why Edward was so thin, for he barely touched his food. He would sit and stare at it, eat a few mouthfuls as though they might harm him, with a fearful air, each mouthful chewed for a long time before swallowing as though it were painful to do so.

"Do you not like the food? Would you prefer something else? Eliza is a good cook, I am sure she could make something to tempt you," Maggie tried once but he only shook his head as though she did not understand. He took his porridge plain and refused any of Eliza's tempting treats.

Once a week, Walter would come to the cottage. He was a taciturn man from the village whom Doctor Morrison had employed to travel once a week to Leamington Priors and return with a bottle of the sulphur-smelling spa waters, of which Edward was to take a small cup each day. Walter also brought food supplies as ordered by Eliza and did the heavy chores, cutting and stacking wood, pumping several buckets of fresh water each day for Eliza's kitchen, and more for Agnes to do the laundry once a week. He had a dappled grey pony named Daisy with a small cart for errands and Maggie would sometimes offer Daisy a wizened apple from storage, still sweet but wrinkly, which the horse accepted with much snuffling and good-natured nudges of her velvet nose against Maggie's hand.

"Walter is at the door," Maggie said to Edward one day. "Do you want to give Daisy an apple with me? She does love them so."

"No," he said, from the depths of his book on astronomy, but there was an odd crack to his voice and his shoulders tightened. She was reminded of the first time she had seen him, the impression of fear which had receded since they had come to know one another.

"Does Edward not like Daisy?" she asked Agnes, who was sweeping the hallway as she passed.

Agnes's eyes widened. "Why? What has he done this time?"

Maggie stopped, confused. "Done? He has done nothing. I only asked him if he wanted to feed Daisy an apple, but he seemed vexed."

Agnes glanced both ways and dropped her voice to a whisper. "He's afraid of horses."

"Afraid of them? Why?"

"I don't know. But when he first come here, Walter brought Daisy round to the door, like he always does, and Edward was coming out of the parlour and Daisy whinnied at him and he screamed, not just a bit surprised like but terrified. He went back into the parlour and slammed the door shut and he won't never go near the door if there's the sound of hooves or he knows Walter's about. I expect it is the lunacy," she pronounced. "Being afraid of things one ought not to be. You've heard his nightmares. They ain't normal for a grown man, neither is fearing horses. It's all part of his affliction. That's why the doctor must come and treat him, in the third room."

"The third room?"

"Upstairs."

Of course. The third room. Maggie had dismissed it in her mind, thought it was perhaps a storeroom. Curious, she climbed the stairs and opened the door.

Nothing. A chair in the shadowy corner of the room. Another chair. A small table with a drawer to one side. A large ceiling hook, perhaps from usage as a storeroom in the past. Otherwise, it was clean and empty. Edward had spoken of a male companion before Bridget, who might have been put to sleep in this room, for it would not have been appropriate for him to share a room with two women. Just a disused bedroom, nothing more interesting.

In February it snowed. Maggie woke to a blueish light and saw the garden changed to a white blanket. Eliza muttered about delays to Walter's deliveries and Agnes tutted about trying to bring in water and wood, but Maggie hurried out in the garden without even waiting for breakfast or Edward to open the door. He followed her.

"At the Hospital, if it snowed, they'd let us out to play in the snow if we were good," she said, turning to him with a smile.

"To play?"

Her face was bright with excitement. Those days were her happiest memories, the short but glorious wild freedom of being allowed out to play in the snow, let loose from the monotonous routine of each day. Snapping icicles from low-hanging rooftops, throwing snowballs, sledging on whatever they could find, including broken shovels or old sacks.

He shivered. "It is very cold, would you not prefer –" He

broke off as she scooped up a handful of snow and threw it at him, hitting him squarely in the chest.

Edward gasped and stepped back, then tentatively scooped up a handful himself, at which she picked up her skirts and ran down the garden, his first attempt missing her by inches. "You will have to try harder than that!" she called to him, still running.

For a moment he stood, the cold snow in his hands, staring at her, then laughed and ran after her, stumbling over hidden molehills and fallen branches, but gaining on her, his second shot catching her shoulder.

She turned to face him, laughing, a ball already flying towards his face, but he ducked just in time, and it sailed over his shoulder. "So you do know how to play," she called, both of them quickly stooping for more snow, aiming, both missiles landing at the same time, on her skirts and his arm.

By the time they returned to the house, their clothes were wet through and both of them had to change before returning to the parlour. Maggie took longer and Edward found himself alone in the parlour, before the roaring fire Agnes had set when she had seen the state of them, and the hot tea and ginger-cakes Eliza had made. He needed none of them. There was a warmth inside that did not come from fires or tea, but from running, which he had not done for many years, from hurling snowballs and making them as fast as he could, from ducking and chasing. From laughing. His heart still beat fast, as though he had suddenly been brought back to life from the dead, life itself racing through his body. How many years had it been since he had laughed so much? Since he had been so happy? Had he ever? He could not recall.

Maggie returned to the parlour, hair still damp but in dry clothes and smiled at the sight of Edward's face. He greeted her with a warm smile, but his cheeks, always so pale, were flushed with a rosy glow.

"I have not laughed so much in years," he told her and there was wonderment in his voice.

She chuckled as she poured the tea. "Then prepare yourself to laugh a great deal more over the coming days, for Eliza says the cold is staying and there may be more snow tomorrow."

The days that followed were some of the happiest either of them had ever known, for the snow fell again and again, until they were almost up to their knees in the garden, their change of clothes always hanging up in the kitchen to dry, despite Eliza's tutting at the space they took up and Agnes' amazement that they should enjoy being out in the cold so much. Maggie worried that their play might make Edward's spirits what Doctor Morrison had called "recklessly high," but he was so much happier, running and laughing, more animated than she had seen him thus far. It must surely be good for him.

When the sparkling snowy weather turned wet and muddy by the end of February, forcing them to stay indoors on most days or risk Agnes' wrath at their muddy footprints, Maggie sought other entertainment. She found a pack of cards in the drawer of the table and Edward asked her if she knew how to play a game called vingt-un.

"No, will you teach me?"

"You must get to twenty-one points with the cards you are dealt, one card at a time. No higher, or you lose."

They played for hours, exclaiming over wins and losses, but other distractions were needed for the long, wet days.

"Can you play?" asked Maggie, looking at the pianoforte.

He shrugged. "A little."

"I have never heard you play."

"I was not encouraged to do so."

"Will you play for me?"

"What would you like me to play?"

"Do you know *Silent Worship*?"

He rose without answering and sat at the pianoforte and began to play. With no hesitation, he played from memory, and played well.

Midway through the piece, she said, "Start again."

He frowned. "Why?"

"Please?"

He began again but this time Maggie stood to sing.

"Did you not hear my lady
Go down the garden singing
Blackbird and thrush were silent
To hear the alleys ringing."

He stopped playing and stared at her. "Where did you learn to sing like that?"

"We all sang in the choir. Some of the great composers played concerts to raise funds for the Hospital. Handel was one of its most ardent supporters, he wrote a piece called the Foundling Hospital Anthem. You play well, will you not continue?"

He played and, by the third verse, he joined in with her and she was surprised to hear a strong, deep voice from him, not what she would have expected from his slender frame.

"Oh, saw you not my lady
Out in the garden there

Shaming the rose and lily
For she is twice as fair

Though I am nothing to her
Though she must rarely look at me
Though I can never woo her
I'll love her 'till I die

Did you not hear my lady
Go down the garden singing
Silencing all the songbirds
And setting the alleys ringing

Surely you heard my lady
Out in the garden there
Rivalling the glittering sunshine
With the glory of golden hair."

They finished, grinning at one another.

"You have kept secrets from me," Maggie said. "Now that I know you can play and sing so well, we must do so more often." She wanted to ask when he had been taught to play, but mindful of not bringing up his past, she refrained.

"*I* have kept secrets? When you sing like a… a nightingale?"

When Maggie awoke the next morning, she could hear a familiar man's voice and when she made her way into the parlour, she found Doctor Morrison eating breakfast.

"Ah Maggie, good morning to you. I have arrived for Edward's treatments. We will spend most of the day on them, and I will return to Leamington Priors this evening when we are done."

She made a curtsey. "Yes, sir. He is better than when last you saw him, I think. He still has nightmares, but he has been taking more exercise in the garden and I believe –"

Doctor Morrison interrupted. "There is no need for changes to his routine, Maggie," he said. "Today, he will receive his regular treatments."

"Yes, sir. Shall I fetch Edward?" She was still unsure of what the treatments might be.

"No, we shall prepare the treatment room first. Let us go there now."

He rose from the table and strode up the stairs, carrying a leather bag, Maggie following.

"Now," he said, once they were in the third room. "Let us set up the chair."

He stepped briskly to the corner and pulled the chair into the centre of the room. It seemed ordinary enough, a solidly built wooden chair with arms, but now that it was out of the shadows Maggie saw that it had large metal rings secured to the sides and back, and leather straps with buckles attached to the arms. She frowned but the doctor was already opening the drawer of the table, from which he removed sturdy chains, which he proceeded to fasten to the chair's rings. The chains rose to a single large metal ring connecting all three of them.

"Wind down the ceiling hook, Maggie."

Maggie stared at where he was indicating. Behind the second chair in the far corner of the room was a large handle, which connected to a windlass on one of the ceiling beams. Tentatively, she turned it.

"The other way," instructed the doctor, engaged in taking

several items out of his bag, including a bleeding bowl and various glass bottles.

Maggie tried the other way and the ceiling hook slowly lowered.

The doctor nodded approvingly and attached the hook to the metal circle. "Now wind it back up to tighten the chains."

She did so.

"Excellent. You may fetch Edward now. And call down to Agnes, tell her to come up."

Dread settled in Maggie's stomach. Edward was to be bled, that much she could see, but what was the purpose of the chair? What was in the many bottles that the doctor had brought with him?

In the corridor, she hesitated, unwilling to bring Edward into the room, which now felt ominous. Putting off the moment she called down the stairs.

"Agnes?"

"Are you ready for me?"

Maggie did not know what she meant, but evidently she had expected the call. "Yes."

There was a clatter of footsteps and Agnes came up the stairs carrying two empty brass buckets and a handful of cleaning rags, as well as a pail of fresh water. She edged past Maggie and went into the third room, putting the items down as directed by the doctor., Coming back out, she looked inquiringly at Maggie.

"I'm to fetch Edward," said Maggie helplessly. She wanted to ask Agnes for reassurance that nothing terrible was about to happen, but the girl only nodded and clattered back down the stairs.

Maggie stood for a moment before she raised her hand and knocked.

"Come in."

She opened the door. Edward sat opposite the door on his bed, fully clothed.

"Doctor Morrison is here, for your… treatments."

He stood at once, but he was more pale than usual, and his hands were shaking.

"Are you well? I could ask him to… delay?" Almost asking for herself rather than him, for she had a mounting dread in her stomach.

He shook his head and clenched his hands into fists, as though to make the shaking stop, walked past her and into the corridor. He hesitated for a moment outside the third room, before he swallowed and entered.

Maggie followed.

"Good morning, Edward."

"Good morning, sir."

"Take your usual seat and we shall get started."

Edward lowered himself into the chair, making the chains rattle.

"Your shirt."

Edward removed his jacket and waistcoat, handing both to Maggie without looking at her.

"Very good." The doctor was busy mixing up powders in a small cup, adding a few drops of liquid from one of the bottles to create a paste.

Slowly, Edward peeled off his shirt and Maggie took it. His skin was very white.

"We begin with blistering, Maggie. I shall apply this paste to Edward's back and chest. Blistering draws out noxious humours, which often abound in patients who are afflicted with melancholic thoughts."

"What is that, sir?" Maggie dared to ask, indicating the paste.

"Ground blister-beetles, combined with pepper and mustard. We apply it to the skin, and by midday or so it will have raised blisters on his skin."

Maggie stared as the doctor applied the paste in little mounds over Edward's back and chest, then wrapped him in a strip of linen to hold the paste in place against the skin.

"Now, we shall proceed to bleeding him, which of course has long been efficacious in such cases and many other ailments. Pass me the scarificator from the table."

"The?"

"Scarificator. The small brass box."

She passed it and he removed the bottom half, revealing twelve tiny rotating blades. He pulled back a small lever on the box, then held it over Edward's arm. Maggie wanted to stop him, but Edward seemed in a daze, making no attempt at refusal.

"The bleeding bowl, Maggie, if you would be so good. And a clean strip of linen."

She fetched them and stood helpless as Doctor Morrison pushed down on Edward's arm with the brass instrument, which made a click.

"It arms the blades, you see," explained the doctor, as though Maggie had eagerly asked for details. With his thumb, he pressed a knob and Edward flinched. Blood began to flow, the doctor lifting the instrument away to show the twelve tiny cuts made in Edward's skin, now bleeding rivulets into the bowl.

"Hold that there for a few moments, Maggie. Then we will do the other arm."

She held it, staring into Edward's face, but his eyes were on the floor as the blood flowed out of him. After a few moments, the doctor wiped and applied a dressing, before repeating the operation on the other side.

"There, we are making splendid progress," he said with satisfaction. "Let us move on to the enema."

"Sir –"

"Yes, Maggie?"

"Surely – all these treatments on one day, sir, is it not too much for Edward to bear all at once?"

The doctor frowned at her. "Thomas Willis has observed that lunatics are less susceptible to such pain as you or I might feel, Maggie. They can bear heat or cold, fasting, wounds and so on, far better than a sane person. Indeed, such treatment often has a beneficial effect on them. When Edward was first brought here, he had regular cold baths in winter and, even now, I only allow him to wash in cold water."

Maggie said nothing. Who was she to question a physician? He must know what was correct, but Edward's white face and hunched shoulders made her stomach clench, it could not be right to visit so much pain on him.

The doctor smiled. "You are very young and unused to this line of work, Maggie. You will learn. Bridget, now she was a very handy woman with Edward's treatments. She could even do the bloodletting and blistering all by herself, indeed, she took something of a pride in it. Sadly, I lost her services to an asylum who valued her experience. But I shall train you up just as well, you will see."

He had Edward remove his breeches and lie down on his

stomach on the bare wooden floor while he administered the enema by means of a large pewter and wood syringe. Edward remained silent throughout while Maggie looked away, embarrassed and horrified. She would have liked to have left the room, to grant Edward some sense of dignity, but knew without asking that she would not be allowed.

"Now," said the doctor. "We will leave him to feel the effects, I do believe it is midday and I am in need of sustenance. Eliza being the good cook that she is, I shall be well tended to, I believe. Come, Maggie."

"May I stay with him, sir?"

"A faithful companion indeed! If you wish to."

He nodded his approval and swept from the room.

"Leave, Maggie," murmured Edward.

"I cannot leave you alone and in pain."

He grimaced. "The cramps and their… results are not something I would wish you to witness, Maggie. They are humbling enough when I am alone."

She winced. He was already in pain from the blistering and bloodletting, now the cramps would grip his belly and bowels until he had voided everything in the pail left here for the purpose. All she could offer him was dignity. "I will wait downstairs," she said gently. "If you have need of me, call for me."

He grimaced in pain as another cramp came but nodded and she backed out of the room.

In the parlour the doctor was sitting down to a bountiful meal of sliced ham, a wedge of cheese, fresh-baked bread and a pie, as well as a dish of strawberries, seed cake and a pot of tea.

He ate heartily over the next hour, apparently oblivious to the groans and sometimes cries of pain from upstairs. Maggie had food to eat with Eliza and Agnes in the kitchen, but sat, all appetite gone, her hands clenching under the table. The other two women were sombre, but did not speak, so that the three of them sat in silence, making the sounds above them even worse.

As Doctor Morrison came to the end of the meal, he called for Agnes. "You will help Maggie make all tidy upstairs. Let me know when you are done."

"Yes, sir," said Agnes, fetching a second pail of water and more cleaning rags.

Upstairs, Edward sat on the chair in exhausted silence. The room stank, but Agnes made short work of cleaning away the chamber pot, pail, and dirtied water that Edward had used to clean himself. Maggie opened the window to bring in fresh air and used clean water and soap to ensure his hands were clean and wiped his sweat-riven face with a strip of linen. He seemed barely able to sit upright, body half-folded in on itself in the chained chair.

Once Agnes had left, the doctor made his way back to them.

"Let us see about these blisters, eh?"

He unwound the linen strips and Maggie gasped, for Edward's chest and back were now covered in raised blisters, each more than two inches across.

"Have you not seen blistering before?" enquired the doctor as though making polite small talk.

"No, sir."

"Well now, we will snip each one open to release the effluence that has gathered and dress each wound. Some physicians leave them undressed, but I am of the opinion it is better to dress them."

The paste was wiped away, then the doctor used a scalpel

to cut open each blister and drain away the liquid within it, before dressing each one. Maggie swallowed hard as Edward gritted his teeth so as not to exclaim with pain as each one was cut open and dressed.

"Now to our last treatment of the day," said the doctor, apparently well pleased. "Cox's Swing."

"Sir?"

He indicated the chained chair. "It is known as Cox's Swing. Joseph Mason Cox oversees Fishponds Asylum, near Bristol. He is a preeminent physician in the field of lunacy. His book, *Practical Observations on Insanity*, is a most excellent source of reliable and efficacious treatments. The patient sits in the chair, which is hoisted upwards, so that their feet are comfortably off the ground. We revolve it in one direction for forty turns, until it is very tightly wound, before releasing it, so that it revolves very rapidly in the other direction. The rotation causes nausea and dizziness, as one might expect, which has been proven to be highly beneficial patients suffering from lunacy."

Maggie took a deep breath but couldn't stop the words spilling out. "It seems… unkind, sir?"

He chuckled. "You are soft-hearted, my dear. Let us proceed."

"Please." It was the first time Edward had spoken to the doctor. "Please, sir… not the chair."

Maggie suppressed a gasp. Edward had borne being bled, blistered, his bowels emptied in the most violent fashion, yet he was afraid of the chair? How bad would it be?

"Now, Edward, I expect better of you." Swiftly, he fastened the straps round Edward's forearms and tightened the buckles.

"Maggie, turn the handle so that the chair is raised from the ground."

She hesitated.

"Come along, Maggie."

She turned the handle with difficulty, straining against his weight. Inch by inch the chair lifted, until even Edward's long legs could not keep his feet on the ground.

"Higher."

A full foot from the ground.

"That should do it. Now, you must help me to rotate the chair for forty turns. There are mechanisms that do this, but I am afraid we must make do with this more primitive system here."

One either side of the chair, they turned it, while the doctor counted and above them the rope holding the hook on the ceiling grew tight.

"One… two… three… five… ten…. fifteen… twenty-five… and forty."

It took all of Maggie and the doctor's combined strength to hold the chair in place.

"When I say the word, Maggie, you must let go and step back *promptly*, you understand?"

"Yes, sir."

"Very well. *Now*!"

She let go and stepped back and the chair, released, spun so fast that Edward became a blur. He let out a cry and fell silent. The chair spun so violently that as it came to the end of its natural rotation, it began to re-rotate in the other direction, before slowly coming to a halt.

Edward was white-faced, swallowing repeatedly, his eyes

unfocused. It was a horrible treatment, but at least it was over. She hoped the doctor would now leave.

"Excellent. And again."

"Again?" Maggie stared in horror at the doctor.

"Well, of course, Maggie, one rotation would barely be enough, now, would it?"

"How many…?"

"We will continue for about two hours."

"Two *hours*?"

"If you grow fatigued, I will call for Agnes or Eliza. They have helped in the past. But I am sure you can manage the first hour or so."

They wound the chair and let it go. Again it spun, again Edward cried out. This time when the chair stopped, he retched and Maggie held a pail to his mouth, into which he emptied yellow bile, for he had not eaten at all that day. There was nothing in him to be voided.

"Very good. Again."

"Please stop, sir, he is so unwell!"

"My dear girl, Edward is well used to this treatment. When he first came into my care and was less… tractable than he is now, I used this for an hour or two, three or even four times a day, for well over a month. It made a huge difference to him in the early days, so much so that now I need only visit him once every two months."

Over and over the chair was wound and released. Each time, Edward cried out, gripping the chair with his bandaged arms, retching and retching again, even though there was plainly nothing left in his belly, not even the yellow bile.

"There now," said the doctor, checking his pocket watch after an eternity. "That should do it." He wiped his sweating forehead with a handkerchief. "Bless me, I believe I need a drink after that."

Maggie followed him onto the landing to watch him go downstairs to the parlour, calling for Eliza as he did so, then hurried back into the room.

Edward was sitting where they had left him, a broken doll, arm and legs loose, face porcelain-pale, eyes closed. She knelt at his feet.

"Edward?"

His eyes opened and tried to focus on her, staring into her face as though he could barely see her. "Maggie." His voice was a croak.

"He will go soon," she whispered. "He says he is done."

His eyes met hers for an instant, before they closed again. "Thank God."

She put her hand on his, pity overwhelming her, and stayed there for a few moments, but got to her feet as she heard steps in the corridor.

"Well now, Edward, I think we are finished. You will soon feel the benefit of our work. Maggie, help me take Edward to his bedroom."

He could barely walk, his knees buckled under him, his arms draped over their shoulders without holding on to either of them. Between them they managed to get him back to his room and lay him on his bed, where Maggie pulled up the sheet and blanket over him. He lay silent, face white, eyes closed, breathing shallow.

"I will see you in another two months, Edward," said the doctor from the doorway, but there was no reply. "He will sleep well tonight," he added with satisfaction. "The swing results in what Cox calls "refreshing slumbers," and he is quite right."

Maggie thought that anyone would sleep after being exhausted, terrified and in pain for hours on end, but she did not speak. If the doctor thought her too critical, he might dismiss her and find another woman to take on the role of caring for Edward and she did not want to leave him to the none-too-tender mercies of what such a woman might be like, given the impression she had gathered of Bridget, who had taken all too keen an interest in 'treating' Edward. Wordlessly, she followed the doctor down the stairs to the front door, where she handed him his hat and coat.

Doctor Morrison appraised her. "You have conducted yourself well enough, Maggie. You may have found some of my methods harsh or surprising, as you have not seen them before, but from now on you will know what to expect and will not question their effects. Lunatics must sometimes be treated in ways that seem unkind to the untrained eye, but it is to keep them as well as they can be in themselves. They cannot be allowed to become too spirited or disturbed."

Maggie kept her eyes on the floor. "Yes, sir."

"Very well. I will return in two months to repeat the treatments and, until then, you will continue in your efforts. I think we will do well together, you and I, as you grow used to your position."

She could not wait for him to leave. "Yes, sir."

The carriage wheels crunched through the gravel, and he was gone at last. Maggie rested her head against the closed door.

He was a monster.

There had been no need to treat Edward so, she was sure of it. In what way had he been too spirited or disturbed? He had been happier than when she had first met him, of that she was sure. He had smiled more often. He had laughed. And now he was broken, purged in every possible way till he could barely stand, fearful and in pain. The Hospital letter she had been given came back to her, in which she had been exhorted to *execute all lawful commands with Industry, Cheerfulness and good Manners.* Her jaw clenched. She might have to obey her master in carrying out Edward's treatments, but she would find ways to make his life kinder, to build his strength up for the doctor's visits. Perhaps one day he could be well and strong enough to refuse the treatments, to leave this place even.

She climbed the stairs again and went to Edward's room, where she found him asleep, his skin paler than she had ever seen it, sweat still in his hair. She knelt by his bed and lightly touched his cheek and hair. "I will look after you, Edward," she whispered. "I promise I will do everything I can to keep you safe and make you well."

He did not stir. She rose, took away the burning candle and went back to the parlour downstairs, sitting in a chair and thinking about what she could do, what small comforts she might provide between the doctor's visits.

He lay in silence, not asleep. Another round of the treatments had been survived. There would be two months to recover before it happened again. Would it be enough? His strength ebbed a little further every time it happened, yet there appeared to be no escape from Doctor Morrison and his theories, from his incarceration and treatments here. From the madness everyone assured him he suffered from.

Yet this time had been different.

Someone had cared.

Maggie had tried to intervene. She had tried to stop the treatments. Even questioned Doctor Morrison. Failed, of course, because she was a servant, and he was both an eminent physician and her master. It was not her place to question him. Edward did not blame her for failing. His heart was too full. Someone had stood up for him, had tried to shield him. Had cared enough to try and help him. And now, just now, thinking him asleep, she had whispered to him. Had made him a promise. Said she would look after him and make him well. Was that even possible? That he could be well? He had spent so many years with his father demanding to know what was wrong with him, being told there was some defect in him by everyone around him, being treated for his affliction. It was hard to believe he could ever be well. But Maggie had said she would do everything she could to make him well, and if she believed it, he too would try to believe it of himself, would try to gather what remained of his strength and recover his health, his sanity. He would try because she believed in him.

That night, for the first time he could remember, he did not have a nightmare.

The next day was cold and rainy. Maggie brought up a jug of hot water for Edward to wash, taking over the task from Agnes. He watched her pour it into a basin and frowned at the steam rising from it.

"The doctor says I am only to have cold water."

"In this weather, everyone should keep warm, and there is plenty in the kitchen."

He hesitated, but gave a small smile at the determined face she was pulling and nodded. "Thank you."

She nodded back and left the room, feeling as though she had won a small victory against the absent doctor. Perhaps he was a great physician, but Maggie had seen and experienced bullying at the Hospital and she knew a bully when she saw one. She was certain that there had been no need for the treatments. Edward had nightmares and was timid of the world around him, but that did not make him dangerous or in need of treatments. Surely it would be better to show him kindness and allow him to grow in confidence? At any rate, a jug of warm water could not undo the doctor's treatments, even if they were efficacious, which she doubted.

"There's cream for our porridge," said Eliza, in a generous mood after being praised for her housekeeping by the doctor.

"I shall take some to Edward."

Eliza was wary. "Doctor Morrison says he is to eat plain food, nothing rich or it will spoil his constitution."

Maggie nodded as though she agreed. "Very well," she said. "Can I take the cream and the honey with me for my porridge?"

Eliza was about to reply but got distracted by the cat bringing a still-live mouse to drop at her feet. In the ensuing screeching, Maggie made good her escape with a small jug of cream and the pot of honey. Back in the parlour, she stirred in honey and cream to the two steaming bowls of porridge, then returned the jug and pot before their absence could be noticed and commented on. By the time she had returned, Edward had made his way downstairs and was seated at the table. She joined him and began eating from her bowl. At the first spoonful he looked up in surprise, but Maggie only went on eating her porridge and pretended not to notice him. He stared at her for a moment, then went back to eating the porridge without comment. She was pleased to see that he managed to finish all of it.

After breakfast she begged an ointment from Eliza and used it to dress his wounds, both the blisters and the cuts, hoping to soothe the pain he must be in, but they did not speak of the treatments.

From that day onwards she took over fetching his washing water and breakfast, making sure that he had hot water and that his breakfast was both ample and tasty, spreading fresh-baked bread thickly with good butter or cutting extra slices of pound cake, saying she was still hungry. Eliza occasionally laughed at her, saying she was eating them out of house and home, but Maggie would only tease back, saying that it was good to have a generous cook, which made Eliza happy and stopped her asking any awkward questions. The nightmares still plagued Edward most nights, but they grew less frequent.

The warmer days of late March and early April were now upon them. The yew and holly trees, along with the tall laurel hedges, had kept the garden green, if not exactly colourful aside from the flashes of red holly berries, but now spring growth appeared in the garden, as the hawthorn, copper beech and ash came back to life. The oak made its late appearance as the days grew warmer and brighter. Meanwhile, there were daffodils and crocuses, violets and primroses in the woods and new shoots on the roses. In the stream, the wriggling mass of tadpoles, when inspected more closely, were growing tiny legs. The weather was kind, the sun shone most days and there was warmth in the air. There was asparagus in the kitchen, made into a delicate soup or served alongside the roast lamb as a special treat on Easter day, after the tedium of Lent's restrictions. There were so many eggs that they could have them coddled or with ham, or in the rich custards that Eliza prided herself on making to serve alongside puddings. Maggie tried to make Edward eat more, but she had a sinking feeling as Easter passed. Doctor Morrison would arrive soon to treat Edward, for he had said he would return every two months and that time was almost up. Perhaps if she fixed Edward's mind on the future, beyond the oncoming assault, he might be better able to withstand it.

"We could plant more flowers outside," she said one day. "Abercrombie's book on gardening talks of bulbs for springtime and roses for the summer. It is too late for this year's spring, but perhaps we could plant some bulbs for next year. And if we were to plant fruit trees in the garden, we could pick fresh fruit from the trees in summer and make preserves. The book says a young tree will bear fruit in perhaps three years after planting."

Her enthusiasm warmed him. "We can ask Walter for what we want. What kind of fruit trees would you like, Maggie?"

"Apples? Pears? Perhaps a quince. I once ate quince preserves and they were very good."

Standing by his window that night, looking up at the full moon, Edward felt a rush of gratitude and happiness. Maggie intended to stay. She planned to stay with him for years, perhaps, if her talk of planting flowers and fruit trees were to be believed. He had been dreading the next visit from Doctor Morrison, but perhaps now he could face it, if she were by his side. Slowly, he unlaced his shoes and removed them, then stood a moment longer looking up at the moon before pulling the curtains closed. He would sleep well tonight, he thought. No nightmares. And tomorrow they would send Walter to buy plants for the garden. He began to unbutton his jacket.

A sound outside in the lane.

The hooves of many horses.

He frowned. Who would be driving so late through the village, even on a full moon night? He thought of looking out, but horses… He turned away from the window even as he heard a hammering at the door.

CHAPTER 2
The Midnight Carriage

MAGGIE WOKE WITH A START TO HEAR EDWARD shouting. Of late, the nightmares had been both less violent and less frequent, but this one sounded worse than usual, and she hurried towards the door, grabbing at the lamp, fumbling for the catch. But as she opened the door, she let out a scream herself, for in the dim light of the corridor Edward was being manhandled down the stairs by two men, who had him gripped by an arm on either side.

"MAGGIE!"

"Edward!" Panic seized her, she ran down the first few stairs to catch up with them and grabbed at him, but one of the men holding him used his other arm to shove her backwards, so that she fell back onto her behind. By the time she had regained her feet they were already forcing him through the front door, even though he struggled in their grip and shouted again.

"MAGGIE! HELP ME!"

"I am coming!" she cried out. "ELIZA! AGNES!"

Eliza and Agnes burst out of their room and ran down the stairs behind her, all three rushed through the door where, in the shadowy moonlight, Edward was being forced, struggling, into a large carriage pulled by four horses. The door slammed shut as Maggie grabbed at the arm of one of the men.

The man turned and Maggie gasped and stepped back in surprise, his skin was black, she saw, so that the whites of his eyes shone in the uncertain light.

"What are you doing to Edward?"

"I am taking His – him – home," said the man.

"This is his home!"

"To his true home," said the man, pushing Maggie away, not roughly but firmly. "Step away, girl."

"I am his companion; I look after him! You cannot take him away without Doctor Morrison's permission."

"You need not fear for him. He will be taken care of."

"But – you cannot simply take him, he is not well, he is –"

"Unwell, I know." He stepped up onto the carriage, taking his place by the impervious driver.

Maggie pulled at the carriage door, but she did not know how it fastened and in the shadows her fingers were clumsy. Edward's pale face pressed against the window, his eyes wide with fear. He shouted again to her, voice now muffled by the barrier between them.

"Maggie!"

"Let him out!" she screamed at the men. "Help me!" she cried to Eliza and Agnes, but they hung back, scared.

"Move," said the man and the driver beside him brought down the whip.

Maggie reached up and grabbed at the dark man's arm as the carriage wheels began to roll, but he tugged sharply away from her, and the button of his sleeve came off in her hand. She stumbled backwards and then the carriage was gaining speed, and even as she ran after it, she knew it was too late. Edward shouted something but she could not make out the words.

The carriage was gone.

Maggie stood shaking in the dim light as the sound of the hooves and Edward's shouts faded away.

"You've got nothing on your feet," said Agnes at last, her voice cowed.

Maggie stared down at her bare feet, cold and muddy from the lane.

"Come back inside," said Eliza more practically, putting an arm about Maggie's trembling shoulders. "There's nothing we can do for now. The Doctor will tell us what's what."

Maggie allowed herself to be led back into the cottage, where Eliza lit candles and lamps and Agnes brought a basin and a rag to clean the soles of her feet, one of which was cut and bleeding.

"I'll get a clean rag to wrap it," said Eliza.

Maggie could barely feel the cut. Slowly, she opened her hand and looked down at the silver button lying in it. On its polished surface were an acorn and a bulrush, their stems bound together with a coronet.

"What is it?" asked Agnes, leaning forward to look at it.

Eliza bustled back and knelt to wrap a clean strip of cloth round Maggie's foot. "That's a livery button, that is," she said.

"A livery button?"

"Grand families have their manservants wear livery with their coat of arms on the buttons."

They all peered at the acorn and the bulrush, the tiny coronet. "Whose livery is it?" asked Maggie.

"Don't know, never seen that one. There's the Earl, he's got a boar on his, and I've seen two carriages with coats of arms pass by, one was a stag and one was a spear with waves. Never seen an acorn and a bulrush with a crown."

"Why would someone kidnap Edward?" Confusion and fear washed over her again. "They took him without his shoes, just grabbed him and forced him into the carriage. What will the Doctor say?"

"We didn't have no say in the matter," said Eliza, sitting back on her heels. "Two men against us womenfolk, we couldn't have fought them, now, could we? The Doctor will have to make enquiries. You can show him that button. We'll send word at first light with Walter. He'll drive into town and leave a message for the Doctor to come at once. You can write, can't you?"

Maggie nodded. The three of them made their way into the parlour where Maggie took down the paper and quill pen and carefully opened the ink, then wrote in the neat script she had been taught:

To Doctor Morrison

Sir,
A carriage and two strong men came for Edward in the middle of the night and did not tell us where he was to be taken and being only women, we were unable to stop them. One of the men wore this button. Please send word of how to proceed.

Yours respectfully,
Maggie, Eliza, Agnes

As soon as it was light, Agnes was dispatched to Walter's house to deliver the letter, which had been neatly folded up and contained the livery button, with instructions that he should ride into town and take it to Doctor Morrison at once. He was to put the letter only into his hand, for Maggie knew that discretion would be important. The doctor would not want anyone knowing his business and that would surely include his patient being taken away in the dead of night, with no warning or explanation.

But the letter Walter returned with late that morning did not give them much comfort.

> *Edward has returned to his family. You will remain at Ivy Cottage to await my further instructions. A new patient will join you within a few weeks.*

Eliza and Agnes seemed consoled by the note when Maggie read it to them, going about their daily chores as though nothing had changed. But Maggie wandered from room to room and all around the garden, even down to the stream and back, several times that day. Waiting for another patient seemed impossible to her – that she should forget all about Edward, ask no questions as to his wellbeing or whereabouts, only accept that he was gone and another put in his place as though one man or another were the same – how could she do so? She thought of his shouts, his frightened face, how he had reached out to her and called her name. Returning to his room, which contained the scent of him, she ran her hand over his bedlinen, seeing his shoes, which had been left behind. Wherever he was now, he was barefoot. Where was he at this moment? Were people being kind to him? And why? Why had Edward been taken away?

She slept fitfully that night and the next, waking often,

thinking there was hammering at the door or that she heard Edward shout, lying in the dark room, hearing Eliza and Agnes' breathing, unable to sleep for worrying about Edward.

She tried to remember every detail that might help her understand what had happened. He had been at Ivy Cottage for eight years, had come there from a school. He was twenty-two and therefore of age yet was still kept here. He seemed sane enough to her, apart from a few oddities, such as his fear of horses and the nightmares. She thought of his height, his deep blue eyes, his refined features. The lady visitors at the Hospital would surely have given him sweets had he been a child there, for he was more handsome than any man Maggie had ever seen. But broken and sent away from his family, into the clutches of Doctor Morrison.

Where was he? Back in his true home, the man had said, but where was that, what did it mean? If he had a family somewhere, why had they now taken him back? And without warning? At midnight in a carriage none of them had ever seen before?

Where was Edward now?

Edward gazed around in despair. The room was large but dusty, clearly the maids no longer cared much for it since it no longer had a purpose. There were holland covers over a few items but otherwise it was as before, one of the few places in the house he remembered with any fondness. He had run up the stairs to it after escaping from her. But his mother had followed him.

"You will take up your rightful rooms at once."

"I will not. I will stay here."

"You cannot possibly stay here. The servants will talk."

"Let them."

"If they talk, you will end up back in that… place."

"Good. Send me back there."

She stared at him in horror. "You cannot. You must take up your rightful place now that he – that they – are gone."

It was unthinkable, what she was asking of him. It was impossible, what had happened. Not one, but both of them gone. He could not comprehend it, could not make it seem true. He kept expecting one of them to appear and yet the house was silent, no stamping of boots, no raised voices. She was all alone and she had sent for him, was asking for him to… it was impossible. He paced the room in his stockinged feet, back and forth, back and forth, under her anxious gaze.

"Where did you even tell everyone I was?"

"At school."

"I am twenty-two years of age!"

"University. Then travelling."

"One lie after another."

"Would you have preferred we told the truth of what you are?"

"A lunatic, you mean?" he asked and she flinched at the word. "There is no pretty word for it."

"You are… afflicted… with a… melancholic disposition…"

"So afflicted that you have had me in the care of a physician for the last eight years who specialises in the care of lunatics. Locked into a cottage and its garden, unable to go anywhere else, on the threat of being put into a harsher institution."

"We did what we thought was best."

"And now you need me and so… I am no longer mad? Am I cured, do you think?

"You… the title, the estate…"

He gave a bitter laugh. "Ah, of course. The title and the estate. Heaven forbid we lose those."

"If you can only –"

"What? Play the part of a sane man long enough?"

She was silent.

He shook his head and laughed again, but it had a sob within it. "Oh, that *is* what you wanted. I must play a part. I must not fail or –"

"If you were married, if there were an heir…"

He stopped pacing and stared at her. "Married?"

"It would secure…"

He sat down in the window seat, legs suddenly weak under him, stared out over the gardens he had not seen in eight years. "I must play a part long enough to marry and sire an heir and then what? I can be safely locked away again?"

"If you marry and sire an heir, the title and the estate will be safe and you… if you feel able to take your place, you could…"

"Be free?"

Silence.

"You are allowing me a chance to escape my gaol? If I can do what you ask, if I can fool everyone, if I can behave myself well enough, then perhaps I will be allowed to remain free? Is that what this offer is?"

She looked down.

"I will take that as your assent."

"Then you will do it?"

"I have one request."

"Anything."

"I need Maggie here."

"Who?"

"Maggie. She is at Ivy Cottage. Bring her here."

"We cannot have someone here who knows –"

"I cannot do this without her."

"Why?"

He could think of many reasons, but one above all. "Because she is the only person who cares for me."

"She –"

He held up a hand to stop her. "I cannot do any of what you are asking without her." His voice cracked and his eyes welled up despite himself. "Bring her to me or I will truly run mad." He felt his breathing grow rapid, so that he was panting, a dizziness creeping over him.

She took a step backwards.

"Send for Maggie," he repeated, turning his back on her so that she might not see the tear that was rolling down his face. "I will not leave this room until you do."

He heard the swishing silk of her skirts as she left the room. Would she send for Doctor Morrison, to have him locked away again? Or for Maggie, to set him free? He leant against the cold wall, touched the peeling paper. Could he do it, even with Maggie by his side? Could he do what was being asked of him, after eight years locked away? He did not know, yet he had to try. This was the first time he had been offered a chance to escape, to reach out for a different life, to be free of the word he had been tarred with.

Lunatic.

Could he escape that word now? It might be his only chance, but without Maggie, he would fail. He needed her strength to find his own.

He needed her here.

Maggie woke again and heard the clock strike midnight, turned over in her bed, listening to the soft sleeping noises from Eliza and Agnes. Her mind would not be still. *Edward, Edward, Edward.* It was all she could think of.

A hammering at the door. She was sure of it. And yet she had imagined it so many times now it could not be true.

But it came again and she sat bolt upright, clutching at her blanket, Agnes and Eliza stirring beside her. She rose to look out of the tiny window and there it was again, the midnight carriage and its four horses, the stolid driver.

She ran down the stairs, opened the door, stared up into the dark man's face. The same man who had taken Edward.

"Are you Maggie?"

"Yes."

"You must come with me."

"Why?"

"He is asking for you."

"Edward?"

"Yes."

"Is he safe?"

"Yes. But he has been asking for you and I have been sent to fetch you."

Maggie's heart hurt at the idea that Edward had wanted her at his side and she had not been there, that he had been all alone. She would go to him at once, she would go to – "Where are we going?"

"To Buckinghamshire."

Maggie vaguely knew her counties; geography had not been much taught at the Hospital but there had been a map on the wall. She could picture Buckinghamshire, a county closer to London than where they were now. They must have travelled through it on their way to Ivy Cottage.

"Is that his home? Or a – a hospital?" What if it were somewhere like Bedlam, a place full of lunatics, some of them dangerous, not like gentle Edward?

"It is his home."

"Am I to care for him there?"

"I have only been told to fetch you."

She did not like the way he refused to answer questions fully. "Why have you come at night?"

"For discretion."

Maggie hesitated. It was madness to step into a carriage at night with two unknown men, to go somewhere, she knew not where, only that it was in Buckinghamshire. But if Edward was there, if he had asked for her repeatedly… the thought of him, desperate, asking for her repeatedly, made up her mind in an instant.

"I need to pack my things. Tell Eliza and Agnes –"

"There is no time. Dress. Tell no one. Leave everything. More clothes will be provided."

She turned away without speaking and made her way back upstairs. Softly, she took her clothes and shoes, dressed in the darkness, fumbling with her laces, feeling about her for her coat. She thought of the Bible and the letter she had been given, her spare clothes, but she had been told to take nothing and so she came back down the stairs and addressed the man still standing on the threshold.

"You swear you are taking me to Edward?"

He nodded, turned and opened the carriage door, pulling out small steps. Inside a low lamp was burning. "We'll be there by dawn," he said. He held out a hand to help her in, but

Maggie shrank away from his touch and climbed in by herself. He closed the steps and then the door. The carriage rocked as he took his place beside the driver, then jolted as it moved forwards. Maggie pressed her face against the window, but already Ivy Cottage was swallowed up in the gloom, the horses gathering speed. Her face rocked into the glass like a cold slap. She sat back and looked around.

The low light of the lamp showed an interior that put Doctor Morrison's carriage to shame. She was sitting on vast soft cushions, made of a sumptuous velvet in a rich dark colour, perhaps a dark blue, although it was hard to be sure in the dim light. The roof was covered with elaborate pleats of the same velvet, drawn towards a circle outlined in silver scrolls. At the centre, the image she recalled from the man's livery button: the acorn and bulrush, bound by a coronet, in silver. Swagged curtains framed the windows; a dangling tassel might summon a servant from the driving seat. Maggie edged away from it. On the seat opposite her was a thick woollen blanket, soft when she touched it. At first, she did not use it, but despite her coat she was cold and eventually she wrapped it about her, bringing instant warmth.

The carriage rocked onwards. Maggie could see little out of the window. For a while she felt nauseous, from the rocking of the vehicle or from fear or both. But after some time the warmth of the blanket, the endless motion and her tiredness from three nights of broken sleep made her lean back against the thickly padded backrest, drowsiness overcoming her. She slept.

She half-woke when they pulled into the dimly lit stable yard of a coaching inn, felt the carriage jolt as fresh horses were harnessed to the carriage. The change happened twice more, and each time Maggie peered about for signs of where they were. In one yard a boy pressed his face against the glass to look in and was cuffed round the head by an unseen man for his insolence. They were always gone again in a short space of time, pulling away from each inn and back onto the roads, Maggie dozing again as they drove on into the night.

In the cold light of an early dawn, she woke with a dry mouth and bleary eyes, limbs stiff with cold. Pressing her face against the window she saw ornate gold and black gates swinging open, the wheels crunching on fresh gravel through an endless avenue of towering trees lining a well-kept road. Maggie pushed at the window to open it. Cold air struck her, but now she could lean out and what she saw ahead left her open mouthed.

A vast building, set amidst gardens and grounds. A castle-like façade, with two turrets and a wooden door large enough to drive a carriage through. She had barely taken it in when the carriage swept round in an arc, forcing her to lean to one side to keep her balance, and then stopped.

A lurch and a crunch of gravel as the man jumped down and came to the door, opening it. He folded down the steps and held out his hand and this time Maggie took it, stepped down, her limbs protesting.

"Welcome to Atherton Park," said the man. He turned to the driver. "To the stables," he said, and the carriage pulled away, disappearing round the corner the vast building. "Follow me," he added to Maggie, and strode away from her, rounding the side of the building, away from the vast front door. Maggie stumbled after him, limbs heavy and clumsy.

"Wait," she said.

The man turned. Up close, now that there was more light, she saw that his skin was not really black, but dark brown, his eyes also a deep brown. He was dressed in a rich blue velvet that matched the interior of the carriage, the jacket heavy with silver frogging, his buttons shining.

"Who are you?" she asked.

"My name is Joseph," he said.

"Whose livery is it you wear?" she asked, expecting him not to answer

"Buckingham."

This meant nothing to her. They were in Buckinghamshire; he had told her that much. He had already turned away, was walking down the side of the building till he came to a smaller door, on which he rapped smartly. It was opened at once by a boy in matching livery, who bobbed his head at Joseph and gaped at Maggie.

"Less of your staring," said Joseph. "Go tell Mrs Barton I'm back. Come," he added to Maggie.

He walked briskly through a vast empty corridor, the flooring a dark timber, the walls painted a pale greeny-blue and hung with stern portraits of grand men and women, all of them with expressions of superiority. Hurrying after him, Maggie saw a white ceiling intricately moulded with swirls and highlighted in gold leaf above her.

They came to one staircase and another, everywhere decorated with grandeur like the Governors' 'court' room at the Hospital, the walls painted or papered, gold touches everywhere and sweeping staircases, making Maggie feel small and lost. If Joseph were to leave her here, she would not even be able to find her way out.

They came to a smaller staircase and a corridor, less grand

than those lower down in the house, although there was still a dizzying array of doors. Joseph stopped outside one and gestured Maggie forwards.

"He's been asking for you day and night," he said, and opened the door into a dimly lit room.

Maggie almost cried out in relief, for there, on a plain wooden bed, somewhat too short for his long frame, was Edward, asleep in his clothes, the rumpled sheets and blankets suggesting that he had slept but restlessly, a lamp burning low on a table. She advanced into the room on tiptoe so as not to waken him, looking about her in curiosity.

It was a room for children, a nursery, for there was a globe and a blackboard, dusty but still with faint marks of long-ago chalk. She could see another bed through an open door, also too small for a grown man. The green curtains were faded and the room, although large, felt neglected, as though its occupants had long gone.

"Does he – is he – is this his home?" she whispered.

Joseph nodded silently.

Maggie had known so little about Edward, she now realised. He came from a grand family, a rich family and yet… "Isn't this a nursery?"

"He would not go to the rooms set aside for him."

Maggie saw a stool in a corner of the room and took it, placed it by Edward's head and settled herself, waiting for him to awaken. The blanket had fallen from his shoulder, and she pulled it up to keep him warm. When she looked over her shoulder Joseph was watching her.

"Are you thirsty?"

She realised, suddenly, that her mouth was very dry, she was indeed thirsty. "Yes. Is there some water?"

"I will fetch some," he said. "And tea?"

"If it is not too much trouble," she said, her voice still low, unwilling to wake Edward by speaking too loudly. "Thank you."

He hesitated, then disappeared from the doorway. She could hear his heels down the corridor, brisk, confident in this house. Her relief at seeing Edward drained from her. Where was she? Some grand house, where Edward, it seemed, belonged, and yet he was sleeping in an abandoned nursery, wearing the same suit he had been taken in, crumpled and sweat-stained. His clothing had been simple, but always clean. Were they not looking after him? Joseph had said Edward had been asking for her and clearly whoever lived here had grown desperate enough to send for her, to send Joseph out again on the long journey, traveling dangerously by night to avoid notice. She gazed down at Edward's sleeping face, his skin pale, hair tangled on the pillow, one foot uncovered, knees bent to fit in the small bed made for a child.

The fire in the grate was laid but not made and the room was chilly. Maggie looked about for a tinderbox and saw one on a small side table. She lit the fire, kneeling and blowing gently to encourage the flames to take hold. As she finished, she heard fast footsteps again and Joseph appeared in the doorway bearing a tray.

He looked startled at the sight of her on her knees by the fireplace.

"What are you doing?"

"The fire needed lighting."

He put the tray down. On it were two glasses of water and two bowls of steaming porridge. "Cook sent us this, she'll send up more when His – when he awakens. I've taken most of my meals up here when I'm attending him."

"You have been attending him?"

"Briefly. Within two days it was clear we'd have to fetch you, or he'd not settle down." He rubbed his face. "I've not had much sleep, this past week."

"Is Doctor Morrison here?"

He shook his head, seemed for a moment as though he were about to explain further, but closed his mouth.

Maggie made short work of her glass of water, passed Joseph one of the bowls of porridge and took the other for herself. It was thick, hot and well-made and she ate it gratefully. If Edward should awake, she must be ready to care for him.

Edward woke, but kept his eyes shut. Perhaps if he kept his eyes closed long enough, when he opened them, he would be back in Ivy Cottage, but he already knew he was not, knew by the too-small bed that would not fit his long frame, by the fact that he was still in his clothes. His stomach clenched in cold fear at the thought of another day here, another day of being cajoled or coerced, threatened with the imminent arrival of Doctor Morrison when all he wanted was to see Maggie's face again, her wide eyes, her ready smile, to feel her comforting presence nearby, a friendly face to help him through what he must endure. He had begged for her to be sent for, but who knew whether she would come or whether she would be too scared to do so, whether Doctor Morrison might withhold her? The morning sunshine made the light seem blood-red through his eyelids. He could hear the crackle of the fire and could smell porridge.

"Do you not have clean linen for him?"

Edward's eyes flew open. Maggie. Sitting by his bed, turned away, towards Joseph, who at once saw that he was awake. The expression on Joseph's face alerted Maggie, who turned to him.

"Edward!"

Happiness rushed through him. She was here. He was safe. No matter what else happened, she had come, she had come to him.

"Maggie," he croaked, his voice hoarse from the past few days.

"Edward! Are you well? What happened? Why were you brought here? What is this place?" All her questions came tumbling out in a rush.

Relief washed over him at her concern. He had been right to beg for her, she was the only person he could trust to care for him in this awful new situation. Pulling himself upright in the bed, he pushed back his unkempt hair. "I am well enough; I am glad to see you."

She returned his smile, then frowned. "But where are we? What are we doing here?"

Joseph cleared his throat. "You must come downstairs with me."

"Why?"

"I was told to take you there at once, I only brought you here so you could see one another and eat. She'll be waiting."

Maggie turned, frowning, to Edward, but he waved one hand at her, his face weary.

"Go."

Maggie stood to follow Joseph.

"Wait." Edward gazed at her, miserable. "Promise me you will come back?"

"Of course I will come back," she protested. "I have not come all this way to run away the moment I leave your side."

"You have not yet heard what she has to say," he said.

"Who?"

"My mother."

Maggie followed Joseph down the first staircase and then another. He showed her into a vast room, lavishly decorated in primrose yellow with ornate furniture, gilded looking glasses and large vases of flowers. Sitting by a fire burning below an elaborate stone mantelpiece, in an imposing velvet armchair, was an older woman. She was dressed in black from head to toe, although even Maggie, ignorant of current fashions, could tell that the dress was silk and expensively made. The woman had Edward's face, the same vividly blue eyes, the same high cheekbones, but her pale skin was lined, and Maggie was reminded of Edward after Doctor Morrison's treatments, the same exhaustion showing on an otherwise beautiful face.

The woman stared at Maggie but did not speak. Maggie bobbed a curtsey and stood, uncomfortable under the woman's scrutiny. There was another woman in the room, standing to one side, neatly dressed in grey. She was older than Maggie, but younger than Edward's mother, with warm brown eyes and a pleasant face. She gave a small nod when Maggie caught her eye. A servant of some sort.

At last Edward's mother spoke.

"He has done nothing since he arrived back here but lash out and scream to leave Atherton, to be returned to Ivy Cottage. We have had to confine him to the rooms he has chosen and tell the servants that he is overcome with grief. My maid, Duval here, waited on him while Joseph collected you." She looked Maggie over, her lip curling with disdain. "Are you his mistress?"

"No!"

"Then what are you to him that he should demand your presence here?"

"I am his companion, ma'am, hired by Doctor Morrison to look after Edward, I –"

"*Edward?* You call him Edward?"

Maggie gulped. What had she done wrong? "Is that not his name, ma'am? It is what I was told to call him."

The woman narrowed her eyes. "The man you call Edward is Edward Robert John Atherton, the twelfth Duke of Buckingham. He is the master of Atherton Park. He is addressed as His Grace or to those with whom he is familiar, as Buckingham. I am his mother, the Duchess of Buckingham. You address me as Your Grace."

A dizziness came over Maggie, whether from tiredness and fear or from this sudden news that Edward, gentle fearful Edward, was a duke. It could not be true. She had known he must be from the gentry, and had guessed, once she had seen this house, that his family must be rich, but a duke? And yet… all the comforts they had enjoyed at Ivy Cottage. A simple cottage in a tiny village and yet there had been feather beds and cream with their porridge, ample supplies of food and fuel, and Doctor Morrison to care for a young man considered mad and sent away from his family… now Maggie understood why there had been no shortage of money, no expense spared in Edward's treatments, however unpleasant they were.

"But…"

"But what?"

"He has been at Ivy Cottage for years, I was told…"

"He has been there since he was fourteen years old."

"Then why has he been brought back now? Has Doctor Morrison said he is cured?" For a moment Maggie was hopeful, for after all she had never seen much wrong with Edward, and the doctor's treatments had only weakened him, not changed his behaviour except to make him quieter and sicker.

"His father and elder brother have died."

"Both?"

"His father died of an apoplectic fit four months ago and my older son died in a hunting accident more recently. Edward is the only heir. If he does not take up the title, the whole estate will go to a distant cousin. Which cannot be allowed to happen."

Maggie stayed silent. There was too much information coming at her; she was still trying to imagine Edward as a duke. Would such information make him better or worse? Would the responsibility be too much to bear, would it make him ill again?

The Duchess cleared her throat, then spoke reluctantly, as though what she was suggesting was displeasing to her. "I have an offer for you. We have one social season in which to find Edward a bride and get him married. If we leave it any longer, it will cause gossip. Edward has…" She paused. "Edward has insisted that you be always by his side. Not just at home, though that would be preferable. He wants you to be at all the social occasions he must attend during the season, he says he has not the strength, the – the confidence to partake in them otherwise. Obviously, the Duke of Buckingham cannot be seen to require a nursemaid, people will talk. I have devised a plan. You will stay here, posing as a distant cousin of the family so that you can keep Edward calm without anyone realising you are effectively nursemaid to a lunatic. Once he is safely married off, you will be paid one thousand pounds, and you will leave Atherton Park and never speak of your time here again." She stared at Maggie. "Do I make myself plain?"

The offer and the sum of money were breathtaking. A thousand pounds would allow Maggie to live comfortably for years. But… "What happens when he is married?"

"He will sire an heir, which will secure the estate and the title for another generation."

"I meant, what will happen to Edward?"

"He will live here, unless his madness is too obvious, when he will be kept elsewhere, as he was before. The title and the estate will be safe." She shrugged again and, in that moment, Maggie despised her casualness, as though she were speaking of Edward occasionally taking the sea air or the waters for his health, as and when he chose, not the reality of being locked away from the world, subjected to the torment of Doctor Morrison's treatments.

"Well?"

Maggie wanted to ask for time to think. Everything was too much, she was still trying to understand all she had been told, but the Duchess was not granting her time to think. Among the thoughts whirling through her mind was the line from the Hospital's letter to her when she had been sent out into the world: *Lying is the beginning of everything that is bad; and a Person used to it is never believed, esteemed or trusted.* Maggie felt muddled and uncertain of what exactly she was being asked to do, what would happen, what her assent might lead to. What was most important?

Edward. She would be with Edward, and that was all that

mattered for now. She would care for him as she had done at Ivy Cottage. That part, at least, was simple. But she was to pose as a cousin? Pose as a lady? That she could not imagine, but it did not matter for now; all she needed to do was care for Edward. Everything else was unimportant. Even the money, a life-changing sum. She set that thought aside. Perhaps he would be happier with a wife and a child, perhaps it would help him. He might find a woman who was kind and gentle, who could lift his spirits. And if all else failed, Maggie could return with him to Ivy Cottage, or somewhere like it, and life could go on as it had before.

"Yes. I will stay."

The Duchess took a deep breath, whether of relief or apprehension, Maggie could not tell.

"Very well. Leave me now. You will spend the day upstairs in the nursery. Neither you nor Edward must leave those rooms unless otherwise instructed. Food will be sent up to you. Joseph will attend to you both. I will send for you later today when I have had time to plan. Go."

Maggie bobbed another curtsey and followed Joseph back to the nursery rooms.

Edward was standing by the window and turned as the door opened, Joseph backing away, leaving them alone. "Did she frighten you off?"

Maggie shook her head. "You asked for me to be by your side while you find a wife," she said, "and I will be. I will do whatever will help you find happiness."

"Is that what marriage will do?" he asked in a low voice. "Make me happy? Make me well?"

"I don't know," said Maggie. "But it might. If you had a good wife by your side... someone you... love."

He gave a small unhappy laugh. "I am not sure that is how the *ton* views marriages. It is a cattle market. Best breeding and most money wins the auction."

"The *ton*? What is that?"

He threw himself down into an armchair, legs under him, shoulders hunched, his old posture. "The rich and powerful. The finest society. The people with whom we shall be forced to spend our days in order to secure a wife my mother and the rest of society deems appropriate to be a duchess. You'll see when the social season begins."

"The social season?" All these new words, new meanings, things she had never heard of, which tripped so easily off Edward's tongue. A world of which she had known nothing at all.

"It is when the *ton* goes to London and sets up its marriage market. Young ladies are presented at court, available for sale to the highest bidder. Endless balls, picnics, walks, dinners, luncheons, social calls, house parties at estates like this one, until at last everyone is sick of one another and returns to their homes to wait out the summer months and go hunting, before starting all over again."

"Not in the summer?" asked Maggie, trying to imagine what he was describing.

"It begins in the autumn, September to November, that is the Little Season. Then home for foxhunting and Christmas. The season proper begins again from January, although the greatest crowds form in March, since there is better weather for picnics and pleasure gardens. By July it is done, the marriage bargains have been struck or one is left on the shelf for another year and considered a failure if you are a woman, or a promising rake if you are a man." He sighed. "It is supposed to be the time when the gentlemen sit in Parliament, which follows those timings, so their families accompany them to London. That is how it started, I suppose, but it has now turned into a marriage mart. That is what I will be facing to find a bride. I am not sure there will be room for finding love."

Maggie nodded. What could she say by way of comfort? The picture he had painted was bleak. "At least you will be out in the world," she tried.

"At least I will have you by my side," he replied. "You will keep me safe, Maggie."

"I will do my best. You forget that I must pretend to be a lady. I am not sure I will succeed."

"Then we will both be pretending. I to be sane, you to be a lady. We will have to help one another."

She held out her hand. "It is a bargain," she said, trying to make him laugh, but he took her hand in his and shook it, eyes serious.

"A bargain," he repeated.

Food was brought by Joseph at noon, a large tray containing soft white bread, good butter, thickly sliced ham with a salad of fresh leaves, as well as baked apples served with cream. With it came a teapot and cups, as well as fresh cold water.

"Your cook is very generous," observed Maggie.

Edward tilted his head at Joseph. "Is Mrs Barton still the cook?" he asked Joseph.

"She is, Your Grace."

"Will you ask her to send up her seedcake tomorrow? And her bread pudding."

"Are those delicacies from your childhood?" asked Maggie.

It was the first time she had seen Edward respond with enthusiasm to something from his past.

"She was very kind," said Edward. How often he had escaped his father's rages or his mother's icy silence by creeping down the back stairs to the servants' dining hall and the great kitchen, where Mrs Barton would stand him on a chair and allow him to stir her seedcake mix, or let him layer slices of bread in a dish, ready to pour a custard mix over it, foods which would later be served in the nursery for dinner.

"Her Grace has asked that you both join her in the drawing room after you have eaten," said Joseph.

The warm apples and cream went dry in Maggie's mouth and it was hard to swallow, but she tried to smile and nod as though this were a delightful summons, mindful that she must not let Edward's fears rise up. He had already put down the dish from which he was eating, his appetite gone as quickly as hers.

The drawing room, grand and spacious as it undoubtedly was, made Maggie feel as though she could not breathe. She sat stiffly by Edward, facing the Duchess, Joseph and the maid. Joseph was better dressed than Edward, who sat barefoot and hunched in his working man's clothes, wretchedly uncomfortable beneath his mother's cold gaze.

"What did you say your name was again?"

"Maggie Stone."

"That will not do at all, it is a housemaid's name. You will be known as Margaret. Margaret…" She paused. "… Seton. I believe there are some Setons in the north who have acceptable connections. If anyone asks, we will imply you are distantly related to them." She nodded to herself, rapidly inventing. "You will be a third cousin once removed on my side of the family. Your mother made an unfortunate marriage and your father recently died, leaving you to my care. You will address His Grace as Cousin Edward and he will address you as Cousin Margaret, to allow for the closeness which your role as his nurse may require. We cannot have any suggestions of impropriety, we have enough to conceal as it is." Her lip curled, as though the idea made her feel ill. "In addition, you will call me Aunt Caroline. We must maintain the falsehood of being related at all times."

Maggie, who had spent years wishing she had a family, could not, at this moment, think of anyone to whom she would less like to be related than the Duchess, with her cold eyes and forbidding manner.

"As few people as possible must know who you are and of our plan." The Duchess looked down at her hands, counting. "Doctor Morrison, of course, should treatments be necessary. For now, I have asked him to stay away, as regular visits by a physician may draw unwanted attention. Joseph will act as His Grace's valet from now on. We cannot risk hiring a new valet who does not know of his affliction. My lady's maid, Celine Duval, will dress you and correct any failings in your manners. That is three people, and we must not allow any other people to know the truth. His Grace's natural grief at the loss of his father and elder brother, the sudden shock of becoming the Duke of Buckingham, all of these can be used as excuses for any behaviour that may seem less than... normal, but overall he must appear sane. We cannot have servants gossiping or the *ton* suspecting anything is amiss. There can be no whispers, no suggestion of anything untoward. He must find a bride and be married by the end of the season."

She turned to look at Joseph and Celine. "You will both, always, refer to Margaret as Miss Seton."

"Yes, Your Grace," they chorused.

"Margaret, you will address them as Joseph and Duval."

Maggie blinked, confused.

"What is it?"

"Joseph by his first name but Celine by her surname?"

"Yes. That is how it is done. Footmen are referred to by their Christian names. A maid, also. But a lady's maid is given the distinction of being called by her surname. You will have to learn these things." She closed her eyes and sighed. "If it is possible."

"I am a fast learner." Maggie lifted her chin. "Aunt Caroline," she added for good measure.

"Very well. Duval, take Margaret to the Wisteria Bedroom. Arrange for her to be…" she looked Maggie up and down, evidently displeased by what she saw "… appropriately dressed, at least for now. Do whatever is necessary, purchase whatever is required. You can ensure she has a more extensive wardrobe when the season starts, but she must at least pass muster as a member of the family until then, should we receive any visitors or be seen in public. His Grace must choose a room he is happy with since he refuses to use the ducal suite. However, neither His Grace nor Miss Seton are to be seen outside the nursery by any of the servants or outside the house until they are properly attired. That must be our first matter of business."

Maggie glanced at Edward, who gave her a small nod.

"Yes, Your Grace," murmured Celine Duval, before turning to Maggie. "Please follow me, Miss Seton."

CHAPTER 3:
The Wisteria Bedroom

MAGGIE FOLLOWED CELINE ALONG ENDLESS CORRIdors, while the maid described the rooms they were passing.

"The Rose Bedroom, the Peony Bedroom, the Hyacinth Bedroom. This is the Wisteria Bedroom."

Maggie was shown into a room that took her breath away. She had expected a utilitarian servant's quarters, perhaps one more elegant than those she had been used to at Ivy Cottage: a small room with a bare wooden floor, a plain bed, a wooden chest of drawers for her belongings with a candle or lamp on it, a white chamber pot. Perhaps, given the elegance of the house, there might be a rug on the floor, a small looking glass to check her appearance. Instead, she was standing in a large room with a thick carpet woven in cream and lilac. Two huge windows overlooked gardens, each draped with lilac silk curtains which hung down to the floor. There was a four-poster bed draped in the same fabric and the walls were papered with a delicate pattern of wisteria flowers trailing down from their vines. Maggie stood on the threshold, hardly daring to step inside.

"And your dressing room is just there." Celine waved towards an open door. "It is small, but pretty enough."

Maggie stepped carefully onto the carpet, afraid of leaving dirt on it from her boots. She followed Celine through the door into a room half the size of the bedroom but full of light from another large window, painted in a lilac that echoed the paper of the first room. It contained two clothes-presses, both in a dark polished wood with floral inlays. A basin and jug were on top of one, the other held a lamp. Close to the window was a delicate long-legged table with a large looking glass and a writing set on it, completed with a silk-covered stool before it.

"Your dressing table," said Celine. "I will find you a *necessaire*, Her Grace has more than one."

Maggie had no idea what a *necessaire* was but did not like to ask. "May I return to Edward now?" she asked instead. "He will be feeling anxious about choosing a room."

Celine guided her back to the nursery.

"I will look out clothing for you," she said as they walked. "This evening, I will show you what I have available and measure you for other things. You have no other clothes with you at all?"

Maggie shook her head. "I was not given time to bring anything. I only have what I am wearing."

Celine shook her head. "Men. Joseph should have let you bring whatever you had need of, although... Her Grace will not allow you to be seen dressed as you are, so only your underclothes would have been useful, in truth. I will attend you later."

"Thank you," said Maggie, grateful for Celine's calm acceptance of the situation. Hopefully, the maid could be relied on to help her navigate this strange new world.

In the nursery, Edward was gazing out of the window again.

Maggie crossed the room to his side. "Your mother says you have a set of rooms on the floor below this one."

"I won't stay in those rooms." He didn't turn to look at her.

"Why not, if they belong to whomever is the duke?"

"They were my father's. And my brother's after him."

"They are yours now," she said gently. "If they offend you, if they hold bad memories, I'm sure you may change the décor. Or choose other rooms." She could not help a small laugh. "It is not as though Atherton Park lacks rooms to choose from."

He gave a half smile.

Encouraged, Maggie pressed a little further. "I have been put in the Wisteria Room. It is very pretty."

He looked out of the window. "Then I will take the Iris Room."

"Where is that?"

"Next door to the Wisteria Room."

She was surprised that he could recollect all the rooms and where they were in relation to each other. "Shall I ask Joseph to make it ready for you?"

"I am not allowed to leave this room until I am properly dressed," he reminded her, his face sullen again.

Maggie settled herself in a small nursing chair, set low to the ground. "We shall make ourselves comfortable here for now," she said. "I can sleep in that side room, if we are not to be seen by anyone. Although who would see us, anyway, and why would it matter?"

"You look like a maid," he pointed out, not unkindly. "I look like a farm hand. The servants would prattle if they saw me dressed like this, my mother will not hear of it. She will not rest until a tailor has been sent for."

"How many servants are there? I have only seen Joseph and Celine and know of the cook."

He laughed out loud. "There are almost two-hundred-and-fifty servants at Atherton Park," he told her, amused. "You have not seen them because we have been carefully managed, kept out of sight, taken to my mother only when everyone else has been told to stay out of the way."

She gaped at him. "Two-hundred-and-fifty? What do they all *do*?"

He settled in a chair and rubbed his face as though refreshing his memory. "Do you want a list? The estate manager, the steward, the butler, the housekeeper. They all have assistants because they have so much to do, so an under-steward, an under-butler, an under-housekeeper. The footmen, I believe there are eight of them. Maids of every kind and every description, from Duval all the way down to a scullery maid, there must be two or three dozen of them, including the dairy maids and the girls who work in the still room. The laundry maids, there are five of them who do nothing but wash the clothes and linens in the laundry house. The cook has an under-cook, six girls and two kitchen boys under her. There's a boot boy to polish everyone's shoes. The hallboy. The stablemaster, the coachmen and the grooms, the stablehands and stable boys. A farrier. Probably a tiger. The gardeners and their assistants, there are more than forty of them alone. The gamekeeper and his assistants. Groundsmen. A gatekeeper."

Maggie gaped at him. "A *tiger*?"

Edward laughed out loud. "A young boy who sits behind a gentleman when he is driving his own carriage, to hold the horses when he is out of the carriage. Like a tiny groom, I suppose."

Maggie shook her head. "How is it I have seen none of them?"

"You can see the gardeners from the windows sometimes, and the groundsmen. Indoors you will not see servants unless you have summoned them. My father…" He paused. "My father used to say he did not wish to see any of the maids unless it was in chapel for prayers."

"Is there a village nearby, a church?"

"We have a chapel here."

"In the *house*?"

"Yes."

"It is more like the Hospital than a real house," said Maggie. "With laundry-houses and a chapel and so many staff. What are we to do all day, if we are not allowed out of this room?"

They searched the room, removing holland covers to reveal a dappled grey rocking horse, from which Edward turned away. The side room contained only a simple bed like the one in the main nursery. Other holland covers covered a chest of drawers, inside which they found playing cards as well as an old pair of battledores with a decrepit shuttlecock.

They passed the afternoon playing vingt-un, then progressed to a game of battledore and shuttlecock, though their shuttlecock flew poorly, its feathers badly crumpled.

"We must have a new one to play properly," said Edward, as the shuttlecock fell to the floor yet again.

Late in the afternoon, there was a discreet knock at the door and Celine appeared. "I have brought some clothes from

Her Grace's rooms I think may fit you. Can you try them on now? I can adjust them in the coming days."

"Go," said Edward. "I need to catch my breath after that game."

On the bed in the Wisteria Bedroom were laid out a white lawn nightdress trimmed in fine lace and five dresses. Two in wool: a dark grey with a lilac ribbon trim, the other a rich brown trimmed in an elaborately pleated silk of the same shade. There were two muslin dresses: a deep violet with prettily puffed sleeves and a dark green one with gold threads making up a floral pattern at the hem. The last dress was a deep rich blue silk, plain in style but beautifully finished, with tiny sequins glittering across it like stars and a gold braid trim.

"That one is an evening gown," said Celine. "You will need at least one for now."

Maggie stared at the clothes. While they were all beautiful, the blue silk was like a fairytale dress, she had never seen anything so fine. Even the rich ladies who had visited the Hospital had been dressed in day clothes, not an evening gown like this one.

"Won't the Duchess mind?"

Celine's mouth twisted. "These are old clothes," she said. "Her Grace has not worn any of them for at least five years. They are no longer the latest style, but they will do very well when I have altered them. A young lady would generally wear something lighter, but the household is in mourning, so these are appropriate for now. When we begin the season, you will wear more stylish clothes in brighter and lighter colours."

Maggie touched the blue gown. "I have never worn a silk dress," she murmured.

Celine smiled. "It will suit you," she said. "When I have

prepared those, I will find you a spencer and a pelisse to go over your gowns, otherwise you will freeze when you go outside in a muslin. For now, I will look out a shawl for you, Her Grace has dozens. Meanwhile," she pointed into the dressing room, "I have found you an old travelling *necessaire* of Her Grace's, from before her marriage."

A polished wooden box was on the dressing table, with a key set in the lock.

"Open it," encouraged Celine.

Carefully, Maggie turned the lock and lifted the lid, to reveal a green velvet lined upper compartment, in which lay a silver comb, brush and a small hand-held looking glass, along with empty little glass pots, each with a silver lid.

"For cosmetics," said Celine. "In Her Grace's youth, all ladies wore a great deal of face powder, with rouge. They blacked their eyelashes also. Nowadays a young lady would not use such items, she would appear immodest. Perhaps a little rouge, only, for a ball. I will provide you with some when we go to London, also perfume. For now, I will bring you tooth powder. For cleaning your teeth."

A second compartment under the first revealed several ivory-handled tools, including a toothbrush, a silver toothpick and tongue scraper, nail cleaner and tiny scissors. There were also hairpins and an additional brush.

"For brushing clothes," said Celine. She pressed down on a section of the box and a hidden drawer appeared out of the side, holding two delicate necklaces, a tiny ruby cross on a gold chain and a string of shining pearls. "You will need some jewellery," she said.

Maggie drew back, suddenly nervous. "Her Grace…"

Celine smiled at Maggie's fearful face. "Her Grace wears

diamonds and emeralds. She has boxes of jewellery. These are nothing to her. But if you wear no jewellery at all, it will look odd. Her Grace wishes you to look like a member of the family, so you must be dressed accordingly."

"I have never used a toothbrush," confessed Maggie.

"You use it like this," said Celine, picking up the toothbrush. "Dip it in the tooth powder, it is salt with peppermint oil, then brush each tooth. When you have finished, you spit it out and use this." She showed Maggie a bottle which proclaimed, on an elaborately decorated label, *Eau de Bouche Botot mouthwash*.

"Gillyflowers, cinnamon, ginger and anise. You rinse your mouth with it, for sweet-smelling breath. Then spit it into this cup."

"What are gillyflowers?"

"Like cloves," said Celine.

Maggie took a tiny sip. It was very strong-tasting when in her mouth but left a pleasant enough aftertaste once she had spat it out.

Maggie had been used to cleaning her teeth with a corner of a wetted rag, when she had done washing her face with it. "I had no idea ladies used so many products."

Celine laughed out loud. "That is nothing to what Her Grace uses. She has every kind of powder and cream you can imagine in her dressing room. But she worries about her beauty fading with age. You are still young; it takes nothing for you to be beautiful."

Maggie shook her head. "I am not beautiful," she said honestly.

Celine put her head on one side. "You are not perhaps a great beauty, they are rare enough in this world," she conceded.

"But you are pretty. And when you are elegantly dressed, I am sure plenty of young men would think you beautiful."

Maggie shook her head again. "We used to have lady visitors at the Hospital," she said. "They would walk amongst our tables while we ate and amuse themselves by picking out what they called aristocratic faces, perhaps the illegitimate offspring of important men, or even acquaintances of theirs. They gave sweets to those they thought most beautiful." She looked down. "I was never given a sweet." And it had stung, whatever the chaplain said about vanity it had still stung as the years went by and sweets were freely given to those with larger eyes or longer lashes, cherubic curls or pouting lips, while her face was passed over every time, unworthy of note.

Celine was horrified. "And they called themselves ladies? Treating orphans as an amusement?"

"They were welcomed by the staff, as they might make donations to the Hospital."

Celine tutted. "A real lady should not treat children so. And you *are* pretty, you will see. You have a sweet face. Now come, I must undress you."

"I can undress myself," said Maggie, drawing back.

"All ladies have help to dress and undress."

"I am not a lady, as you know."

"You are a lady while you remain in this house, Her Grace has decreed it so. Come."

In the dressing room more items had been added, including a boot brush, a pretty lace fan, lavender soap for washing and a small bottle of rose perfume.

"We can buy something else in London," said Celine. "My mother was very fond of rose perfume and taught me to make it. I made it from the roses that grow here at Atherton, but

Her Grace does not wear it. She likes perfumes from the grand shops, from Paris especially."

Maggie unstopped the tiny bottle and breathed in the sweet fragrance of the rose garden. "It is lovely," she said, with real feeling and Celine smiled.

Celine undressed Maggie, who, despite feeling uncomfortable, complied. Celine, however, knew her business, for as soon as she was down to her shift she tried two of the dresses on Maggie, pinning and tucking and making little notes to herself, before giving her a clean shift.

"There. This one is my own, I will take your shift to be washed and it will be dry by the morning if I hang it before the fire." She grew brisk. "I will send to Mrs Brooks in Atherton for underclothes, she can have them ready in under a week." She took a measuring tape out of her pocket and measured Maggie's waist, bust and hips, as well as her calves, then sat down at the dressing table and drew out a sheet of paper and a quill and began to write, murmuring under her breath. "Four caps, three chemisettes, two nightgowns, three petticoats, twelve shifts…"

"Twelve?" Maggie stared.

"…three short stays and two longline corsets." Celine thought for a moment. "From the milliner, we will order three pairs of silk stockings and six of cotton for now. And ribbons to tie them."

Silk stockings? Maggie could not even imagine such luxury.

"You will not be much in company while the house is in mourning. Later, when we travel to London, we can buy better silk stockings." She gave a shrug, "The ones available locally are good enough, but not the finest. Her Grace will not wear them."

"I have never worn silk," Maggie said.

"Ah? Then you will find them well enough for now. Now for your shoes." She glanced at Maggie's worn boots and clearly found them wanting. "I will order slippers and a new pair of boots from the cobblers. They will do for now. In London, we will find what we require."

Maggie could not imagine what Celine had in mind: what more could she possibly require?

"I will have one of the maids, Jane, attend you. I will oversee her, but as I must look after Her Grace, I will require help at dressing times."

Maggie felt a rising panic. "What if she realises I am not a lady?"

Celine smiled. "She is from humble origins herself; she will not notice small signs that an experienced lady's maid would spot. You need only let her do her work."

Maggie tried to focus on her own concerns. "May I see where Edward will sleep?" If he should have nightmares, she would need to know her way to his room.

Once Maggie was re-dressed in her own grey wool, Celine led her out of the bedroom. "Would you like to see the ducal rooms?" she asked.

Maggie nodded, curious at why Edward found them so little to his taste.

Celine took her on a long walk, to a different part of the house.

"Her Grace's rooms are there," she said, indicating a door. "And the ducal rooms are here."

The suite of rooms traditionally reserved for the Duke of Buckingham was both magnificent and unwelcoming. Maggie instantly saw why Edward disliked them. Made up of four rooms, there was a large bedroom, a comfortable dressing room, a small room intended for ablutions with a shining copper bath, and a private drawing room or study, with armchairs as well as a writing desk. Impressive though the suite was, the décor was heavy and overbearing, with dark bulky furniture and an oppressive red as the main colour, making the rooms seem gloomy despite the large windows. Having four rooms all to one person made them feel empty rather than luxuriously opulent, as though one were alone and shut away from all human company. The suite might remind Edward of his past life at Ivy Cottage, where he had been kept in comfort but seeped in loneliness.

Since Edward had refused to use it, the ducal suite had been left to languish in darkness, its windows shuttered, and furniture draped over as though the rooms were closed up and the rightful owner absent. Celine and Maggie returned to the Wisteria Bedroom corridor, where Celine showed her the Iris Room, which shared a wall with Maggie's bedroom. The Iris Room favoured rich purple, a little overpowering but less gloomy, and boasted only the main bedroom with a small dressing room, like Maggie's.

On Maggie's return to the nursery, she found the Duchess and Joseph with Edward.

"He cannot be dressed like that," snapped the Duchess. "He looks like one of the farmers. Use his father's and brother's clothes for now, while new ones are ordered."

"I will not wear their clothes." Edward's pale skin was flushed, his neck blotchy, hands in fists at his side as he stood with his back to the window.

"It will take at least a week to have new clothes made, even if a tailor comes here with his assistants and does nothing but cut and sew day and night."

"So be it."

Maggie was surprised by Edward's stubbornness on these matters, but he would not budge and insisted he would continue to wear his "farming clothing," as the Duchess referred to his suits.

"You cannot go anywhere or be seen by anyone until this is dealt with," the Duchess said. "And you will eat in this room. We cannot have the other servants see you like this."

"We will spend our days in the nursery, then," said Edward. "Since you treat me like a child, it seems the best place."

The Duchess swept out of the room in a fury, leaving the four of them in a long silence.

"Order the tailor from Aylesbury," said Celine at last to Joseph. "They will gladly come if they think they can claim to be clothing the Duke of Buckingham. I will order a seamstress to make the undergarments. His Grace and Miss Seton will remain here for a week, and we can be done by then, I am sure of it."

Celine and Joseph left and, soon after, Maggie and Edward were sent food, two large trays of it, including a soup of spring greens, pigeon pie, tongue, asparagus, mushrooms, stewed pears and a syllabub.

"All this for us?"

Edward gave her a look. "You have not yet dined amongst the *ton*," he said. "This is nothing."

The food was very good although they could not finish it all. Afterwards Celine brought the nightdress and the toothbrush with the tooth powder and mouthwash for Maggie to use, along with a green shawl to drape over herself. Joseph brought a matching set of toiletries for Edward, who reluctantly agreed to wear a clean nightshirt so that his shirt could be washed and dried.

"Goodnight, Edward," Maggie said once they were alone again.

"Goodnight, Maggie."

The side room had been where the nursemaid would have slept, Maggie supposed. The bed, freshly made up by Celine and herself, was comfortable enough, but she had only been asleep for a little while when Edward's nightmares began.

"PLEASE!"

Startled awake and unused to her surroundings, Maggie at first struggled to find the door into the nursery.

"FATHER! NO!" and a scream, worse than she had ever heard from Edward.

She burst into the nursery at last, tripping over her feet in her haste to reach Edward's bedside. The lamp's dim glow revealed him, bolt upright in his too-small bed, arms flailing as though seeking to stop someone. Maggie grasped his arms, brought them down, put her arms about his shoulders.

"Edward! Edward, it is me. Maggie. Edward?"

At her voice, he slumped, as though suddenly released from some unseen struggle, leant into her arms. "Maggie. Oh Maggie."

She felt tears, wet on her bare arm and held him closer to her. "Edward. It was a nightmare. You are safe now."

He pulled away from her embrace, now fully awake. "I am sorry."

"There is nothing to be sorry for. "Will you tell me of what you dreamt?"

Silence.

"Never mind," she said gently. "Will you sleep now? Shall I leave my door open? I could barely find it in the dark," she added.

"No, I will – I will sleep."

Carefully she made her way back across the room to her bed. Once there she wiped his tears from her skin and lay back down. What horrors had there been in this house, she wondered, that had led Edward down the path of lunacy?

Within a day, lured by a generous purse, a local seamstress and her assistant were installed in an unused small parlour and set to work sewing over a dozen shirts for Edward, then moving on to nightshirts, while a hasty order of cravats, stockings, shoes, boots and slippers was made to local suppliers, sending Edward's measurements to them. A tailor with three assistants and a carriage full of rolls of cloth arrived from Aylesbury, was allowed brief access to Edward in the Iris Room, dressed only in one of his new shirts for fear of them even catching a glimpse of his current attire, before taking over the parlour as the seamstress left, the four of them cutting and sewing for days. Maggie would have liked to have seen how their work was progressing, but Edward wanted nothing to do with them. Various parcels had also arrived with the tailor, including hat boxes and a parcel containing a beautiful long silk robe in shimmering peacock blue.

"A banyan, Your Grace," said Joseph, unpacking it and shaking out the folds. "For morning or evening wear when you are at home without guests. Worn over your shirt and breeches."

"My father never wore them. He said they were like a woman's frock."

"They are very comfortable; most gentlemen wear them."

Edward waved him away. "This fuss over clothes is absurd." Once the clothes were complete, he would have to face the rest of the household, from whom he had so far been locked away, as well as be free to go outside, to see once again the gardens and grounds of his childhood, which held few pleasant memories. He stared out of the large windows, looking down onto the formal gardens below, hands gripping the windowsill. Maggie had been called away by Celine for another fitting and every time he was alone, the memories of his past rose up within him, making him fearful of what was still to come, which only emerged as testiness towards Joseph, which was unfair, making him only feel worse.

In the Wisteria Room Maggie watched Celine undoing a large parcel, a delivery of everything that had ordered from Mrs Brooks, the bed now piled high with snowy white linen, from caps and nightgowns for sleeping, to a heap of petticoats, chemisettes and shifts. There were also short stays and two longline corsets. A box from the milliner provided the promised pairs of cotton and silk stockings as well as two sets of ribbons to hold them up.

The cobbler's efforts arrived the next day, one box containing two pairs of kid slippers for indoor use, one pale cream, the other a dark blue. They felt invisibly soft on Maggie's feet, as though she were only wearing her stockings and made her footsteps silent on the thick carpets and even on the wooden floors. The other box contained a pair of brown leather ankle-height boots, which appeared a great deal less sturdy than Maggie's current boots, but were far more elegant, fitting tightly round her ankles and boasting pointed toes. Laced into them, Maggie took a few cautious steps. She would have to walk with more care for any dirt or puddles, should they ever be allowed outside again. She often caught Edward staring out of the windows and was unsure whether he was longing to go out or whether he felt unsettled by his surroundings and was happy being kept indoors, away from any people or places from his past.

The nursery rooms were their world, as though they were back at Ivy Cottage, but with a larger staff of unseen servants to wait on them. Only Joseph and Celine were allowed to enter, Joseph setting and lighting the fire each day.

"I feel like a scullery maid," he said to Celine.

Whatever food they requested would be brought to them and Maggie took the opportunity to try and feed Edward better, asking for cream and sugar to be served with his morning porridge, serving him more potatoes with his meat.

The days passed slowly in the dusty nursery. They found a globe, along with old games and toys and played with them as though they were children once more. Skipping ropes, hoops and whips, toy soldiers, spillikins and the board game of Fox and Geese kept them occupied for some time. Between and during games Maggie tried to draw Edward out on his childhood.

"Did you have a nursemaid?"

"I recall a few of them, they came and went."

"Any favourites?"

He shook his head. "They favoured my brother because my father did. I was too shy for their liking."

"Did you go to school?"

He looked at her oddly. "I had a tutor until I was sent to boarding school."

"Was he kind?"

"He was not unkind. But it was my brother everyone cared for. He was the heir. It was his education that mattered the most."

"And school?"

He swallowed, put down the battledore they had been playing with. "I hated it," he managed at last. "It was full of bullies and my brother did nothing to protect me, he thought it all in jest, but I could not bear it." Day after day of little torments, never-ending pranks or threats. Every day having to be on his guard. "Then I went to Doctor Morrison."

Maggie did not wish to ask questions about the doctor. She had seen his treatments and, according to the doctor himself, what she had seen had been as nothing compared to Edward's early days there.

For the first time in his life Atherton Park was rid of the two men who had made him miserable there, although what was to come still frightened him. What his mother wanted of him, to take up his place in society, to be the Duke of Buckingham, was as though a door to possible freedom had been opened and yet was guarded by demons. How was he to manage, when his last eight years had been spent locked away and called a lunatic? How was he to manage, to pretend to be something he had not been prepared for? His only shred of hope lay with Maggie. If she would remain at his side, he might be able to confront the daunting task that lay ahead of him. He would have liked to better express his feelings to her, but she knew nothing of what his life had been like so far. It would only horrify her. "I am grateful you are here," he managed, after a long silence had fallen between them.

Maggie reached out and touched his hand. "I would not have left you alone," she said. "I was glad that you sent for me. Whatever is to come, we will manage it together."

For all her reassurance to Edward, Maggie still found herself each night worrying about what she had agreed to. These days, playing in a locked-up room, with only Celine and Joseph admitted, was another version of Ivy Cottage, as though nothing much had changed. She could not imagine what was to come. At least Celine and Joseph knew who she was and could help her with the deception. When Edward fell asleep one rainy afternoon and Joseph came to ask if they needed anything, she took the opportunity to speak with him.

"Have you served here since you were old enough to go into service?"

"I have been part of this household since I was six."

"*Six?*"

"I was a pageboy to Her Grace. A wedding gift from her father. It was fashionable for grand ladies to have a little blackamoor attending you."

"But you were a child. Where was your mother?"

"I was taken from her and sent to England."

"From where?"

"Jamaica."

"I don't know where that is."

"The West Indies." He strode across the room and spun the globe. "Here."

She followed him, bent over the globe to see where he indicated. "So far away?"

"It is where spices and sugar come from. My mother was a slave there."

"And your father?"

He shrugged. "Probably. I never knew him."

"And you were brought here to be a…"

"A pretty gift," he said. "Like giving his daughter a new necklace to celebrate her advantageous marriage."

"I'm sorry."

He sighed. "It is a long time ago now. Thirty years."

"You knew Edward when he was growing up?"

"Yes."

"What was he like?"

He glanced at the sleeping Edward. "A gentle child. Not like his brother and father. His father was a big man and noisy with it, you could hear him coming five rooms away. He stomped and swore and shouted at dogs, horses, servants and even his own family. His brother was a copy of their father. Whereas Edward… he was quiet, shy even. He loved animals, he'd wander all over the estate looking at birds, deer, fish. He'd sit so still and quiet you could barely see him, then he'd come home and read about animals and plants, try his hand at drawing them. He was promising at it, used to beg for a drawing instructor. He learnt to play the pianoforte almost alone. His father couldn't make him out at all. The only interest the Duke had in animals was shooting them. He used to say Edward would have been better off being a girl, at least they could have married him off."

Edward stirred and woke, and Joseph grew silent again.

"Did you sleep well?" asked Maggie.

Edward gave a half-nod, his face turned away from her. "Call for tea," he said.

Maggie felt uncomfortable speaking to Joseph as though she were his superior. "Would you bring up some tea, please, Joseph?" she said.

"Yes, Miss Seton," he answered smartly and left the room.

It was like playing a game, pretending to be a fine lady with servants and using a different name. The children at the Hospital sometimes played Master and Servants, a game where the Master or Mistress would pretend to be very grand indeed and order about all the Servants, giving them more and more elaborate things to do, but part of the joke was that they could not do anything for themselves. They would order a cup of tea but ask the servant to raise it to their lips, as they could not do anything so exhausting as picking up a cup themselves. Yet here it was real, she could not go and put on the kettle herself, she did not know where the kitchen was in this vast house and would surely get lost trying to find it. Instead, she had to dispatch Joseph, order him to bring tea as though she were his mistress, and he in turn must call her Miss Seton, a name that belonged to no-one, made up on the spur of the moment by the Duchess, just as once Maggie's true mother-given name, whatever it had been, had been changed. At least she was still Margaret, though no-one ever called her that at the Hospital, so even that felt odd and overly formal, as though she were in trouble.

The roaring fire, hot tea and even the warming ginger biscuits Mrs Barton had sent up with Joseph did nothing to take the chill away from Edward. He had heard Joseph's last words as he awoke. *He used to say Edward would have been better off being a*

girl, then at least they could have married him off. No need to ask who had said that, Edward had heard the words enough times directly from his father's lips, he had made no secret of how he felt about Edward, that he was a disappointment compared to his brother. His father would have been happier if Edward had also been a hunter, or even a rake about town, either option would have made sense to him. Edward had felt it keenly, the disappointment, the baffled repugnance of his father. He had not even tried to be more like his brother, for it was all too obvious that it was simply impossible, that their temperaments were so disparate that Edward could never hope for his father's approval, and so he only hid away from him more and more.

But he had Maggie by his side now, there was a small comfort in that. A person whom he could trust, who had promised to stay by him and make him well. If such a thing were possible. At Ivy Cottage he had half believed it was. Here, he was unsure again.

"Your Grace, the tailor left last night, your wardrobe is complete, and Her Grace has requested that you move into the Iris Room today and are dressed appropriately from this afternoon onwards."

"I'm to be set free, am I?" Edward tried to sound nonchalant, but his stomach turned over at the thought of being seen by more people, of leaving the safe world of the nursery.

"Yes, Your Grace."

"Your dresses are also ready," said Celine to Maggie. She had spent days constantly sewing, one dress or another laid across her knee while she altered sleeves and bodices or shortened hems, for the Duchess was taller than Maggie. Edward and Maggie were eating a midday meal of roast chicken sandwiches and honey cake, along with a dish of preserved plums and tea. "This afternoon you can have a bath, and then I will dress you as a lady should be dressed, while Joseph dresses His Grace. Then you will be free to go anywhere in the grounds that you choose."

"A bath?" Maggie had never had a bath. There had only ever been jugs of cold water and basins, with washing cloths and soap.

"I have had the footmen bring up a bath to your room," said Celine to Maggie. "The maids have been filling it for the last hour. His Grace also has a bath being filled in his room." She made her way out.

"Are you looking forward to being free to roam?" Maggie asked Edward.

He did not answer, only passed her a slice of honey cake.

"Thank you," she said. The hot tea and sweet cake gave her confidence for what was to come, but Edward did not finish his portion.

"Your bath is ready, Your Grace," said Joseph from the doorway.

Edward left in silence. Maggie made her way to her room, where the dressing room was full of steam. A vast copper bath had been filled more than halfway. Soaps and three jugs filled with more water were on the table, while two large linen cloths lay nearby ready to dry her when she was done.

Feeling shy, Maggie undressed and at a nod from Celine, cautiously climbed into the warm water and lowered herself into it. The level rose as she did so, covering most of her body. The sensation of being enveloped in warm water was extraordinary and Maggie could not help letting out a sigh of delight.

Celine giggled. "Now the soap."

The room's air took on the scent of lavender from the soap, then of rosewater which Celine added to the large jugs of warm water to rinse Maggie's hair. Wrapped in one of the large cloths as Celine used the other to dry her hair, Maggie admired the new underclothes laid out for her, with the brown woollen dress she had chosen to wear. It was a fine weave, trimmed at the hem and the end of its long sleeves with a pleated brown silk, worn with a chemisette with frills about the neckline.

The new clothes required the help of Celine, Maggie realised. It would be impossible to dress by herself from now on, since most of the items fastened at the back. This was why ladies had a personal maid. It made Maggie feel helpless not to be able to even dress herself. Even the youngest children at the Hospital had been encouraged to put on their own clothes as soon as they were able, the older ones assisting them only if necessary, with staff poking fun at them if they could not quickly learn to manage alone.

"Your hair," said Celine, just as Maggie was certain they were done.

"What is wrong with it?"

"You cannot wear plaits; they are for children."

Maggie would have protested, but she supposed Celine was right. She submitted to having her plaits undone, her hair brushed and pinned up at the back.

"When we go to London you can have your hair cut," promised Celine, speaking through hairpins held in her mouth.

"Cut? I do not want my hair cut!"

"Just at the front," soothed Celine. "I will curl it for you. It looks odd without curls at the front. Every lady of fashion has her hair so."

"I should go downstairs, Edward will surely be waiting," fretted Maggie.

Celine laughed. "A gentleman's grooming takes every bit as long as a lady's," she assured Maggie. "And Joseph has been waiting to dress His Grace properly for some time, he will not skimp. Take a moment to look at yourself."

The looking glass showed a lady, there was no doubting it. Hair pinned up at the back, a ruffled chemisette, the dress altered to suit her size and height, the new boots. Maggie felt as though she were staring at someone else, one of the lady visitors at the Hospital perhaps.

"I found a pelisse and some gloves," said Celine. "They are not new, but they will do."

The pelisse was a dark blue while cream kid gloves fitted comfortably if slightly too large on Maggie's small hands.

"It sits a little long," fretted Celine of the pelisse.

"It does not touch the ground," Maggie reassured her. "It will not drag in the mud." Anxious to be with Edward, she made her way down the stairs, every step feeling odd in the new clothes and boots.

But there was no sign of Edward in the drawing room, only the Duchess, who observed Maggie in icy silence.

"Will I do?" asked Maggie at last, as much to break the silence as to get the Duchess' seal of approval, which did not appear to be forthcoming.

"You look like what you are supposed to be, a poor relation," said the Duchess. "It will do for now."

Maggie could not imagine how her warm, beautiful clothes could possibly make her look poor, but she held her tongue and was glad when Joseph appeared in the drawing room doorway, his face bright with an odd mixture of pride and pleasure as he announced: "His Grace."

Maggie stared. She had never seen Edward in anything but his baggy woollen suits, always in dull browns. Now he stood before her transformed. A well-cut jacket in dark grey, beneath it a silk waistcoat in dove grey. His shirt was an immaculate crisp white with a high pointed collar and a cravat, expertly tied. Beneath it all, perfectly fitted black breeches and high polished boots. The fitted clothes drew attention to his height and neat waist, but also lent breadth to his shoulders. His hair, she was glad to see, had not been cut short, perhaps he had refused, but the unfashionable length had always suited him and now, set off with his new finery, he was both elegant and handsome, his pale skin seeming brighter next to the white linen of his cravat.

The Duchess stared at him for a few moments, then gave a small nod. "At least now you look passable." She walked past him and out of the room.

"I think you look more than passable," said Maggie. "You look very elegant. How do you feel?"

Edward rolled his shoulders. "Uncomfortable," he said. "I never did like all the fuss of these kinds of clothes, it's the only thing the doctor did for me that I agreed with, putting me in those baggy suits like a labourer."

She couldn't help smiling. "Well, we both have fine new feathers." She indicated her new outfit with a shrug and a smile, as though they were absurd, although a part of her hoped he might compliment her.

He gave a half smile but did not comment on her new clothes. "At least now my mother will allow us the freedom of the grounds."

"Then shall we take a walk?"

In the doorway she hesitated about which way to go.

"Left," Edward said, sharply.

"Is there something pretty that way?"

"There's a fountain."

"And the other way?"

"Nothing worth seeing."

They walked along the crunching gravel paths until they came to a formal garden. Neat box hedges cut into sharp lines, everything stiffly perfect. At its centre was a three-tiered white stone fountain, water cascading from level to level. Maggie peered into the depths of the lowest basin. The water was sparklingly clear, the bottom of the basin visible, despite its considerable depth.

"No fishes and plants here," she said.

He sat on the rim and looked into the water, beyond it. "No life. Only what looks right and proper, nothing behind the façade."

"We could add fish. And waterlilies."

"I'm sure my mother would find some objection to it."

"You are the master of Atherton Park."

He shrugged. "I don't feel like it. I feel like an imposter. I was never raised to be the Duke; I was always the spare. Everything revolved around my father and my brother, his heir. I was always an afterthought. It didn't matter what I wanted or who I was, if it wasn't about the two of them, it had no importance." He stopped. "It doesn't matter. Shall we walk on?"

She followed him. "But it does matter. *You* matter."

"I matter now because I am the Duke of Buckingham. If I were not, I would be back in Ivy Cottage, most probably for the rest of my life. You know that to be true, Maggie."

She bowed her head. She knew he was right, but it was a sad truth and somewhere in Maggie it was also a fact that made her angry. That a family should try to forget about their son when it suited them, only to hastily recall him from confinement when they needed him again, was a poor way to behave. But it was not her place to say such things, and she did not wish to add her own feelings to Edward's, upsetting him further. She wanted Doctor Morrison to stay away from Atherton Park and Edward as long as possible, and the only way to achieve that was for Edward to remain calm, to give the Duchess no reason to send for the doctor, no reason to suppose Edward needed his ministrations.

"Your mother mentioned a rose garden," she said instead. "Will you show it to me?"

He gave her a wry look, the look he gave when he was amused by something. "You sound like the girls who used to try and woo my brother," he said. "They were always trying to get him alone somewhere, in the hopes that he would propose."

"And it did not work?"

"He was too wily for that. He would always agree and then call to everyone that they must all come and see the rose garden, or the orangery, or wherever else the young lady had tried to get him alone. And so they would find themselves with a whole crowd of people and no chance whatsoever of snaring him."

"Did he not want to be married?"

"He was young, he was having fun in society. Why get married? There was no need yet. My father was hale and hearty…" He trailed off. "Let us return to the house," he said abruptly, and strode away, Maggie trotting after him to keep up, feeling she had asked the wrong questions, allowed feelings to rise up in him that were unhelpful to his wellbeing. She should not have asked personal questions, must stick to topics of less import.

Maggie found Edward in an armchair in the library, head buried in a book. Quietly she searched the shelves and found a large and heavy atlas, which she managed to balance on her knees, exploring the maps it contained with interest. She hoped that her presence might induce Edward to speak again, but he remained silent for the next few hours, until there was a rap at the door and Celine appeared. She curtseyed to Edward. "Your Grace, Joseph is waiting for you in your rooms."

Edward nodded and left the room as though expecting this summons.

Celine turned to Maggie. "I am here to dress you for dinner."

Maggie was confused. "I am dressed."

"A lady changes clothes for dinner, into something more elegant. Your silk. I have already dressed the Duchess and she is most particular about punctuality. Come."

Back in her room, Celine made short work of removing the brown dress from Maggie and helping her into the blue silk, then tidying her hair. She pulled out the blue kid slippers and laced the ribbons holding them in place so that they would not fall off. Finally, she drew out the string of pearls and clasped them round Maggie's neck. "There," she said, turning her towards the looking glass.

Maggie had been dressed in cast offs, but the clothes she was now wearing were beyond anything she had ever dreamed of. She allowed her hand to stroke the blue silk of her dress, shifted from one foot to the other to feel the delicate kid slippers softly move with her. The tiny sequins glittered, catching the flickering light of the candles.

"*Tres bien*," said Celine with satisfaction.

"Thank you," said Maggie.

Celine followed her down the stairs but stopped at the dining room door. "Watch what Her Grace does and do likewise," she whispered.

Maggie had been so engrossed in the novelty of her clothes that she had not thought that this was the first time she would eat with the Duchess. Suddenly cold, her bare arms turned to gooseflesh, her stomach heavy.

A footman bowed and opened the door to her.

The room was huge and the table at its centre vast, it would easily have seated twenty people around it, but at present there was only the Duchess and Edward, seated one at either end of it, with a third place laid for Maggie by the Duchess' left hand. The room shimmered with dozens of candles and the table was laid with a bewildering array of dishes, as well as elegant tableware and glasses. Two more footmen stood stiffly by one wall, awaiting orders.

Edward rose to his feet as Maggie entered the room. She hovered for a moment, unsure of herself.

"You are late, Margaret," said the Duchess. "We expect punctuality in this house."

"I am very sorry," said Maggie, throat dry. "… Aunt Caroline," she remembered to add after a too-long pause.

"Take your place," said the Duchess, indicating the setting by her.

Maggie reluctantly sat, wishing she were closer to Edward, who was absurdly far away.

"You may serve the soup, Barnaby," said the Duchess to one of the footmen.

The soup was asparagus, a delicate creamy concoction. As soon as the footman had finished serving it, he removed the tureen in which it had been presented and the other footman replaced it on the table with a beef steak pie, which joined the platters of mutton and stewed celery, roast pigeon, a fricassee of rabbits and one of mushrooms, Spanish peas, almond cheesecakes and an elderflower jelly. Maggie watched carefully to see how the Duchess ate and tried to imitate her, taking absurdly small mouthfuls.

"You have been out today," began the Duchess, in a stiff attempt at conversation when the silence had grown unbearable.

Maggie looked at Edward, who said nothing.

"Yes, Aunt Caroline," she said. "We walked in the gardens."

"The rose garden will be in full bloom by late May, it was laid out by Edward's grandmother."

Maggie privately doubted whether a previous Duchess of Buckingham had done anything so close to manual labour as to lay out a rose garden, but she nodded as though this was interesting information.

"You may wish to ride while you are with us," said the Duchess in an even stiffer voice after another endless silence. "The head groom will find you a suitable horse."

Maggie had never ridden a horse and the idea of learning was frightening; the horses pulling the carriages had been so large. "Thank you, Aunt Caroline," she said meekly.

The rest of the meal continued in silence. Maggie ate what she could reach but did not dare ask for dishes to be passed to her.

"We will proceed to the drawing room," decreed the

Duchess at the end of the meal and there followed another uncomfortable hour of silence in the drawing room, where Edward disappeared behind a book again and Maggie stared into the fire and hoped to be set free as soon as possible.

"You may leave us," said the Duchess to the footman in the end. He left the room and she turned to Maggie and Edward. "Now that you are dressed appropriately, we can begin your education," she said. "Neither of you are fit to partake in society at present, since you have been lacking in education these past…" She trailed off, then stood. "We will begin tomorrow." She swept out of the room.

CHAPTER 4:
A Lady's Education

MAGGIE WAS WOKEN IN THE WISTERIA ROOM BY THE curtains being opened. A maid she had never seen before was busy tying them back, before laying out the green muslin dress ready to be worn along with clean undergarments.

"Morning, Miss Seton," she said when she saw Maggie's eyes were open. "I'm Jane. I've brought up your water and Duval says she'll be in to do your hair shortly. Duval says I'm to look after you as she must see to Her Grace first thing. I'm to learn how to look after a lady," she added, sounding excited.

Maggie nodded without replying, fearful of saying the wrong thing. Evidently, Jane saw Maggie as a junior member of the family and a wonderful opportunity to better herself by progressing to the giddy heights of lady's maid.

With Jane's keen attentions, she was quickly washed and dressed, remembering to use the toothbrush and tooth powder as though she had always done so. The green muslin floated about her. She had to touch it to make sure it was real, it felt so light on her.

"It's a sunny day," said Jane anxiously, perhaps fearing that

Maggie's silence indicated displeasure. "I thought it would be warm enough for the muslin, seeing as it's almost May. But I'll fetch your shawl."

"Thank you," said Maggie, wanting to assuage Jane's fears. "You have done very well," she added encouragingly, and Jane beamed and bobbed her a curtsey.

"Thank you, Miss, I'll do my best for you. I'll brush your hair now, ready for Duval, she's not yet taught me how to do hair."

Celine arrived moments later and demonstrated a simple hairstyle for Jane's benefit, the hair drawn up into a braided bun behind. "Miss Seton will have her hair cut when we go to London," she said. "I will teach you to do ringlets at the front. For now, make sure the back is very smooth."

"Yes, Duval."

"Breakfast is ready, follow me, Miss," Celine added to Maggie.

Breakfast meant sitting with the Duchess and Edward, which made everything feel stiff. Where Maggie and Edward had once toasted bread together before the fire while talking, or eaten hearty bowls of porridge, breakfast in the drawing room was an altogether different matter. There were four kinds of cake, a brioche, a seed cake, a honey cake and a plum cake, along with coffee, tea and hot chocolate. Maggie carefully helped herself to a slice of seed cake, before hesitating over the drinks. She had never drunk coffee or hot chocolate.

"May I pour you some hot chocolate? I think you will like it," offered Edward.

She nodded gratefully and accepted the tall thin cup she was given, which sat in an odd saucer, with a raised circle in the centre to hold the cup more firmly in place. She took a small sip. It was like drinking a pudding, very thick and rich with spices and sugar, topped with a froth that vanished on her tongue. Edward caught her eye and smiled at her expression of amazed pleasure.

"I like it better than coffee myself," he said, sitting beside her with his cup. The Duchess, sitting opposite them both, made no comment, only sipped her cup of tea.

"Send for Jenkins and Mrs Russ," she told the footman who had been standing stiffly against a wall.

"Yes, Your Grace."

He left the room and the Duchess leant forward and spoke rapidly. "Jenkins is the butler. Mrs Russ is the housekeeper. They must both see you now that you are fit to be seen and neither of them can know who you are, Margaret. I cannot allow more people to know what is happening."

Maggie saw Edward's shoulders tighten. Her chocolate cup trembled.

A man and a woman entered the room, both perhaps in their fifties. Jenkins had dark hair, Mrs Russ might have had red hair in her youth, but it had faded to a reddish brown. Maggie tried to stand up as they entered the room, but Edward grabbed at her hand, giving a tiny shake of his head.

"Jenkins, Mrs Russ," said the Duchess. "His Grace has come home to take up his rightful position as master of Atherton Park."

Jenkins bowed and Mrs Russ curtseyed. "Welcome home, Your Grace," they chorused.

"May I say on behalf of all the staff how sorry we all are for your losses, Your Grace," added Jenkins.

Edward nodded without replying.

The Duchess intervened. "We are also joined by Miss

Margaret Seton. She is my third cousin once removed. Her father recently died and left her to my care. She will be living with us for the foreseeable future."

They both bowed and curtseyed again, although not as deeply as for Edward, Maggie could see the degrees of importance accorded to them both. She dipped her head in response, trying to emulate Edward's slow, gracious movements.

"That will be all," said the Duchess. "Send for Duval and Joseph." Jenkins and Mrs Russ left the room.

Celine and Joseph appeared moments later, and the Duchess turned to the other footman. "You may go, Bartholomew. We are not to be disturbed."

"Yes, Your Grace."

The door safely shut behind him, the Duchess turned her gaze on Maggie.

"Stand up and curtsey."

Maggie did so.

"Don't *bob* like that. That's how a maid curtseys. Slower. Slower than that. Never mind, you will have to practise. Sit down."

Maggie sat, feeling thoroughly inadequate.

"Can you read and write?"

"Yes, Your Grace," said Maggie, offended at being considered illiterate.

"You call me Aunt Caroline," the Duchess corrected her coldly. "You must practise, or you will slip up. You will write a sample so that I can assess your handwriting. Can you dance?"

"No."

"Play an instrument?"

"No, but –"

"Draw?"

"No." Drawing lessons had been reserved for the boys at the Foundling Hospital, in case it should help them with future trades.

"Can you ride a horse?"

"No."

"Sew?"

Maggie was relieved. At the Foundling Hospital she'd been one of the best sewers, her stiches neat and even, her mending and darning invisible. "Yes," she said firmly.

The Duchess narrowed her eyes. "Plain sewing or embroidery?"

"Plain."

The Duchess sighed.

"I can do netting," said Maggie, stung at having her skills so obviously dismissed.

"Well, that is something at least. Duval, you will provide threads and beads for Miss Seton so that she can do netting. She can start by making herself a reticule. And you will teach her embroidery. Meanwhile you will prepare a sample of embroidery she can have with her when company are present, that will make it appear that she is working on something."

"Yes, Your Grace."

"She has a beautiful voice," said Edward.

"I beg your pardon?"

"Margaret… *Cousin* Margaret has a wonderful singing voice."

The Duchess raised her eyebrows.

"You would do well to make the most of it, if you want her to appear accomplished," said Edward. "You are determined to think poorly of her, but you are making a mistake."

The Duchess gave a cold nod, then continued addressing

Joseph as though she had not been interrupted. "Tell the stables to find a horse for Miss Seton and have her taught to ride, she must begin at once." She paused and Maggie thought she saw her swallow. "His Grace will also need a suitable mount, for use both here and in London."

Joseph, too, seemed reluctant in his response. "Yes, Your Grace."

Both avoided looking at Edward, and he stayed silent.

"Very well," said the Duchess, after a long pause. "I will hire drawing and dancing masters, and a singing instructor. They will have their work cut out to have you both ready for society in only four months." She turned to Celine and Joseph. "You will assist their education in whatever form is necessary, be it the need for a dancing partner or informing Miss Seton when she does not behave in a manner befitting a lady."

Maggie's handwriting was reluctantly passed by the Duchess as acceptable, and their days began to take shape. Upon rising, they were dressed by Jane and Joseph, made their way to breakfast, allowed a brief walk in the gardens, then began their education for the day, continuing until past midday, when they would eat a simple repast, before recommencing lessons until late in the afternoon. They were allowed very little free time.

"If you are unoccupied at any time, you will take up your embroidery," insisted the Duchess.

Maggie carried a small bag containing her silks and other embroidery needs with her at all times. Luckily her neat stiches in plain sewing meant that her cross-stitch came along well enough to complete a sampler that was not considered disgraceful, after which Celine set about teaching her other styles of embroidery, which Maggie took well to, stitching leaves, flowers, water and birds in ever increasing complexity. She often found herself taking it up when servants were in the room, for their endless presence made her anxious. Having spent their entire lives around the nobility, surely they would take one look at her and know her for a maid?

"They will judge me," she confided to Celine, but Celine shook her head.

"They feel sorry for you. They think you were brought up without much money and now must find your way in a grand house with the Duchess as your aunt criticising you. They do not whisper anything else about you."

"And Edward?"

"They are glad to have Edward home. Atherton Park needs a master, and his father was not always... kind."

Only a few days went by before Celine had Maggie try on a new article of clothing.

"It is a riding habit, Old John the stablemaster has said he has a horse for you and will bring it round the day after tomorrow."

The dress Celine was offering was different to what Maggie had worn so far, a stiff woollen dress with long sleeves in a deep red, far wider and longer in the skirt than any of her other dresses.

"It leaves room for you to sit in the saddle without any impropriety," said Celine, speaking through the pins held in her mouth. "It is too big, but it will do while you learn."

The morning came and Joseph summoned Maggie to the front door, where a groom was standing with a chestnut mare.

Edward stood behind her, framed in the doorway, unwilling to come any closer.

"Morning Miss," the groom said. "Old John chose Lacey himself, he says she's a gentle one, just right for a lady to learn on."

The saddle had two padded pommels, one pointing straight up, the other curving to one side.

"You'll ride with your legs to the left, Miss, unless you've already learnt to ride to the right?"

"I've not learnt to ride at all," protested Maggie.

"Left boot in my cupped hands, Miss, then when I do say 'Up,' I shall lift, and you must spring up so I can lift you up onto the saddle."

Maggie tried to follow the instructions.

"Up."

She tried to push herself upwards as the groom lifted, but she was a little behind him and so instead of a smooth spring upwards, there was a lift followed by a jump when the lift had already lost its power. Instead of finding herself in the saddle, she was pushed against the horse, which stepped away, leaving her stumbling, one foot still held by the groom, now exposing too much of her leg, almost to the knee. He quickly let go of her foot.

Several more clumsy attempts were made, with Maggie's cheeks growing flushed with embarrassment at nearly falling into the groom's arms, when Edward stepped forward.

"Let me help."

"But Your Grace…"

But Edward had already approached Maggie and was holding out his cupped hands for her foot.

"I don't think I am very able," gasped Maggie, feeling foolish.

"Of course you are. Your foot," insisted Edward.

She placed her left foot in his hands, her right hand on the horse's back.

"Up."

She sprang and this time she and Edward were perfectly in synchrony, his lift giving her spring power, and she was suddenly solidly in the saddle, Edward guiding her foot so that her right knee wrapped round one part of the pommel, her left leg snug beside it, held in place with the second part. The excessive folds of the riding habit had maintained her dignity throughout the movement, now spreading out around her so that only the tips of her boots stuck out from the fabric.

Relieved, she looked for Edward, but he had already retreated to the steps. His hands, she saw, were shaking.

"That's it," said the groom encouragingly. "And now hold the reins. Like this." He demonstrated, then passed them to her to hold, which she did, awkwardly.

"Not so tight," he said. "Don't pull. Elbows down and in and I'll take you for a walk."

"I don't –" began Maggie, but the groom had already led the horse forwards on a leading rein, and it took all her concentration to balance, tightening her thighs around the twin pommels, trying not to tighten the reins out of fear. But as the swaying of the horse's slow plod continued, she relaxed. She was taken round the grounds for a brief walk, then returned to the front door, where Edward, smiling, watched her dismount, which she managed, although she landed ungracefully, stepping on her long skirts.

The lessons continued daily, and after the first few Maggie learnt to get into the saddle with the groom's assistance, rather than Edward's.

"Just as well," said Edward, "I think the *ton* would be horrified to see a duke acting as a groom, don't you?"

"Won't you join me for a ride?" she asked.

But he hung back, face uncertain. Meanwhile, she learnt to trot and canter, although she was too afraid to gallop as yet.

The drawing master who had been hired was a delicate young man, whose worn shoes and shabby clothes indicated he badly needed this work. He was clearly overwhelmed to have a Duchess' family member to instruct, bowing and scraping to not just the Duchess but also Maggie.

"My niece's education has been sadly neglected," said the Duchess when he arrived. "She has not been given drawing lessons and yet she will need to demonstrate some basic accomplishments in polite society. There will not be time for her to learn everything she should already have mastered, so I would suggest that you limit your instruction to botany. Teach her to draw and paint flowers, that will be enough."

"As Your Grace sees fit," stammered the young man, flustered in her presence, dropping paper and paintbrushes onto the library floor.

Maggie knelt to help him collect them while the Duchess raised her eyes to the heavens and swept out of the room, leaving Celine and Edward as chaperones.

Once she had gone, the drawing master grew in confidence, taking a few flowers from the ornate display on a nearby table and showing Maggie the shape and texture of the stems and leaves, how to consider where the light was coming from, and which part of the image should be shaded. By the end of their first hour together, Maggie had sketched a tolerably good iris. To make rapid progress, it had been decided that the drawing master should stay for three weeks, sleeping in the servants' quarters, and that Maggie should receive three hours a day of instruction, exclusively focused on sketching and painting flowering plants. A large portfolio, bound in a patterned green paper, had been provided for her to keep her better works in.

"But who would ask to see them?" she asked the Duchess at breakfast the next day.

"All young ladies keep examples of their accomplishments near at hand," said the Duchess. "When making calls to the house, ladies and gentlemen may ask how you have been entertaining yourself and that is your cue to indicate a sampler of embroidery or your drawing portfolio, which visitors may ask to examine. It is only civility on their part of course," she added with a sniff. "Few people have any real interest, but it is part of polite conversation, and you cannot have nothing to show should they ask. That would look most peculiar."

Edward watched as Maggie bent to her work. This absurd concoction of lies was part of everything he had disliked about life at Atherton Park and in London. Perhaps Maggie was being instructed in haste, but was she really unlike all the young ladies of the *ton*, after all, who were no different except that they had been practising their accomplishments since they could walk? Were they not all engaged in the same falsehood? Edward doubted any of them were fascinated by netting or embroidery. Perhaps a few truly did enjoy drawing or music, but he remembered his father saying that young ladies only displayed their accomplishments until they were married and then forgot all about them, which hardly indicated a true interest on their part.

Later that day, before the evening meal was served, Joseph took Maggie into the dining room, where he explained the tableware, glassware, seating arrangements and where guests should be seated according to rank.

"I'll never remember all that!"

"You won't have to remember all of it, your hostess will already have thought of it, and the footmen will pour into the correct glass, but you must remember the silverware at least. Let's begin. This is a sugar sifter, which you would use on your berries. Sugar tongs would be used for lumps of sugar in your tea."

Maggie nodded.

"Now spoons. This is a berry spoon, this is a marrow scoop, that is a salt spoon and next to it a mustard spoon. This one is your soup spoon and this one a dessert spoon."

And so it went on, while suppers continued to be the worst part of the day, stiffly formal, eaten mostly in silence, which at least allowed Maggie to silently practise her spoons and knives in her head, even while her earlobes throbbed painfully from Celine's ruthless piercing of them with a needle so that she might wear earrings.

Prayers on a Sunday took place in Atherton Park's chapel, a beautiful space where morning sunshine lit up the carved plasterwork of the arched ceiling. The tall columns were painted the same dark blue as the carriages, while the pews were a delicate pale shade of the same colour, with a beautifully tiled floor. At first Maggie found sitting in the front pew alongside the Duchess and Edward odd, but after a few weeks she grew used to it. After the sermon, they would leave first, to the bobs and bows of the entire staff who were gathered there for prayers, over two hundred each week, making the chapel seem like the church in a small village. As soon as the first Sunday was over, the Duchess had Maggie registered as an inhabitant of the local parish. Maggie had expected this to be difficult, but the vicar recorded her false name without question.

In all their morning walks Edward always led them to the left.

"If you leave the house and walk to the right," Maggie asked Celine one morning, "what do you come to?"

Celine thought. "Gardens. Then the lake."

"Nothing else?"

"The stable block is that way too."

"Is it close by?"

"Yes, but hidden behind a copse by the house. Most stable blocks are set out of view, but they need to be close at hand for when a carriage or horse is sent for."

Maggie nodded. She thought about Edward's fear of horses, how he had helped her mount because she was struggling, but also how quickly he had retreated once she was safely in the saddle, his shaking hands. She remembered, too, how first the Duchess and then Joseph had been uncomfortable when discussing Edward's need for a horse to ride.

Later that day, Joseph summoned her to review her table

etiquette skills, but once alone in the dining room she grasped the opportunity to find out more.

"Why does Edward not like to ride?" she asked.

Joseph looked away. "Some gentlemen are not fond of the hunt," he said.

"It is more than that," she persisted.

Joseph sighed. "His Grace had… an experience when he was younger, which…"

"Which what?"

"He liked to ride well enough," said Joseph, speaking fast as though to get the story over and done with. "He had a pony, a dappled grey he called Pigeon. He loved that pony, rode it all over the estate, had a good seat, after a while he didn't even need a groom with him. But his father insisted he should have a real horse, a larger one and Edward didn't want to change, he wanted to keep his little pony, even though he was getting too big for it. You've seen his long legs." He stopped.

"And?"

"And his father had Pigeon shot in front of him. Said if he wouldn't give him up, he'd take him away and Edward would have no choice but to get a full-size horse." He swallowed. "There was blood spattered on Edward's face. He fainted."

Maggie gaped at him in horror.

"How could he be so cruel?"

"The Duke was a hard man. He had no tenderness to him, and he tried to stamp out any sign of it he saw in Edward. He did not value virtues such as gentleness or kindness, he thought them weak, fit only for women. Pigeon was only one such occasion, there were plenty of others, but that is the reason why Edward is fearful of horses. It is not because he cannot ride or is afraid of them as animals. He was an excellent rider but after that day he would shake if he was around them and when his father tried to make him mount another horse he screamed. That was when they sent him away to boarding school."

"At least he was away from his father."

"You would think so. But he was broken by then already and boys in such schools… they are brought up to rule, to spot the weak within their ranks and toss them aside. They tormented him. He would come home in the holidays weeping, begging his mother not to send him away again and every time he grew more desperate until he tried to drown himself in the lake and after that… they sent him to Ivy Cottage."

Maggie sank onto one of the dining chairs, legs grown weak beneath her. "Their own son?"

"Doctor Morrison told them what they wanted to hear: that he was mad, a lunatic, that he could be taken off their hands and either cured or simply kept away, a secret."

"Didn't anyone ask after him?"

"The spare? No. The heir was loud and visible enough in society, so they said Edward had gone to some school in Scotland, I believe. When he was old enough to have left school, they changed their story to say that he was at university, then fond of astronomy, that he was travelling, that he was… who knows? Who cared? No-one. By then his older brother was dashing about London with every pretty miss and her mama trying to secure him as a husband and every young rake trying to cheat him at cards. Who would even recall that there was a younger son?"

Maggie stood silent for a few moments. Everything she knew about Edward had changed in an instant. She had already doubted that he was a lunatic but had not trusted her feelings against the word of an eminent physician and

Edward's family… his own mother. Now she saw how Edward had been broken, not because his mind was weak, but because his father and those around him had taken everything that was good about him and thrown it back at him as a weakness, had crushed his spirit until he could take no more and, once broken, had further tormented him in the name of caring for him until he no longer knew what was true about himself and could only cower in fear from those who approached him. And then, this beast of a father and his thoughtless bully of a son had died and suddenly Edward had been worth something in the family's eyes, had been the way to secure the title and the estate, the vast riches which would otherwise have passed to someone else, leaving them behind, worthless without him.

The singing instructor professed himself delighted with Maggie's voice and found little to improve in it, only introducing her to various new songs that she had not previously known, since most of her singing had been choral works or religiously themed. Now she was to sing appropriate arias from operatic works or well-known songs that other young ladies would have been taught to sing. She learned them quickly and when the instructor was not there would beg Edward to accompany her on the pianoforte, which he would do so long as there was no-one else around.

"It is not considered a manly instrument," he said, when she asked why he was so reticent.

"But you play it so well."

"I will play it whenever you wish to sing."

One morning Maggie turned right instead of left. "I wish to see Lacey," she told Edward. "I have an apple for her."

He hesitated, followed her at a distance, lips tight, as she approached the stable block, a large low building set around a courtyard with a wide and high gateway, large enough for a carriage and horses to enter or exit. To the side, a fenced-off ring, strewn with gravel.

"What is that?"

"A training ring," said Edward. "It is called a *manege*."

In the yard, they were met by an old man with a hunched back.

"Your Grace. It's good to see you."

"Old John."

The man smiled at Maggie. "And you'll be Miss Seton that's been doing so well with Lacey. I'm the stablemaster, everyone calls me Old John, my son's John now, he's the head groom."

"I brought an apple for Lacey."

"And there she is, waiting for you."

Lacey's curious face poked out of one of the boxes, and Maggie went towards her and fed her the apple, while Edward stayed in the centre of the yard, as far from any of the horses as possible.

"Can we come more often?" she said when she returned to him.

"As you wish." Lacey was no doubt like a gentle beast, but his heart was pounding. His experience in this very yard still made him shudder, but he did not want his fears to hold Maggie back. He was glad to leave the yard, to leave the smell of horses behind and for his breathing to slow.

But two weeks later when Lacey was brought to the front door for Maggie's riding lesson there was a handsome black horse alongside her, with both Old John and a groom in attendance. Maggie, already at the door, hesitated.

"Good morning, Old John."

"Good morning to you, Miss. I've brought this fine fellow along for His Grace to see."

"Are you sure?" she asked him. "It seems unwise when Cousin Edward has not ridden for years."

"Let's see, Miss," said the old man, unperturbed. Edward emerged behind Maggie, and Old John touched his hand to his cap. "Good morning, Your Grace."

"A new horse?" asked Edward curiously.

"Yes, Your Grace. But a shy one, flighty. He'll be needing a steady hand, but one of my lads will take good care of him. He's a fine horse, just needs more care. He'll walk alongside Lacey this morning with Miss Seton riding. She'll show him the ropes, being so gentle herself."

Edward looked the horse over from the steps, then slowly walked down towards it, raised a hand to its neck. The horse shifted under his hand, nervous.

"There now," he said softly. "There now. I won't hurt you."

The horse stamped its feet and Maggie put out a hand towards Edward, afraid for him. But Old John touched her arm and shook his head silently.

Maggie frowned. "It looks –" she began, wanting to say *dangerous*, but Old John shook his head again and put a finger to his lips.

"Needs some care, that one," he repeated. "I'll see which of the lads can be trusted to bring him on."

"No," said Edward, not turning away from the horse, one hand still on its neck. "I'll take him for myself. What's his name?"

Maggie stared. Edward, who had refused to ride, who seemed afraid of horses, was offering to tame and ride a horse Old John considered flighty?

But the old man nodded serenely. "Merlin, Your Grace."

Edward took the reins from the groom and walked the horse forwards. "I'll take him to the manege to see what he can do."

"Yes, Your Grace."

Half an hour later Maggie completed her own riding lesson, returning to the manege, where Edward had Merlin on a leading rein, making him walk, trot and canter, following the circular training arena round first one way and then the other.

"Why did you buy an untrained horse for His Grace?" Maggie asked Old John, who was watching Edward.

"He's not untrained," explained Old John. "You could ride him. But so far he's needed a firm hand and His Grace don't like to treat his animals that way. He'll make him into a gentler beast before he rides him."

Maggie was curious. "Did you know Cousin Edward would take him on when you bought him?"

Old John nodded. "I hoped His Grace would," he said. "I've known him since he were a little lad, I know what kind of horse might draw his attention. Being shy himself, he must feel he is the master, not the beast to be trained."

Maggie gave a laugh. "I think you might be a physician," she said. "Or a magician."

"I ain't a book-learned man," said Old John. "But I do know horses."

"And dukes?"

He chuckled. "And dukes, or some of 'em," he conceded.

By June the rose garden was in full bloom and there was a heady perfume in the air. Now that the stable block was no longer out of bounds, Maggie and Edward occasionally walked down as far as the lake. The first time they did so, Edward stood for a long time looking over it, the gentle ripples on the surface, the ducks swimming by. He thought of the last time he had been here, the cold of the water closing over his head, eyes tight shut, willing himself to be gone from this life in which he felt trapped without an end in sight, then the distant sound of shouts and splashing and being grabbed, yanked to the surface, the sudden rush of air and light and coughing and choking as he was dragged to the shore by one of the gardeners. Within days, he had met Doctor Morrison for the first time.

"Did you come here often as a child?" Maggie asked.

He shrugged, trying to let go of the memory. "Sometimes. My brother was too fond of playing pranks on me though, even if we took the rowing boat out, he was always trying to find a way for both of us to end up in the water."

"Could we go in the boat now?"

He hesitated, the memory still lingering but the day was sunny, and Maggie was at his side, he had played by the lakeside many times before that fateful day. Perhaps he could reclaim it as a happy spot again.

"The boat is just there," he said at last. "You will have to help me push it into the water."

After some effort they got the boat halfway into the water, then Maggie got in and he pushed off, leaping in beside her, so that the boat rocked and she shrieked, frightening the moorhens nearby. Edward took the oars and found they were easier as a man than they had been as a boy. He rowed them slowly around the small island in the centre of the lake, where wild ducks and geese made their nests. The sun and the gentleness of the boat's movement allowed the memory to fade a little, made him think of something else.

"I wonder how the frogs are doing at Ivy Cottage," he remarked.

"Do you think of it often?"

"Only to be grateful for being far away from it."

"Are you happy here?"

"It feels different now than it used to." He did not say, now my father is gone, now I am no longer the lesser brother. "I could be happy here if I did not need to… do all these things that are expected of me."

"You will go brown," Celine admonished Maggie when she saw her come in from the first day at the lake. "You must carry a parasol, or the *ton* will think you a rustic."

"I cannot even sit in the sun?" Maggie sighed, but she carried a parasol with her from then on. The lake became a favourite place as Edward took pleasure in rowing Maggie about, and even tried to teach her to row beside him, the boat turning in circles for a while until they found a matching rhythm. Thanks to the parasol, her own skin stayed pale while Edward's changed to a healthier hue and his arms grew stronger from rowing the boat.

July came, the days too hot and tedious for Maggie to bear any more learning. Sometimes, she would glance at Edward and make a small pleading gesture with her hands, as though at prayer, and he, trying not to smile, would announce that he needed to rest, that he was tired. This excuse always made the Duchess uncomfortable, as though she feared Edward might suddenly start ranting or behave in some way like a madman, so she would hastily nod her agreement and let them go free.

They would escape where she could not find them or would never think to look for them. To the lake, to the stables, sometimes down to the kitchens, where the maids would stare at them wide-eyed but Mrs Barton the cook, ever unflappable, would welcome them with a cup of tea and let them help her make some small treat, Maggie rolling pastry while Edward filled jam tarts. They would wait until the delicacies had been cooked, then take them outside to the lake or gardens and eat them still warm, letting the sunshine fall on them.

Edward had been putting off speaking with his steward, Mr Wilson, who managed Atherton Park, but now he asked for a meeting with him and found him to be a man of good sense and with practical ideas in which Edward took an interest. Merlin had given Edward more than just riding confidence.

"There are some cottages on the estate that have fallen into disrepair, I will ride out tomorrow to see them with Mr Wilson," he told Maggie one day.

She watched him set off from the window, marvelling at how much he had changed, how he strode confidently out to where the groom was holding Merlin, got into the saddle with ease, his posture elegant, his shoulders and chest broader than they had been at Ivy Cottage, when he had been all limbs. Here at Atherton Park, where he was shown deference and care by all the staff and could find his way into the unexpected role of duke, he seemed to be growing into his manhood, shrinking again only when the Duchess criticised his progress.

There was an endless stream of rules for every possible social interaction. Maggie was not to speak of or ask anything personal, nor even to compliment a person's dress, as it might seem too familiar. She was not to laugh overmuch; she was not to discuss politics. The hostess at a dinner would begin by turning to the guest on her left and speaking to them until the second course was served, when she would turn to the guest on her right and speak with them. Guests would follow the hostess' lead.

"What do I speak of, then?"

"The weather. The health of absent family members. You can admire something in the room, such as a portrait. Speak of something suitable which you have just finished reading, though not love poetry, it is not respectable for a young lady. Anyway, it will be for the gentleman to entertain you at dinner by choosing suitable topics of conversation, you need only reply appropriately. Also, a gentlemen may offer you wine, as it is not polite for a lady to call for wine herself. You may accept or decline, although you should give a reason for declining, so as not to seem ungrateful for the attention paid to you. Edward, practise with Maggie."

"Cousin Maggie, will you do me the honour to drink a glass of wine with me?"

"Yes, thank you, Cousin Edward," she replied, awkwardly.

Edward nodded to Joseph. "Two glasses of wine," he said.

Joseph poured two glasses and passed them both on a silver tray. Edward took both and passed one to Maggie with a small bow.

"Bow in return," instructed the Duchess.

Maggie gave a bow. It felt like a ridiculous movement when seated, but Edward only raised his glass and took a small sip. She copied him.

"Very well," said the Duchess. "Now you will know what to do. If you prefer to decline, simply say, "Thank you, but I am not accustomed to much wine at dinner and I have just finished a cup with His Grace," or whomever most recently offered you a glass. Or indicate that you still have a full glass and offer your thanks. That will do. If there is a choice, choose white or champagne, but you will find the wine has usually been chosen for the meal."

Maggie privately hoped that no-one would ever offer her wine or indeed speak to her at all, it was all too complicated, she had enough to do with remembering which way to turn her head and keeping up endless small talk.

"You would do well to read some popular novel currently in circulation," added the Duchess. "There is one called *Pride and Prejudice* which has been widely read of late. It is written by a lady, so they say, and no doubt most young ladies and even some gentlemen will have read it, so you will seem up to date."

The drawing master having completed his work and the singing instructor likewise, it was time for a dancing master to be hired, even though the hot days of summer hardly seemed suitable for much physical exercise. Edward also needed to be schooled.

"My niece's education has been sadly neglected," the Duchess said to the dancing master. "And my son was never fond of balls when younger, he was too busy... hunting and so on. He will have to improve himself alongside her."

Maggie wanted to laugh at the idea of gentle Edward going hunting, but the simpering dancing master was too busy adjusting her posture to notice.

"Your Grace need have no fears, I can assure you that within a few weeks they will both be the delight of any ballroom."

"They had better be," said the Duchess. "I am in correspondence with Lady Jersey, and she assures me that vouchers for Almack's will be dispatched to us as soon as the season opens." She considered for a moment. "You will also instruct them in the waltz," she added. "It may not be required, but I have heard that it is being danced more often now, even in respectable circles. It would not do to seem behind the times, and it may well lead to a... hastening... of affections for a suitable partner."

"As Your Grace requires." The dancing master bowed. Maggie wondered whether he was physically able to address the Duchess without bowing. But she appeared satisfied and left the room.

"There are not many steps to master in order to be able to perform most dances at a ball," began the dancing master. "So, we will commence with the travelling steps, these include the Allemande, the Chassé, the Waltz, the Fleuret and the Strathspey." He nodded to the accompanying pianist, and they began.

By the end of the first lesson Maggie's head was swimming with trying to recollect everything. He had said there were only a few steps, but they ran into one another, and she kept forgetting which was which. Edward, she could tell, had already received this kind of instruction, the steps coming back to him.

"Step, close, step, hop!"

Maggie landed from her hop and the dancing master looked horrified.

"Land with *delicacy*, Miss Seton. Your Grace, do not *bounce* so much, you will lose dignity."

"I am too much a spring lamb and you, apparently, too much a carthorse," whispered Edward, his eyes gleaming with humour.

"Shush," begged Maggie, trying not to laugh. "I have forgotten what the *tems levé* part is. Why are there so many words?"

"Today we will progress to the setting steps," said the dancing master with every indication of apparent confidence that Edward and Maggie could even remember the travelling steps.

And on it went. From travelling steps to setting steps, then flourishes and punctuation steps. The dancing lessons occasionally required Celine and Joseph to join them, to better understand the criss-crossing of partners through sets.

"And *smile*," reminded the dancing master for what felt like the hundredth time in the past hour. "A mis-step with an easy smile may be forgiven, while perfect steps with a sullen demeanour will not."

Maggie pasted a smile onto her face and giggled when she saw Edward doing the same.

"No giggling," remonstrated the dancing master. "A lady does not laugh out loud, for fear of seeming reckless in her manner."

Maggie bit back her giggles, thinking of the times when Edward and she had been reduced to helpless fits of laughter at some foolish incident, like the time Maggie had lost a shoe in the stream or when an apple had fallen on Edward's head.

Was that reckless behaviour? It had only seemed good-natured to her, raising Edward's spirits. She made sure her face was appropriately composed with only a small smile showing but did not dare meet Edward's eye in case he made her laugh again.

But they progressed over the weeks that followed. Maggie's steps and landings becoming daintier, Edward's statelier. The dancing master professed himself satisfied that they were able to perform a minuet, a cotillion and a quadrille to his satisfaction.

"Today we will begin the waltz," he said. "Now, you will know that this is a new dance and was until recently considered unsuitable for a respectable ball, but it has grown in fashion and so it is wise, as Her Grace has suggested, to be at least competent in it, should it be called. As a matter of etiquette, the dance is more… intimate, owing to the close proximity of the couple. It is therefore appropriate that it should only be danced where a lady has been chosen for a gentleman to dance with by either her chaperone or the Master of the Ceremonies. A gentleman should not propose it himself to an unknown lady for fear of seeming too forward in his attentions. It is often danced by those couples who are recently engaged or where there is strong evidence of an understanding. With those points understood, we will proceed to the correct starting position."

Edward and Maggie stood opposite one another.

"Closer together. Your right arm about the other's waist," instructed the master. "Then the left, hold it up, curved above your head, and clasp your partner's hand, thus creating a circle through which you will face one another."

They stepped closer, their faces now only a hand's breadth apart. Maggie felt suddenly shy. She and Edward had touched many times, of course, he offered her his arm several times a day, she touched or held him when his nightmares were bad, but now they were standing pressed together, hands clasped, his other hand firm on her waist. She had thought the fuss over the waltz overblown by the dancing master and his endless rules, but now that the dance was to begin, she understood why this dance had been frowned upon. There was an intimacy to it.

"And begin the travelling step we have learnt, and as you do so, you rotate," instructed the master.

She trod on Edward's toe at once.

"I'm sorry!"

He shook his head, smiling, his steps neat and precise. Maggie focused and slowly the rhythm became smoother. Edward's hand tightened on her waist, and she felt him begin to guide her, their steps synchronised so that there was a sway to the dance, the spinning no longer jerky little adjustments of direction but fluid, soft. Maggie gazed up at Edward through the circle of their arms and saw his face serene and certain. It made her smile, and he smiled back.

"The left arm now lowers, the lady places both hands on the gentleman's shoulders and the gentleman places both hands on the lady's waist, continue the rotation."

Maggie placed both her hands on Edward's shoulders, surprised for a moment to find them broader and firmer than she had expected. He was growing stronger from eating better and exercising more. The thought made her happy, and she held onto him more tightly, confident in his strength. His hands tightened about her waist in response, guiding them to a faster pace. For a giddy moment, Maggie was being whirled around, held in his strong hands, entirely in his control, so that she need only feel the music and respond to it, without worrying about the steps, which suddenly came naturally to her, guided as she was by Edward's certainty.

"Somewhat too fast, Your Grace, but very poised. I believe we may consider the waltz instruction complete."

Maggie wished the master had not called a halt so soon. The rest of the dances, even when they had grown better at them, had been enjoyable but always requiring of thought, counting the steps in one's head or being careful not to step the wrong way, and the dancing master had always had something to say about whatever they were doing, with endless reminders of form and etiquette. But the waltz, for a moment, had been different, as though she and Edward were alone together inside the music. She had seen – no, *felt* – his confidence in directing their progress around the floor and it had given her the freedom to enjoy the moment, to feel herself graceful in his arms, responding to his guiding touch.

Edward stepped away from Maggie, disappointed. He had put up with the other dance instruction, it had all come tediously back to him from his younger days as a boy and he had done his best to be a good partner to Maggie, improving his steps so that he might perform them well. And they had laughed together sometimes and as she improved, he felt they made a creditable pair, unlikely to disgrace themselves at a ball. But the waltz had been… it had been unlike the other dances. Putting his hands on Maggie's waist, he had felt the music through her movements, and it had made his movements more certain, had given him a growing confidence that had allowed him to hold her more tightly, to steer her, guide her. And she had followed him, he had felt her grow soft under his hands and allow him to lead her. He wanted that feeling again, the two of them graceful together, entwined in the music. There was something about it that gave him confidence. That made him want more.

That evening at supper the Duchess made an announcement.

"We will go to London for the Little Season. We will send word ahead for Atherton House to be made ready and will set off next week."

Maggie put down her soup spoon and looked at Edward, who had also stopped eating.

"So soon? Parliament does not open until November; I will not be required to attend until then."

"We need time for Atherton House to be at its best and for all of us to have new wardrobes, as well as to try out a few social occasions and ensure you are both ready for the full season in the spring."

The rest of the meal continued with an anxious silence hanging over them. The long summer days, Edward's healthy colour and more confident posture had lulled Maggie into thinking their days would progress like this forever, now she was harshly reminded it had all only been preparation for what was yet to come.

That night Edward's nightmares, which had lessened, came back with a vengeance, Maggie heard him cry out and hurried to him, found him sweating and wide-eyed, bolt upright in his bed.

She sat on the edge of it, stroking his arm. "All will be well, Edward."

"Will it? I dream of making a fool of myself, of people pointing and laughing, of being married against my will to a woman whose face I cannot see... I..." His breathing was growing faster, and she clasped his hand in hers.

"Edward, I will be by your side. You have done so well here... it will be the same in London, you will grow in confidence and find that you can manage everything perfectly. Breathe slowly, Edward, slowly."

He looked at her, fearful, struggling to steady his breaths. "Will I?"

"Yes," she said firmly, although she did not feel anything like as certain as she sounded. His anxiety made her anxious too, she imagined making some foolish mistake, despite all the months of instruction she had received, by which everyone would know her for a maid. Edward's chances of being accepted in society ruined, a sad return to Ivy Cottage. Back to Doctor Morrison and his brutal treatments.

Atherton Park was thrown into disarray over the next few days. Servants hurried about, meals were far plainer than Maggie had seen to date, in the last days a simple tray was sent up to each of their rooms. Maggie carried her tray to Edward's room and ate with him there, finding it a relief not to spend awkward meals with the Duchess. The larger unused rooms were full of holland covers to protect the furniture from dust during their absence. Every carriage in the stables had been pressed into use, sending goods, servants and clothing to London.

Even Merlin and Lacey departed.

"Two of the grooms will ride them to London," said Edward, gazing out of the window, "so that we can ride while we are there."

"Is there a lot of riding in London?"

"Most of the *ton* make it their business to walk or ride on Rotten Row every day when the weather is fine."

"What an odd name. It does not sound like somewhere the *ton* would like to be seen at all."

"It is in Hyde Park. I believe it was originally known as the *Route du Roi*, which is French for King's Road. It was ordered by William the Third, but the name was corrupted. I have been before. It is pleasant enough. I used to ride with Mother in the open carriage. I don't recall much else about London."

His hands were gripping the windowsill. Maggie laid one hand on his. "It will not be so bad," she said, though she knew nothing of what it would be like.

"It will be unbearable," he said, and left the room.

The day before their departure they received an unexpected and unwelcome visitor. Maggie was partway through being dressed when there was a knock at the door, revealing Edward, half dressed and flustered. Jane stared at him in amazement and Maggie tried to smooth over his intrusion.

"What *are* you doing here, Cousin Edward? I have not yet done my hair. Jane, my brush. And will you please find my pink brooch, it is in there somewhere," knowing full well no such item existed.

Jane, eyes still wide, hurried to the dressing room.

Edward's voice was a hoarse whisper. "Doctor Morrison is here."

"What? He cannot be."

"I have just seen him arrive."

Maggie swallowed. "Get dressed," she managed. "I will be downstairs in a moment."

"I cannot find a brooch," said poor Jane, coming back into the room as Edward closed the door behind him. "Is His Grace alright?" she added.

"He is well, he only wished to say I was late, Her Grace needs me for something," improvised Maggie. "Can you do my hair as quickly as possible, Jane?"

She hurried down the stairs as soon as she could escape from Jane's careful grooming, going first to the drawing room and then the morning room in search of Edward, before finding the Duchess and Doctor Morrison in the library, the two of them standing over Edward, who was seated on a low stool as though being punished.

"You are still under my care, Edward," Doctor Morrison was saying, with a kindly smile. "You have only to say the word and I will take you back to Ivy Cottage. If it all seems too much for you, if you cannot face the season in London, you have only to send for me at any time."

Edward did not answer.

"I see that he is struggling," said the doctor to the Duchess, who appeared fearful. "It is already a bad sign that he felt unable to leave Ivy Cottage without Maggie." He gave her a disdainful glance. "You will keep me informed of his progress, Your Grace, so that I can advise you on the best possible treatment for him."

The Duchess looked worried. "If he can only be married off…"

"That is certainly our hope, Your Grace. But should he show signs of being unable to maintain a façade of sanity, it would be better to withdraw him from society once more until we can be certain his behaviour will not tarnish his reputation amongst the *ton*. Once doubt has been sown… it may be too late to be mended."

The Duchess nodded; her hands tightly clenched together.

"Edward, you must reassure Doctor Morrison that you are able to… to face the season."

Edward gave a small nod.

"Speak, Edward," said the doctor. "If you cannot speak when spoken to, it bodes badly for the season to come."

Edward raised his face. His expression was miserable. "I will do my best."

"Very well," said Doctor Morrison. "I must be on my way, but I will keep a close eye on his wellbeing," he said, and Maggie heard his words as a threat. He left the room, the Duchess following him, both ignoring Maggie as they passed her.

Edward put his head in his hands. "I will fail, I know it."

She knelt before him. "You will *not* fail. You have done so much, changed so much for the better since we came back here. You have grown better in yourself, anyone can see it."

"I thought I was doing well but they… when they doubt me, it makes me doubt myself. I wasn't born to be the Duke, Maggie, I was only…"

"Stop it. You *are* the Duke now, born to it or not. Mr Wilson thinks you are doing well, he was delighted with your interest in the cottages, in the management of the whole estate."

"We have not been anywhere, met with anybody. We might as well have been back at Ivy Cottage. Now we must go into society, be amongst people who will ask questions, who will watch me at every moment, who will judge whether I am worthy of marrying their daughters…"

"Any woman would be lucky to marry you."

"Lucky to marry a lunatic?"

"You are *not* a lunatic."

"Doctor Morrison—"

"I don't care what Doctor Morrison says. I have spent more time with you than he has, and I say you are sane."

He gave a tiny laugh and took her hands in his. "I am sane when you are with me, Maggie. You give me hope that I can be the man everyone wants me to be."

She shook her head. "You need only be the man you are, Edward," she said. "You are more than enough."

"Do not leave me, Maggie," he said, raising his blue eyes to meet her concerned gaze. "Promise me you will stay by my side."

"I promise."

CHAPTER 5:
London

THE JOURNEY TO LONDON MADE MAGGIE FEEL ILL. The endless rocking of the carriage was part of the reason, but seeing Edward grow ever more silent and anxious as the miles went past, and the Duchess grew ever more watchful, as though he were about to bolt, caused a hard knot of fear in Maggie's stomach. She did not even feel she could converse with Edward as she would like to, to try and make him smile or even laugh with absurdities, under the Duchess' eye. If only she and Edward could have had a carriage to themselves. As it was, when they stopped at coaching inns and were shown, with great deference, to private parlours in which to eat, Maggie had to watch as Edward ate less and less, his face tight with anxiety. They ate in rigid silence and returned to the carriage, for further jolting miles. The servants were travelling ahead of them, so that they could be ready to attend them at each coaching inn, but even Joseph and Celine's friendly faces gave Maggie scant comfort. They stayed overnight in an inn and were shown to rooms which were comfortable enough, but Maggie spent most of the night listening out in case Edward should need her and the next day found the carriage's rocking worse than ever, swaying between nausea and sleep, hour after weary hour.

They entered London in the late afternoon, but it still took hours to reach Atherton House. The streets were better than the country roads but full of people and other vehicles, slowing progress to a crawl, even though the heraldry of their carriage gave it precedence.

At last, with twilight falling, they pulled into a vast square of grand houses, with pretty gardens in the centre. The carriage drew to a halt in front of an imposing house, the door swiftly opened by a footman.

"Welcome home, Your Grace, Your Grace, Miss Seton."

Maggie's legs felt weak after not moving them for many hours, but she managed to climb out of the carriage, then stood gazing up at the house. It stood four storeys high, with a basement underneath it, and, she was later to discover, both gardens and a mews for the stables at the back. Atherton House stood on the south-eastern side of Grosvenor Square and was one of the largest houses, built when the square was first developed, more than eighty years previously.

News of their arrival having spread, they were welcomed by the butler, Webb, and the housekeeper, Mrs Green, while a flurry of footmen tended to their luggage, so that they were soon installed in their new bedrooms to change for dinner. Jane had been allowed to travel with them as Maggie's personal maid and was wide-eyed at being in London.

"I shall get lost, Miss," she whispered, once they were shown to the Willow Room and Edward had been put next door in the Oak Room. All their main luggage had already arrived ahead of them, in large trunks and boxes, so that they had travelled only with what they needed to make them comfortable for the journey. Jane hurried to begin unpacking. "I've been at Atherton Park since I was first in service, but I've never been here, and Mrs Green looks fierce."

Maggie had similar feelings but could not allow them to show, so she only gave what she hoped was a reassuring smile. "I am sure you will do well, Jane," she said, looking about her. The layout of the space was similar to what she had at Atherton Park, but here the decoration featured Chinese wallpaper showing a delicate scene of willow trees and colourful songbirds in blues and greens.

"Duval says you're to go shopping for all sorts of finery," breathed Jane. "I shall look forward to dressing you for the balls and dinners and grand parties, Miss. I'll have so much to tell the other maids when we go home for Christmas."

Christmas felt a very long way off to Maggie. She could only hope that they would last that long without making any errors or Edward being unable to bear the pressure of this new life.

Once dressed for dinner, she knocked on Edward's door and found him in the Oak Room, where panelled wood and a wallpaper of green oak leaves and golden rampant lions was both grander and gloomier compared to the Iris at home.

"Are you ready for whatever lecture my mother has planned tonight? Edward asked, a wry twist to his mouth.

"Tomorrow morning, we could visit the stables and see Merlin and Lacey," she suggested.

His face brightened. "How do you always know the right thing to say to cheer my spirits? Come, let us face Mama together."

The dining room was as large as the one at Atherton Park

and the dinner, if anything, more elaborate. Crawfish soup, lamb, roast beef and mutton, veal collops and peas, sweetbreads, fried artichokes, green truffles, fruit in jelly, calves' ears, damson tarts and more. When Maggie had first come to Atherton Park, she had felt obliged to try everything, but by now she was accustomed to choosing only what she had a taste for and leaving the rest.

"I will take Maggie to Gunter's for an ice tomorrow," said Edward, when the silence had gone on longer than was bearable. He addressed Maggie. "It is a pastry shop with the best ices and dainties in town, and it is only a couple of streets to the east of here, in Berkeley Square."

"You will go nowhere without my express permission," ordered the Duchess. "Neither of you are fit to be seen until you are more appropriately dressed. You both look positively shabby. Three weeks should do it. Until then, we are not at home to callers. We will make it known that we wish to enter society very slowly, owing to our recent bereavements. Besides, everyone will know that we will need new wardrobes, since we were absent for most of last season and in mourning until recently."

Later, Maggie protested to Celine.

"Shabby?"

Celine laughed. "For London and the *ton*, yes."

"But Edward looks elegant and I – I am dressed perfectly well, even if they are hand-me-downs."

Celine shook her head. "Her Grace is right," she said. "Your clothes look outmoded, and His Grace's are not cut as well as expected for a duke. The tailor from Aylesbury did well enough for the countryside, but we need a London tailor to do the job properly. Besides, His Grace has put on some weight and is broader in the shoulder, I think, from all the exercise. We will be keeping the tailors and modistes busy in the next three weeks. You do not have anything like enough clothes."

"I have six dresses."

"That would not be enough were it three times over," said Celine.

The Duchess lost no time. The next morning, she began putting her plans in place.

"Joseph has gone to Weston the tailor to have him call on His Grace later today. He will take all necessary fittings and be entrusted with commissions for every part of his wardrobe. My modiste will call on me here tomorrow. Celine, you will see to it that Margaret is appropriately dressed. Remember that how she is dressed will reflect on our family. The young ladies of the *ton*, especially those whose families may be noble but, shall we say, lacking in funds, must look at her and imagine that they, too, will be so dressed once they marry Edward and become the Duchess of Buckingham. Spare no expense. They must be dazzled, they must not question anything about Edward's suitability and a lavish display of fripperies will distract them. I cannot wear anything too bright as I am still in half-mourning, so Margaret's clothing is of the utmost importance."

"Yes, Your Grace."

Maggie sat silently. Here they were, the social season now close at hand. The endless lessons and preparation would soon be at an end and the drive to find Edward a wife would begin in earnest, his wealth and title laid out as bait for unwitting families keen to make a good match, Maggie's clothes there to turn the heads of foolish young girls barely out of their nurseries, daydreaming of being a Duchess, of wearing beautiful clothes and spending their lives flitting from one social occasion to another. And the truth? The truth was that it was all a snare, a trap. A young woman would perhaps find herself rich and titled, yes, but her husband might be taken from her as soon as she had borne an heir, leaving her in the icy control of Edward's mother. Maggie shivered.

"Your shawl?" offered Celine.

But the cold feeling in the pit of Maggie's stomach would not go away.

That evening Celine came to Maggie after dinner, ready to make a list of places to shop. "We will begin tomorrow morning. Joseph will accompany us, and we will take the carriage. We will use Her Grace's modiste, Mrs. Pontet in Pall Mall. She can measure you and we will choose from the latest fashions. But we will also need ribbons, hats and more silk stockings. Shoes and boots from Wood. A riding habit."

"I have a riding habit," protested Maggie.

Celine laughed. "You cannot possibly be seen in that old thing," she said. "You will require a made-to-measure habit and a hat. Most days you will ride in the carriage with Her Grace on Rotten Row, but on some occasions, you will ride out with His Grace, and to do so you must be immaculately turned out." She ticked each item off on her fingers. "Fans. Perfume. Parasols. Gloves. Muffs, they are worn very large at present so Her Grace's older ones will not do. Opera dress with a hooded cloak. Pelisses, spencers, reticules, chemisettes and fichu, feathers for your hats and hair. Fancy dress."

"Fancy dress?"

"Oh, there is always at least one fancy dress ball, where you dress up in a costume. And often a masquerade as well."

"Masquerade?"

"A fancy-dress ball but where you wear masks. Some consider them risqué, as one cannot be sure with whom one is dancing, but everyone goes anyway." She gave a sly smile. "Of course, mamas who are trying to marry off a son or daughter will drop hints about what they are wearing. I am sure Her Grace will let it be known what His Grace is wearing so that the young ladies will know to whom they should make themselves pleasant. Anyone on her list, for sure."

"List?"

"Every lady has a list of suitable matrimonial prospects for the season," said Celine. "Her Grace will have one for His Grace."

"Who is on it?"

Celine shook her head. "She will tell you herself," she said, reluctantly. "His Grace will be informed of the women Her Grace considers most worthy of his time and attention and on whom she would look most favourably."

The ribbon counter at Harding, Howell & Co was bewildering. Hundreds of ribbons, ranging from so narrow they might have been used for embroidery threads, up to lavishly wide strips of silk that would easily have covered a hand, intended for dress sashes and bows on bonnets. The range of hues was greater than Maggie had ever seen, from a green so pale it was goose-egg white, to the darkest forest green; a bold scarlet transformed into daintiest pink, navy blue lightened to a spring sky.

Woollen braids, gauzy silk wisps, rich velvets. Stripes, scalloped and picot edges, stiff-tight woven linen and slippery satin.

"Ribbons are every lady's friend," Celine said, in her element. "The plainest outfit can be transformed with ribbons. Your bonnet and sash, *naturellement*, but also trim for your neckline and sleeves, to tie your dancing shoes or weave through your hair, your fan's loop for your wrist, the finish on a basket. Besides which there is ribbon embroidery to finish a gown's hem, if your modiste employs someone skilled. Poor ribbon work can look very clumsy, but when it is done well it can be so pretty. I am a fair hand at it myself," she added as she fingered a narrow pink ribbon. "This, you see, if you worked it well it would make rosebuds, then a fresh green for stems and leaves."

Maggie nodded as though she were fully aware of all these uses but in truth, she had never even owned a single ribbon until she had come to Atherton Park. It would have been seen as a frippery by the Hospital.

"We will require a fair few, given how many items we need to trim and finish," said Celine. "Do you choose those you most take a fancy to, and I will select those I know we will need."

Maggie stood frozen with indecision. How to choose? Matron's voice echoed in her head: *The girls of the Hospital are clean and neat and that is all that is required of them in the way of looks.* She reached out to stroke a shimmering peacock blue silk three inches wide. Celine had secured the services of an assistant and was pointing here and there, rattling off lengths and discussing the merits of each fabric for their intended purposes.

"A good choice," she said, noticing what Maggie had touched. "Perfect for a bonnet tie. Three yards."

"I didn't…" Maggie began, but Celine was not listening, she was indicating in rapid succession a wispy rose-pink, a deep blue velvet, and a white satin.

"For your stockings," she said of the white satin.

A giddy sickness rose in Maggie. Soon she would be wearing white silk stockings embroidered with tiny pink roses, held up with the white satin ribbon, while pulling on a bonnet trimmed and tied with the peacock blue… it was too much. She wanted them, these beautiful things, wanted them so desperately. They were everything she had never had and had sometimes, wickedly, envied in others, but they were also everything she had been told were above her place, unnecessary frivolities leading only to vanity and pride. And all of it was false, a lie. Would they be able to tell, these leading members of society who had seen hundreds, perhaps thousands of their own kind, would they take one look at her and know that she was only play-acting the part of a lady? Surely they would. At least Edward had been born to this life; some of it still came naturally to him from his early days. But everything Maggie had learnt to enable her to get through the season had come in the last few months; she had no prior knowledge to fall back on. She would like to stop here, to declare that she could not do this, but then Edward would face them all alone and she could not leave him to do that.

"I feel…" she began, and touched her throat, where the contradictory feelings were gathering.

"Are you unwell, Miss?" asked the assistant, catching the gesture and looking concerned.

"No, I just… felt…"

Her protestations were waved away. A chair was brought at once, another assistant dispatched for refreshment.

"I'm sorry to be such trouble," Maggie murmured, blushing hotly at all the fuss, the heads turning as she took a seat by the ribbon counter. She was a fool: falling sick at buying a few ribbons, what sort of nonsense was this?

"Trouble, Miss? Not at all. Shopping can be very tiring for a lady," said the assistant, evidently well trained in the art of soothing rich women and their imagined frailties. Behind the assistant, Celine smiled warmly at Maggie and nodded when a delicate cup and saucer were proffered, before turning back to the selection process while Maggie sipped the hot tea and tried to smile at the second assistant whose entire job it now was to hover by her side in case she should faint or do something else ladylike.

"Gloves," said Celine, consulting her list. "And perfume."

The scents at the dark wooden perfume counter at perfumer Floris gave Maggie a headache. Celine had her try samples of more than fifteen different perfumes, some in fresh citrus, others in a too-strong woody vetiver. As Celine was picking up another bottle Maggie touched her arm.

"Celine, I prefer the rose perfume you make yourself," she said. "I know it may not be made by a grand perfumer, but it is warm and delicate, and it reminds me of walking in the rose garden."

She expected Celine to argue that a home-made perfume was not good enough but instead the maid dipped her head with a pleased smile. "I am glad you like it so much. It reminds me of my mother." She inspected the vast array and pointed. "In that case, we shall simply purchase a bottle worthy of storing it."

A tiny but beautiful rose-hued glass bottle with a silver cap was purchased and Maggie hurried back outside where the air, even if it did include dung from passing horses, did not at least give her a headache from too many rich scents packed into one space.

By the time they had finished shopping, Maggie was surprised there was any room left in the carriage. They were surrounded by boxes, beautifully presented and wrapped. Taking up the most room were hat boxes, five of them, with another three to be delivered. Two ready-to-wear gowns were laid in a far larger box, where minor alterations only would be required, to be done by Celine. Outside, larger boxes had been strapped onto the carriage, including two vast boxes which one might reasonably expect to have something substantial in and actually only contained two muffs, one a rich brown fur, the other a delicate confection of white silk and swansdown, which Maggie said to Celine was like packing a cloud into a box.

"A lady can keep private items in there as well as in her reticule," pointed out Celine, practically. "Her fan, a handkerchief, some ladies even use them to conceal private correspondence."

Maggie believed one could easily keep a bourdaloue inside muffs as large as the ones they had purchased, in case of unexpectedly requiring to relieve oneself, but she supposed that was not a ladylike thing to say, let alone think, so she kept the thought to herself.

Celine also purchased a bunch of blue-jay feathers.

"What are they for?"

"I have a plan for your riding habit and hat."

"A special riding hat? Won't a bonnet do? We have bought enough of them."

"It is like a top hat, but for a lady," explained Celine. "You have not worn one until now as there was no-one to see you and they need to be made to measure. But you cannot go riding without a hat."

At 37 Golden Square Maggie was fitted for a riding habit by Mr S. Clark, a gentleman's tailor, who took endless measurements as well as one of Celine's blue-jay feathers, tucking it next to his notes.

"Why does the modiste not make riding habits?" she asked Celine, once they were back in the carriage.

"A few do now," admitted Celine. "But Her Grace prefers things done traditionally, and riding habits have always been made by men, to give a more tailored look. Now, we will need some items for your reticules. The modiste will make a few for you, to match your dresses or compliment them, but you will need items to carry inside them."

"Such as?"

"A sewing étui."

"A what?"

"A little sewing case, with needles, pins, thread, scissors. In case you should be out and have anything happen to your clothes, so that it can be remedied."

Celine added a tiny silver vinaigrette, a small purse, a cosmetics case from Pear's made out of green-tinted sharkskin leather which contained a face powder called Almond Bloom with matching rouge in Liquid Blooms of Roses, Rose Lip Salve in a round silver cachou tin, a pocketbook to keep notes in with a tiny silver pen to accompany it, a carved ivory fan and half a dozen dainty handkerchiefs trimmed with exquisite lace. Most of the items were minute, the cosmetics cases measuring just two inches, so that they might all fit comfortably within a dainty reticule. They ordered visiting cards marked

Miss Margaret Seton, Atherton House, from a printer, to be delivered as soon as possible and which would reside in a small scroll-decorated silver case.

They visited Lock & Co., Hatters to the Nobility and Gentry, at No. 6, St. James' Street, where an eager assistant named Patrick measured Maggie's head and then showed a selection of riding hats, deftly sketching the one Celine nodded at and adding all the measurements to it.

"We keep all our customers' details. If you should wish for another hat at any time, you need only send word and we will have one ready for you the very same day, if required." He made copious notes about what had been planned for her habit and assured her that the design he had in mind would be "everything wonderful," checking through a vast selection of silk ribands on display and nodding when Celine tapped a suitable blue, which matched the jay feathers she left with him.

The riding habit, when it arrived a few days later, was breathtaking. A rich blue with gold frogging and buttons down the front and on the cuffs, in a military style. The large white box from Lock & Co., simply but elegantly marked with their name in swirling black writing which Celine had placed next to the habit, contained a beaver felt riding hat in a warm brown, decorated with a blue-ribbon trim and a spray of the blue-jay feathers which exactly matched the habit.

"And the boots," said Celine with pride.

A pair of half-length riding boots in brown leather from Wood were finished with blue silk tassels.

"All that just for riding a horse," marvelled Maggie.

"A lady is very visible on a horse," pointed out Celine.

"And riding in Rotten Row, which is mostly where you will be, is not riding in the countryside, for sport or to get somewhere. It is riding to be *seen*. There are ladies who have several riding habits."

"This one will do for me," said Maggie, stroking the hat. "It is all so beautiful."

The clock chimed and Celine startled. "It is time to go riding. Joseph will already have prepared His Grace."

Maggie stared at herself in the looking glass. The riding habit was tighter than her current dresses, with a thicker fabric, the skirt falling in multiple folds at the back. Her hat was a perfect fit, as were her boots and new gloves. She felt both held in and weighed down with the entire outfit, as though she had gained in stature and importance. She knew now why the Duchess moved with a stately gait. The clothes were doing the same to her as she made her way down the stairs, the skirt looped over one arm.

By the door, Edward inspected her. "Are you sure there is enough fabric on that thing? And enough gold buttons and frogging?"

"Is it too gaudy?" Maggie's spirits dashed. For a moment she had felt truly elegant, encouraged by Celine's admiration.

Edward shook his head. "I am only teasing," he said. "I did not mean to poke fun at you. You look every inch a lady and it will be my pleasure to be seen with you on Rotten Row."

"You despise the idea of being seen on Rotten Row."

He nodded. "But I will have you with me and that will make it bearable. As usual. You make all these absurdities bearable. Now, may I offer you my arm as we make our way outside?"

She took his arm, her other arm holding up vast swathes

of the blue fabric. The warmth of Edward's smile and his arm made her feel confident. *You make all these absurdities bearable*, he had said, but it was as though it were he making this strange life seem possible for her, rather than her looking after him. She could rely on his care of her to get through this, their first real social outing.

The stables housed two carriages and eight horses: a large town carriage drawn by four horses, and an open-topped phaeton drawn by two, as well as Merlin and Lacey for riding. The reunion with Merlin and Lacey was warm, and once in the saddle they found their way to Hyde Park and the wide, sandy bridleway of Rotten Row, where there were already numerous riders, carriages and pedestrians making their way up and down, all of them elegantly dressed to see and be seen. It was soon clear that Edward and Maggie excited interest, for they were at once both so well dressed as to be important and yet their faces were unknown, so that they were the recipients of polite yet puzzled nods as they rode by. But by the time they had made their way to the end and back, the *ton*, well briefed on all their members old and new, had put two and two together and accurately identified them, with Maggie catching the odd murmur of "Buckingham," as men nodded to Edward.

"I have made a list of the most suitable debutantes this season," the Duchess announced that evening after dinner. "Edward, you will pay particular attention to these names and seek them out at gatherings, so that you can ascertain which ones seem to you the most suitable as a potential bride."

Edward picked up a book and appeared to immerse himself in it.

Unperturbed, the Duchess produced a sheet of paper and proceeded to read from it. "Miss Elizabeth Belmont, daughter of Viscount and Countess Godwin. A mouse of a girl, but that could work in our favour. Her family would fall over themselves for a duke."

"Why is her surname different from that of her parents?" asked Maggie, confused.

The Duchess sighed. "Because Belmont is their surname, Godwin is the title. Just as Edward is not referred to as Atherton." She returned to her list. "There is an heiress, Lady Honora Fortescue. Only child of the Marquis and Marchioness of Halesworth. Suffolk. She inherits everything but the title. They say she is bold; I am not sure she will do. Although, if she ends up having to run the estate by herself, it might be necessary to have a firm hand…" She made a face, but then put a small mark next to Lady Honora Fortescue's name. Miss Belmont's name received a different mark.

"Lady Anna Huntington…"

Maggie watched Edward's face as the various names and titles passed, how his hands gripped the book. No pages were turned as the Duchess enumerated the possible brides.

"Viscount and Viscountess Lilley and their daughter Lady Frances Lilley."

"But their surnames…" began Maggie, quickly subsiding at the look on the Duchess' face.

"Barely been seen in town since she was presented three years ago and still unmarried, her family are always saying she's only shy, but I'm not risking her being sickly or mad, she's altogether kept too much away to be certain. And she's often at the seaside in Margate, more than anyone ought to be unless they have need of the sea air for some reason." Her name was crossed off the list in one certain stroke of the quill.

"Lady Celia Follett." She shrugged. "Not really on the market. She has been promised since she was a baby to the Earl of Comerford. She's being presented at court this year, she will have one social season and then marry him as planned, so she's irrelevant. She also has a deformity of the hand, which is most unfortunate. Besides, I met her three years ago and she was pert, had a great deal too much to say for herself. Asked far too many questions." Again, the crossing-out.

Maggie wondered whether Lady Celia and the Earl were happy with an arranged marriage, but she doubted whether anyone would have bothered asking them. Edward would suffer the same fate: a woman being chosen, not for her good heart or pleasant character, not for any thought of love or at the very least companionship or friendship, but only because she would not ask too many questions, would be sufficiently overawed by the prospect of marrying a duke to go along with the plan, knowing nothing about her future.

"You will excuse me." Edward stood up, made a perfunctory bow to his mother and left the room.

"I think I should…" said Maggie, glad of the excuse to stop listening to the list. She hurried after Edward and caught up with him on the stairs.

"A list!" He leant against a wall. "A list, as though they were brood mares at an auction, so that I might better choose from amongst them. Nothing about whether we might suit one another, about what they are like, unless my mother considers it worth noting that they are "too pert" … it is worse than I expected."

Maggie nodded, not knowing what to say, for she agreed with him.

He sighed. "It seems the whole world is mad, and yet I am the one called a lunatic."

Maggie shook her head. "You are not a lunatic," she said. "It is a strange world, and it demands strange things of you, things it perhaps ought not to…"

He took her hand in his. "I wish the world saw things as you do, Maggie," he said. He squeezed her hand. "At least I have you by my side to remind me I am not as mad as they say I am." He released her hand and resumed climbing the stairs. "I will try not to wake you tonight."

"You always say that as though I resent it," she reminded him. "I do not mind. I am glad to comfort you when the bad dreams come."

They had come to the doors leading to their rooms.

"Goodnight, Maggie."

"Goodnight, Edward."

Maggie sat on the edge of her bed, hands absentmindedly undoing her hair, dropping hairpins here and there. The Duchess' list had unsettled her more than she cared to admit to Edward. It was so coldly done, without emotion, only a hard assessment of each girl and her family. Were the mamas of the *ton* currently making their own lists? Edward would feature on them, of course, a young handsome duke, rich and actively seeking a wife. What would they say about him in the privacy of their homes? What cutting remarks might they be making even now, assessing his wealth and power, knowing nothing about the Edward she had grown to care for, a man uncertain of himself but with a kind heart and a warm laugh when they were alone, with the bluest eyes and hair that caught the sunlight when he rode out... None of this would count for anything, to the mamas. Would he be judged only on the diamonds their daughters might wear, the grand homes, carriages and servants they would have at their disposal, the sums they would be free to spend at the modiste of their choice. Was that all Edward was to them? He was worth so much more. How might she help him find someone who would see him for himself? Who would love him as he deserved to be loved.

By the end of September, the Duchess deemed them ready for their full debut into society.

"Lady Godwin's dinner and Lady Halesworth's ball will be enough of a start to the season," she decreed. "It will give people a chance to see us and to know that Edward is serious about finding a wife this season. After that, there will be no difficulties in finding enough people who are interested in him, and a quick engagement and marriage will be our intent. Preferably by the end of this season. June is always a good time of year for weddings, before the *ton* return to their homes for the summer."

The night before Lady Godwin's dinner Maggie awoke to Edward's shouts and hurried to him.

"I cannot breathe," he gasped.

She sat on the edge of his bed, stroking his arm, his shoulder. "You can," she assured him. "Breathe, Edward. Breathe."

"But if I cannot... if it is like this at the dinner..." He pulled away from her, staggering to his feet, pacing the floor, his breathing ragged and too fast. She followed him and as he came close to a wall, pushed him against it so that he could no longer pace the room, pressed a hand against his bare chest, her warm skin against his cold shaking body. "I will be there. You will do splendidly, I know it."

It took a while before she felt his muscles relax under her hand, heard his breathing slow. When she lifted her hand away, he nodded, still trying to breathe normally.

"Lie down, now," she said and he obeyed her, touching her hand again for reassurance.

"Sit with me," he murmured, and she did so, perched on the edge of his bed, watching his eyes slowly close as he grew calm. She did not leave the room until he was asleep, her stomach tightly knotted with worry.

Celine oversaw Jane as she did Maggie's hair, the back scooped up into a braided bun, the front curled into elegant ringlets after a hairdresser had been called to the house to cut the front of her hair shorter so that it could be more fashionably arranged.

"Keep *still*, Miss," Jane begged.

Maggie tried. But she was worried for Edward. Tonight would mark his social debut. No doubt she would be seated somewhere else, not by his side. What if he became afraid, began to breathe too fast, to grow dizzy? What if they asked questions about his whereabouts all these years and he stammered or withdrew into silence? If the evening went badly, word would sweep round the *ton* that the Duke of Buckingham, on paper such a desirable catch for any young lady, was strange, odd, eccentric… a lunatic. What if questions were asked, what if the servants' rumour-mill, so deadly accurate, were to begin churning?

"There," said Celine. "Your hair is done. See how well you look. Jane, you may go down to your dinner."

Maggie stood in front of the looking glass, clutching her reticule. The blue silk she was wearing made her look cool, though her colour was heightened, her cheeks over-pink. Her neckline was low, revealing too much cleavage.

"It seems immodest," she murmured.

"You can see more than someone standing in front of you," pointed out Celine.

"Can I go to him now?"

Celine nodded and Maggie hurried towards the door, then turned on the threshold.

"Thank you," she managed. "I appreciate all you have done to make me… fit for this."

You must not be afraid," Celine said gently. "You are more a lady than plenty I have known."

Maggie knocked on Edward's room, but there was no answer. Cautiously, she opened the door, but the room was empty. Panic overtook her. Had he run away while she was having her hair curled into the absurd ringlets? Was he cowering somewhere, refusing to attend the dinner? She hurried out of the room and down the stairs.

"There you are. We have been kept waiting for you."

The Duchess, magnificent in a dark plum dress, glittering with diamonds, a heavy velvet cloak on top. And by her side – Maggie let out her breath – Edward, immaculately dressed in formal black with white shirt and cravat, white silk stockings and black buckled shoes, holding his gloves and looking entirely in command of himself.

"I'm so sorry," murmured Maggie, hastening down the stairs to join them. Joseph held out her dark blue velvet cloak with a white fur trim and before Maggie knew it, they were in the town carriage outside, Maggie sitting uncomfortably close to the Duchess, Edward opposite her.

The carriage moved off and Maggie tried to catch Edward's gaze, but he stared resolutely out of the window into the dark streets. Was he angry with her? A tight ball of fear lodged in her stomach.

There was no real need for the carriage, for the Godwins were only two squares away. Their daughter, Miss Belmont, was clearly to be the focus and purpose of the evening. Having been recently presented at court, she was now out in society and what could be more advantageous than for their dinner invitation to be the first accepted by the Buckinghams, since the Duke was clearly the most eligible bachelor of the season to come?

As they arrived Maggie looked over Miss Belmont, who was a small, dark-haired young woman, with pale skin and wide brown eyes. She gave an immaculate curtsey when introduced to Edward, but Maggie could not hear her, although her lips moved, so softly did she speak. Would she suit Edward? A kind person would be good, but would such gentleness survive the Duchess?

Edward was trapped in endless courtesies, the bow over his hostess' hand, the firm handshake with his host, the offering of an arm to Miss Belmont to take her into dinner, the tedious small talk first to the daughter and then the mother, who was all but simpering at him as though she were the debutante, not her daughter.

The dining room shone with candles and glass and silverware, the dishes, from jugged hare to pheasants, fillet of beef, mushrooms, roast lobsters and more, were completed with a dazzling array of sweets, from tiny colourful jellies to iced biscuits, apricot puffs and even lemon ices, although Edward could not have sworn to what he had eaten, nor to what it tasted like.

Although the ladies went through the motions of retiring, the men kept their port drinking to a minimum, evidently keen to ensure Edward spent as much time as possible with the daughter of the house.

In the drawing room an older woman made small talk with him, possibly Miss Belmont's aunt, placed there to gather information on him and report back to the family on his manner and character. The correct manners and words came from him as though he were only a puppet and all the while he was horribly aware of the never-ending scrutiny. As for his mother and Maggie, he could smell their fear that he would slip up, that he would be exposed for what he was: the spare who had become duke, the lunatic released from his cell only to play a part.

From his hosts and their friends, he could feel the greedy desire to secure him. Their smugness at having already got one up on the rest of the *ton* by having him attend their dinner as his first social outing. It would allow them to boast, to imply there might already be some kind of understanding between the families, that it was only a matter of time… their daughter Miss Belmont had been officially presented, the Duke was bound to… and yet, their covetousness making them all too willing to forget to think, to ask questions. Did it not concern them that nothing had been heard of him for years? Did they not think it odd that he had not been at either the funeral of his father nor that of his brother? Their questions, when they came, were so weak, so easily brushed aside, that he almost wanted to tell them the truth. He only murmured something about travel, a distant uncle, an interest in astronomy and they were nodding at once, of course, of course, so good for a young man to travel and have interests before settling down, this last with over-joyful smiles, as though this were an engagement party and not merely the prelude to the social season proper.

He both despised and pitied them all, so caught up in their foolish social rules that they could not see what he was, a broken man, a man who might fool them all but only for so long before the cracks showed, before they caught a glimpse of what was underneath and then? Perhaps they too would lock him away. Perhaps, he thought, he should be afraid of them. But the thought of being taken back to Ivy Cottage, where he could live quietly with Maggie, as he had done before… at this moment he would gladly exchange this life for that one. He could even endure Doctor Morrison if he could have Maggie by his side.

What frightened him tonight was Maggie. He could barely take his eyes off her. She had been beautifully dressed and coiffured and as far as he could tell she was managing to make her way through the evening without fault, but her eyes frequently sought his and there was fear in them. He wondered whether she would give up after this evening, whether she would refuse to keep going with this charade and leave him to manage by himself. And he could not do it, he admitted to himself. He was coping only because she was there, where he could see her, giving him courage to get through this evening, this scrutiny, this bid for his right to remain in the world and not be locked away again. The idea of her leaving, of being frightened away…. His heart beat faster at the thought, a wave of dizziness swept over him.

"Edward?"

She was at his side, one hand resting on his for just a moment.

"I feel dizzy,' he said in a low voice, conscious of the need not to be overheard.

Her voice lowered to a murmur. "Breathe," she said. "Breathe, Edward. All is well. I am here with you."

He wanted to hold her hand but that would be noticed, instead he looked into her eyes and his shoulders relaxed under her warm gaze. He thought back to her hand on his naked chest in the nights after bad dreams, the touch of her skin against his, how it had always soothed him, and tried to breathe more slowly.

"What would I do without you?" he asked after a few moments, and she only shook her head.

"You do not have to think of that. I will always be here if you need me."

His racing heart slowed at her confidence, her certainty. "You are not frightened away?"

"Not if you are with me."

He could not resist it; he touched her hand again. "Thank you," he murmured.

"Go," she said smiling. "You are supposed to be making conversation."

In the carriage on the way home the Duchess nodded, pleased. "It went well," she said. "Next week will be the Halesworth ball. You must both ride or walk daily in Rotten Row," she added. "Now that you are beginning to make acquaintances it is important to be seen."

Edward wondered whether she had even noticed his moment of panic, or whether she had simply overlooked it while courting the Godwins. Soon he must face the next social hurdle, their first ball.

Despite her fears, Maggie found the Halesworth ballroom enchanting. A vast room, with a gleaming wooden floor reflecting the light of hundreds of candles. Looking glasses everywhere, vases of ornate flower arrangements everywhere in vivid autumn shades of orange and yellow, with red berries here and there. In an adjoining room, every kind of drink and delicacy were laid out, from shining ices to tiny piled-up iced biscuits in a myriad of colours. And jellies, cakes, puddings, each exquisitely presented on delicate stands. Maggie found a glass of champagne pressed into her hand and was presented with a pretty paper fan, on which were written the planned order of dances for the evening, along with space to add the names of her dance partners, should she claim some, to be included with the aid of a delicate silver pencil.

"May I claim the first dance?"

Maggie turned to find a young man bowing before her.

"I – yes, of course," she stammered, trying to hold both the pen and the glass of champagne while opening the fan.

"Allow me," he said, and took the fan and the pen, added his name to it with a flourish, bowed again and left her standing flustered.

She put down her champagne on a side table, unfolded the fan and examined the elaborate handwriting. Bamber, was it? She had never heard of him and what an odd first name, unless it was his surname?

"May I request the second dance?"

And so it went on. Maggie could barely move from her spot, nor seek any refuge or rest, as one man after another bowed and wrote their names onto her fan. At last she moved until she was entirely hidden by a vast floral display and gaped at the fan in disbelief. Name after name, most of them surnames, she supposed, as they did not sound like Christian names at all.

"You hiding as well?"

Maggie realised she was standing next to a tall young woman with fair hair who was leaning back against the wall in a bored attitude. Unlike most of the women in the room, she had short hair, brushed forwards and curled at the front. Maggie hastily tried to think of the appropriate thing to say.

"I just needed a moment to collect myself…"

"Deadly dull, isn't it? And we haven't even started dancing yet, then there'll be small talk to make."

"I'm sorry," Maggie murmured, "I don't know your name. I am –"

"Margaret Seton, distant cousin to the Duchess of Buckingham, who's taken you in and is currently busy marrying off the Duke of Buckingham. He's the catch of the season, for sure. Must be helping your chances along too?"

"I –"

"I'm Lady Fortescue."

"Lady Fortescue?" Maggie thought back to the Duchess' list and wondered if this was the woman she had mentioned. What was it she had said about her?

"Lady Honora Fortescue, daughter of Lord and Lady Halesworth, heiress to the Fortescue Hall and estate," said the woman. "If you want the whole of it. Lady Fortescue will do."

"Are you – are you looking forward to the dancing?" stumbled Maggie, appalled to discover that she was speaking with the host's daughter and mindful of all the lessons in polite conversation she had received. This one was not going quite as she had expected.

"Oh, don't feel the need to prattle to me," said Lady Fortescue, examining her fan. "There's no need. Tiring enough being on the marriage mart and making small talk with the men without having to try and be polite to other ladies as well. Who's on yours?

"My?"

"Fan."

Maggie mutely held it out.

"Ah, Bambers for the first, is it? He's all right. Bit of a drip but means well. Once helped me climb through a window when my Pa was coming and wouldn't have been best pleased to see me standing around outside with the menfolk when I was supposed to be dancing inside. Lord Seymour, he's a bore. Earl of Radcliffe, make sure he keeps his hands to himself, he's a rake and doesn't care who knows it. Mowbray – he's going to be a count one day, not a bad sort, might be worth a try I suppose. Pembroke's a bit of a dish, afraid you don't stand a chance, he'll get to choose the pick of the bunch this year. Lymington. Decent. Montgomery." She shrugged. "Passable. Only a second son, no title, but they've got pots of money, so you'd hardly go short. Mowatt. One to keep an eye on, he's due to inherit a pretty big pile and become a viscount as soon as his uncle Lord Barrington dies, which can't be long now. He's an invalid, always at the seaside in Margate with Mowatt dancing attendance on him." She sighed and handed back the fan. "First half are the usual crew. How's His Grace, is he a good one or shouldn't I bother? His brother wasn't worth the trouble, even if he was going to be a duke. Bit of a bore and crass with it. Sorry for your loss, by the way," she added as an afterthought. "My condolences and all that sort of thing."

Maggie found herself liking the woman, even though she was not at all what she had been expecting. "His Grace is a good man," she said, unsure of what else to say about Edward.

"Looks a bit more refined than his father and brother. Not your hunting fishing shooting type?"

"He rides," said Maggie tentatively. "But he prefers books, and he is looking forward to attending the theatre."

"Oh, that sort," said the girl. "Not my type, but no harm done. I should think Buckingham will have his choice this season, even Pembroke won't be able to outdo him. He's only a viscount, though he is rich as Croesus. But girls love a duke, don't they? Fall over themselves for the chance of being a Duchess and outranking everyone for the rest of their lives. Scarcity value, I expect. As for the mamas, they'll be chasing him down like hounds to a fox. Hope he's got a strong constitution; he's going to need it. Anyway, we'd better get started. The first dance is coming up and Bambers is looking about for you, poor chap. You'd better go and rescue him. I'm with Mowatt. I'll check on how that uncle of his is doing."

And she was gone, striding rather than gliding across the floor, tapping sharply with her fan on the arm of a young man with brown hair, who turned and bowed to her, then led her to the dance floor, where couples were forming up into a set.

Another man was making his way towards Maggie when she heard a welcome voice.

"I think I should add my name to your dance card, Cousin

Margaret. I cannot forsake you all evening, it seems neglectful on my part, even if you do seem busy."

Maggie's shoulders dropped with relief at the sight of Edward, who gave her a small bow, his body turned to edge the other man away.

"Oh, yes, of course, the…" Maggie glanced down at her fan "…the waltz is free, Cousin Edward."

"Then I will claim it," he said, taking her fan and adding the name Buckingham to it.

The man behind him managed to rally.

"I hope you have a dance left for me, Miss Seton?"

"I do," said Maggie politely. Edward turned away from her as the man added his name. She had a sudden desire to catch Edward's arm and ask him to take him with her, but of course he was headed towards his first dance partner, Miss Elizabeth Belmont, the tiny mouse of a girl who was firmly stuck to a wall and seemed unwilling to dance at all, her cheeks blushing scarlet at his approach.

Maggie endured the first four dances, stepping neatly through her paces while counting in her head or making repetitive small talk with her partners, who were attentive enough. By the sixth dance she was beginning to wish she could stop all this nonsense and rest somewhere quietly, perhaps with Edward, where they could laugh at all this formality and not feel constantly watched. The level of scrutiny she was under was nothing compared to how the room watched Edward's every move, the mamas edging forward their daughters to try and get into his eyeline, the young women simpering and flirting with him if they got the chance. But at last it was the turn of the waltz and she saw more than one woman's face turn disappointed when Edward headed towards her for this more intimate dance.

"At last, someone with whom I am not obliged to make small talk," he said.

"Shall we dance in silence?"

His smile grew broader. "We can try. We will look most odd compared to all the other couples, I'm sure. People will think you are offended with me in some way."

"We can try to look taciturn with one another, then they will be unsure who is displeased with whom."

He chuckled. "Very well. No smiling. You have my word."

The music began and they lifted their arms, creating once again the circle through which they would gaze at one another, and took their first steps.

Gazing without smiling or speaking at Edward was a strange experience. At first, Maggie found it uncomfortable, knowing that they were being observed by all, but as the music lent her grace, she forgot about the onlookers all around them. Because she could see only Edward, as though they were alone, she could lose the tightness she had felt all evening, instead relaxing, as their arms changed position into the more intimate hold, her hands on his shoulders, his hands on her waist. For a shocking moment she imagined his hands on her bare skin, only a few layers of fabric away. Her cheeks grew warm, but the music kept her movements fluid, allowing him to guide her about the room. Her face stayed solemn, not because of their teasing agreement to seem taciturn, but because of the intensity of feeling that was building in her, the music and the sway of the dance. Edward's eyes.

Edward gazed down at Maggie. He had thought to claim the waltz only to rescue Maggie from the tedious looking man bowing over her hand, but he knew that was not true, she had danced with plenty of tedious looking men all evening and he had not claimed her for himself. Only when he had glanced at his partner's fan and seen the waltz coming up soon, had he made his way to Maggie. He remembered how it had felt to dance the waltz together, none of the boring steps and turns, the exchange of partners required in other dances, this dance had felt different to him and it felt different again now. Her body soft under his hands, her warm brown eyes steady on his, her hands on his shoulders. He felt, suddenly, manly, in a way he had never felt before, having been told year after year that he was not as much of a man as his father, his brother. But there was something so feminine and graceful about Maggie, so trusting in how she let herself be guided about the dance floor, that he felt himself grow in confidence, in the pleasure of holding her, being responsible for her movements, for steering her smoothly past other couples without even looking at them, maintaining the gaze between them. Their silence, which he would have found awkward with another woman, he found strangely intimate, as though the two of them were entirely alone together and comfortable in one another's presence, no false chatter or artificial attempts at flirtation, only a true connection, a sincere union.

And the waltz was over. Edward wanted to tell the musicians to play it again, to prolong the moment, but instead there was a smattering of applause from the dancers and the chatter of the crowd.

"Can I take you for an ice?" Edward asked.

Her lips parted in a ready smile at the idea, but the Duchess had appeared at their side, trailing a young woman behind her who was showing off a spectacular cleavage and hair so full of feathers she looked like a plump partridge.

"You will remember Miss Lindley, Edward, perhaps you would care to take her for an ice, the room is stifling."

He had no choice but to bow, take the proffered hand and walk away with the woman, disappointment heavy in the pit of his stomach. He wanted to look back at Maggie, but that would be impolite to the young woman he was escorting, so he did not, hoping to return to Maggie later. But the Duchess played a more active role in managing the evening than he would have liked. She steered him towards certain dance partners, endlessly introduced him to young women to escort somewhere for something, if not ices then a drink, or something to eat as the evening wore on.

It was past two in the morning when they finally tumbled into their carriage and, exhausted, made it back to their bedrooms with barely a word passing between any of them.

Maggie sat on the edge of her bed and carefully removed her dancing shoes. Her feet ached. She understood now why Celine had bought so many pairs. Delicate as they were, she could not imagine them holding up for many more balls. She thought the evening had gone well, she could not see any faults Edward might have made, and she hoped she had made none herself. Mostly she had felt nervous, except for when she and Edward had been able to dance together. She smiled at the thought of it, hoped that going forward there would be at least one dance at every ball that she would enjoy. Jane had sat up for her, and, sleepy-eyed, she helped Maggie undress.

"Was it very elegant?" she asked.

"It was," said Maggie. "But I am so tired."

The dress off and her nightgown on, Jane dismissed, Maggie fell into a deep sleep.

She woke to bright sunlight streaming through the windows and the sight of Celine opening the curtains.

"Is it very late?"

"Half past ten. Her Grace is already at breakfast. How was the ball?"

"I think it went well. Is Her Grace pleased?"

Celine laid out a dress. "She has not said anything."

Maggie hurried to wash and dress, then made her way downstairs. The Duchess stood up as Maggie entered the morning room and swept past her without a word, leaving Maggie standing uncertain and alone except for Joseph.

"Shall I order more tea?" he asked.

She nodded and sat down at the table, where cake, rolls, bread for toast and dishes of butter and preserves were laid out, even though it was already eleven, evidently the household staff made allowances for late nights at balls. There were also six bouquets of flowers, neatly arranged in vases, which appeared odd all clustered together as the floral arrangements in the house were usually larger, placed elsewhere and these were each very different in style between them. There were some letters nearby on a silver tray and two small parcels wrapped in brown paper, each fastened with a strip of white lace tied in a bow. Maggie took a piece of cake and ate some of it, still only half awake and wondering at the Duchess' evident annoyance. She rethought the events of last night. Had either she or Edward behaved incorrectly? Had there been whispers? A gloom settled over her. They had failed in some way, failed at the very first hurdle.

"Is His Grace not yet up?" she asked, as Joseph returned with a pot of fresh tea.

"He is up," said Joseph, "He will join you shortly, I am sure."

He placed the tea close to her and then gestured towards the flowers and parcels. "Your deliveries."

"Mine? What do you mean?"

Joseph seemed to be trying to hide a smile. "The flowers are all addressed to you, Miss Seton," he said. "As are the parcels from Brown's."

"Who has sent me flowers?"

"I believe some of the gentlemen with whom you danced last night."

Maggie gaped at him. "That can't be."

Joseph picked up one of the vases and brought it closer to her. Amongst the flowers was a small white envelope, which he offered to her. She opened it, still uncertain, and read it aloud. "To Miss Seton, with compliments, Lord Frampton." She stared up at Joseph, amazed. "Are they all…?"

"They are all addressed to you." He handed each card over, and she read each message with increasing astonishment.

"And the parcels from Brown's," Joseph reminded her, when she had finished.

"Brown's?"

He passed her the two small parcels and she pulled at the lace strips, which undid to reveal cardboard containers of exquisitely iced biscuits. One contained gingerbread iced in white, onto which appeared to have been painted roses, as though on to a miniature canvas. The other contained lemon biscuits in the shape of sunflowers, the icing tinted bright yellow with green stems. They were tiny works of art and Maggie exclaimed over them.

"Brown's is the best maker of iced biscuits in London, they specialise in gifts for ladies from gentlemen who wish to show their regard."

Maggie stared at the biscuits and flowers. "Last night…"

"Was a triumph," said Joseph, smiling. "Everyone there believed you to be who you said you were. His Grace was considered charming, he is the catch of the season and you –" he gestured towards the table of gifts "– you have evidently made an impression on the gentlemen of the *ton*."

"But the Duchess…"

"… is not pleased that you are being seen as a good match also," explained Joseph, voice lowered. "The *ton* believes you to be a relation of the Duchess and therefore of good breeding. Regardless of a dowry, there are rich men who will consider you a suitable bride."

Maggie shook her head, flushing scarlet. "I didn't – I gave no – I would not –"

"There is no harm done," said Joseph gently, seeing her flustered. "You played your part as planned and it worked. His Grace will be offered any bride he chooses, and you are under no obligation to accept any gentleman's attentions. The flowers and biscuits are a sign of a job well done."

The door opened to admit Edward and Joseph stepped away from Maggie and returned to his place by the wall.

They attended only one social occasion a week, as a result keeping their scarcity value, the Duchess receiving endless invitations but turning most of them down with the excuse that they were only attending a very few parties due to their recent losses, that they would be delighted to accept further invitations come the full season which would get underway more fully in March. Maggie would have been happy enough, for all seemed to be going well, had it not been for a conversation she overheard early one morning, when she came down to breakfast and found the drawing room empty, but heard voices coming from the morning room, one of which filled her with a familiar dread. She slipped back out into the hallway, then moved closer to the sound, recognising Doctor Morrison's voice, speaking with the Duchess.

"I am delighted to hear things are going well, Your Grace," he was saying, "though we must remember that what we see on the surface may not be the full truth. His Grace is still afflicted, and we cannot know in what way it may manifest at any time. We must maintain caution, especially when the season proper starts and greater demands are made of him."

"Can he not be cured at all?" the Duchess replied. "He seems to have made great progress, better than I would have expected."

"Alas, these afflictions rarely disappear altogether, Your Grace. We have only to think of His Majesty... but you must not worry yourself. Should he become ill again at any time, we can always withdraw him to the countryside, possibly to the comforts of the Dower House, so long as a bride can be found as soon as possible."

Maggie stepped carefully and quietly away from the door, then sat in the drawing room, her appetite entirely gone. Was Edward never to escape the doctor? No matter how well he was doing, would these doubts always hang over him?

On the fourth of November Parliament opened and Edward would be expected to attend. Maggie's nerves rose. This was one place to which she could not accompany him.

"You will do well, I am sure," she whispered as he set off. Certainly, he looked the part, immaculately dressed, and at least he had attended enough social occasions to know he could hold his own.

Edward sat through the endless rituals and pomp of the opening. The Prince Regent gave a speech.

"My Lord, and Gentlemen, it is with the deepest regret that I am again obliged to announce to you the continuance of his Majesty's lamented indisposition."

Edward swallowed. *Indisposition.* Is that what they were calling it? The King himself, locked away from his rightful role, because of his madness, or his indisposition. While he, Edward, was sat here, where the King should also be, masquerading as a well man. Would it last? Could it last? The King had managed to hide it well enough for many years, but finally it had been too much to bear, and the madness had broken through the façade, had revealed itself and he had been locked away, allowing for the Prince to become the Regent.

"The great and splendid success with which it has pleased Divine Providence to bless his Majesty's arms, and those of his Allies, in the course of the present campaign, has been productive of the most important consequences to Europe. In Spain the glorious and decisive victory obtained near Vittoria has been followed by the advance of the allied forces to the

Pyrenees, by the repulse of the enemy in every attempt to regain the ground he had been compelled to abandon, by the reduction of the fortress of Saint Sebastian, and finally by the establishment of the allied army on the frontier of France. In this series of brilliant operations, you will have observed, with the highest satisfaction, the consummate skill and ability of the great commander Field Marshal the Marquis of Wellington, and the steadiness and unconquerable spirit which have been equally displayed by the troops of the three nations united under his command..."

It went on. More speeches, more ritual and ceremony. There was little for Edward to do, only to nod, to shake hands with various men who introduced themselves to him, nod his head at the condolences, bow to acquaintances already met during the social occasions he had attended thus far. In the carriage on the way home, he allowed himself to relax again. Perhaps it would not be so bad. There were topics of interest to be discussed, he had always enjoyed reading about matters of the world and now he would take part in them, might even contribute something useful. If his *indisposition* would not rear its ugly head, would not take such glimpses of liberty away from him. It was already late in the day, and he made his way to his room, refusing food, needing to sleep, to rest after the nerves of the day had faded.

"I've joined a gentleman's club," Edward told Maggie.

"Which one?"

"Boodles."

"Someone mentioned a club called Whites," she said,

thinking back to past conversations at various dinners and parties.

He shook his head. "That was my father's club. I don't want to spend my days being told what a fine fellow he was by his friends. I want a place of my own." He looked at her. "Why are you smiling?"

"I like seeing you make your own choices, deciding who you want to be."

"There are too many choices I'm not allowed to make for myself," he said. "I must at least have some say in my life. Even if it is only the club I frequent."

"Are the men there friendly?"

"I have met a Mr Mowatt and a Lord Lymington, both of them seem pleasant enough."

Maggie took pleasure seeing Edward grow interested in the matters of the day and how he might contribute to the governance of the country. He read the morning papers with care and attended his club, where he met with and discussed political matters with other men. She wished that he could be allowed more time to live this new life before selecting a bride, for he needed time to grow into his opinions and choices, but she doubted such time would be granted him.

Meanwhile they attended the balls and dinners the Duchess deemed most suitable. Maggie began to look out for Lady Fortescue at these gatherings, for she made a refreshing change from other young women of the ton, whose conversation was very circular and limited. Lady Fortescue, as an only child, would inherit her father's estate and therefore took more of an interest in its day-to-day running than most young women.

"Our steward is growing advanced in years," she confided

to Maggie. "We may have to replace him one day, it's a shame his son has no abilities to follow him. How is your steward?"

Maggie had to confess she had had no dealings with him.

"Worth getting to know them," said Lady Fortescue, "They manage everything. Staff are always a problem, though," she added, shaking her head. "We've just taken two new girls as maids from the Foundling Hospital. They're not bad but one of them screamed when she first saw Hector."

Maggie, thrown by the mention of the Foundling Hospital, could only manage, "Who is Hector?"

"Pa's dog. Nice little spaniel, wouldn't hurt a fly. Turned out the poor girl had never seen a dog, can you imagine? Of course, they know nothing about life outside of the Hospital."

Maggie tried to give laugh. "Imagine," she said. She had only seen a dog once when she had been younger, and it had come in with a delivery man.

"I go along there sometimes, Mama's a great supporter of the Hospital. You can join us one day if you like."

Maggie swallowed. The idea of walking amidst faces she knew well, while amongst the ranks of the lady visitors, was a horror too great to contemplate. "I am afraid the Duchess keeps me very busy," she managed at last.

"Well, just say the word if you'd like to accompany us," said Lady Fortescue. "We go often enough."

Parliament was to be adjourned on the twentieth of December, but in view of the poor weather, most of the families left a week or so earlier. On the fifteenth, Maggie stood with Edward outside Atherton House, wrapped in her coat and furs.

"Will you be glad to be back at Atherton Park?" she asked.

"I'll be glad not to have to socialise for a while," he said.

The Duchess emerged in time to hear him. "When we return you will find out what a real social season is like," she said, taking the footman's hand to step into the carriage. "And we will expect a wedding by the summer."

The day-and-a-half journey back passed in a cold silence which no furs or footwarmers could thaw.

CHAPTER 6:
Winter

THEY HAD BARELY RETURNED TO ATHERTON PARK when the Duchess received news that her brother was unwell and decided to attend him, setting off again for Derbyshire with Celine and two of the footmen.

"You will have to have a small Christmas," she said before leaving. "I had hoped to hold some dinners for our local acquaintances, but I will not expect you to do so without me. The servants' ball, however, must go ahead. It is traditional, and the staff will be disappointed if it is not held. Mr Wilson will arrange everything; you need only show your faces for a dance or two."

Maggie watched the Duchess' carriage depart, and her spirits rose for the first time in months. She had not realised how much she had been crushed by her constantly disappointed or coldly watchful presence.

The weather turned savagely cold in the two days before

Christmas Day, and heavy snow fell. Maggie was awakened not by the ever-attendant Jane but by Edward, who bounded into her room, dressed in a thick cape and boots. "Come, Maggie! A snowball fight before breakfast, what say you?"

She laughed at his wild enthusiasm, the lightness that his mother's absence had created. "Out of my bedroom this moment, I am not even dressed!"

"Be quick about it," he said, tugging on the bell-pull for all he was worth, so that a frightened Jane came panting into the room moments later, having run all the way from the basement.

They waded out through the knee-high snow and threw snowballs at one another before retreating to the drawing room for breakfast.

"We will toast our own bread," said Edward, dismissing the footman.

He knelt before the fire and scorched their toast a few times until he improved, while Maggie poured hot chocolate. Curled up on sofas opposite one another, they ate and drank and talked, not of any of the past few months but instead of Merlin and Lacey, of whether it would snow even more, of what food might be served at the servants' ball and with whom they should dance.

Edward seemed to mind the cold even less than Maggie. She retreated to the drawing room, where she sat watching him out of the window as he spoke with the gardeners about a new layout he had in mind. It was good to see him having his own ideas for Atherton Park. When he returned to the drawing room he called for his steward.

"Mr Wilson, as there are only two of us, the servants' ball can be held the evening of Christmas Day, we will not mind having a tray for dinner. And spare no expense, make it the best ball you have ever had."

On Christmas Day they opened gifts. The Duchess had left a book on politics for Edward and Fordyce's Sermons for Maggie, which they made no comment on, only set aside.

Maggie had embroidered slippers for the Duchess and Edward had bought her perfume from Floris, but both gifts had gone with her to her brother's house.

"My gift for you, Maggie," said Edward, passing her a small wooden box, elegantly carved.

She opened it to find a string of coral beads, a fashionable item for young women to wear with white muslin dresses in the summers.

"Thank you, Edward, it is very pretty."

He stood to fasten it about her neck, his fingers warm against her skin.

"These are for you." She had embroidered half a dozen handkerchiefs for him, not only with his initials but with trailing ivy stems and tiny, barely-there frogs, all in white silk, so that they could only be seen up close.

He laughed at the tiny frogs, tracing their shapes with one fingertip. "What fine needlework. Thank you."

The servants' ball took Maggie by surprise. The ballroom was radiant with boughs of greenery and red ribbons, tables groaned with food in the adjacent dining room and over two hundred men and women, dressed in their best, were unrecognisable from their daily roles. Maggie wore a green silk dress and she and Edward entered the ballroom to a round of applause, after which Edward made his way to the housekeeper Mrs Russ and bowed, and Maggie curtseyed to Jenkins the butler, the two couples leading the first dance. They danced another four dances until they were exhausted, for these were no stately dances, but hand-clapping whirling country dances, which left Maggie panting and holding her side.

"And now we will leave you, so that you can *really* enjoy the evening," announced Edward after proposing a toast to them all.

"Three cheers for His Grace!" called out Joseph and the cheers rang out loudly as they waved goodbye and left the ballroom, making their way back to the main house.

"Wait, Maggie."

She turned on the stairs to find Edward following her. "Yes?"

"I have something for you." He held out a little package, wrapped in paper.

"You already gave me a gift."

"This was the one I really wanted to give you, but I thought Mother might not approve."

"What is it?"

"Open it."

She unfolded the paper and found a gold locket. She opened it and gazed in wonder at the miniature of Edward inside. The painter had caught the vivid blue of his eyes and his gentle expression, even on such a tiny scale. "Edward. It is… it is lovely."

"I wanted to give you something to remember me by."

Her throat tightened. "I will never forget you, Edward," she said, her voice low. "I do not need a portrait of you for that. I gave you those handkerchiefs to remind you of Ivy Cottage. Should you ever find yourself there again, know that I would come to you at once, if you found a way to send me word, wherever I may be. But I will treasure this. Thank you."

He nodded. It seemed as though he might be about to say something more, but then only nodded again and went back down the stairs, disappearing into the drawing room while Maggie stood and watched him, the gold locket clasped in her hand. Once in her room she put it carefully away in the tiny drawer of the *necessaire*.

The Duchess was delayed at her brother's for a further two weeks due to the heavy snowfall and they passed their days mostly indoors, singing, reading to one another, occasionally tramping down to the stables through the thick snow to pat the horses and feed them apples.

"If only life could always be like this," said Edward one day, when Maggie was in the middle of reading aloud to him.

She glanced up from the book. "Like what?"

He gestured at the room, the two of them. "This. We are free to do as we wish, we are happy. I have not had a nightmare for three weeks, have you noticed?'

She had. "Your life *can* be like this, Edward," she said, closing the book and leaning forward.

"Not with my mother and Doctor Morrison waiting for me to fail."

"You are the Duke of Buckingham," she reminded him. "Your mother could move into the Dower House and leave you to manage things as you saw fit." She tried not to think of what she had overheard, that the doctor might consider locking Edward in the Dower House.

"She will only do that if I marry."

"You will find a good wife," she said, trying to sound as though there were no doubt in the matter. "I am sure of it."

He gazed out of the window. "I hope I find one with whom I can be as happy as we have been these last few weeks."

Their quiet happiness was shortlived. By the end of January, the Duchess had returned and deemed that, no matter how bad the roads, it was time to travel to London. The journey was made in the savagely cold weather that had now descended over the country. The carriage was full of woollen blankets and fur wraps, footwarmers filled with hot coals had been placed at their feet, all of them were wearing so many layers of clothing that their outer coats would barely fit over the top. Both Maggie and the Duchess used their giant fur muffs and at every coaching inn they all huddled around the blazing fires drinking cups of hot soup, desperate to feel warmth. Even in the well-appointed private bedchambers they occupied for the night, Maggie had to add her furs and wraps to the covers provided and wear her coat over her nightdress.

"I have never known such cold," said Celine, her teeth chattering as she helped Maggie dress.

"Are you all warm enough in the servants' carriage?" asked Maggie, concerned.

"There are enough of us in the carriage to huddle together," said Celine. "It is the best heat, to be close to another person."

Maggie, who sat opposite Edward and the Duchess, could not imagine huddling together with the Duchess.

Atherton House was shrouded in a deep fog, but Maggie was grateful for the warmth and comforts provided. The servants were kept hard at work lighting and caring for more fires than usual to keep the rooms warm, and Maggie kept a shawl always wrapped about her.

"The fog does not seem to have abated," said the Duchess to the housekeeper.

"It is still very bad, Your Grace, but it was worse. At Christmas it was so thick no-one dared venture out for fear of getting lost."

"Let us hope it improves," said the Duchess. "The season will be hard pressed to commence if no-one can go out of their houses for the cold and fog."

Maggie woke very late. Her bedroom fire had already been lit, but she had not heard the maid. The room seemed darker than it should be, and when she pulled back the curtains to look out she stared in surprise, for the world outside had disappeared altogether into a thick fog, so dense that she could not even see into the centre of the square, could barely even see the railings and steps directly below her, by the front door. There was only a thick whiteness and an eerie silence, unlike the usual clip clop of hooves and the rolling of wheels. Maggie pressed her face against the glass but could still see nothing at all.

"No-one can go out today," reported back Joseph when she came to breakfast. "Coachmen are walking their coaches if they must take them out, with lanterns. It is like night-time out there."

They spent three days in thick fog, which eventually cleared but the weather remained misty, the cold still bitter.

There was nothing to do but spend time at home, reading, sewing, writing. Some of their meals became less elaborate, for it was difficult to get reliable supplies.

When Maggie awoke on the first of February, for a moment she thought she was back at the Hospital, where winters had been cold, and they sometimes had to break the ice in their wash-basins before they could wash their faces of a morning. But no, she was under the thick covers in the Willow Room, and a maid had scurried in and was on her knees at the fireplace.

"Sorry to be late, Miss, we had to light more fires than usual, what with the snow." The maid hurriedly got the fire going and jumped up as Celine entered the room.

"You should have lit Miss Seton's fire earlier," she scolded.

"Sorry, Duval," said the girl, scampering from the room.

"More snow," exclaimed Celine, opening the curtains. "But the fog has lifted, at least."

Maggie climbed out of bed, bringing a whole blanket with her, wrapped about her nightdress. She stood with Celine at the window and gazed out over the square, which looked entirely different, carpeted in thick pristine snow over every part of the gardens and houses.

"Up to your knees," said Celine. "It'll take most of the morning for the streets to be clear. They say the Thames has frozen over. There might even be a frost fair if it holds. There hasn't been a big one for twenty-five years."

"What's a frost fair?"

"Skating and all sorts, on the Thames."

"That can't be safe!"

"It is if it freezes solid. I've heard they even had fires on it, last time."

"Fires on the ice?"

Celine nodded, moving to gather Maggie's clothing for the day. Maggie was grateful to see not only a blue woollen dress but a thick shawl to go with it.

"If you go out later for a walk, wear furs and take your muff."

Bundled up in layers of clothes, Maggie and Edward stepped out into a world transformed. Everywhere was white and the air so cold it was hard to breathe. But wrapped in her warm woollen dress and thick furs, her boots and a vast muff, Maggie felt oddly warm.

"Except my nose and lips," she said to Edward. "They feel like they're going to entirely freeze, and I shall have a face made of ice."

He stopped at once and turned to her, removed his gloves and placed his warm hands on her cheeks. "Better?"

She felt a sudden rush of warmth to her neck and cheeks that had nothing to do with how warm his hands were. It was so intimate, Edward standing so close to her, his skin touching hers, somehow different from the night-times when she would lay her hand against his skin, to calm him from his bad dreams. "Y-yes," she managed.

He took his hands away again, the rush of cold air replacing his warmth immediately. "Tell me when you need me again," he said. "Take my arm. We don't want to slip and fall on this icy street."

She took his arm, enjoying the warmth of his body next to hers.

"There," said Edward as they came to the river's edge, large railings marking the end of the pavement, set well above the water's edge.

Maggie stared down. The Thames, usually so fast flowing and a dark murky colour, was now entirely still and covered with snow, turning it from a moving river into a sparkling winter wonderland. Already there were gaily coloured tents set up at various points and people hurrying about setting up more, walking where before they would have drowned.

"What are they all doing?"

"Setting up the Frost Fair. Shall we go? They will have all sorts of merriments for us to enjoy."

She was still amazed by the sight below them. How could it be possible to walk on the ice without fear? "How thick is it?"

"I'm not sure. They say thick enough for hundreds, perhaps thousands of people to go out on it, all together. I even heard there's to be an elephant."

"An elephant? On the ice?"

He nodded, grinning. "Shall we go to see it tomorrow?"

"What if the ice breaks and the poor creature drowns?"

"They wouldn't take it out unless they were certain it was safe."

The next day they ventured out to explore the Frost Fair, Maggie holding tight to Edward's arm, the ground beneath them so slippery it was hard to stay upright.

"Penny for the plank, sir."

Edward paid a boy two pennies so that they could descend from the shore down onto the ice on wooden boards, laid there to make the descent safer and cleaner.

"He'll want two more to let us off the ice again," said Maggie. She knew the pennies the boy would earn today would be food in his belly, perhaps a little money for his family.

"He will," said Edward jovially. "I don't begrudge him it," he added. "He's a smart boy to have thought of it, and after all, otherwise we'd have been trying to climb down and landed poorly, you know it."

"Like the time I knocked you over with a snowball?"

"You dare bring that up again? Are you not afraid I will seek my revenge?"

Maggie giggled. "Are you not afraid I will only win again?"

Edward held out his hand to help her down the last part of the plank and onto the ice. She stepped out tentatively, afraid, still, that it would break beneath her even though it was obvious from the sight ahead of them that it was unlikely. If the ice could hold carriages with horses, tents, and several hundred people already enjoying the novelty, it should be safe for two more.

The first tents and stalls had created a shopping avenue of sorts, while latecomers had pitched more sporadically about the giant field of ice.

Walking along the avenue, Maggie was surprised by the variety of food and drink. There were stalls for tea, coffee or hot chocolate, the latter heavily spiced and sugared, as well as every kind of gin and ale, from Wormwood Purl to Brunswick Mum. Thick sandwiches of roast beef or mutton were wrapped in raw cabbage leaves to keep customers' hands clean while they ate. There were baked apples and gingerbread, shaped as hearts or snowflakes, stands with toys, books or pieces of jewellery shaped from cut steel.

There were drinking and dancing tents, from which lively fiddle music leaked out and into which various men disappeared, often walking less steadily when they emerged or with a woman on their arm who had not accompanied them there. Further out on the ice two large structures had been built out of wooden poles. They held up swings ridden by giggling girls, pushed by their admiring beaus, often soldiers, dashing in their red cloaks. Nearby there were skittles, with eager groups of men and women playing. Sledges topped with miniature sails as though they were ships were available for the children, who climbed onboard and were dragged about the ice by older boys, charging a penny a ride.

"What are they?" asked Maggie, seeing a dozen or so stalls that were handing out paper leaflets.

"Printing presses," said Edward, heading towards one.

The printing presses were producing commemorative poems. They read a few before Edward bought them both printed slips, which declared:

Amidst the Arts which on the Thames appear,
To tell the wonders of this icy year,
Printing claims prior place, which at one view,
Erects monument of THAT and YOU.
Printed on the River Thames,
February 4,
in the 54th year of the reign of King George the III.
Anno Domini 1814.

One printer, a man named George Davis, had gone a step further, creating not just poems or amusing sayings but an entire book of one hundred and twenty-four pages: titled *Frostiana; or A History of the River Thames In a Frozen State: and the Wonderful Effects of Frost, Snow, Ice, and Cold, in England, and in Different Parts of the World Interspersed with Various Amusing Anecdotes*. He had typeset and printed the title page on the ice and the book itself promised a wide range of topics, from histories of extreme weather to *Ice Palaces and Icebergs*, information about how to save someone from drowning, as well as how to make a fruit ice-cream. Apprentices were busy hanging up copies of the title page to dry and Edward stopped by the stand and paid for a copy of the book to be sent to Atherton House, which address occasioned a great deal of bowing and scraping.

"We surely have to add that to the library," said Edward as they strolled on, "since we were here in person to see it being made and experience its delights. Perhaps we can give the recipe to Mrs Barton, and she can make us an ice-cream to remember this day."

He seemed happy and light-hearted, and it made Maggie's spirits rise to see him like this, although she did wonder if, one day in the future, he would come across the book and think of her, think of the day they had spent laughing together in a strange white world so unlike their everyday life. Would he be married and safe with his family, perhaps have children? Or would he have been taken back to Ivy Cottage or elsewhere to live out his lonely days recollecting the few days of freedom he had ever known?

They waited to see the elephant, which plodded slowly across the ice, surrounded by crowds of wide-eyed spectators who broke into rapturous applause as it reached the other side in safety. Maggie watched in awe, she had never seen such a beast, towering above them all, its grey wrinkled skin and strangely dangling ears like no other creature she had ever seen.

"They say they can suck up water with their trunks and spray it at you," said Edward. "A good thing all the water here is ice."

"Buckingham!"

They turned to see Lord Comerford making his way towards them.

"Comerford," said Edward with pleasure. "Are you here alone?"

He made a face. "I'm supposed to be meeting Lady Celia Follett, but I haven't caught sight of her yet. Miss Seton," he added, bowing.

"Lord Comerford." Maggie curtseyed.

"I've seen the Godwins," Lord Comerford said to Edward, as though imparting helpful information. "They're over by the swings."

"Thank you," said Edward politely.

"Lady Follett is just there," said Maggie. "In the red coat."

"Ah yes," said the earl. "Much obliged. Good day to you both."

They nodded their farewells as he made his way towards the woman to whom he was supposedly engaged. Maggie wondered whether he was pleased to see her or felt any dread in being promised to the young woman. He had pointed out the Godwins and their daughter Miss Belmont, which made her wonder if the whole of the *ton* considered the alliance a done deal for Edward.

"You look doleful, are you too cold?"

Maggie startled out of her thoughts. "No, no, I am well," she said, reluctant to spoil the adventure.

"Good," he said. "I will buy you a hot chocolate to keep you warm and then we must seek out our turn at skittles."

He made no mention of the swings. Was that omission on purpose or accidental? Was Edward deliberately avoiding the Godwins?

The sweetness of the hot chocolate, spiced with ginger and cinnamon, warmed Maggie's hands and belly, turning her mind away from sad thoughts of the future and back to the glittering present. Everywhere was the smell of meat roasting on large braziers, from goose and mutton up to a vast ox.

"Is it wise to have so many fires?" Maggie asked.

"Who knows, but the ice seems thick enough still and the smell is making me hungry."

"You are always hungry these days," said Maggie, as they received thick slices of bread stuffed with roasted goose and pickled red cabbage. It amused her to see Edward eating something so inelegantly served after months of fine fare and delicate table manners at Atherton Park and Atherton House.

He grinned and took another large bite. "I think I must still be growing," he said. "My tailor will be most displeased with me if all my coats become too tight."

Maggie thought he could do with eating more, so she encouraged him to buy the hot baked apples and spiced and iced gingerbreads on offer. Some were in the shape of an elephant to commemorate its appearance on the ice, though the shape had clearly been carved by someone who had only seen one for a very brief glimpse, appearing like a large circle with the addition of an extended trunk.

"I can eat no more," she finally protested.

The skittles reminded her of playing games at Ivy Cottage, the first time she had heard Edward laugh out loud. Watching him throw the ball, she contrasted how he had been then, a spindly fearful youth in labourer's clothes, barely able to eat for fear of the purging to follow. Now, he was a handsome laughing young man, his cheeks flushed with the cold, dressed in the finest tailoring London could offer and sporting a fearsome appetite. Maggie offered up a silent prayer that he might always be this way, that no matter what the future held, he would at least be happy and healthy, that nothing and no one might take that away from him again and reduce him to helpless misery.

Back at the plank to shore they found a young man loitering nearby, dressed well enough but very much the worse for drink.

"Spare a penny for the plank, sir?" he asked Edward. "I've lost everything I had on me on the Wheel of Fortune."

Edward paid his penny as well as theirs, slipping the little boy a few extra coins at Maggie's whispered request.

"God bless you, sir," said the drunken man, wandering off unsteadily.

"He should think twice about which stalls he frequents in future," said Edward, shaking his head with a grin.

It was twilight by the time they returned to Atherton House, cold but happy, so well fed that they barely touched their dinner. The Duchess retired after only a short time in the drawing room.

"Will you play the pianoforte, Edward?" Maggie asked. It would be a perfect end to the day.

"Only if you will sing."

She nodded and he sat at the pianoforte, rifled through some of the music and then pushed it away and began playing from memory the song they had sung together back at Ivy Cottage. She joined him in singing the first verse.

"Did you not hear my Lady
Go down the garden singing

Blackbird and thrush were silent
To hear the alleys ringing..."

"Although it is hardly the time for gardens," Edward pointed out, pausing for a moment. "Perhaps we should change it." He thought, then sang.

"Oh, saw you not my Lady
Walking at the frosty Fair
Shaming the glittering snow
For she is twice as fair.

Though I am nothing to her
Though she must rarely look at me
And though I could never woo her
I love her till I die."

Maggie laughed. "And then?" She picked up the refrain.

"Surely you heard my Lady
Go through the snow lands singing
Silencing all the songbirds
And setting the sleighbells ringing..."

Edward responded,

"But surely you see my Lady
Dancing across the Thames
Rivalling the glittering icicles
With a glory of golden hair."

"Such a fine composer," she teased.

"It is easy with a pretty tune and such magical surroundings as we had today," he replied. "And we sing well together, do we not?" His voice was warm, and Maggie wanted, for a moment, to bask in that warmth, to revel in the closeness that it implied, their natural affinity, their ease when they were together alone. But he was looking at her with eyebrows raised now, waiting for an answer.

"We do." It was all that she could manage, but it was a feeble response for what she felt and perhaps he thought the same. A flicker of disappointment appeared and vanished again across his face, as though he had hoped for more.

"I like to hear you sing," she tried again, wanting to give more, to show him that she shared his joy of the moment. "It makes me think you are happy."

"I am happy when I am in your company," he said but it sounded too much like the pale compliments handed out at every social occasion they had attended so far, without true meaning between them. They were both silent, uncertain of how to proceed, what response would be appropriate.

They were interrupted by Bartholomew the footman, asking if they wanted hot drinks.

Edward shook his head and Maggie likewise.

"I think that might be the servants' way of encouraging us to retire for the night," said Maggie with a small laugh when Bartholomew had disappeared.

Edward stood. "Probably," he agreed. "In that case, may I offer you a candle to light your way upstairs?"

They each took a candlestick, the two small lights flickering as they made their way up the stairs. They paused on the landing by their respective doors.

"Good night, Edward," she said, reaching for the door handle.

"Maggie?"

"Yes?"

"I am…" He hesitated.

"What is it?"

"I am glad we had this time together. Not just today."

She nodded, her face serious. "So am I."

He made her a small bow. "Goodnight, my lady."

She curtseyed. "My lord," and entered her room, but when she sat on the bed, she could hear him next door, still singing the song.

"Though I am nothing to her,
Though she must rarely look at me,
And though I could never woo her,
I love her till I die."

CHAPTER 7:
Almack's

ALTHOUGH THEY HAD RETURNED IN TIME FOR EDWARD to take his place in Parliament, on the first of March he was back at Atherton House within two hours of leaving.

"The Prince Regent asked for Parliament's opening to be delayed until the twenty-first," he said. "And it was agreed. So there will be nothing to do for three weeks."

"You mean there will be extra time for social calls, picnics and pleasure gardens, and the men will all be expected to attend," said Maggie wryly.

"You have learnt the ways of the *ton* far too well, I think."

"A pile of invitations has been delivered," she said. "Your mother has been sifting through them, picking and choosing what she thinks are the best occasions at which to show our faces and finery."

Edward nodded but remained silent. Maggie contemplated the ticking clock the Duchess had set in motion when she had said that there must be a wedding before the season was done. It was March. There were fewer than five months left, for although parliament would officially conclude on the thirtieth of July, many families would begin to leave London earlier, during June, especially if the city grew too hot. Now that the days were growing longer the most intense twelve weeks of the season would commence, as every family sought to see and be seen, to conclude the season in a blaze of glory and avoid a whimpering failure.

"For tomorrow's ball," said Celine the next morning, looking through Maggie's gowns, "I think perhaps the green?"

"We've just been to a ball," protested Maggie.

Celine straightened up and looked at her, bemused. "I fear you do not understand what the true social season is like," she said. "How many invitations do you think you will be accepting while we are here?"

"Perhaps one a week?" offered Maggie, already knowing the answer was wrong. "That is what we did during the autumn."

Celine laughed. "At least two balls a week."

"Well, that is not too bad," said Maggie, relieved.

But Celine was not finished. "The theatre and opera two to three times a week. Perhaps a private dinner once a week, with family connections or where there might be a significant interest in His Grace from a family. Those are the evening appointments. During the day, you will call on other families or be called on, depending on Her Grace's at home days. There will also be other daytime activities: picnics, luncheons, carriage rides and ices at Gunther's. Riding or driving in Rotten Row on a daily basis. Then there will be pleasure gardens, not as frequently but from time to time. Church on Sundays."

Maggie stared at her, heart sinking. It was too much. Edward had managed, with the odd struggle, the very limited events they had undertaken so far, she had been proud of him, but this sounded far too much for anyone to bear.

"There will be more than one social activity every day," concluded Celine, as though Maggie might have missed this point. "And most evenings, you will not be home until well past midnight. You may lie in later than usual but of course you must still be up and ready to make or receive calls from midday onwards."

"How does anyone manage it?" asked Maggie, aghast. "How will Edward manage it? He will be exhausted and…" She wanted to say frightened, but held her tongue, not wanting to diminish him in front of Celine, but Celine's face was already showing a sad pity.

"I am sorry for His Grace," she said, her voice quiet. "The season can be pleasant for those who enjoy social occasions, but for someone like His Grace I am sure it will be very taxing. Especially when he will be so much in demand."

"Will he? Surely there will be plenty of other young men who are eligible for marriage?"

"He is a *duke*," said Celine. "There are fewer than thirty in the whole country. It is nearly as good as marrying a prince. And he is not only a duke, but also very rich, young and handsome, when most of the others are old or already married off, and a couple are not that rich because they are inveterate gamblers. Every lady in the *ton* with an unmarried daughter has His Grace at the top of their lists."

"Does he get a say?" asked Maggie, the words tumbling out of her mouth. Anger rose up in her at the way Celine was speaking, as though Edward were a valuable horse up for sale, instead of a young man who had been unable as a boy to withstand a bullying father and had crumbled, before being shut away as a madman when, Maggie was certain, he was no such thing, though he might be unable to behave as the *ton* would like him to.

Celine looked down, as though Maggie had chastised her.

"I'm sorry," said Maggie, touching her arm. "I know you are only speaking the truth of how things are. I just…"

Celine nodded, still silent. When she spoke, her voice was very quiet, as though she feared being overheard. "I am glad His Grace has you by his side."

"But he won't have me forever," said Maggie. "As soon as he is married, I will be told to leave, and they will expect... so much of him. He is growing in strength, but I am not sure…" She trailed off, uncertain of what she was trying to say, only that she was fearful for Edward. So much was demanded of him, and she could see him trying to grow into the role he had never expected to take on, yet at the same time his mother believed him a lunatic, ready to shut him away again at a moment's notice. And if he were married and shut away, his wife would have no choice but to keep up the same façade they were engaged in now, a pretence that all was well, a constant lie to the rest of the *ton*, year in year out. A lonely life for everyone involved and yet what was the alternative? For a moment she wondered if life in Ivy Cottage might be better for Edward. They had been happy enough when Doctor Morrison was not attending. Could Edward live there, or somewhere like it, without the doctor coming to administer treatments? Maggie would gladly live with him, care for him. There had been many happy days together at Ivy Cottage and even at Atherton Park when the Duchess was absent.

It was obvious that the Little Season had been just that, a pale imitation of what they must face. Every day except Sunday was filled with a schedule which was so busy that Maggie could not understand how anyone bore the endless social demands. They rose at ten and breakfasted, after which the Duchess would retire to her rooms where she would manage household affairs, speaking with the cook and housekeeper and writing letters. Edward and Maggie seized these opportunities to visit the horses, walk in the garden and generally avoid any social obligations, bracing themselves for what was to come. The so-called morning calls were conducted between two and four in the afternoon and were so formally short that they frequently visited three or four houses each day, staying for less than half an hour at each before taking the carriage to their next destination. All the houses were within the confines of or only a few minutes' drive from Grosvenor Square. If they were not calling on someone, there was always some social occasion in which they were to partake, from visiting the pleasure gardens of Vauxhall to riding out with someone, or a picnic on the warmest days. Their only supposed respite was on Thursdays, the day the Duchess had determined to be her at home day, when they had instead to receive company for the two hours set aside for this purpose, making the same small talk repeatedly with each new guest. The weather, the delight of such-and-such a dinner or ball previously attended, varying degrees of simpering at Edward and heavy-handed mentions of a young woman's accomplishments and keenness to settle down, then farewells, followed moments later by greeting new guests and the whole to be done again. Often, more than one set of visitors arrived simultaneously, which meant Edward had to try and split his attentions between several young women without causing offence by paying particularly marked attention to any one in particular.

A brief escape was possible at five, to walk or ride in Hyde Park, though this necessitated a change of clothing both before and afterwards. It also required constant nodding and bowing or curtseying to those they encountered and on the dreariest occasions an overly-keen mama and her daughter would hint so heavily to join them that they would spend the rest of the hour making yet more small talk, received with excessively rapt attention by the daughter.

A small dinner at home would lead on to a supper out or a ball, often not returning home till one or two in the morning. Maggie's feet were constantly in pain from the dancing and the late nights took their toll; some days she could not rise early enough for breakfast. Although there was endless elegant food provided at many of the gatherings they attended, the restrictions on how she should eat – tiny mouthfuls and unending small talk – meant that often she went hungry until she could get home and ask Jane to bring her something simple: a bowl of soup with bread and butter or some cake and fruit.

During breakfast at the beginning of the second week in March, the Duchess was smug as she checked through a silver tray of cards, letters and invitations.

"Lady Jersey has been so good as to send vouchers, as I expected."

Edward sighed.

"Vouchers?" asked Maggie.

"To Almack's."

No explanation was forthcoming, and Edward was looking unusually grim-faced, so Maggie waited until she could ask Celine.

"It is the most fashionable and sought-after invitation of the season," she explained. "There is a ball every week for twelve weeks during the season, in some very grand rooms in King Street, just behind St James' Square. You cannot get in unless you have been invited by one of the lady patronesses. There are seven and each week they hold a committee meeting to decide who will be invited. Everyone in the *ton* wants a voucher. Of course, Her Grace is very well connected and has a very eligible son to marry off this year. That is why the vouchers have been so readily sent. They will probably even be offered again, should it go well. Almack's is *the* place to secure a high-quality marriage partner, because only the very best families with the most eligible sons and daughters will be admitted entrance. If her Grace did not have a son to marry off this year, it is possible she would not have received a voucher. But she has His Grace. And…" Celine stopped.

"And?"

"And since the *ton* think you are Her Grace's niece, you are also considered a good marriage prospect."

"How can they think that when they believe I am only an impoverished distant connection?"

"It is still a connection. There are wealthy families without titles who would think it very fine to be at all connected to a duke."

Maggie shook her head. "It would be impossible, anyway. I am not who they think I am, and I can't spend the rest of my life lying about it."

Celine's eyebrows went up. "You might find a rich husband. It is not nothing, do not dismiss it too quickly."

"I am only here to make Edward feel safe," said Maggie. "When he is married…"

"When he is married off, he may be put away again," Celine said bluntly.

"And if he is, I will go with him if I can," said Maggie. She leaned towards Celine, earnest. "Celine, if they send me away before the marriage, and afterwards he is locked away again, will you find a way to reach me and let me know where he is? I cannot bear to think of him without someone by his side to look after him."

"You would spend all your life caring for him?"

"Yes."

"There are others who could care for him."

"I saw how he was when no-one around him cared." Gaunt, afraid, poorly dressed, barely speaking. He had become almost unrecognisable since, filling out to a healthier weight, elegant in tailored clothing, his skin glowing, a new confidence showing itself, his smiles and laughter when they were alone. She did not want all of that to fade away again.

The much-feted Almack's came as a disappointment to Maggie, despite the size of the ballroom, which was close to one hundred feet long, decorated in white and a pale straw-yellow, with blue drapery, large double-tiered crystal chandeliers and a gallery for the musicians. Adjoining the ballroom were an anteroom, a tea-room, and a card-room. But despite the vaunted exclusivity, the rooms felt very crowded and overly warm.

"Twisted Lady Jersey's arm, I see." Lady Fortescue appeared at Maggie's side. "Hope you ate a good dinner before you came."

"Why?'

"Worst food in London, Almack's. Stale sandwiches, stingy on the ham. Watery lemonade, no alcohol and dry cake. Hardly appetising."

Maggie choked back laughter at the way Lady Fortescue could humble even the most hallowed of institutions. "I did not know it was so poor. I did not eat before we came out."

"Ah well, you'll just have to starve. In future, should you be coming here again, tell your cook to send up a good pie beforehand and leave you a wedge for your return home." She sighed and shook out her dance card, dangling from her wrist. "Here come the menfolk, brace yourself."

Maggie's dance card filled rapidly enough, and she watched as Edward dutifully made his way from one young woman to another, bowing and adding his name to various cards, though he looked sombre as he did so.

Lady Fortescue circulated before returning to Maggie. "His Grace in a bad mood tonight? Can't be weary of the marriage mart already, surely? He's barely started."

"He is not fond of these larger gatherings," Maggie said.

"Is anyone?" asked Lady Fortescue. "Here we go then, first dance. Tally-ho."

The usual ballroom experience followed, although the crowded room gave less space than usual, despite its large dimensions. Maggie danced, but was concerned about Edward, who, even when dancing with a partner, seemed less and less happy.

"May I have this dance?"

Maggie looked up at a tall young man sporting a loud waistcoat. "I am so sorry, the next dance is taken… sir," she finished, unsure of the man's name. While many of the young women had apparently memorised every available man's name and title, she frequently found herself uncertain.

"Radcliffe," drawled the man. He took her fan from her hand and inspected it, raising one languorous eyebrow. "Frampton? Surely not. Man's a bore. You'd do much better with me. Don't you think, Frampton?"

Maggie followed his eyeline and saw that Robert Sinclair, the Earl of Frampton, had joined them in time to hear Lord Radcliffe both insult him and try to steal his dance partner.

"I am afraid my fan says otherwise, Lord Radcliffe," she said sharply. "I have already given my word to Lord Frampton, and I do like to keep my word." She turned away from him and gave her best curtsey to the Earl. "Lord Frampton. I believe you were about to escort me to the dance floor?"

The Earl offered her his arm and she took it readily, moving away from Lord Radcliffe.

"I am sorry Lord Radcliffe was so rude," she said gently, aware

of the tightness in the Earl's body.

The Earl softened as they turned to face one another, and the

dance began.

"He is not… as gentlemanly as he should be," he managed, no doubt skimming over a variety of words he might have liked to use but considered inappropriate in front of a woman.

"He is not," agreed Maggie with a smile. "We shall try to forget about him."

The Earl smiled back and nodded, and when the dance was finished, he kissed her hand. "I hope to see more of you now that you are returned to London," he said.

Maggie smiled, but had no chance to leave the floor, immediately being claimed by her next partner.

The girl with whom Edward was dancing was a slip of a thing, he could barely feel her, but he could hardly breathe, as though there was a great weight pressing against him. All around the edge of the ballroom were not just glittering jewels but the glittering eyes of the *ton*, the young women watching his every move, their experienced mamas calculating the odds of ensnaring him, their fathers mulling over his worth, so that the whole of the ballroom was like a net closing in on him, forcing him into something which felt wrong, though everyone around him insisted it was right and even he himself could not put his finger on what was wrong. What *was* wrong with choosing an amiable, suitable bride and growing to love her? What *was* wrong with following what everyone else had done for generations? It had worked well enough for everyone to continue along this path and yet there was a growing unease in him that had nothing to do with the clothing or the dance steps or the manners, all of which he was now accustomed to and even Maggie was managing well enough…

Maggie. He saw her dancing with Lord Frampton, a bright smile on her face which enhanced his feeling of unease, rather than calming him as the sight of her usually did.

The music ended and he barely managed a short bow to his partner before leaving her.

Air.

He needed air, he could not breathe, each breath in was a struggle, he… usually he would have wanted Maggie but now, he did not want to see her, only wanted to get out of this accursed place and find somewhere to be alone, regardless that his name was down for the next four dances and that he would be leaving his partners stranded. The music began again and now it seemed as though it were being played out of tune, the door to the street below seemed very far away…

Maggie scanned the room. Where was Edward?

"May I be so bold as to claim a second dance this evening?" began Lord Frampton, bowing low before her.

"No!" said Maggie too quickly. Edward. She must find Edward.

Lord Frampton looked startled.

"I mean – I do beg your pardon," Maggie said, her voice cracking. "I am not quite feeling myself. The heat… I beg you will excuse me."

"Allow me to accompany you to a quieter part of the room," said Lord Frampton at once, holding out his arm.

She could not refuse, so she followed unwillingly, still craning her head, searching for Edward.

He led her to a quieter part of the room, where Miss Belmont and Lady Fortescue were standing.

"Ah, Lady Fortescue," he said with relief. "May I leave Miss Seton with you for a few moments while I fetch her something to drink and an ice? The room is very warm."

"Thank you," managed Maggie, taking the seat he had indicated for her, still looking about her for a glimpse of Edward.

"You're doing well," said Lady Fortescue, watching him depart. "Known him since he was a baby. Make a decent husband, Frampton. Good heart."

"I need to go outside," gasped Maggie, struggling to her feet. She felt dizzy.

"You can't go out there without a chaperone," said Lady Fortescue. "That's where the men are smoking."

"I need to find Cousin Edward," said Maggie. "He is – he was not feeling well, earlier."

Lady Fortescue frowned at Maggie but nodded. "Alright," she agreed. "I'll stand by the door where I can keep an eye out for you. Nip out and have a quick look for Buckingham. If you can't see him, or you have any trouble, just call."

They made their way through the crowded ballroom and past the dining room, down the stairs and into the main foyer, where tall columns decorated at their tops as palm trees loomed over them.

"Be quick," said Lady Fortescue. "Can't be seen to be hanging around here."

Maggie hovered in the doorway. Edward might simply have stepped outside for a few moments to collect himself, to have a rest from the endless social interactions in which he was obliged to take part. Outside were dozens of carriages awaiting their owners and, off to one side, a group of men smoking, but she could not see Edward among them. As he did not smoke it would have been unlikely anyway, but she had hoped he might have followed an acquaintance. She peered out into the darkness. There! Disappearing down a dark street, unmistakeably Edward's figure, striding away. She opened her mouth to call to him, then realised she could not as it would bring immediate and unwanted attention. Nor could she run out of the building and follow him. She could only stand and watch as he disappeared, then turned and ran back inside.

"Did you find him?" asked Lady Fortescue.

Maggie wanted to confide in her but she could not risk any details spilling out by mistake so she only said, "He has gone home, I think, he must not be feeling himself."

Lady Fortescue shrugged. "Rum lot, men," she said. "Never understood them myself. Leave him to it. Better get back to the ballroom. We'll have left a bunch of partners wondering where we got to."

Maggie managed two more dances before she found the Duchess and whispered that Edward had left. The Duchess, a fixed smile on her face, swiftly bundled both of them into the waiting carriage and ordered the driver to take them home at once.

"You saw him leave?" she said.

"Yes. He went down a street close by."

"Which one?"

Maggie pointed.

The Duchess' lips thinned. "Gentlemen sometimes have… needs," she managed at last. "We will say no more about this. I will let Lady Jersey know that you felt ill, and we had to retire for the evening, and that Edward accompanied us out of consideration."

Maggie did not reply. Neither she nor the Duchess spoke again and when she reached her bedroom and had been pre-pared for the night by Jane, she turned her face into the pillow and wept.

Edward made his way blindly down the nearest street that would take him away from the group of men smoking and the various carriages and drivers hanging around the outside of Almack's. His heart felt too fast in his chest, his breathing matching it, he could feel himself grow dizzy, for a moment he was afraid he would faint here, in the dark, where no-one would find him. The dark and the cool air were a relief from the noise, heat and lights of the ballroom, but he could not seem to slow his breathing. One hand to his chest, he leant against the wall, willing himself to stay upright.

"Good evening, my lord."

A woman appeared opposite him from an open doorway, through which spilled a low light. She was dressed elegantly, except that her gown was so low-cut as to be entirely indecent.

"Good evening," muttered Edward.

"Were you looking for someone?"

"No, thank you."

The woman smiled and stepped away from the doorway, making her way over to Edward. Her lips were stained red and, although her hair was fair, her eyelashes were sooty-black. "Are you sure, my lord? Because most gentlemen on this street are looking for a… companion. Someone to spend time with, in a friendly manner."

He knew what she was; some of the young men at his club Boodles had talked of visiting such a woman. A few had invited him along to one of their favourite haunts, but he had always said no. If he had not been locked up in Ivy Cottage there would, no doubt, have been an occasion or two when he would have been taken to a woman like this to complete his education as a young nobleman. Visiting these establishments would have been part of his life, but he had shied away from his acquaintances' suggestions, uncomfortable with their winking invitations.

"I was just looking for some quiet."

The woman moved closer. "Oh, I understand, my lord, I

do. It can be very demanding, Almack's, for a young gentleman. All those mamas, all their pushy daughters simpering, maybe your parents nagging at you to hurry up and be wed. But there is plenty of time for all of that. Sometimes all a gentleman wants is a little peace and quiet, a place to lay his head and leave his cares behind him."

Edward nodded. She described it so accurately.

She rested a hand on his arm. "I have a quiet room inside," she murmured. "You will be undisturbed. Perhaps a rest and a nightcap are all you need to gather your thoughts, my lord?"

He hesitated and her smile broadened. Her hand slipped down his arm and clasped his hand. "Come," she said.

He stared at her, then breathed, "Maggie."

Her eyebrows raised for only a moment before she smiled more widely. "I can be your Maggie," she agreed. "Will you tell me your name?"

But Edward pulled his hand sharply away and strode so fast down the street that he was gone before the prostitute, startled, could call him back.

His heart was beating so hard he could almost hear it. Not from the encounter with the prostitute but from a sudden realisation.

Maggie.

He loved Maggie.

He desired Maggie.

It had been the touch of the woman's hand. Until now, his hand had only ever been clasped with warmth and affection by Maggie and, in that moment, he had understood why Almack's had made him feel ill when he had attended enough balls by now to have grown used to them. The sight of Maggie smiling in Lord Frampton's arms was a culmination of the slow dread that had been growing in him and that dread came not from a general disinclination to marry, it was that he did not want to marry any of the women he was supposed to choose from. He wanted to marry Maggie.

He leant against a wall in the dark street and tried to marshal his thoughts. He must marry, there was no doubt on that score. But he loved Maggie, that was now so clear to him that it was as though a thousand candles had been lit all around her, a blaze of certainty.

And yet.

He was accustomed to thinking that she belonged in his world. She was dressed for his world. She took part in all the events of the *ton*.

She was part of his household.

But so was Kitty the scullery maid down in the kitchen, and to his mother, to the whole of the *ton* if they knew her origins, Maggie was no better than Kitty. A union between them would be unthinkable and yet it was all he could think of.

He let out a groan. He had escaped a madhouse only to plunge into true madness. But the thought of marrying someone else and watching Maggie leave forever... that was not possible, it would destroy whatever happiness and confidence she had built up in his life.

He walked the streets all that night and when he returned to Atherton House as dawn broke, he was no closer to finding a way forward, leaving him to be swept along by the current, unsure whether to swim against it and risk everything or allow it to take him to a safe but unwanted shore.

In the days that followed, he found himself gazing at Maggie as they went about their days. Did she feel something more for him than friendship and kindness, the care she had always shown? He did not know how to ask her and still his own feelings for her grew stronger.

CHAPTER 8:
Masquerade

A S THE WARMER DAYS OF LATE APRIL SETTLED INTO springlike picnics and pleasure gardens, as well as the daily riding in Hyde Park, Maggie was aware of the Godwins making certain that Miss Belmont appeared at every event the Buckingham household attended, her pale face emerging from ever more elaborate bonnets and dresses, while Lady Anna Huntington's parents continually invited them to dinners and near-daily walks. Although Lady Fortescue did not seem even slightly interested in Edward, Lord and Lady Halesworth made it their business to ensure her presence wherever Edward was, with the result that Maggie, who liked her forthright manner, was beginning to regard her as a friend.

"Lady Jersey is holding a masquerade," sighed Lady Fortescue, trailing behind Edward who was walking arm-in-arm with the silent Miss Belmont around Rotten Row. Directly behind them walked the Duchess and Lady Godwin. "We'll all have to be dressed up in something ghastly. Last year it was some dreadful sea theme. You should have seen the room; it was nothing but sirens and the navy. One would have thought we'd all been conscripted."

Maggie nodded, although she was more intent on watching Miss Belmont and Edward together. Was this who the Duchess had in mind for Edward? She was so delicately built she might be crushed with one hand, and she rarely spoke. When she did it was a whisper. Perhaps that was why the Duchess favoured her, for Maggie could not imagine this girl doing anything other than what she was told... by the Duchess, no doubt.

"We will turn back now," said the Duchess. "We have the Galpin ball tonight to prepare for."

There was much bowing and curtseying as the families left one another and amidst it all Lady Godwin smiled pleasantly at Maggie. "I am so glad there is a young girl like yourself at Atherton Park," she said. "My Elizabeth can be shy, but a family member such as yourself will draw her out when... well, I will say no more for now."

Maggie managed to fix a smile on her face and complete her curtsey, before climbing into the open carriage in which she and the Duchess had arrived. Edward was busy mounting Merlin, who had been kept waiting once the Godwins had met with them and suggested they all walk together.

"Lady Godwin suggested her daughter might be joining our household soon," said Maggie, wanting to see the Duchess' face.

"Good. Then the deal is almost done." The Duchess gave one of her flinty smiles.

Every time the Duchess spoke of Edward's future marriage in this way Maggie's stomach turned over, with... with anger, yes, surely it was anger that made her emotions rise up like this. How dare she treat Edward's future happiness as a deal, as though they were buying a piece of land or ordering a new horse for the stables. And she was outraged also on behalf of Miss Belmont. The poor girl had no say in all of this, she was sure of it, and yet the decision already seemed made, both families closing in on the couple at the centre of their plans, forcing Miss Belmont towards a life Maggie could not believe she would enjoy, forcing Edward to marry someone he'd barely spoken with.

Yes, it was anger, she was sure of it, anger at the injustice of it, the cold-hearted nature of the whole business. She would not allow the other feeling to rise, the one that felt like sickness, something desperate in her, a desire to stop this whole charade, a desire to… a feeling that grew stronger when she thought of Edward, of the touch of his hand, the warmth of his skin against hers. The nights when he screamed her name and she came running to him, held him in her arms to bring him back from the darkness of his dreams, how they danced together…

No. Enough. That feeling was… not real, it was only… only… but she could not even put a name to it, because if she did, she would have to acknowledge something that was not possible. It was not possible. She must focus on Edward's happiness, and his happiness and safety lay in finding a suitable bride as soon as possible and securing her hand. Edward had been changeable in this past month, sometimes charming and happy, at other times wistful, retreating to his books or spending more time away from the house, in Parliament or at his club. She supposed this was a good sign, that he was becoming more his own man, able to go about his life without Maggie there to reassure him, but it also made her feel lonely. Her days felt empty when he was absent, despite the continuing onslaught of social gatherings.

"I told you there would be a masquerade," said Celine when Maggie mentioned it. "The theme is The Queen of Queens. It is Queen Charlotte's seventieth birthday this year, as well as the Grand Jubilee of the House of Hanover, which will celebrate one hundred years this summer. As the masquerade is in honour of the Queen, everyone will be dressed as they were in her youth."

"With the giant hooped skirts?"

Celine nodded. "The modistes will be delighted. Can you imagine how much silk will be used to make just one such dress?"

"Can't you just use the Duchess' old clothes?"

"You know better than that. We must make haste to order your costume and the Duchess', before everyone places their order and the modistes get overly busy."

"And what will the men be wearing?"

Celine giggled. "You will think they have all become dandies overnight," she said. "They will be very colourfully dressed. Oh, and wigs," she added suddenly. "We must order wigs for you all."

On the night of the ball, Maggie stared down at herself and back in the looking glass. "How did anyone ever wear such clothes?" she asked Celine.

Her dress was white and gold, with a waist drawn in so tightly she could barely breathe, gold high heels which made every step precarious, and a white powdered wig adorned with gold stars, which was so high she was certain it would topple at any moment. Her face was powder-white, with brightly painted red lips, over which she was to wear a white mask outlined in gold sequins which Celine was currently fastening. The mask would cover most of her face, leaving only her red lips uncovered. The skirts of her dress billowed out on both sides as far as her outstretched arms.

Celine giggled. "Have you not seen the portrait of Her Grace as a young woman?"

Maggie had, though she could hardly believe it was the Duchess. A beautiful girl, in a vast blue dress, face coquettishly turned away but her eyes still meeting the viewer's, the hint of a smile. "She was very pretty."

"She was the talk of the *ton*. Everyone wanted to marry her. There was rumour she might even be suitable for the royal family. But the Duke secured her."

"Did they love each other?"

Celine emerged from straightening Maggie's petticoats, her face serious. "The Duke was not always… kind," she said. "Her Grace did not have an easy marriage. His Grace was a difficult man to love."

"Does that not make her more inclined to ensure Edward's is a love match?"

Celine applied a little more powder here and there to Maggie's face and wig, standing back to get the full effect. "Those who have not known such a thing may struggle to imagine it," she said.

"His Grace will be ready by now," said Maggie. "I should go down."

In the corridor Joseph met her, holding out her cloak.

"Remember, it is a masquerade," he said. "You do not disclose your identity. There will be no receiving line, no announcements of rank, you simply enter the ballroom with your invitation. Only the footmen will know who you are. Unless they are bribed to share the information, of course," he added.

"Bribed?"

"You do not know what the mamas of the *ton* will do to identify their prey," said Joseph darkly. "I have seen them slip a footman money to point out which gentleman is the person they seek, so they can send their daughter to stand close to him and wait for an invitation to dance."

"Truly?"

"Oh, truly."

Walking with care so as not to turn her ankle, Maggie made her way down the staircase, one hand firmly on the bannisters.

"Your Highness." Edward stood at the bottom of the staircase, gazing up at her, his blue eyes shining. Accustomed to seeing him in sober colours, Maggie could not help but be enchanted by his costume. He wore a suit made in golden velvet, with lavish ruffles on his white shirt and gold braiding and buttons. He had refused a wig. His natural hair curls were tied back with a ribbon, the colour matching the gold of the velvet. White silk stockings, black shoes fastened with gold buckles. There was something in his air that spoke of confidence, a certainty to his stance which made her smile.

"You look like a princess," he said, as she reached him.

The Duchess nodded frostily. "Well done, Duval," she said to Celine, who was hovering behind Maggie. "You have done a good job."

"Is that supposed to be a compliment to Margaret, Mother?" asked Edward.

"She is dressed as she should be," said the Duchess. She was laced into a similarly shaped gown, dark purple silk glittering all over with tiny gold sequined stars. She gestured to Celine, who hurried forward and fastened her mask, an elaborate half-face confection in the shape of a crescent moon. It made her easy to recognise, but Maggie suspected that the Duchess was not keen on being anonymous, but rather preferred to see and be seen. Perhaps she wanted to be known so that the various mamas of the *ton* could seek her out and ask for assistance in identifying her son. Joseph helped Edward with his mask, a full-faced gold and black affair, behind which Edward disappeared entirely into an unknown person.

The carriage would not fit all three of them at once, due to the vast skirts of the two women, so the first carriage took the Duchess and Edward, while Maggie climbed into the second carriage.

"I hope you enjoy yourself tonight," said Celine, leaning in for a moment to adjust her mask.

"Thank you," said Maggie.

Arriving, she took a moment to rebalance herself in the golden heels, walked carefully up the stairs, to where a footman held out his hand for her invitation. He glanced down at it, nodded and bowed her into the room, with none of the announcements of names and titles which Maggie had come to expect.

The ballroom was vast, adorned with statues of gilded cherubs and multi-coloured feathers in vases, displayed as though they were flowers. The sight of hundreds of people in the glorious costumes with fantastical masks was dazzling and Maggie paused for a moment to take it all in. For once she felt free. No-one knew who she was, so she would not continuously feel watched. If she should chance to make an error, she would not be found out by the *ton* or reprimanded by the Duchess.

She could see the Duchess in her purple gown, so she drifted towards her through the crowd and stood to one side, where she could hear her speaking, but not be easily seen, given the mask which must be obscuring some of the Duchess' view of the ballroom.

One woman after another came up to her, bowed their heads and made small talk, before inevitably enquiring after what they were seeking: Edward's whereabouts. Maggie watched as the Countess of Bedford made her move.

"His Grace is here tonight, of course?"

"Of course." The Duchess smiled. "You will know him by his clothing… let us simply say that it matches his hair."

The countess gave a pleased smile and drifted away, though Maggie noted that her elegant glide turned faster as she made her way to her daughter and whispered in her ear. The daughter, sporting a sparkling pink gown that barely allowed her to get through doors, along with a glittering sequined facemask, nodded eagerly and began looking about her. Maggie silently cursed the Duchess. If she was going to do this to all the suitor-seeking mamas of the *ton*, what was the point of a masquerade?

Sure enough, within half an hour, it was all too obvious that the young ladies of the *ton* had found Edward. Wherever he went in the ballroom, a stream of women followed him. If he asked someone to dance, the rest of them waited on the edges or sulkily accepted second-best partners. As each dance finished, they arranged themselves as close as possible to him, preening and coquetting.

Maggie did not have much time to observe Edward, however, for her hand was sought for each dance. Reluctantly, she acquiesced to one after another, men dressed in elaborate costumes in every possible colour of velvet and silk, for once lavish peacocks instead of severely elegant Beau Brummells.

A man in blue silk held her hand a little tighter than the rest. "You will not mind if I disclose myself?" he asked, as their dance came to its midway point.

Maggie smiled. "Lord Frampton," she said, for the Earl's voice was familiar to her and she had found him a kindly person.

He returned the smile. "I am glad to find you know me, even at a masquerade," he said. "I knew you at once, even across the room. It is the way you carry yourself, graceful but without false elegance. Some of the young ladies of the *ton* think very highly of themselves and it can seem more like arrogance. I would always rather have grace combined with friendliness."

"You have been a good friend this season," murmured Maggie. "I have been grateful for your consideration."

His hand tightened on hers. "I am glad to hear you say it," he said, his voice warm. "I have enjoyed your company this season more than I expected. I am not so much a social butterfly myself. Finding a lady who is so at home within company is a relief to me, I confess."

Maggie stifled a laugh. The idea that she was being complimented on her skills in society by a man born and bred to the *ton* was absurd. "You are kind to say so," she said. "Though my preference is for quieter company and for the countryside."

"Really?" he asked eagerly. "It is how I feel myself. I am – I am glad to hear you say so."

Maggie turned her head to search for Edward. She could not see him however, so she looked back at the Earl and smiled as the dance finished, sweeping a curtsey that would have made even the Duchess proud.

There was a smattering of applause as the dance ended and a brief interlude, during which various couples wandered away to refresh themselves with ices or drinks and new couples formed around the floor, ready for the next dance.

"I hope to see you at the Gillinghams' dinner?" Lord Frampton said, still at her side.

She nodded, unsure of whether they were in fact attending, although since they attended everything, it was a fair assumption. Edward had vanished from the room. Maggie cast her mind back to which lady she had last seen him with and decided it had been someone with blue butterflies in her towering wig, but Maggie was unsure of her identity, and the lady, too, had disappeared from the room.

Might Edward have taken her somewhere private? Might he be about to propose? Had the Duchess impressed on him, out of Maggie's hearing, that he should make up his mind tonight and choose one of the ladies she had so firmly pushed forward? A cold shiver rippled down Maggie's body and her eyes prickled, as though she were about to cry. The idea that Edward might be married to a woman who might not care for him, who might not stand by him, protect him from the possibility of being locked away again...

The opening strains of music. A waltz was about to start. Maggie looked about her for a discreet way to leave the dance floor, having no desire to dance with anyone. She stepped backwards and bumped into someone standing just behind her.

"Please forgive me, I…"

"May I have this dance?"

For a moment she thought it was Edward but the man

standing in front of her was dressed in a rose-coloured silk costume, with a full-faced mask and a brown wig.

"Of course," she said, then immediately regretted her assent. She had been too well trained, she thought bitterly, trained to overcome how she was feeling, which was miserable and most certainly unwilling to dance a waltz with some strange man. But the instructions had all been firm on this, she could not refuse to dance unless she refused to dance all evening. And it was too late now. The man lifted his arms, and the waltz began, Maggie following his steps and movements with little interest, still looking about her for Edward.

"Are you looking for someone?"

"I – a person with whom I am acquainted…"

"His Grace the Duke of Buckingham? Every other lady seems to be searching for him."

Maggie stared. The eyes behind the mask were very blue, beneath the dark brown wig a tendril of golden hair had escaped. "Edward? Edward!"

"Shh, you will give me away."

"But your clothes… your hair…"

"Joseph had a second costume prepared for me. I could not bear another night of being followed everywhere." They changed direction, gazing at one another through the oval created by their arms. "And as you can see, the ruse has worked. The ladies are searching for my gold velvet, and it is nowhere to be seen."

"I thought…"

"What did you think? That I had been dragged into a quiet spot by some especially persistent young miss, hoping for a proposal?"

"Yes." The cold fear that had run down her whole body, the way tears had risen in her eyes at the idea… what was that?

"I have been careful to avoid them all," he said, and his voice was serious. "There is only one woman here I would care to be alone with."

Maggie's stomach churned. So, he had found someone. "And who might that be?" she enquired, trying to keep her voice light. "Do I know her?"

"I don't know," he replied. "If we dance towards that side of the room I will try and point her out to you when we reach her. She is very beautiful," he added with a smile.

Whom could he mean? It could not be Miss Belmont, for he knew Maggie had met her repeatedly. But then who? None of the young women with whom he had danced, walked, on whom he had called, had taken his fancy. Besides, if he had fallen for any of them the Duchess would have promptly given the match her blessing, for all of them had been deemed suitable, eligible, even desirable, for Edward to pay court to. He had only to say the word and the wedding would be arranged in as much haste as was possible without appearing unseemly.

She stumbled over his feet, then tried to regain the rhythm of the waltz, which had felt so magical before, but the previous grace and flow of it had deserted her. She felt clumsy, awkward, as though dancing without music, without a partner, all alone and in the way among the whirling couples, unwanted in their midst and uncertain of her steps.

Slowly they moved across the ballroom, towards the outer-most edges of it. Edward steered them, still dancing, through a door and into a side room which was empty save for a full-length looking glass on one wall and low velvet benches set around the edges. This was the room where all the ladies at the ball came to change into their dancing shoes if needed or to check that their feathers and wide skirts were uncrumpled from the journey. For now, it was empty, and Edward stopped their rotations, but did not let go of Maggie, so that one of his hands was on her waist, the other clasping her hand but lowered, so that she was held within the circle of his arms, her back to his chest, her face towards the looking glass.

"There she is," he said, his voice low against her cheek. "I told you she was beautiful."

Her laugh of dismissal died in her throat, for he tightened his hold on her and bent his head. She watched in the looking glass as he kissed her shoulder, felt his lips warm on her bare skin, spoke in a half whisper, her voice shaking. "Edward…"

"You know me," he said softly. "As I know you."

Slowly, he turned her in his arms so that she was facing him, then let go of her, reached up and pulled away his mask, which he dropped to the floor. His hands went behind her back, brushed gently up her neck before untying her mask, which he cast aside as he had with his own.

"There you are."

She gazed up at him, lips parted in expectation, full of desire for his touch. Her hand reached up to touch his cheek, and she felt the hardness of his jaw. She had touched his face many times during his nightmares, but never like this, pulling him towards her. His hold on her tightened as his lips touched hers, soft at first and then more passionately as she responded, somehow knowing what to do, instinctively wanting more, wanting every part of their bodies to be entwined. She clung to him, a moan escaping her lips.

"Gracious, Lord Sedgewick is a terrible dancer," came a

giggling voice just outside the doorway. "I swear my toes are black and blue."

In a moment, Edward had knelt and picked up the two masks, lifting his own to his face, passing Maggie hers as two young women entered behind them. Maggie, flustered, turned her back on them to use the looking glass as she tried to fasten her mask. Edward fastened his own, bowed to them all and left the room.

"Who was that?" asked one of the women, turning to watch him go.

"Don't know," said the other, sitting on a bench, unlacing one slipper and examining her stockinged feet. "Gentlemen ought to be given more lessons before they attend balls, if they can't be trusted to get through one dance without sending their partner home with a limp."

Maggie's trembling fingers somehow managed to fasten the mask onto her face. She turned to leave and came face to face with the Duchess.

"Are you ready to leave? It is almost two o clock."

"Yes," was all Maggie could manage.

"I will take Edward in the carriage. You can follow on in the phaeton."

She stood and watched as the Duchess took Edward's arm and steered him out of the ballroom, saw him look back over his shoulder at her but could not make out his expression beneath the mask he wore.

"Are you leaving?" The Earl of Frampton was by her side.

"I – yes," was all Maggie could manage.

"Allow me to escort you to your carriage?"

She hardly heard him, only saw his arm and took it, followed him outside and took his hand as she climbed the carriage steps, nodded at whatever he was saying, waited for the carriage to take her away. The open carriage suited Maggie, she needed the cold night air on her face, her neck. She took off the mask and lay it beside her, tilted her head back and closed her eyes, the better to remember every word, every touch, every moment that had passed between them but above all to revel in the rush of feelings that filled every part of her. Edward had kissed her. The feelings she had held for him, had tried to suppress, came rushing up in her, suddenly vivid and undeniable. She had thought it was only her concern for his wellbeing that made her feel anxious when he walked or talked or danced with other women. But that was not it. She loved him. The fear she had felt when she had thought he was about to show her his future bride had turned into overwhelming desire for him as he had kissed her and now she wanted only to be close to him again, to press herself against him and feel his lips on hers, to whisper words to him, to hear what he might whisper to her.

The ride was too short to cool her flushed cheeks. She entered Atherton House with her mask dangling in her hand, her heart beating fast at the knowledge that she would see Edward again shortly.

But of course the Duchess was standing in the hallway with Edward, passing her cloak to the footman. "We can only be grateful there is not another ball tomorrow night," she was saying as Maggie entered, "I am quite worn out. Goodnight, Margaret," she added, catching sight of Maggie and evidently expecting her to go immediately to bed.

Maggie hesitated, but to pause too long would look odd and so she made for the stairs. "Goodnight, Aunt Caroline." She could not bring herself to utter Edward's name without her voice shaking, so she began walking up the stairs, desperate to glance back but afraid to do so would show her feelings on her face.

Edward called her back. "Margaret."

She turned at once, eager for the very sight of him.

He stood silent, one hand on the banister, his gaze steady on her. "Goodnight, Margaret," he said at last, his voice low and warm.

"Goodnight, Edward." Her voice shook, but she smiled, knowing from his tone that there was more he wanted to say, that only the Duchess' presence was stopping him. For a moment longer she gazed at him, then walked quickly up the last stairs and turned into the corridor to her room.

At once the Duchess turned inquisitorial. "Did you dance with Miss Belmont?" she demanded.

Edward could not recall, but no doubt he had; he had danced with her at most balls this season. "Yes."

"Good."

She paused, as though about to say something else, but Edward needed to be alone with his thoughts, with the feelings rushing through him. "Goodnight, Mama."

"Goodnight, Edward."

He took the stairs two at a time but paused for a moment outside Maggie's door. If he were to knock softly, she would come to him, he knew it, but that was too much, too soon. He was not sure that he could restrain himself if she were in his arms again. And there would be a difficult path to tread ahead, he knew that. It would be wise to sleep now. In the morning, they would speak together in private, they would find a way to be together, he would hold her close again and touch her lips with his, would whisper to her the words he had been denied speaking. In his room he lay smiling in the dark, waiting for a new day to dawn on this, their secret joy.

Maggie awoke to full daylight as Jane pulled open the curtains. For a moment tiredness from the night before overcame her and she closed her eyes again. But the masquerade came flooding back to her and she sat up in bed, cheeks flushed, heart beating faster.

Edward had kissed her.

He had *kissed* her.

And he had known who she was, the intimacy had not been meant for someone else. He had removed both their masks and gazed into her eyes before he kissed her. And his hands on her body… his lips on her neck… the shining blue of his eyes…

"The blue, Miss?"

"What?"

Jane stood waiting; a blue muslin dress draped across her arms. "The blue?"

"Yes… yes of course, Jane, thank you."

She had to wait for long agonising moments while Jane carefully dressed her in the shift, laced her stays, put on the stockings and tied her garter ribbons, adding the petticoat and finally the dress with its endless array of buttons. Her shoes. Her hair. All of it seemed to take far longer than it usually did. She did not much care how she was dressed, all she cared about was finding Edward. Finally released from Jane's care, she all but ran down the stairs, smiling when she heard his voice coming from the drawing room, then came to a sudden halt in the hallway as a man stepped out of the shadows and she came face to face with Doctor Morrison.

"A word, Maggie."

She gasped as a cold hard knot lodged in her stomach. "Doctor Morrison."

"Is there a room where we can be alone?"

She swallowed and made a small gesture towards the morning room, glancing towards the drawing room, hoping against hope for Edward to appear.

"His Grace is speaking with Her Grace," said Doctor Morrison, catching her gaze. "As you can imagine, he has some explaining to do." He stepped briskly into the morning room and stood back, waiting for Maggie to join him. Once she did so, he closed the door behind her.

She waited for him to speak. Perhaps he knew nothing.

"I told you that I would be watching, Maggie," the doctor said, his voice kindly. "I may not be exalted enough to attend these social occasions to which, through deceit, you have found yourself invited. But I have my... eyes and ears within this world. And what I was told unsettled me. I have heard of a growing closeness between you and His Grace, a fondness, which I had hoped would progress no further. But last night, Maggie, last night, *you were seen.*"

She opened her mouth, but he shook his head. "Do me the courtesy of not protesting innocence, Maggie. You were seen. Edward waltzed with you, and then... you kissed."

She stood silent, heart pounding, unable to meet his eyes.

"Evidently, I was not clear enough when last we spoke. Let me make myself absolutely clear, so that there can be no doubt whatsoever. If any such intimacy occurs again, I will have no qualms in telling everyone who you are and that Edward is a lunatic."

Her stomach lurched "He will be locked away again!"

He smiled an unpleasant smile. "Then I, his family's trusted physician and expert in this matter, will once again take him into my care. For as long as is necessary. For the rest of his life, quite possibly. And I will be paid handsomely for doing so." He leant closer to her. "Or you will see to it that he marries and marries well by the end of the season, in which case both you and I have been promised a payment acknowledging the successful completion of our task. And we will go about our lives again, as though none of this ever happened. Choose, Maggie, but see to it that you choose wisely. You are not to speak with His Grace unless it is absolutely necessary. You are not to dance with him nor spend any time alone with him. Do you understand me?"

The polished wooden floor shone her reflection back at her, the floating dress, the careful ringlets of her hair. A lady, through and through. But her outer appearance concealed a fast-beating heart and the knowledge that any chance at happiness had been snatched away.

"Do you understand me?"

"Yes, sir."

He was gone, but the polished lady still stood there, her reflection marred by tears.

Edward had awoken to a fierce rush of joy. The sunlight streaming in his window echoed his feelings and he had hurried Joseph through his dressing, anxious to find Maggie and speak with her. They would have to find somewhere private, and he thought at once of the mews, where only the horses would be privy to their whispered conversation about how to proceed.

But as soon as he ventured out of his room, Bartholomew, the footman, found him.

"Her Grace wishes to see you, Your Grace."

He nodded. She would have some invitation to mention or some other such nonsense. He did not care. The quicker it was over with, the faster he could find Maggie. He strode to the drawing room and found his mother standing there, her face white with rage.

"Miss Elizabeth Belmont."

"What of her?"

"You will marry her."

"Lord and Lady Godwin's daughter? The mouse?" He gave a despairing groan. "Is that all you think me worthy of? A girl who is scared of her shadow? Do I get a say in the matter?"

The Duchess met his gaze with a steely glare. "No."

"I do not get to choose my own bride?"

"You have proven yourself incapable of making sane decisions, Edward. Perhaps it is not your fault, you were not raised to be the Duke of Buckingham, and you…became… ill and were taken away for treatment. Perhaps I should have left you there. Perhaps it would have been better for you, but the estate and title would have been passed away and we would have lost everything."

"*You* would have lost everything."

She lifted her chin. "I would have lost a great deal. But there are hundreds of people who rely on our family. Who knows who would have replaced us? Perhaps someone who would have treated them poorly. I had to try. And I thought you were doing better than I had expected, despite a few… incidents." Her nostrils flared. "But this… this is too much."

"What is?"

"This affection for a maid."

He stared at her, his heart thudding.

"You were seen, Edward."

"By whom?"

"Doctor Morrison."

"Doctor… how could he have seen anything? He was not there."

"He was… informed."

"He set spies on me?"

"He was right to," she spat. "Kissing a maid!"

Anger pushed up inside him. "Do not call Maggie a maid."

She fixed him with her gaze again. "That is what she is, Edward. A maid. An orphan raised by the Foundling Hospital, sent to Doctor Morrison as a servant, to care for you in your affliction."

He put his face close to hers. "She is the only person who has shown me any loyalty, any care, any kindly feeling. For years. Perhaps ever."

She looked down. "I am sorry you think so."

"You think differently? Do you wish to name someone else who cared for me? You, perhaps?"

"I –" Under his angry gaze she faltered.

"As I thought." His own mother making such a weak attempt at declaring any sort of feeling for him was unexpectedly wounding. His body tried to return to its old ways, shoulders hunching against the pain, head dropping. He fought against it, but the fear crept up in him. "So I am to marry Miss Belmont, and when you lock me away again, she must do as she's told, is that it? Will she be brought to me once a year to breed with, a mare brought to stud to keep the Atherton line going, to secure the title? Is that all she is to you? Poor girl. Wife to a locked-away husband. And I? Married to a woman who barely knows me, shut away from my own home and family."

"She is the best possible match for you."

"You cannot imagine anyone else better suited to me?"

"You will propose to her."

"Will I?"

"Yes."

"And if I do not?"

"Then you have lost your wits again and I will have to call on Doctor Morrison's services."

"Refusing to marry a woman I do not love on command is enough cause to lock me away as a madman?"

"Refusing to marry a woman of your own station because you have crazed notions of being in love with a maid? Yes."

They stood staring at one another, but it was Edward who first dropped his gaze. "I love her," he whispered.

"You will not speak to her again unless you must do so in public. You will not be in a room alone with her again, not even during your night-time… disturbances. You will marry Miss Belmont. If you refuse to comply, Edward, you will return to Ivy Cottage." His lips opened and hope entered his eyes, but she shook her head. "Without her. If you do not comply, she will be sent away at once."

Standing alone in the morning room, Maggie tried to stop her tears falling, but they would not, despite wiping her face more than once. Swallowing, she turned to leave, anxious to return to her room where she could be alone without being seen by any passing servants. Stepping into the hallway, she heard footsteps coming and hastened towards the stairs just as

Edward burst out of the drawing room, his expression that of a desperate man. He stopped at the sight of her, the two of them standing for a moment, eyes locked together in mute misery, before Maggie turned and ran up the stairs, a sob escaping her as she reached the landing. Edward stood watching her flee, his hands in fists by his side.

CHAPTER 9:
Proposals of Marriage

MAY PASSED IN A WRETCHED HAZE. WHOLE DAYS would go by when Edward and Maggie did not speak to one another. Mealtimes were silent. When Edward screamed at night, as he did often and more violently as time passed, Maggie would sit trembling in the darkness of her room, not daring to go to him, listening to Joseph trying to comfort him next door.

Outside of Atherton House, the social season continued, inexorably demanding their presence. They walked, they rode, they attended picnics and balls, church on Sundays, even a few weddings as the *ton*'s marriage mart started to bear fruit. The young women who knew they were not being considered for Edward chose other suitors, whether for love or money. Maggie changed her dresses repeatedly, from morning dresses to walking dresses to riding habits and evening gowns, allowing Jane to pick and choose as she wished, having lost any pleasure or interest she might once have had in the lavish wardrobe and the regular additions to it that her modiste was all too happy to provide as the season progressed towards its final stages. By the end of June, many of the *ton* families would head home to their estates, as the summer sun made London too hot and too malodorous for their sensitive natures. The men might need to stay or come and go for the final sessions of parliament at the end of July, but even they would head home as soon as possible. Time was running out.

Where Maggie had once hoped for Edward to be happy and healthy, free to make his own choices, now she could only hope for a quick marriage to a suitable woman. Her own desires, her own feelings for him were not only utterly impossible, they were also dangerous to him. She pushed them down when they rose up in her. The only way she could care for Edward was to keep him free. And that meant married, to a woman of the *ton*. And so she attended the parties and encouraged the young women who flocked to Edward, stepping out of their way, nodding and smiling when they indicated they wished to join them on a walk. Edward's freedom was all that mattered, she told herself, even though the idea of him marrying another woman gave rise to an ache inside her that grew each day that she saw him bow and smile to one lady after another, offer his hand to help them into their carriages, partner them in dance after endless dance. In the brief moments of their days when there were no social obligations or Parliamentary sessions, a stream of important-looking men made their way into Edward's study and then left, looking well pleased. Maggie could not fathom their purpose in visiting him, until, at a more than usually dull ball, she overheard the Duchess speaking with an elderly man.

"Your Grace. I wanted to say again how greatly we have

appreciated His Grace's interest in our efforts at the Foundling Hospital where I am a governor."

The Duchess' expression stayed carefully blank. "His Grace is interested in so many charitable institutions," she said at last. "I do not think he has yet apprised me of his attentions to the Hospital. Will you tell me more? I do so admire your work there."

"He has made a *most* generous donation to our funds." The gentleman smiled. "But he has also made arrangements that several children each year should join the Atherton estates both here in London and in Buckinghamshire, to be servants or apprentices. It is more than we could have hoped for from such a young man, to already be so thoughtful of the needs of those less fortunate."

"He is very charitably minded," agreed the Duchess, her voice lacking all warmth. "I will let him know his bequest has been well received, Lord Gibbs."

Maggie turned away, aware that her eyes were filling despite her best efforts to seem unaffected, but over the course of the month she heard from more than one source that Edward was busying himself with charitable works, from supporting the building of a new site for Bedlam at St. George's Fields in Southwark, to large donations to the Philanthropic Society, whose efforts centred on beggar children being taught crafts.

"We are most grateful for your generosity, Your Grace."

Edward nodded and stood up to shake the hand of the representative of the Marine Society, which sent poor boys into the navy. "I am keen that children especially should be well cared for and find their place in the world."

These moments of charitable efforts were the only part of Edward's day that brought him pleasure. The silent mealtimes were unbearable, the invitations continuing unwanted pressure. Maggie's compliance with the need to marry him off was a constant source of hurt. If she had begged him to embrace her again, to kiss her, to marry her, he would have risked even the torments of Ivy Cottage again, only to have her by his side, but instead she avoided his gaze, turned her face away from him and spent her days and evenings all but ushering young women towards him.

His nightmares grew worse. In them, Maggie was taken from him by force, or he was dragged away from her, closed up in a racing carriage taking him back to Ivy Cottage. Or he was back in Ivy Cottage already and the doctor was administering his treatments. He would wake screaming, sweating, and where before Maggie would have come to him, now she did not. Instead Joseph would hurry to him, would try to calm him, speaking gently. Edward was grateful for Joseph's care, but he longed for Maggie's warm embrace, her voice whispering to him, her hands clasping his. Being lost to his nightmares again without her presence was a loneliness he thought he had escaped.

For Maggie, hearing Edward cry out and be unable to go to him was a torture. She would pull the bell frantically for Joseph, knowing he would go to Edward's room, grateful that Edward had someone by his side when she could not be there.

As May came to an end, Edward's nightmares grew ever worse and one night, after she had heard his shouts and Joseph's hurried footsteps, she waited until Joseph left the Oak Room and opened her door, waylaying him as he left.

"The nightmares are getting worse."

He nodded.

"I am grateful to you for caring for him so well," she whispered.

He hesitated. "May I speak with you?"

She nodded, led him to a little alcove along the corridor where two chairs were placed, for servants who needed to wait up at night until the family returned from balls or dinners. She sat and indicated the other chair.

He hovered, uncertain for a moment, then took the chair and leant forward. "I have something to ask you."

"What is it?"

"Will you marry me?"

"Joseph!"

He reached out for her hand. "When I first brought you here, I hoped only you would care for His Grace, that he could be free again, for he has never been mad. I thought Her Grace was foolish to propose what she did, I was certain you would fail, that you would be exposed and yet you managed it, you held your own through all of the season and I came to admire you."

"Joseph…"

"You are brave. Kind. Intelligent. We could go far away from here, there are many opportunities for a footman who has served a duke. In a lesser household I could secure a position as a butler. You would not need to work. We could live a good life together, I know it."

She laid her hand on his.

"I can't, Joseph. I wouldn't wish to marry you without loving you. It wouldn't be right."

"I would be kind to you, Maggie. A life shared with a good person by your side is worth striving for. When His Grace marries, they will let you go, and I would be happy to go with you and build a fine life together."

She gazed into his deep brown eyes. "You know whom I love, Joseph. It would stand between us."

He sighed and let go of her hand. "You should tell him how you feel."

She shook her head. "He needs to marry. He needs to be safe."

"And you think marrying a woman he barely knows, who will come under his mother's control, will protect him from being locked away again?"

"I will find a way to get rid of Doctor Morrison."

"How?"

She shook her head. "I do not know. But I will find a way."

"He should dismiss the doctor himself."

"The Duchess would never allow it."

Joseph leant forward. "He is the master now. He is the Duke of Buckingham. He outranks her."

"The King outranks us all and he has been set aside for the Prince Regent."

"Because he is truly out of his wits, poor soul. Edward is not, never was, mad. He was frightened and broken and sent away so that his father could pretend he did not exist. He is quite sane. And he has grown into his manhood under your care, Maggie. He is not the poor boy he was when he first went into Doctor Morrison's so-called care. He is finding his courage and true self. But he needs more time. And he needs a loving and loyal wife."

"Miss Belmont…"

"Miss Belmont is a mouse. She will be crushed by the Duchess in a matter of months, if not weeks. He will fall prey to doubts about himself, he has had less than a year to believe those doubts to be untrue." He reached out and took Maggie's hand again. "If you will not marry me, tell Edward how you feel, at least. Give him the chance to decide who is the right woman for him to marry."

"If he tried to marry me, he would be locked up as mad for the rest of his life."

"If he loses you, he will lose himself. Think on it, Maggie." He rose to leave but paused by the doorway. "And my offer still stands, Maggie. Should you ever wish to leave the Buckinghams, you have only to ask, and I will leave at your side."

The first of June brought an end to the Duchess' already waning patience. The *ton* was racked with sudden excitement. The Duchess of Buckingham had announced a house party complete with a lavish ball, to be held at Atherton Park in mid-June. To be holding such a huge event so late in the season could only mean one thing.

"Is it true the Duke is going to propose? Or already has?" an eager young lady asked Maggie as she stood watching the dancers at a ball that night. The Duchess had insisted that they continue to be seen at social occasions.

"He has not yet proposed to anyone that I am aware of," Maggie said, struggling to keep her voice steady.

"Then he must be going to do it when they all arrive, and the big ball will be an engagement ball to round off the season. How exciting!" Without even waiting for a confirmation or denial from Maggie, the girl took off for her mama on the other side of the room, to whisper in her ear.

Late the next morning the Duchess stood, annoyed, by the front door. Finally, she called for a footman. "Where is His Grace? We are late for the Galpins' picnic."

The footman appeared mildly surprised. "He is gone, Your Grace."

"Gone? Gone where?"

"Back to Atherton Park, Your Grace. He left this note for you."

"Thank you, Bartholomew, you may go."

Maggie watched as the Duchess tried to keep her expression calm as she read the note. "Edward has returned to Atherton Park with Joseph. He does not intend to return to London before the end of the season."

Maggie stared at her. For once, even the Duchess did not seem to know how to proceed. "Will we follow him?"

"We have no choice but to do so." Her jaw tightened. "Ring the bell for Webb and Mrs Green. We leave within the week. But no one must suspect anything is wrong."

Meanwhile the word swept round the *ton* that the Atherton house party and ball was the only place to be seen this summer. It would round off the season with a triumphant success for the Duchess, and for one gloriously elevated young debutante, who would oust all the other contenders to become a duchess. The only question remaining was who. Who was the winner of the season? The *ton* counted and counted again. Some debutantes had already secured engagements, so it could not be them. Others were unlikely. It was agreed it must be someone of high rank; the Duchess would not stoop so low as to favour a girl from an untitled family; the family were not, after all, in need of wealth. So only a titled woman would do. The *ton* narrowed it down to the three most likely women: Lady Honora Fortescue, Miss Elizabeth Belmont, Lady Anna Huntington. The Duchess would say nothing when these names were mentioned, but all three of their families had been invited to the event, so the curiosity intensified even more. Maggie heard the odd comment by young rakes which made her think they were going so far as to place bets on the outcome. Ungentlemanly though it might be, they were only carrying out in coinage what the rest of the *ton* was doing with tongue-wagging. The three families with daughters in the race preened and hinted in public. In private, they summoned modistes and dancing-masters, sacked and hired ladies' maids, grilled and drilled their daughters on how to behave themselves and generally panicked that their greatest opportunity was about to be lost if they failed in what was turning out to be the final and most important event of the season. A dukedom was at stake for the first time in years and they were damned if they were not going to try for it. Even the fathers, usually outwardly scornful of the mothers' machinations, showed an interest. They went out of their way to bump into Edward at Parliament, had their stewards send them reports of Atherton Park and his other estates so that they could talk knowledgeably of whatever issues Edward might be interested in. When word got about that he had expressed some interest in a botanical print the drawing masters were summoned to ensure each of the girls could reliably sketch flowers.

Those young ladies who had not yet secured a husband were determined to still be in the running. They cajoled every contact they had to put them in front of the Duchess one more time, to see if an invitation to the great event would be forthcoming. Two young women received proposals but asked their ardent suitors to wait until the summer, in the hopes that they might still be considered, should one of the chosen three prove to be lacking in some important criteria. The suitors, knowing full well why they were being asked to wait, were by turns insistent and sulky, rightly feeling that they had been demoted to second choice. But even they, with hurt feelings, had to acknowledge that a young woman would be foolish indeed if she did not at least hold out until all hope was lost to become a duchess.

Celine was dispatched to the modiste with two already beautiful gowns in their possession but as yet unworn, one in a rich purple for the duchess, one in delicate pink for Maggie, with instructions to make them even more elegant, to be worn at the house party's ball. Maggie only shook her head when asked if she wanted to specify the alterations to be made. She had no interest. The exquisite clothes that had once seemed so delightful had lost their charms with Edward gone.

Maggie spent as much time as she could keeping to her own rooms when in the house, until she was summoned to the drawing room by the Duchess the day before their departure.

"Lord Frampton is in the library."

"Lord Frampton?"

"He knows we are leaving town. He says he wishes to speak with you."

"With me?"

"In private."

"Why?"

The Duchess stared at her; jaw clenched. "A gentleman only asks to speak to a lady in private for one reason."

Confused, Maggie stood waiting for a further explanation. What she was hearing could not be right.

"Margaret."

"Yes?"

"Lord Frampton is waiting. I hope you know what your answer should be."

"My answer?"

The Duchess' voice was tight. "Lord Frampton is about to make you an offer of marriage, Margaret. I hope you know better than to accept him. It would be an utter disgrace for an earl to marry someone like you under false pretences."

Maggie stared at her. "An offer of *marriage*?"

"Oh, you need not put on a pretence, Maggie, I am sure you knew it was coming. All these past months amongst the *ton,* you saw your chance and grasped it with both hands. A young earl with no parents to guide him when choosing a wife? How convenient that Robert Sinclair, Earl of Frampton, should find himself dancing with you so often. You could not have Edward, so you cast your net wider, is that it?"

"I was not… I have never sought…" Maggie was flustered and bewildered.

"He is waiting," the Duchess repeated. "Go to him and get

this over with. You will refuse him as graciously as you are able, then go to your room."

She swept away and Maggie forced herself to walk to the library. She hesitated with her hand on the door, took a deep breath and entered.

The Earl was standing by one of the windows, wringing his hands. Maggie felt a swell of pity for his nerves. As she entered, he corrected his posture, bringing his hands to his sides for a smart bow.

"Miss Seton."

"Lord Frampton. It is a pleasure to see you." And it was. She was fond of him; he had been a kind and gentlemanly figure throughout the social season. She had thought of him as a friend and had not realised he had seen their relationship in a different light.

"I am glad it is a pleasure to you," he said clumsily but with a hopeful smile. "May we sit together for a moment?" He indicated seating by the fireplace, and she joined him there, wondering whether she should allow him to speak or whether it was better to intervene before the proposal was made, whether that would be more ladylike or even simply kind. But she did not make up her mind fast enough, for the Earl was already speaking.

"I have greatly enjoyed your company this past season," he said, leaning forwards earnestly. "I – since the death of my dear mama, I have been – well, lonely. Frampton Hall is a good home, and I am at my happiest there. I am not much of a town person. But I thought to myself that I must do my duty and find a bride this season and so I came to London with that express intention. And I – I found it harder than I expected, Miss Seton. I do not have the guidance of family, excepting my Aunt Catherine, who is a most excellent person but has particular ways of thinking. She – well, she believes that finding a bride is only about suitability. Rank. Wealth. Breeding. But I should like – that is, I should prefer to also consider love, Miss Seton. I should like to love my wife."

Maggie's heart ached for him. There was a kindness and a goodness to him that she wished was being bestowed on someone else, someone able to make him happy. "Lord Frampton, I –"

"Please call me Robert, Miss Seton. I should also make it clear that I do not require my future bride to bring a dowry. I have more than enough and so I am glad to say that such considerations need not be of concern in this instance." He paused, a little breathless. "Let me be plain. I have concluded that while I greatly esteem many of the charming young ladies of the *ton*, it is only in your company that I have felt the happiness which I would wish to find in a marriage and therefore, I ask that you do me the honour of becoming my wife. Will you marry me, Miss Seton?"

Maggie wanted to reach out and place her hand on his, but was afraid it would be taken for assent, so instead she put her hand against her heart.

"I am sorry, Lord Frampton, I cannot marry you."

Pain flickered across his face. "Do your affections lie elsewhere?"

Edward. They lay with Edward. Impossibly. She thought of the Duchess' horror and anger at the idea of her saying yes to the Earl and multiplied it a thousand-fold to what she would say if she could see into Maggie's heart and know how much she longed to be with Edward. But the Earl was waiting for a reply, and she did not want to prolong his pain.

"My affections are as yet… unclaimed, Lord Frampton. But I am not ready for marriage. I wish to stay with my family until I am older."

His disappointment turned back to hope. "I would wait for you," he assured her. "However long… I am still young myself, Miss Seton, there is no hurry. If there were an understanding between us, I would be more than happy to wait."

He was a good, kind man. For a moment, something flickered in Maggie. Should she say yes? What, after all, could the Duchess do? As the wife of Lord Frampton, Maggie would be safe and loved, elevated to the rank of countess, an unthinkable leap in her fortunes. She would be married to a good man. Making a life with Edward was an impossibility while Robert… Robert, extraordinarily, was actually a possibility.

But Edward was everything to her and she could not live a lie.

"I am sorry, Lord Frampton," she repeated. "I do not wish to hold you to a promise which you might come to regret. I hope that you will find another lady who will make you happy."

He set his jaw, stood and bowed. "I will take my leave of you Miss Seton," he said, his voice wavering ever so slightly before he pulled it back to firmness. "Should you ever reconsider… you know where to find me. I shall remain your devoted friend."

Maggie rose and curtseyed, met his unhappy eyes. "As shall I, Lord Frampton," she said gently. "And I am grateful for and honoured by your offer."

He bowed again and left her, striding out of the room, no doubt to retreat to the privacy of his waiting carriage where he could weather the sting of her refusal alone.

Maggie watched him go. Celine would have chastised her.

Throw away the very real opportunity to become a countess, for an imagined and impossible romance with Edward, something that would never be allowed to happen? What madness was this?

"It is I who am the lunatic," Maggie murmured to herself. "It is a wonder Doctor Morrison has not put me in Bedlam."

The journey back to Atherton Park was long and silent. Maggie stared out of the windows as the carriage rocked along the roads, mile after mile. She tried to think of ways in which she could free Edward of Doctor Morrison. She dozed from time to time, her tired mind unable to find a way forward.

They stopped at a coaching inn for the night. Maggie nodded eagerly at the offer of a tray of supper brought to her bedchamber and spent the evening alone, retreating to bed early. The next day, her only consolation was that each mile travelled brought her closer to Edward.

She sprang out of the carriage when they drew up. Ignoring all the other servants who were gathered to welcome them, she hurried to Joseph.

"Where is His Grace?" she asked, her voice low.

Joseph's face was serious. "Visiting the Dower House."

"The Dower House? Why?"

He shook his head, reminding her of the listening ears surrounding them. "He has been there most days."

Maggie looked down at her clothing. A pale blue muslin gown and kid slippers, they were hardly the thing for the walk across the grounds and down beyond the stable block, especially after the recent rain, but she did not want to take the time to change.

The Dower House stood a half mile from the main house, a handsome mansion set within its flower gardens. Maggie had seen it from a distance but had never been inside. Merlin was nibbling at the grass outside and she stopped to pat him, feet sore from the gravel. The front door was ajar, and she pushed it open, stepped into the large hall, which felt cold and empty, despite its elegance.

"Edward?" she called out.

There was no answer. She opened the door on her left to find a parlour, elegantly painted in rose pink, with delicate plasterwork in white. There was a thick carpet, couches and chairs, side tables, all draped in holland covers, lending the room a ghostly air, as though it were waiting for someone to come and reclaim it from its forgotten state.

"Edward? Edward!".

There was no reply. She left the parlour and headed up the stairs.

Edward sat on the bed in the main bedchamber, shoulders hunched, staring down unseeing at the swirls and flowers of the carpet. A gracious room, well decorated. The whole of the Dower House was elegant; no Dowager Duchess could complain of being mistreated by being sent to live here, so he, a mad duke, could hardly complain if this were to be his fate. He was unfit for society, unfit for the role he had not, after all, been born to play. Being sent here to live out his days was a kindness. There would be staff. Loyal servants who could be trusted to keep their mouths closed and not gossip. Enough to live well but without risking unwanted tattletales. Perhaps

Joseph might come with him. He was a good man, a man with heart.

Edward thought of the young women to whom he had been introduced. They were pleasant girls, doing their best, as was he, but however much they lied about their accomplishments or personal charms, were any of them telling as big a lie as he was? No. One of them would be chosen, would wear his ring and be crowned with a Duchess' coronet, would believe herself to be lucky… and then she would find out the truth, that she was wanted only to breed, to secure the estate by providing an heir as quickly as possible, that her husband would see her only a few times perhaps, enough to sire a child and the rest of the time he would be closed away, hidden in the Dower House. What a lonely life for her. What a sad life. He hoped, at least, that she might find solace in their children.

Their children. Would he be allowed to see them? To have some joy in their existence, or would he be kept at a distance, for fear of frightening or corrupting them with his madness? Would they, too, be watched incessantly for any signs of strangeness, or inability to take on the mantle of heir?

"Edward?"

Her voice, calling from somewhere below. Ah, Maggie. Would she, perhaps, come and live with him here, care for him? He could bear anything, if she would be by his side. They could live quietly here, bothering no-one. But what sort of a life would that be for her, caring for him all her days, not allowed to… to marry, to have children. The thought of Maggie marrying made his stomach turn over. It would mean her leaving him, going away to her own household, where she would one day be loved by another man…

"Edward?" Her voice again, louder this time, closer.

The idea of Maggie marrying another man brought jealousy flooding through him. But if he were to declare that he loved Maggie? That he wanted to marry her? A duke, marry the maid hired to care for him? He could already feel the cold clamp of the buckles on Doctor Morrison's cursed chair closing around his wrists. The bleeding, the purging, the vomiting, leaving him shaken and whimpering, without even the solace of Maggie's soft hand on his, her warm brown eyes on his. Because they would send her away at once. If he should ever say that he loved Maggie, he would be locked up for the rest of his life and she would be sent far away. He would never set eyes on her again. In her place would be some monstrous nurse unworthy of the name, a woman who would grip his arm even harder than Doctor Morrison, who would agree with whatever the physician prescribed, who would keep her cold eyes fixed on him to ensure his compliance. Maggie, his beloved Maggie, would be lost to him forever.

She stood in the doorway before him, her shawl slipping from her shoulders, slippers muddy, cheeks flushed pink from the cold brisk walk to find him. "Edward! What are you doing here?"

"Doctor Morrison said he would lock me up in the Dower House. I thought I should look over my future home."

She stared at him, eyes filling with tears.

"Seven bedrooms," he said. "A dining room that seats twelve. Do you think I shall be allowed guests, Maggie? Do you think people will want to stay and stare at the mad Duke of Buckingham?"

"You are not mad," said Maggie. Her voice trembled and he wanted, more than anything, to stand and take her in his arms, but that way led to never seeing her again. And, surely, that would be true lunacy, to do anything that might lead to such a fate.

"Ah, but you're wrong, Maggie," he said, struggling to keep his voice even. "I must be mad, because Doctor Morrison says so, and so does my mother, the woman who gave birth to me. They should know, should they not? And after all, I do have delusions, they are right about that."

"What delusions?"

"That I might be allowed to live my life as I choose? That I might be happy? That I might be allowed to choose a woman I love for my wife?" He gave an unhappy laugh. "That proves to you, Maggie, how delusional I must be. That I should even think to marry for love, when all the *ton* thinks otherwise."

"I would want you to marry for love," she said, her voice very small.

He rose at once and came to her, standing so close that he could smell the warm scent of her, not the delicate rose perfume she wore but her own scent, a smell which made desire rush up in him. "Would you, Maggie?" he asked, and his hands clasped her waist and drew her closer to him. He almost kissed her there and then, found himself gazing at the rosy temptation of her mouth, his lips parting to match hers, before he met her gaze and saw her eyes were full of tears. "Maggie…"

"We cannot," she murmured, voice so low he could barely hear her. "We never can, Edward."

He let go of her waist as though his fingers had been burned, so fast that she rocked backwards as he let go of her. "Never?" He wanted her to fight for them, to say that what they felt was greater than the threat it posed, that she did not care about anything except him. But instead, she shook her head in silence, a tear falling down onto her cheek, followed by another.

He stared at her for a moment, then let out a curse and strode from the room, unable to bear her being so close yet untouchable, there yet not his. Outside he sprang into Merlin's saddle and rode back to the house at a gallop, all but throwing the reins into a surprised groom's hands, then making his way into the hallway.

The Duchess emerged immediately from the drawing room. No doubt she had been watching and waiting at the window. "Where have you been?"

"The Dower House," said Edward curtly, brushing past her and taking the stairs two at a time.

"Edward!" Her voice rang out sharply and he paused at the top of the staircase without turning.

"Yes?"

"There is to be a house party here. Next week. With a ball. At which we will announce your engagement."

CHAPTER 10:
Old John

T HE HOUSE PARTY'S DETAILS WERE SETTLED. GUESTS
would arrive Monday and Tuesday. Tuesday night would
feature an elegant dinner. On Thursday there would be a
lavish ball, and therefore everyone expected Wednesday to be
the day when Edward would ask Miss Belmont to marry him,
thus making the ball a celebration of their engagement. Under
the weight of this expectation, Atherton Park was being transformed. Where the servants usually went about their business
discreetly, silently, rising before dawn to make fires and cook
breakfasts, staying up late to clean dining tables and working
in rooms the family was not using, now they were everywhere.
Indeed, Maggie wondered whether they had multiplied overnight, for there appeared to be more maids and footmen than
she had ever seen before. Every corridor had people rushing
down it, carrying armfuls of linens or vases of flowers, cleaning
implements, firewood and coal. Maggie expected the Duchess
to be outraged but she was everywhere too, directing, criticising, re-arranging work already done.

"Atherton Park must be at its very best," she said, pointing a maid in one direction while shaking her head at another, who was about to place a vase of flowers in the wrong location. "Lord and Lady Godwin must see it at its finest to seal the deal."

Every bedroom would be in use; even the nursery was rearranged to make sleeping space for the extra servants who would be attending with their masters and mistresses. Meanwhile the vast extension to the back of Atherton Park, which consisted of a magnificent ballroom in the centre with an orangery to one side and a dining room to the other, was brought fully to life for the first time since Maggie had arrived at Atherton Park. Dozens of gilded chairs were brought out from under holland covers, looking glasses polished, hundreds of candles were placed ready in their holders, chandeliers were lowered and dusted, gigantic flower arrangements were prepared.

"I heard a French chef is to manage the meals during the house party," Maggie said to Celine, who had come to her bedroom to choose clothes for each day's activities.

Celine tittered. "Monsieur Cerf arrived in his own carriage, with another trailing behind him full of assistants and half a kitchen's worth of bowls, spoons, bain-marie sets, salmon kettles and who knows what else."

"Does he think a duke's kitchen won't have what he needs? What does Mrs Barton say? Isn't she put out to have her kitchen taken away from her and have some French chef lording it over her?"

Celine shook her head. "She knows her true worth," she said confidently. "Monsieur Cerf is only for show. Mrs Barton is wanted all year round because she's one of the best cooks there is. In all the time she has served here, there hasn't been a year gone by without some lady tried to poach her from Her Grace's service."

"Do ladies do that? How underhand."

"Ladies try to poach servants all the time," said Celine. "I have lost count of the number of times a lady has pressed a guinea and a visiting card with their address on it into my hand and whispered that she would be glad to hear from me, should I be looking for a new position."

"And you never said yes?" asked Maggie, surprised. Surely serving the Duchess was a role most servants would prefer to escape from.

Celine smiled. "I am used to her ladyship by now. And…" she shrugged. "I have known her a long time. Now, your dress for the ball."

The thought of the ball, a celebration of Edward's impending engagement, brought a wave of nausea. "Whatever you think best," she said hurriedly.

"The pink silk, I had the modiste attach roses to the bodice and then petals falling down from the skirt," began Celine with enthusiasm, making to open a large box, but Maggie only nodded.

"I will see it on the day, it can be a surprise," she managed with false brightness.

Celine set the box aside. "Then just the green for the picnic," she finished, and left the room.

From Monday, the guests began to arrive, carriage after carriage throughout the day, each one welcomed by Edward and his mother, with Maggie standing by their side, endless bows and curtseys and servants hurrying to unpack luggage before the carriages were driven away to the stable yard, which was bursting at the seams. Every family arrived with their servants in tow. The attics were full and the guest rooms which had lain empty were all assigned. The Peony Room, the Rose Room, the China Room, the Red Room, one after another they were filled.

They had just finished welcoming Lady Fortescue's family when Maggie caught Edward's eye. "I have a surprise for you," she murmured, having checked that the Duchess was busy speaking with Lord and Lady Halesworth.

"What is it?"

"Come," she said, turning towards the first flight of stairs.

He followed her, noting how confident she was at Atherton Park now, how she did not hesitate at every staircase or turn her head this way and that as they went down the corridors, fearful of being lost, uncertain of which rooms were behind which doors.

She stopped outside a set of doors that had brought dread to him for years. He took a step backwards. "Maggie…"

"Close your eyes."

"What?"

"Close your eyes. Please."

He wanted to say no, but he could not refuse her hopeful sweetness. He sighed and closed his eyes, stood still and waiting, felt her hand take his, her warm skin against his, pulling him forwards. He took one step and another, trusting that he was safe, focused only on her hand clasping his. They had so few opportunities to touch.

"Now you may look," she said, letting go of his hand and he opened his eyes.

For a moment he frowned, unsure where he was. The heavy

dark panelling, the dark-red walls, the bulky bed, they were all gone. The room had been entirely redecorated, the walls now a bold sunshine yellow, the panelling stripped away. The new four-poster bed was still large but more delicately made, with hangings of gold velvet and crisp white bedlinen covered with a silken bedspread woven with a woodland theme, butterflies and flowering vines sprawling across a yellow background.

"And your other rooms," Maggie said eagerly.

"Lead me," he said, wanting her hand in his again.

His dressing room had papered walls, pale yellow with hand painted scenes of woods, with deer and a tiny stream along the very bottom.

"You had them paint a frog?"

"Two actually," she said, laughing. "Come and see your study."

His study was a pale green and here again the furniture had been changed, no longer the heavy bullish desk of his father but a more graceful writing table and chair. A large globe on a table, maps of Buckinghamshire and the world on the walls, the curtains a deep green velvet that made the room cosy but allowed in the bright sunlight.

"Is it different enough?"

Her hand was still in his and he raised it to his lips, kissed it, wanting to keep his lips on her warm soft skin forever. "It – they – are perfect." He lowered his voice. "*You* are perfect."

She pulled her hand away, but her smile was sad. "They are your rooms," she said, her voice soft. "They are the Duke of Buckingham's rooms, and that means they are yours. I left instructions while we were away, and Mr Wilson had it all done to surprise you."

"I will sleep here tonight," he promised her. "I will have

the servants bring all my things here. Joseph will not know how to thank you. *I* do not know how to thank you."

"You already have," she said and the hand he had kissed clenched by her side. "Seeing you claim your rooms is thanks enough."

"I will miss you being next door though," he said.

They stood in silence for a moment, aware of the space between them and how vast it was about to grow, yet how easy it would be to close it, only one step forward by each of them…

Edward took a step back. She was too close to him, he wanted only to reach out and hold her, no, more than that, he wanted to lay her down on the golden silk coverlet behind him, amidst the butterflies and flowers and hold her close to him, unfasten her hair and…

"I will sleep here tonight," he repeated. "Ring for Joseph." If someone else did not enter the room soon, he would not be able to restrain himself.

She stepped away from him, her cheeks flushed and rang the bell, cleared her throat. "I am so glad you like the rooms," she said. "They will be something to remember me by. When – when you are married."

It was too much. "How am I to marry if it means losing you –" he began, but behind him the door opened, and Joseph stood waiting. Edward swallowed. "Joseph, you will have my possessions moved into these rooms at once," he managed, though it came out more brusquely than he meant it to.

"At once, Your Grace. And… Her Grace has asked for your presence in the drawing room."

He did not want to go, he did not want to leave her, but staying was impossible. "I will see you later," he managed.

By late Tuesday afternoon all the guests had arrived and there was a fluttering of valets and ladies' maids come twilight, as every lord and lady must be dressed in their finery for the grand dinner, held not in the usual dining room within the main house, but in the one adjoining the ballroom, which had seating for fifty. Lady Godwin lent her own maid to Miss Belmont, so that she was attended by two ladies' maids, in order that nothing should ruin her chances. It was fully expected that some time before the grand ball there was to be a proposal, that, after the party, Miss Belmont would leave Atherton Park only briefly as its future mistress, the future Duchess of Buckingham. She must be presented at her very best, at every moment, for all eyes would be on her.

Down the staircases they came, glittering jewels and silks, perfume and tight cravats, carefully sorted into their proper ranks in the drawing room, ready to enter the dining room.

Maggie watched them all, caught the endless glances of the guests at Edward and Miss Belmont. Everyone was waiting for the announcement that the tiny mouse had somehow snared the prize stallion of the season. Astonishing and yet agreeable, there could be no possible objection, for Miss Belmont was wealthy in her own right and from a family of impeccable breeding.

"Any word of when we're to be told?" Lady Fortescue was at Maggie's side, looking unusually serious.

"Told?"

"If he hasn't proposed already, he'd better hurry up. Can't have an engagement ball without an engagement, can you?"

"He has not proposed yet," said Maggie softly.

Lady Fortescue narrowed her eyes at Miss Belmont. "Perhaps he's had second thoughts," she said.

Maggie shook her head. "His thoughts are not his to command."

"Not even by you?"

Maggie turned to Lady Fortescue in surprise.

"Oh, come now," said Lady Fortescue, looking away but speaking fast. "I'm not blind. I saw you dance together. And anyone who saw that must know where his true affections lie."

A rush of heat rose to Maggie's neck and cheeks. "I –"

Lady Fortescue shook her head. "If he's going against his desires, he should remember it's not just his happiness that's at stake."

There was something odd in her voice, something desperate. Maggie looked at her friend more closely, saw her jaw tight, a glitter of tears in her eyes. "Are you – do you – are you telling me that *you* care for Edward?"

Lady Fortescue let out a bark of laugh that had several people turn. "God, no," she said.

"Then…?"

"Nothing," said Lady Fortescue, draining her glass of champagne.

"I wish you would tell me."

"Not something one can just say."

"Not even to a friend?"

"I would tell you," Lady Fortescue said, "But not in a room like this, where everyone can hear you sneeze, let alone confide…"

"Shall we go elsewhere?"

"Dinner is served," announced the butler.

Lady Fortescue grimaced.

"Later?" persisted Maggie.

"If there is a later," said Lady Fortescue darkly.

The dinner was endless. The array of dishes was beyond anything Maggie had ever seen at Atherton Park, the jewellery on show magnified by hundreds of candles. This was not just the *ton*; this was the very cream of society. Only the most select had received invitations and all of them were eager to witness the event of the season, to see on which head the ducal coronet might be placed, which family were to be elevated to the very pinnacle of titles, beyond which only royalty lay. Maggie turned her head one way, following the Duchess' lead, then the other at her signal, like a puppet. It occurred to her at some point during the tedious hours that her education as a lady must be complete, for she was able to speak acceptable nonsense to anyone seated next to her, able to spout the superficial chit-chat required by the *ton* without hesitation and without even thinking about it.

Opposite her she could see Miss Belmont frozen in place, her face pale and her movements stilted. Lady Fortescue, further down the table, was drinking more than usual. Only Lady Anna seemed her usual self, making spirited conversation with Lord Lymington, apparently oblivious to the fact that no announcement had yet been made.

Edward woke early on Wednesday morning, unused to the new rooms, unable to sleep. His mind was too full of contradictory thoughts. Duty and desire fighting one another, unable to find a path that would guide him to fulfilling both. Tomorrow was the ball. Today all eyes would be on him, everyone expecting him to take Miss Belmont to one side, to speak with her, to return with the announcement they were all waiting for.

Could he do it? For, once done, there could be no turning back for a man of honour. If he proposed to Miss Belmont, he would go through with the wedding.

But he loved Maggie. And what honour was there in marrying a woman without love, knowing his heart belonged elsewhere? His mind was filled with Maggie, it was all he could do not to think of her in every waking moment, not to dream of her each night. He wanted to marry Maggie, but doing so was a dangerous move, one which might find him locked away for the rest of his life. Yet what was his life without her?

He dressed by himself, not bothering with a cravat, leaving his collar loose, pulling on his waistcoat and breeches, his boots, deciding to forgo his jacket; the day would already be warm, and the horses would not care if he were not properly dressed. He ran down the stairs and out of the house, startling a housemaid and one of the gardeners along the way. At the stables, there were only a couple of grooms about, the stable-yard quiet.

Merlin whinnied at the sight of him.

"Hello, my boy. How are you this morning?" Edward made his way to the storage room and scooped up a bucket of oats, which he took back to the horse, who nibbled a few handfuls. Edward offered some to Lacey, boxed alongside Merlin, who snuffled eagerly in his palm, polishing off the rest of the oats.

"All gone," he said, showing both of them the empty bucket. "Enough for one morning, I think."

He stroked Merlin's delicate ears, then leant his face against the horse's forehead. "Why can't it be easier?" he asked out loud. "Every time I think I have made a decision I feel I have failed." He sighed, raised his head again and patted Merlin's neck. "You're a good listener. I had better be getting back now. Perhaps we shall ride later."

He turned to find that Old John was leaning on the stable door, watching him.

"Us servants used to talk about you, when you was a little lad," he said, without any kind of greeting.

Edward couldn't help stiffening. "How unlike my father and older brother I was?" he asked, trying to keep the tightness out of his voice.

"Aye."

Edward didn't reply. He was fond of Old John, but he didn't want to hear this now, the repetition of everything he already knew and feared about himself. That he was unfit to be a duke, how much more suited to the role his father and brother had been, both large, loud, commanding…

"We used to say 'twas a shame you weren't firstborn."

Edward blinked. "What?"

Old John gave him a slow smile. "We used to say how you'd make a right good duke. That you was kind-hearted and loyal, that you looked out for people on the estate and were good to them when you could be, even as a little lad, that you were gentle with animals."

"But my father –"

"Was a bully. And your brother headstrong and thoughtless, God rest both their souls. Your father ruled with an iron fist inside and out and your brother barely thought about this place at all, only wanted the fun of being rich and handsome, didn't want to bother with the duties that come with being master of Atherton Park."

Edward stared at him, speechless.

"You'll be thinking I've overstepped my place, speaking so forthright. But I'm an old man, you can turn me out if you wish, I've served my time now. My daughter would take me in. But I thought, the young Duke don't know himself yet. He do be staring in the wrong looking glass. All he can see is his father and his brother and that's what he thinks a duke is. Perhaps it would ease his mind to know how others saw him. How his servants see him." He straightened up, looking Edward directly in the eye. "You're a good man, Your Grace. A right good duke. The past is gone now. You needn't fear the future, 'cos you'll do well. You'll have to learn a lot, but you've got a good heart. And no-one can do better than a man with a good heart."

Edward had a sudden powerful urge to weep, to throw his arms about Old John and thank him. The old man had gazed into his very soul and seen all his most secret fears and swept them away with his stable broom, to float away on the wind as though they were nothing but chaff, lighter than air rather than heavy burdens. He swallowed and held out his hand. "Thank you," he said, voice gruff. He did not trust himself to say more, but Old John's eyes creased into a smile and his hand was warm and firm in Edward's clasp.

"You're welcome, Your Grace. Now, will you be wanting to ride out?"

"No," said Edward. "No, I have something else I need to do."

Old John watched him go, striding from the yard, and nodded. "Good lad," he murmured to himself. "Good lad."

CHAPTER 11:
Letters

M AGGIE AWOKE BEFORE DAWN ON WEDNESDAY morning and lay staring at the ceiling. Today was the day, everyone knew it. Edward was to propose to Miss Belmont, before tomorrow's ball which would become a celebration of their engagement. By choosing Miss Belmont and paving the way for an heir, he would secure his freedom from Doctor Morrison and his mother, hopefully for good. And as soon as he took that step Maggie would no longer be needed, would most certainly no longer be wanted on the premises by the Duchess.

The grandfather clock in the hallway chimed and chimed again. She wanted, *needed* to speak with Edward. She needed him to know that she loved him. It would make no difference, of course, for he must still choose Miss Belmont. But she needed to tell him, to speak privately with him one last time before they were separated forever.

She pulled the bell for Jane, who arrived after a brief delay.

"Sorry, Miss, I had to wait for the hot water. There's so

many maids downstairs trying to bring up water to the bedrooms."

Maggie nodded without listening; she wanted to be dressed and able to leave the room as soon as possible.

"Your hair, Miss."

"As quick as you can, Jane."

As soon as she was finished Maggie hurried down one floor and along the corridor until she came to the ducal suites, one for the Duchess, one newly made over for Edward. She knocked on Edward's door. No answer.

"Miss Seton?" Bartholomew the footman stood a few paces away, outside the Duchess' suite. "Her Grace wishes to see you."

Maggie would have liked to refuse but there was no way to manage that under Bartholomew's gaze. He knocked. Summoned to enter, she did so and went into the Duchess' rooms.

Matching Edward's ducal suite, there was a large bedroom with blue wallpaper printed with gold pagodas, a dressing room, a smaller room off to the side with a lavish copper bath and a green and gold private drawing room with a desk, at which the Duchess, already fully dressed, was sitting.

"Come, Margaret," she called.

Maggie walked through the rooms until she was in the drawing room and stood in front of the Duchess.

"Be seated."

She sat on the edge of a stiff chair.

The Duchess leant forward. "I wanted to tell you that Edward is to be married."

Maggie's stomach lurched. She thought she might vomit

all over the thick blue carpet beneath her feet. It was too late. He had proposed and Miss Belmont would be his wife. Lord and Lady Godwin would be delighted to have made such a fine match and the Duchess had achieved her goal. And Maggie was… nothing. *Unwanted*. Wanted by Edward, if only briefly, set aside when he had to choose between his feelings and his future.

"He has proposed?"

"Indeed. Your work is done." The Duchess gave Maggie something approaching a stiff smile. "I am… grateful to you, Margaret. You have guided Edward through a difficult social season, given his… affliction… and he is now to be married. To, I think we can agree, a suitable wife, who will not force him to socialise beyond his capacity, and who will prove undemanding."

Maggie said nothing.

The Duchess grew brisk. "And therefore, as your work is done, I owe you the sum upon which we agreed when you first came here." She drew a paper towards her and began to write. "One thousand pounds. My bank in London will honour this promissory note if you present it to them." On top of the paper, she placed a sealed envelope. "References. You will need them to find a position. They say that you have worked in my household as a senior housemaid, that you have been diligent and hardworking, and that I therefore recommend you to any future employer. You will find most doors will be open to you with such a recommendation. You may take whatever items you wish to continue using from your wardrobe, aside from the jewellery. The clothes were all made to fit you and will be unsuitable for Miss Belmont. You will also need money for travel to… wherever you wish to go." She opened a small drawer, took out a coin purse and counted out six large gold coins. "Six guineas."

Maggie stared at the money a lowly ranking maid of all work might make in a whole year, held out by a woman who would spend the same sum on the silk for a couple of dresses, before her modiste had even touched the fabric.

"Take it," said the Duchess, holding it out. "You will have need of ready money. Where will you go?"

"London," said Maggie, her mouth moving by itself, the word emerging without her knowledge or planning. And truly, where else could she go? What else did she know? She had been raised in London, the city was full of opportunities for maids, she would be able to find a position. Slowly, she picked up the promissory note, the envelope containing references and held out her hand, felt the heavy clink of coins as they tipped from the Duchess' hand into hers, the cold humiliation of payment for all she had done for Edward, the weighty return to her place in life, a nobody and nothing in this world, unwanted over and over again.

"I will call for the carriage. It will take you as far as The Golden Grouse, where you will be able to take the stagecoach to London." The Duchess glanced at the clock. "If you pack now, you will make the noon departure. There is one overnight stay at a coaching inn, so you will be in London by noon tomorrow."

"Where is Edward?"

"In the rose garden with Miss Belmont." The Duchess placed one cold hand over Maggie's trembling one. "You should not interrupt them just now. If you wish to leave a letter for Edward, I will see to it that he receives it."

Maggie swallowed. "Yes, Aunt… Your Grace."

"Goodbye, Margaret."

Her voice came out as a hoarse whisper. "Goodbye."

The Duchess stood and Maggie, as though attached to her, controlled by her, stood also, turned and made her way out of the room. She heard the door close behind her and trudged down the corridor and up the stairs to the Wisteria room, every step heavy. Once inside, she leaned against the door for a moment, unable to move further, mind whirling.

Keep Edward safe.

That was the only thought that settled, that she could hold onto. The last thing she could do for him. One dragging step at a time, she made her way into her dressing room and sat at the desk, thinking. Finally, she took up her pen and began a letter.

To Doctor Morrison

Sir,

Your services to our family are no longer required. Enclosed you will find a final payment. I will count on your discretion should you wish to remain a physician of good standing within my circle of influence.

Caroline Buckingham

Carefully, she studied and copied the Duchess' signature on the promissory note into the brief letter, then folded both into an envelope. The sum, perhaps a year's income for a successful physician to the wealthy, was large enough to permanently secure Doctor Morrison's silence and distance, she was sure of it. He would not want the Duchess to tell those within her vast circle of influence that he was a quack or a charlatan, thus ruining his reputation amongst the *ton* and its source of possible further patients. The Duchess' additional six guineas would be enough for now. Maggie would find a position as quickly as possible in London, perhaps in a household where she might hope to rise to a lady's maid or housekeeper one day.

She looked down at her pink muslin dress, a floating delicate thing embellished with tiny pink roses. Her hair was pinned in a manner that she had grown accustomed to and tiny pink rosebuds nestled in it. She gave a wry smile at it in the looking glass. The hair, the dress, they too were at a turning point with her now. Was another way possible?

A letter, written now and swiftly acted on, would see her become the Countess of Frampton. She would live in a castle only slightly less grand than Atherton Park and every day a maid would dress her and do her hair, a maid probably better born than herself, a girl who knew her own family and was of legitimate birth. And that girl would believe her mistress to be part of the *ton*, would believe it without question because it simply wasn't possible that a countess could have been a foundling, could have been brought up to go into service. Maggie would be Margaret forever, for no-one would know her old name or where she came from. She would live a lie for the rest of her life and in so doing would be in fear every day of someone finding out, of one question too many, of making a mistake being made that would cost her dearly.

Or.

She could marry Joseph.

She would never again wear such a dress; she would wear cottons and wools. She would dress herself and her hair would be pulled back in a simple bun, without any fussy ringlets or looped braids. She might enter service, if she could be sure of never been seen by anyone whom she had once dined with or met at a ball. Although perhaps they would not even see her. She could kneel in their library to stoke the fire, serve them tea and they would not see her at all; she would only be another servant to them, a pair of hands, a quiet voice, one of many who existed only to service their needs and desires. Perhaps she might stay at home instead, and bear Joseph's children. He was an elegant and experienced footman, he might even rise to butler one day, or house steward. She would be comfortably provided for. And Joseph would call her Maggie, he would know her origins and not reproach her for them. She could be honest with him; she would not live in fear of making a mistake which would expose her.

Both were good men, Lord Frampton even loved her, she was grateful that she did not have to weigh up riches against love, as so many of the women she had watched this past season must do, resigning themselves to a life of beautiful clothes and elegant coiffeurs and an empty heart.

If she chose to be with one of these men, she faced a choice between riches and honesty. A life of luxury and lies, or one of work and honesty. The women of the *ton* would not have hesitated. Countess of Frampton it was, then. Even Celine would direct her that way.

But. She did not love either man.

And she loved Edward.

It was no good pretending otherwise to herself. This love had existed before that first kiss, before their first waltz. It had been there before she ever stepped into the Atherton carriage at midnight. It had started, perhaps, that first time Edward smiled, that first time she felt the warmth of his skin against hers. She would not have known what it was, then. But she did now. And knowing it made the decision before her far easier.

She picked up the quill and opened the inkwell.

Dear Lord Frampton,

I am conscious of the great honour you did me in offering your hand in marriage. I thank you for your kindness and ask for your understanding in accepting my certain refusal, since my affections lie elsewhere. I hope that you will find a lady who will make you happy, as you deserve to be.

Yours,
Margaret Seton

Dear Joseph,

I must leave Atherton Park, but I shall always think of you with fondness and be grateful for the offer you made me. Please look after Edward, he will need you more than ever now. I hope that one day you will find a good woman to love and that she will bring you great happiness.

Your friend,
Maggie

There was one more letter to write, but she was not sure she could write it yet; already tears had risen to her eyes at the last two she had written. She would pack her chest before writing to Edward.

She glanced about her. What would be suitable for her new life? She gave a little laugh, although it sounded cheerless even to her own ears. Nothing. There was nothing in her lavish wardrobe suitable for the life she would be living. None of the silks, none of the evening gowns. The bonnets were absurdly too decorative, few if any of the shoes were sturdy enough… the riding outfits entirely unnecessary without a horse.

At last she chose, from the back of the press, the dresses Celine had made over for her in the early days of arriving at Atherton Park, two woollens, two cottons and one of the simplest summer muslins from her latest gowns. Half of her undergarments and only cotton stockings; silk would be ruined with regular use. A bonnet that might be called plain if its overly fanciful floral decorations were removed. Two aprons. Two pairs of boots and the very plainest indoor shoes she could find. A velvet reticule. A shawl, gloves and a dark blue wool pelisse with a fur collar to keep her warm in winter. It was still an ample wardrobe, one which would not disgrace a governess from a respectable family, while any maid could only dream of such good quality clothing. It would last her a few years before she needed to replace any of the items. Recalling that there was an old travelling trunk in the nursery, she went to fetch it. Once back in the room that had been hers these last months, she wiped the dust off it and carefully packed her selection, adding the coral necklace Edward had given her. She changed into travelling clothes, leaving some buttons undone for which she would need Celine's help. Round her neck she hung the necklace Edward had given her, the locket tucked into her stays, sitting between her breasts. If she appeared smart while travelling, she would likely be treated better than if she appeared to be a commonplace maid. Finally, she sat back down at her writing desk and wrote a letter, quickly and neatly.

Dear Edward,

I wish you all happiness in your marriage and life with Miss Belmont.

I have been well provided for and will think of you kindly always.

Yours,
Margaret

She folded it but did not place it in an envelope; there was no need. Lies, all of it, but this was the letter the Duchess would see, and it could contain nothing else, or it would never reach Edward's hand, of that she could be sure. So, lies it would have to be. No matter. Her true letter would reach him by safer means. She took a deep breath.

Dearest Edward,

I must call you dearest because you have become so very dear to me. That first day when I met you, when you shrank from any touch, afraid that I would torment you as so many had done before me, even then I felt something for you. I thought it was pity, but it was a bud that bloomed into something far more beautiful. Our days together have been joyful to me because I saw your true self emerge.

And oh, Edward, your true self is magnificent! I have seen you grow into yourself in every way. Your strength, your confidence, your kindness when you saw what power it could have in this world, these qualities are not something to be stamped out of a man.

Be bold, Edward. Be brave. You are everything a duke should be: kind, caring, loyal. You look after everyone who comes into your world, and it is wicked that those who should have cared for you the most caused you to doubt yourself, shut you away and lied to you until you could not tell what was true.

Doctor Morrison is gone for good. I have seen to it. It does not matter how, but know he will never darken your door again.

By the time you read this I will have gone. You do not need a companion any longer, indeed you never did at all, only someone who cared. You do not need to lie anymore. I was the lie, for a sane man does not need a nursemaid; you are the truth: you are the Duke of Buckingham and not just in name. Claim what is yours, Edward, believe that it is yours and it will be.

Do not fear for me, I have been provided for and I will be safe. But I am glad your mother has decreed that I should not stay to watch you marry Miss Belmont. My heart would break. I will strive to be happy for you if I know you are truly happy with her.

She is a good person; I am sure she will make you a kindly wife if you do not let her come under your mother's influence. Keep her close and loyal to you and I believe she will come to love you as I do.

I must go now. Goodbye, Edward. Not a day shall pass when I do not remember you in my thoughts and dreams. In them, you will be everything you deserve to be, and everything I know you are: happy, strong and your own man.

I will always love you. I will always be yours.
Maggie

This she placed in an envelope and sealed, then rang for Celine, who stared at Maggie's packed trunk, her outdoor clothes.

"What are you doing?"

"I am leaving, on the Duchess' instructions. The carriage will arrive for me in a few moments, and I need your help."

"Does His Grace know you are leaving?"

"No, and he must not know. It will only unsettle him, and I cannot do that to him now he has made his choice, I cannot ruin his chance of happiness."

Celine's face showed what she thought of this, but she only nodded. "What do you need?"

"Help me with these buttons. Then I have a letter for Joseph and another which must be sent by the first post. Without anyone knowing."

Celine took the letter and looked at Doctor Morrison's name, gave a slow nod. "It shall be done."

"This is for the Duchess," she told Celine, handing her the folded note to Edward. She held out the envelope. "Will you give this to Edward directly, Celine? Without anyone else knowing?"

"You need to tell him what is in your heart," said Celine. "To his face."

"I cannot. He has chosen Miss Belmont –"

"Under duress!"

"Nonetheless, he chose her. And I… I have told him what I feel, but in a letter which he can discard, if he wishes, so that he does not have to look me in the eye and say he has changed his mind, that he does not care for me. Or that he does, but has chosen Miss Belmont because that is what a duke must do."

"And if he chooses you? Where is he to find you?"

Maggie shook her head. "It is better if he does not search for me. He has made his choice." She hesitated. "I will write to you when I am settled. If – if he is locked away again, send word to me."

Celine stood silent for a moment, then she buttoned Maggie's dress and pulled the bell to summon a footman. Within moments, Bartholomew appeared.

"Yes, Miss?"

"Miss Seton's trunk needs carrying down. You will accompany her on the first stage of her journey to The Golden Grouse."

"Yes, Duval. Shall I take it now, Miss?"

Maggie looked round the room for one last time. She would never again sleep in such a room, instead she would clean it, make the bed, lay out another woman's dresses and toiletries if she was lucky. "Yes," she managed at last. "Thank you, Bartholomew."

Bartholomew shouldered the trunk and left the room, Celine turned to follow him, but Maggie caught her arm.

"Celine?"

"Yes?"

Maggie embraced her. "Thank you. For everything."

Celine's arms came round her back in a warm embrace. "I am sorry to see you go," she said, voice muffled. "I hoped…"

Maggie pulled away, her eyes glistening, her heart thudding painfully in her chest. "So did I," she said. "But it was not to be. I know my place. I have done everything I can for Edward, and now he has chosen a life, a path forward. I need to step out of his way."

Down the staircase one last time, past the grand portraits, past the gilded plasterwork and along the thick carpets, onto the polished wooden floors. A breath of cool air reached her as Bartholomew held the door for her and she stepped out onto the cold hard stone of the steps, felt the crunch of gravel under her feet and climbed into the carriage. She settled herself, then looked out at Celine's anxious face.

"Write to me to tell me you are safely settled," said Celine, one hand on the windowsill of the carriage.

Maggie nodded, unable to speak and the carriage rolled forward, swept round the gravel driveway and headed down the avenue of trees towards the main gates.

The bustling coaching yard of The Golden Grouse greeted Maggie as she stepped out of the safety and comfort of the carriage. The footman set down her pitifully small trunk and bowed to her.

"Goodbye, Bartholomew."

"Goodbye, Miss." He hesitated, then said, in a rush, "Sorry you're not staying at the Park, Miss. We – we all thought you was a – a good influence." He paused, shocked at his daring, then added, "Pardon for speaking out of turn, Miss. I wish you well."

Tears stung her eyes, and she opened them wider so that they would not fall and embarrass them both. "Thank you, Bartholomew. I was very happy there and will think kindly of you all." She swallowed, but could not help adding, "Look after His Grace, he is a good man."

He nodded earnestly. "He is, Miss. I'm proud to serve him."

She patted his arm, touched. "Thank you."

He bowed again and returned to his place on the carriage. The coachman nodded, and the Buckingham carriage moved swiftly out of the yard. Maggie watched it go, her last glimpse of the family crest, the bulrush and acorn, held by the ducal coronet. The dark blue exterior disappearing from view.

"Are you waiting for someone, Miss?"

Startled from her thoughts, Maggie realised the inn porter was speaking to her. "Yes," she said hastily. "The stagecoach. I am travelling to London."

"It'll be along in half an hour, Miss, I'll see you on it safely. Inside or outside?" he added, looking over her clothes with a frown. She had arrived in the Buckingham carriage, a footman had bowed to her, she was too well dressed to be a common maid, but her small battered trunk, a woman alone without a companion, let alone taking a stagecoach, meant she could not be high ranking. Perhaps he thought her a governess or similar, well-bred but fallen on hard times.

"Outside," said Maggie. It would be cheaper, and she must think carefully about how she spent her money. There would be no private carriages, no grand London homes to stay in. But it was a sunny day; the outside of the stagecoach would not be too terrible.

She waited nervously for the stagecoach to arrive. Mail coaches came and went, even the post chaise, faster and more expensive, but, finally, the stagecoach came into view, the interior already full, four people on the outside seats, all men.

Maggie's trunk was swiftly thrown up and lashed into place, before she was helped aboard, climbing up and trying to make herself safe, tucking her skirts tightly about her and getting a firm grip on the railing surrounding her, as well as keeping one hand on her trunk.

The driver cracked his whip and the coach pulled out of the yard, gathering speed. Maggie clutched at her bonnet which was threatening to fly away should the ribbons tying it come undone. This was a far cry from the comfort in which the Athertons travelled, in their private carriage, well-sprung and upholstered, with blankets and footwarmers in the winter, chilled drinks and open windows in the summer for a gentle breeze without any fear of bonnets being lost or the risk of falling from a perilous seat, their servants hurrying ahead at every stage to prepare meals and additional comforts for them as they arrived at each inn along the way. Her new life would be a world away from that which she had known for this last year.

Edward returned to the house unable to hide a smile on his face. He paused for a moment outside Maggie's room, but it was still so early, he did not want to wake her. Well, no, that was a lie, he grinned to himself. He very much wanted to wake her. The idea of her lying soft and warm in her bed, of kneeling by her and stroking her unbound hair, touching her cheek…

That would all come later, he promised himself. He had things to do. He knew every step he wanted to take now; his path was shining clear in front of him. He rang the bell and told Joseph he wanted breakfast in his room to avoid making tedious conversation with the guests who would shortly descend to the dining room. There was only one person to whom he owed an explanation and an apology and that was Miss Belmont. He must put things right with her before he spoke to Maggie, but it would not take long. Hopefully, she would understand; she had a gentle heart, and he would be honest with her. No more lies. No more pretending.

He ate heartily, then washed and allowed Joseph to re-dress him in a more fitting manner. At ten, he made his way to the drawing room where he asked Miss Belmont into the rose garden, causing Lady Godwin to flutter her eyelashes at him as though she were the one being courted.

Outside among the roses he led her to a little bench behind a tall hedge and waited until she had taken a seat. He remained standing, aware that he could not be observed from the windows of the house, where no doubt their curious guests would even now be trying to spot them.

"Miss Belmont," he began. It would be hard to say what he must, but he was done with lying and pretence.

"Your Grace, may I speak first?"

"Of course," he said, taken aback by the mouselike girl having the boldness to interrupt him.

"I know what you are about to say and… I beg you will not say it."

He stared at her. In all their conversations together, she had always acquiesced to anything he said, to the point where he had wondered if she had any opinions of her own at all. He took a moment to recover. "I have been… strongly encouraged –"

"By my parents. By your mother. Not by me." Her eyes brimmed with tears.

He put out a hand and touched hers. "Miss Belmont, I brought you here to…"

"No."

He stared at her.

"No, Your Grace. I will not marry you."

He gave a little laugh, still surprised by her. "I was going to beg your forgiveness for *not* asking you to marry me."

For a moment they both stared at each other. Then she gave a small smile and indicated the bench. "Will you sit with me, Your Grace? I think perhaps it is time we spoke plainly."

He sat beside her. There was something different about her, he thought. Her voice was stronger, she seemed certain of herself.

"You love someone else?" she asked.

"Yes," he said. The honesty of it brought a smile to his face.

"So do I," she said.

"Then why were you so much thrust upon me?"

"I could ask the same of you," she said.

"The woman I love is…" He stopped, not wanting to lie, not wanting to tell the whole truth.

"Unexpected?" she asked, with a small smile.

He smiled back at her. "Yes. You could say that. And yours?"

"The same," she said.

"Will my lack of a proposal be difficult for you?"

She made a little face. "It will cause disappointment for a little while, no doubt. They so badly wanted me to be a duchess."

"I am sorry. I should have known my own mind sooner."

She touched his hand lightly. "It can take a while to know our own true minds."

"I… I am sorry we did not speak like this sooner. I had thought you…"

"A mouse?" She smiled at his awkward expression. "I know everyone calls me that."

He nodded. "I am beginning to see you in a new light, Miss Belmont. I think I like you better now that I hear you speak your mind."

"Are you about to propose to me after all, Your Grace?"

He laughed. "No. But I would like to ask you to be my friend."

She held out her hand. "I would like that."

He shook it. "Will you call me Edward?"

"Only if you will call me Elizabeth."

"I hope you will truly think of me as a friend," he said, standing.

She nodded. "I look forward to meeting your bride, although I think I can guess who she might be."

He looked down at her. "Thank you. I hope to welcome you as a guest here again, when you have secured your own love match."

She took his arm. "I will hold you to that, Edward."

He escorted her back to her parents with a bow, while they immediately dragged her to a private room to be told everything that had occurred.

It was time to go to Maggie. Edward called for Joseph while he opened the drawer of his desk and took out a small leather box. While Joseph helped him out of his boots and into shoes, Edward twitched with impatience. In only a few moments, his happiness would be secured.

There was a sharp knock at the door.

"Enter," called Edward, but the door was already open, his mother framed in the doorway.

"I need to speak with you. Joseph, you may leave."

"Please do not command my servants when I am in the room," said Edward. "I will dismiss my valet when I see fit."

The Duchess' eyes opened wide in shock.

Joseph looked at Edward.

"Thank you, Joseph, you may leave us," said Edward with exaggerated courtesy.

As soon as the door closed the Duchess made her way across the room. "You need to propose."

"I beg your pardon?"

"Do not play the fool with me, Edward. You know full well that tomorrow's ball is planned as an engagement celebration. Therefore, you need to propose. Now. All our guests are expecting it. Lord and Lady Godwin are expecting it."

"I cannot propose to Miss Belmont."

"What on earth are you talking about?"

"I do not love her."

"Love is not necessary."

"Perhaps not to you. It is to me."

The Duchess fixed him with an icy glare. Edward met her gaze squarely. To his surprise, the conversation he had been dreading was turning out to be almost a thrill. The relief of speaking his mind, of *knowing* his mind and being certain of it, of feeling confident in the choices he was making, was like sunshine streaming in through him, the warmth of it deep within him. "I absolutely will not live my future life without love. Too much of my past has been spent without it to forgo it any longer."

"And whom do you propose to marry?"

Edward smiled. "That is none of your business."

"It is most certainly my business, I —"

Edward held up one hand and the Duchess, shocked, fell silent. "I am the Duke of Buckingham. I am of age. My choice of wife is not your business, Mama. I have done you the courtesy of informing you that I will not be marrying Miss Belmont and I have explained this to her also. I will inform you of my bride-to-be's name when she has accepted me."

He made to leave the room, but she spoke. "It had better not be Margaret."

He turned and surveyed her with a cold expression. "And why is that, Mama? Be careful how you respond."

"She has already gone."

"Gone? Gone where?"

"I do not know."

He crossed the room in two strides, his face very close to hers, voice low and angry. "Where did she go?"

She swallowed. "London, I believe."

"London? When did she leave?"

She could not meet his eyes. "I gave her the carriage as far as The Golden Grouse. After that she was going to take the midday stagecoach."

"*When?*"

"This morning, about ten. While you were in the Rose Garden with Miss Belmont."

He stared at her in horror. "But that was more than two hours ago."

"She chose to go."

He gave a half-laugh. "I do not believe you. She would not have left me without saying goodbye. She would not have left at all, had she not thought –" He stopped. "What did you tell her?"

She stood silent before him.

He put his face close to hers, the words coming out through his teeth. "What did you say to her?"

"I said you had proposed to Miss Belmont."

He groaned. "How could you? How could you let Maggie think that I did not care for her, that I had chosen Miss Belmont?"

"Well, she is gone. She took the money I promised her and went."

"You paid her off, so that she would leave?"

"She believed you were going to be married to Miss Belmont, her work was done." She put a hand on his arm. "You believe you love her, Edward, but she is not a lady. She is a maid, a foundling, a nobody. She has no family. You could not possibly marry her. It is better for you – for her – for us all – if she goes. She has money, she has references, she –"

"You gave her references and money. You did what you needed to do to get rid of her, in other words."

"She took them. What does that tell you about her,

Edward? That she saw caring for you as a job. A task. Which she had fulfilled." She handed him the note Maggie had written. "Here, see for yourself."

He glanced down at the note and shook his head. "Unsealed? Meant for your eyes rather than mine?"

"She claimed what was owed to her and left at once, understanding there was nothing else here for her."

The urge to strike her rose up in him, such was the rage he felt. But that was his father's way, not his. He would not allow the baser side of his blood to take over, he would stay true to his own path. He stepped away from her and pulled the bell, summoning Joseph, who, judging by the alacrity of his response, had been hovering outside the door.

"Have my horse brought round immediately."

"Yes, Your Grace."

"If the stagecoach left at midday, she can only have travelled four or five miles beyond the inn so far. On Merlin, I can catch her up within half an hour."

"Edward!"

"Yes?"

"I forbid this!"

Edward laughed out loud. "It is too late for forbidding, Mama."

And he was gone, leaving the Duchess standing alone, a grim look on her face before she pulled the bell and said to the footman who appeared, "Our fastest carriage, at once."

CHAPTER 12:
The Duke of Buckingham

THE STAGECOACH ROCKED ALONG FOR MILE AFTER mile and already Maggie regretted her frugality in purchasing an outside ticket, for the sun was hot and the road dusty, so that she was already too warm and half-choked. It would be a different life now, she realised, but she could cling to one thought at least. She had watched Edward grow in strength and confidence and now that she had sent Doctor Morrison about his business, she could only hope that Elizabeth would be a good wife to Edward and that he would be happy. Still, she could not help the tears that trickled down her cheeks. She would never see him again. She tried to pay attention to the farms and pasturing animals they passed by, while thinking through her plans.

Once in London, she must find lodgings and work. Perhaps she could return to the Foundling Hospital, although now that she had left its confines and seen something of the world, she shuddered at the thought of its limited enclosure. She had the Duchess' references. It should not be hard to find employment as a maid in a respectable and affluent household, where she might in time rise to become a housekeeper. It would be a hard-working life, but she was not afraid of that, only of the loneliness she felt now on leaving Edward and surely that pain would subside? Surely it would. She let go of the rail to wipe away a tear, reluctant to draw unwanted attention.

"Watch out, driver," called one of the passengers who was facing backwards. "You've a fast rider behind you. I think he wants the road."

The driver grumbled but moved the stagecoach a few feet to the left. Maggie could hear the heavy sound of a galloping horse behind them growing closer, and turned to see who could have such urgent business.

Edward! He was urging on Merlin, his face fierce with intent, his eyes scanning the stagecoach and lighting up at the sight of her.

"Stop the coach!" she cried.

"This ain't your private carriage, miss," snorted the driver. "This here's a public stagecoach and if you –"

"Stop the coach!" roared Edward from alongside them and, startled, the driver reined in the horses and the stagecoach rumbled to a stop. Edward leapt down from Merlin and strode to Maggie's side. He held up his hand to her.

"Come down, Maggie," he said, his voice commanding.

"Is this gentleman known to you, miss?" inquired one of her fellow passengers.

"I – yes," said Maggie, her hand reaching Edward's and clambering down from the side of the stagecoach to the ground, where Edward crushed her into his arms.

"Thank God," he ground out. "I thought I'd lost you."

"Sir," said the driver, regaining his dignity as the occupants of the coach stared at Edward and Maggie embracing. "Are you related to this young lady? Because if not –"

Edward let go of Maggie and turned to face the driver. "I am the Duke of Buckingham," he said. "And this young lady is my betrothed. Have your man lift down her belongings. She will be returning home in my private carriage."

"Yes, Your Grace," grovelled the man.

Maggie's belongings were quickly lifted down.

"Drive on," said Edward.

Still full of staring travellers, the stagecoach rumbled away, leaving Edward and Maggie, Merlin and Maggie's trunk alone by the side of the road.

"You read my letter."

He shook his head. "There was no time for letters. As soon as my mother confessed that she had lied to you and turned you out I had to come after you. What did you write?"

She shook her head. "It does not matter."

He touched her cheek. "I should have told you back in March that I loved you, as soon as I realised it myself, that first night at Almack's. I did not have the courage; I was afraid it would lead to being locked away. At the masquerade, I could not contain my feelings, they burst out of me, but afterwards… I am ashamed that I did not fight for you."

"You had a lot to lose," she said quietly.

"And I nearly lost you," he said. "I waited too long and almost lost you, I will not risk that again." He felt in his pocket and pulled out a little leather box, which he opened. In it sat a magnificent sapphire ring set in gold. "I have been carrying this betrothal gift with me for weeks. Will you do me the honour of becoming my wife, Maggie?"

She gasped, touched the ring with one finger, then looked up at him. "It is the colour of your eyes," she whispered.

"My love. Say yes."

It was impossible. It would not be allowed. "Yes."

He slipped the ring onto her finger, before cupping her face in his hands, kissing her lightly, then with more passion. "We will marry at once."

"Are we to run away together?"

He shook his head, serious. "No. I will not run away; I will not go to Gretna Green or hide you as though you are someone to be ashamed of. I love you. We will be married at Atherton Park by special license tomorrow morning, and the ball tomorrow evening will be our celebration."

She stared at him.

"If that plan meets with your approval?" he added.

"I think I am dreaming," she said wonderingly.

"You are not dreaming. Shall I prove it to you?"

Her lips parted. "Yes."

He lowered his face to hers again but the sound of a carriage approaching made them both look up. The Atherton carriage came racing towards them, the four horses sweating as the driver whipped them on, then, seeing them, suddenly slowed, coming to a stop a few feet away. The footman leapt down, opened the carriage door and lowered its steps to reveal the Duchess, her expression wrathful as she stepped out.

"Drive to that tree," she hissed to the driver, indicating a large oak some way further down the road so that they might not be heard.

"I am glad you have found us, Mother," said Edward pleasantly. "Otherwise, Maggie would have had to ride Merlin back to the inn to wait for me to summon a carriage for her."

"You are supposed to be on your way to London by now," said the Duchess to Maggie, ignoring him.

"She was indeed," said Edward. "A good thing I found her, as we are to be married."

"You cannot even consider such a thing," spat the Duchess. "She is nothing but a nursemaid." She turned to Maggie. "You are not even from a respectable family. You are an orphan, from goodness knows what sort of background. Know your place!"

Edward opened his mouth, but Maggie put her hand on his arm. She took a long, slow breath, Matron's "know your place" echoing from her past, and met the Duchess' furious gaze. "I know my worth. I know that I am wanted. My *place* is by Edward's side as his wife."

"You cannot possibly think –" began the Duchess.

"But she can," interrupted Edward. "I have asked Maggie to marry me, and she has said yes. She will be my wife, and the Duchess of Buckingham. And you, Mama, with the greatest respect, will become the Dowager Duchess, and you will move into the Dower House as soon as we are wed. And you will treat Maggie with the respect she deserves and stay out of our affairs, unless you can learn to be civil."

The Duchess stood silent for a moment, so silent that Maggie wondered whether she was going to speak at all. Then a bitter smile spread over her face as she addressed Maggie.

"You played a good game," she said, her voice tight with anger.

Maggie lifted her chin. "It was never a game to me," she said. "It was never a game because I cared for Edward and would have done anything to make him happy."

"And do you think the *ton* will accept an orphan from the

Foundling Hospital, no doubt a bastard into the bargain, as the Duchess of Buckingham? You will never be received anywhere."

Maggie couldn't help it, she laughed out loud. "But I am not a bastard orphan from the Foundling Hospital," she said. "I am Margaret Seton, a distant cousin of the Duchess of Buckingham, taken into the Duchess' home out of the goodness of her heart after I lost both my unfortunate parents, and I have just made a love match with her son the Duke of Buckingham. It is a gloriously romantic story which will enchant all who hear it, and it is your game that has turned against you. If you say otherwise, if you tell the *ton* who I really am, the scandal will reflect on you. *You* will never be received anywhere. A mother who locked up her son when there was nothing wrong with him that could not have been cured by stopping his father bullying him. A woman who lied about his wellbeing to try and marry him off to an unsuspecting respectable family, prepared to allow his supposed madness to taint their bloodline? Who passed off a bastard-born orphan maid as her cousin to avoid any suspicion as to her son's suitability for marriage, all so that she could cling to the estate and title, the wealth, she so much enjoys? I cannot *imagine* what fun the scandalmongers would have with that, Your Grace."

There was silence for a moment, before Edward spoke. "We have a wedding to arrange, so we must return to Atherton Park at once. Mama, Maggie will go in the carriage with you. You may either be civil to her or say nothing at all. I will know if you are uncivil." He turned to Maggie and took her hand, kissed it and led her to the carriage, where the footman stood to attention as she climbed in.

Edward stepped aside as his mother was assisted by the footman, who closed the door behind her. Edward looked in at the window. "I will see you at home, Maggie," he said gently, then glanced at his mother. "Not an uncivil word," he reminded her.

Maggie watched as he swung into Merlin's saddle and rode away, back towards Atherton Park, while the carriage was slowly turned around, to follow him.

When he was out of sight Maggie sat back in the seat and looked at the Duchess.

"I will marry him," she said. "It is not for the money or the title or any of those things that matter to you. It is because I love him. I loved him before I even came here, when he was a nobody and we were happy together in Ivy Cottage. You will not believe that, of course, but it is true."

The Duchess met her gaze with a stony glare.

"Very well," said Maggie. "Then we will not speak until you are ready. Whenever that day comes."

When they arrived at Atherton Park, Edward took Maggie by the hand.

"We have things to arrange, Mama," he told the Duchess as she emerged from her carriage. "I will see you tomorrow morning in chapel for our wedding."

"You cannot marry tomorrow. You would need –"

"A special license, I know," said Edward, finishing her sentence. "I have one. It is one of the last things I did before I left London. I did not know if I could find the courage to use it, but now I am glad I did. We will be married at eight o'clock tomorrow morning. Joseph will take the license to the vicar this afternoon and inform him of my intentions." He gave a little laugh. "It is a good thing she is of age and that you had her registered as living in this parish under the name you invented for her, mother," he said. "You made my task that much easier."

They left her standing on the driveway, her face pale.

Maggie expected Edward to lead the way upstairs, but instead he walked briskly to the end of the hallway, still holding her hand, then opened a door which led downstairs, into the kitchens.

"What are we doing?"

"Giving orders for tomorrow, of course," said Edward cheerfully.

"Aren't you supposed to ring when you want to see a servant?"

"Why stand on ceremony? I prefer to do things my way."

She giggled. "I scarcely recognise you. Charging about telling people what to do."

He grinned at her. "I'm a changed man."

"And what miracle brought that about?"

He stopped at once and came back up a step so that he could put his hands on either side of her face. "You did, of course. You are the miracle in my life. You have taken a broken man and put the pieces back together. You took a poor wretch and turned him into a duke."

"While you took a poor foundling maid and turned her into a lady?"

He shook his head. "You were always a lady. You are a greater lady than half the *ton* will ever be." He kissed her, a soft kiss at first which became more passionate, his hands leaving her face and clasping her waist, drawing her to himself, then broke away from her. "If I kiss you for one more moment I will forget myself and any right to be called a gentleman. Come," and he took her hand again and guided her down the stairs into the kitchen, where a scullery maid gasped at the sight of them and hid behind a door.

"Mrs Barton?" he called out.

Mrs Barton came towards them, surprised. "Your Grace! What are you doing here?"

"I have a task for you, Mrs Barton. I know you can work marvels, but I'm afraid it will be a great bother."

"Anything for you, Your Grace," she smiled.

"I am to be married tomorrow. To Miss Seton."

The cook's eyes grew round for a moment, before crinkling into a deep smile. "Ah Your Grace, that does make me happy to hear. Congratulations to you, and Miss Seton," she added with a bobbing curtsey to Maggie. "He couldn't have done better."

"Thank you," said Maggie, suddenly shy.

"As it is our wedding tomorrow, Mrs Barton, I shall require a wedding breakfast of you. Our guests are all here, and the ball and dinner are already in the hands of Monsieur Cerf. But breakfast tomorrow will come after chapel, where we will be wed. So I need you to prepare your very finest breakfast, for we shall be both happy and hungry. I shall trust you with the bride cake."

"It shall be perfect," promised Mrs Barton. "And I shall be right pleased to make it so."

Edward kissed her cheek. "I know it will be most excellent. The servants are to have cakes and wine the evening after the ball, to drink our health," he called over his shoulder as he pulled Maggie by the hand back up the stairs.

Maggie glanced back to see Mrs Barton's cheeks flushed pink and heard her calling for all her kitchen maids as they neared the top of the stairs, for no doubt they would now have to bake all afternoon and well into the night, though she did not think Mrs Barton would mind, excited as she was for Edward's future happiness. Seeing Edward give instructions, without deferring constantly to his mother, confirmed to her how far he had come from when she first met him.

"If you are making arrangements for our wedding breakfast, I think I should speak to Celine about a wedding gown," she said.

Edward pulled her close to him. "I would marry you in the clothes you are in now," he said.

"Celine would die of shame."

He laughed. "Very well. Go to Celine. Rest after all that has happened today. I will have a tray sent to your room. Tomorrow when I see you again you will be my bride. It has been a long day. We will say nothing to the guests till the wedding is done."

Celine was full of joy at the news but looked surprised at Maggie's choice of a wedding gown from those in her wardrobe.

"So simple?"

Maggie nodded.

"Then I will trim the bonnet with white roses for you and it will be done by morning."

Maggie spent the last few hours of the day in a daze in her room, ate the food sent to her and then went to bed, scarcely able to believe she would be married the next day.

Maggie woke at dawn and had to wait for Celine who appeared holding a fresh white muslin and a bonnet she had trimmed with white silk roses. She knelt at Maggie's feet, making a tiny adjustment to the embroidery on the hem of her dress.

"Joseph has said he will be leaving after the wedding," she said. "His Grace has given him a generous sum and his blessing."

"I hope you will not be leaving?"

"I'll stay with Her Grace when she moves to the Dower House. But I'll finish training Jane before I go, unless you want someone else? You can have anyone you want."

"No, I will keep Jane. I'd have you if I could, but I think you are too fond of the Duchess."

"I'd like to stay with her."

"I wish Edward's mother would be kinder to him, at least. I know she will always hate me; I will have to make my peace with it. But it hurts Edward to have such a cold mother. He cannot forgive her for standing by and doing nothing when his father bullied him, allowing him to be locked away as a lunatic when he was only afraid and hurt."

Celine said nothing.

"I know you have served her a long time," said Maggie. "You must see some good in her, I suppose. I struggle to see it, myself. But I am sorry she cannot be reconciled to the two of us being together, even if only because it makes Edward happy."

Celine sat back on her heels. "She was married very young," she said.

Maggie thought of the painting in the hall, the newly-wed Duchess, barely a grown woman, coquettish and pretty in a magnificent dress.

Celine sighed as she bent to lace up Maggie's rose-coloured slippers. "She was one of the most desirable matches of her coming-out season, considered a great beauty. She could have married anyone she chose. There were men falling in love with her everywhere, and she received many proposals. But she was only a girl, believing in fairy tales. Here was an unmarried duke seeking a wife and she thought it was meant to be. The chance to become a duchess, one of only a handful in the kingdom, was too great a lure. She fancied herself in love and married him despite his reputation for being a rake, possessing a bad temper when he had been drinking."

Maggie sat down on the dressing chair, her face close to Celine.

"Was he unkind to her as well as Edward?"

Celine nodded. "He used his fists on her more than once. She lost a baby girl she was carrying after a beating he gave her. When Edward was little, she tried to stand up for him, but it only made his father worse and in the end she withdrew. She spent most of her days in her rooms, left the boys to the care of a nursemaid and allowed the Duke to do as he wished. They never ate together unless there was company. After the incident with Pigeon, the Duke said Edward must be mad and wanted him locked away and she said nothing, allowed him to hire Doctor Morrison and have him taken away."

"Her own child?"

"She cried all night the day he was taken," said Celine. "I was new here then."

Maggie tried to imagine the Duchess crying and failed.

"She said he would be safer under Doctor Morrison's care than here," said Celine.

Maggie thought of the pale, frightened young man she had first met scarce above a year ago and was unsure. But the Duchess would not have seen the treatments Edward had been subjected to, she would only have received reports saying that all was well. Perhaps she felt reassured that her delicate son was being taken good care of, far away from his father's harsh lessons.

"A mother does not give up a child without a reason," said Celine.

The ledgers at the Foundling Hospital agreed with her. In them were the tragic stories of women who had been abandoned by those who should have protected them; from families and friends to lovers and husbands, leaving them destitute and unable to care for their children. They gave them up only when they had lost all faith in themselves and the world around them, certain that by keeping them they would only visit greater suffering on them. Unable to bear the thought, they had instead turned to the only place that offered hope, left their children within its doors and taken away with them only abiding regret and sorrow, held close to their hearts for the rest of their unhappy lives. The pathetically worthless tokens left by some, who hoped one day to return and reclaim their child, had always been heart-breaking to Maggie, though perhaps worse were those who had left nothing at all, miserably certain of never being able to return.

Maggie nodded. "I will try to find a way to breach the gap between us," she said. "I am ready, now, I think."

"You must have a veil. Wait here."

Celine was back in a short while with a package that she unwrapped with care, disclosing a short but beautiful veil trimmed with delicate lace, which she draped over Maggie's bonnet, covering her face. "It was my mother's on her wedding day. She was a happy bride and wife."

Maggie hugged her. She had been afraid Celine would

bring out the Duchess' wedding veil from storage and she did not like the idea of something both overly grand and tainted with an unhappy marriage.

"And flowers," said Celine. "I have sent Jane for them."

Jane, eyes shining with excitement, arrived holding a bouquet of white roses mixed with pink sweet peas, whose fragrance filled the room.

The chapel was all but empty. Only the Duchess, Celine, Jane and Joseph were invited to be their witnesses, for Edward had shaken his head at the idea of inviting all their guests to attend.

"If I could have only Maggie and myself there, I would," he had said firmly and so it was that they stood together before the vicar and listened to his words echo around them, the scent of roses and sweet peas perfuming the cool morning air.

"Dearly beloved, we are gathered together here in the sight of God, and in the face of this congregation, to join together this man and this woman in holy matrimony, which is an honourable estate, instituted of God in the time of man's innocency…"

The vicar looked up. "Edward Robert John Atherton. Wilt thou have this woman to thy wedded wife, to live together after God's ordinance in the holy estate of matrimony? Wilt thou love her, comfort her, honour, and keep her in sickness and in health; and, forsaking all other, keep thee only unto her, so long as ye both shall live?

Edward's voice was full and confident, answering without hesitation. "I will."

"Margaret Seton. Wilt thou have this Man to thy wedded

Husband, to live together after God's ordinance in the holy estate of Matrimony? Wilt thou obey him, and serve him, love, honour, and keep him in sickness and in health; and, forsaking all other, keep thee only unto him, so long as ye both shall live?"

"I will." She tried to make her voice as confident as his, though it shook with emotion and Edward gently touched her hand with his.

They repeated their vows and Edward put a simple gold band onto her finger beside the sapphire and the vicar pronounced them husband and wife, before blessing them. When the register had been signed, they left the chapel together hand in hand.

"We will return shortly," said Edward to the vicar. "In the meantime, would you escort my mother to the wedding breakfast?"

"Certainly, Your Grace."

Hands clasped, Edward led Maggie out of the house and down towards the stables. Once they were out of sight of the others, he stopped and turned her to face him. "I have already spoken my vows to you, Maggie, but I must tell you again that I love you."

She gazed up into his blue eyes and saw only happiness there, reflecting her own. "Will you kiss me, husband?" she asked, and his lips touched hers in a kiss so gentle and loving that neither could doubt the other's feeling.

"Now come, I must show you to someone before our wedding breakfast," said Edward.

"Show me?"

"It is important," he said.

She followed him, curious, into the stableyard, where Old John was brushing down Merlin.

"Good morning, Old John," said Edward.

"Good morning, Your Grace, Miss Seton."

"Ah, there you are wrong, Old John. This is your new mistress, my newlywed wife, the Duchess of Buckingham," said Edward.

Old John put down the brush and came towards them, then touched his cap to Maggie. "Good morning, Your Grace," he said. "I wish you joy."

"Thank you, Old John," said Maggie and when she glanced at Edward his eyes had welled up. He held out his hand to Old John, who shook it.

Edward cleared his throat. "There will be a celebration for all the staff tomorrow. I've asked Mrs Barton to take good care of you all."

"Thank you, Your Grace. May God bless you."

"Thank you, Old John," said Edward. "Now I must take my bride to our wedding breakfast."

The guests arrived for breakfast in the drawing room, only to be told that it had been moved into the large dining room adjacent to the ballroom and when they arrived there were startled to see not only a more lavish spread than expected but also a white bride cake, decorated with fresh pink and cream roses.

"Come join us," called out Edward. "Celebrate the happy occasion of my marriage to Margaret."

There were some audible gasps as well as a choked-back laugh from Lady Fortescue, before the guests gathered themselves and congratulations began to flow, received with joyful smiles by Edward and Maggie and with forced dignity by the Dowager Duchess. The Godwins, Maggie realised, had already left, for there was no sign of them.

"I am sorry if Miss Belmont had her expectations dashed," she whispered to Edward during the breakfast.

"She is a sweet-natured woman; I hope she will find someone with whom she can be as happy as I am with you," said Edward.

She leant her head on his shoulder for a moment, revelling in the intimacy of the gesture in public.

Much of the rest of the day was taken up with polite conversation with their guests, before everyone retired to their rooms early to begin preparing for the ball.

"I will leave off your shift," said Celine, "We do not want it bulking out the dress, it will sit better this way."

She dressed Maggie, first in her longline corset, which cupped and lifted her breasts and came down as far as her waist, added a pink silk petticoat and tied her white silk stockings with ribbons, her white dancing slippers with rose-coloured ribbons. Finally, she drew the dress over Maggie's head, the pale pink silk bodice and its silk roses giving way to a white silk gauze skirt which, sitting over the pink silk below, took on a rosy shimmering glow when she moved. All over the gauze skirt were worked tiny rosy silk petals, as though they had fallen from the roses on her bodice.

"It is so beautiful," breathed Maggie.

"Wait until you have these," said Celine, turning to the two large leather boxes at her side, one square, one a long rectangle.

"What are they?"

"This," said Celine, gleaming with a secret, "is the Buckingham diamond *parure*."

"The what?"

"A *parure* is a set of jewels," explained Celine. "The Buckinghams have several, of course, but these are the Buckingham diamonds, and they are exquisite."

She lifted the lid of the box and Maggie gasped. Inside, laid out on black velvet, were a tiara, a necklace, two bracelets and a pair of earrings, all made of magnificent, glittering diamonds larger than she had ever seen.

"These are yours now," said Celine with satisfaction. "They are worn only by the Duchess of Buckingham. Some of the other sets are occasionally lent to a relative, but not these. Only you have the right to wear these now."

Carefully, she lifted each item and placed them on Maggie's head, around her neck and wrists, then finally inserted the earrings.

"I feel like a queen," murmured Maggie.

"One more thing."

"There is more?"

Celine opened the second box and lifted out three huge ostrich plumes, creamy white and soft, trembling in her hands. She slid each one into Maggie's hair and pinned them. "See, Your Grace," she said, and Maggie turned to the looking glass.

"I am beautiful," she managed at last, and her voice shook.

"You are," agreed Celine.

There was a knock at the door.

"Enter," called Maggie.

Edward stood in the doorway, in a dark blue silk that made his eyes a richer and deeper hue.

"You look so handsome," Maggie said, smiling.

But he also looked angry. "Leave us," he said to Celine. She curtseyed and closed the door behind her.

"Is – is something wrong?"

He crossed the space between them and pulled her to him so hard that she let out a cry. "How are you so beautiful?" he asked, one arm still holding her, the other hand cupping her face. "How?"

She tried to laugh but his mouth was on hers, his tongue already seeking hers, the kiss so passionate it left her breathless.

"Edward… they will be waiting for us downstairs."

"I do not care," he said. "They can wait."

His movements grew slower. He pulled out each of the three feathers in her hair, dropping them onto her dressing table. His lips brushed her shoulders while his fingers unbuttoned her bodice, allowing the silk and gauze dress to fall to the floor, exposing her corset beneath it and the delicate silk ribbon which gathered the fabric around her breasts.

"If I undo this ribbon…" he whispered and she gasped at the sharp tug he gave, loosening the gathers, so that her breasts, freed from their support, swelled forwards, the tip of a nipple appearing at the edge of the corset. He slid his fingers along the rim of the fabric, pulling at it until both her breasts, still lifted upwards by the corset beneath them, were now fully visible to him. Maggie gazed up at him, trembling at the desire in his eyes.

"I have dreamt of this moment," he murmured, one arm drawing her close to his body so that her bare breasts were pressed against the ridged woven silk of his waistcoat, one hand on her waist, unfastening the tie which still held her pink silk petticoat in place. The silk slipped down her thighs as it fell, leaving her dressed only in her corset, stockings and the

Buckingham diamonds. She nestled into his arms, touching his jaw, running her fingers through his hair.

"You cannot undress me further," she told him. "Or I will be late to the ball."

"I will take you as you are," he told her. "I have all of you that I need. I have your lips," and he kissed her, "I have your breasts," and he cupped one in his hand.

She closed her eyes, revelling in the touch of his hand, before opening them as he lowered her gently down onto the bed, so that she was sitting on the edge of it, while he knelt before her.

"Are you proposing to me again?" she whispered. "I have already said yes."

He put his hands on her thighs and moved them slowly down to the ribbons of her stockings as she leant forward, wanting something from him but not knowing what it was, only that she wanted him closer to her, to feel his body against hers as it had been a moment ago, he felt too far away now, kneeling before her.

He put his hands on her knees and slowly pushed them apart. "Say yes again," he demanded, his voice hoarse.

She did not know what she was saying yes to, only that she wanted everything that was happening. "Yes," she breathed and gasped as his tongue began to explore her. She fell back onto the silk coverlet, writhing under his touch while his hands gripped her thighs and buttocks, one hand reaching for him, wanting more and more but he stopped, standing over her at the foot of the bed undoing his breeches while she watched him, wide-eyed, then moved backwards up the bed so that he could join her on it, crawling up between her legs until he was pressed up against her.

"Yes," she whispered again, reaching up her arms to him, pulling him down onto her, feeling the full weight of him as he entered her, a whimper of pain escaping her lips.

He drew back. "I hurt you."

"Yes," she said again, but she was smiling. "I want it. All of it."

And they were lost in each other, entwined together in pain and growing pleasure until she cried out his name and her cry brought him to a shuddering release.

Afterwards he tried to help her dress, although it proceeded very slowly, as he kissed every part of her as he did so.

"Oh," she said, catching sight of herself in the looking glass as he did up the buttons at the back of her dress. "My dress is crumpled, and half my hair has come down. And your hair is all ruffled," she added, reaching out to ruffle it further. "Everyone will know what we have been doing."

He buried his face in her neck, laughing, kissing her. "You are beautiful, and I do not care that your clothes are crumpled. But I will send Celine to you so that you do not disgrace her, at least. Do I pass muster?"

She shook her head, laughing at him. "No! Your cravat is undone, and your hair is mussed, your breeches have been mis-buttoned and where even is your tailcoat? You must call for Joseph before anyone sees you." She picked up the ostrich feathers and brushed them across his face. "One of us at least must be seen at the ball and you can be dressed more quickly than I."

"I do not want to call for anyone," he said. "I want to stay here with you and do it all again."

She let go of the feathers and came to him, cupped his face in her hands. "Yes," she said. "Yes."

"Now?"

She laughed and kissed him, a long, lingering kiss. "After the ball. After we have danced the waltz together. We will do it all again and wake in one another's arms. Now go."

Celine's eyebrows raised to see Maggie half-dressed and rumpled when she had left her looking perfect, but she only smiled a secret smile and hurried to re-pin Maggie's hair, return the ostrich feathers to their place, straighten and smooth her gown.

"Thank you," said Maggie when she was done. "How do I look?"

"Glowing," said Celine. "And it is not my work that has done that to you."

Maggie giggled. "I am so happy, Celine," she said.

"I wish you joy," said Celine. "I know you will bring His Grace great happiness."

Maggie made her way to the ballroom, where Edward came to meet her at once, kissing her hand to applause and cheers, leading the opening dance with her, a graceful minuet.

"I think I should probably speak with some of our guests," he said, as the dance concluded. "But I shall be back for the waltz."

She watched him walk away, strong and handsome and… hers. The thought of what they had done together, that such pleasure could be theirs over and over again, real happiness lying within their grasp, was intoxicating.

"Congratulations and all that sort of thing," said Lady Fortescue, appearing by Maggie's side. "Bagging a duke in your first season, can't say fairer than that. Inside job, though. Some of the mamas will claim you had an unfair advantage," she added with a grin. "Now they'll have to pick the second-best on their lists."

Maggie grinned back. "I hope with Edward out of the way they might allow their daughters a say in who they marry, and perhaps allow them to marry for love."

"Hardly likely," Lady Fortescue sniffed. "Doesn't work that way round these parts, or are you new?"

Maggie couldn't help laughing. "I think I must be new."

"Ah well, you'll learn. Congratulations, Your Grace." Lady Fortescue offered a curtsey.

"Promise me you won't call me that," said Maggie. "I would prefer you call me Margaret."

"I think you'll find that's only for family and the most intimate of friends."

Maggie hooked her arm through Lady Fortescue's. "Then you must promise to be my most intimate friend," she said. "And right now, my intimate friend Honora needs to help me find an ice before I melt."

"Right you are," said Honora, steering her through the crowd. "Step this way, Margaret."

"And have you found someone yourself this season, Honora?"

"Hard to tell," said Honora, adroitly avoiding the dancing couples and guiding them to a table piled high with tiny glasses of shining colourful ices. "Let's just say there's a chance I've found what I was looking for."

"Mowatt?"

Honora laughed. "You haven't been paying enough attention these last few weeks," she said. "The uncle died and Mr Mowatt is now Lord Barrington, and engaged."

"Then I hope to meet whomever you have in mind, one day soon."

"I'll hold you to that," said Honora, waving her hand at the selection before them. "Lemon, rose or elderflower?"

As the evening progressed Maggie smiled graciously at the many congratulations she received and even responded when someone called her Your Grace rather than thinking they were speaking to Edward's mother, who was standing to one side, her face expressionless as she watched Maggie and Edward circulate.

Maggie made her way over, put out a hand and touched the Duchess' arm, noticing as she did so the stark contrast of the white and pink silken gauze of her dress against the near-black of the Duchess' purple silk.

The Duchess turned her head, face turned stony. "Yes?"

Maggie stepped closer to her, so that she could be heard, even at a murmur. "I hope you will find it in you to be glad for Edward."

"*Glad?* How can you –"

"Edward is marrying someone he loves and who loves him in return," interrupted Maggie. "I know on your wedding day you hoped for the same."

The Duchess' shoulders stiffened. "How dare you –"

"I am sorry your hopes were not met," said Maggie, her hand still on the Duchess' arm. "I am sorry your married life was spent in thrall to a man who was rough, and unkind and did not know how to love or care for you. Who modelled your first son in his image and made you doubt your second son, even though he was born in your image."

The Duchess stared at her, but she did not move away and, emboldened, Maggie took her hand.

"Edward is not mad. He never was. He was broken. As you would have been, had you not built a wall about yourself, a fortress to keep you safe. I am sorry you had to do that. I am sorry you felt you had to give up your son to keep him safe. I am sorry for all you have been through. Edward is mending now, you can see for yourself how he grows in strength, day by day, yet keeps his gentle nature. Perhaps you can begin to take down the walls of your fortress, one stone at a time and show some of your gentleness. I will help you, if you will let me."

"You have… said enough," said the Duchess, but her voice cracked. She had not withdrawn her hand.

"I do not want to be enemies," said Maggie. "I want a family. I have never had a family. I hope Edward and I will have many children. We will make our own family since we have so little between us. But I hope you will come to be a part of it. There will always be room for you." She pressed the Duchess' hand and felt the tiniest response, hardly there and yet there. "I must find Edward now," she said, letting go. "It will be the waltz soon. Excuse me, Aunt Caroline."

"Mama."

Maggie turned back. "Excuse me?"

The Duchess lifted her chin. Her eyes did not quite meet Maggie's. "You should call me Mama, now."

Maggie smiled. "Would that be the correct thing to do, do you think?"

The Duchess' eyes flickered to Maggie's and quickly away. "It would."

"Then please excuse me, Mama."

She walked away from the Duchess, feeling lighter with every step.

"I believe I have claimed this dance?" Edward appeared before her as the strains of the waltz began.

Maggie gazed up at him as their arms lifted together and their hands joined. "The waltz will always be yours, Your Grace."

He smiled down at her. "I will always be ready to claim it. To claim *you*, Your Grace." His hands tightened on her waist. The thought of what those hands had done to her only a short time ago, how and where they had touched her, made her breathless.

"I never knew before now what it was to be wanted," she said and saw his jaw clench for a moment at the thought of the unhappy pasts they had both suffered, but then he smiled. A radiant smile, full of confidence and joy, that made her heart fill with happiness.

"You are wanted, Maggie," he said, as he whirled her around the floor, her body pressed to his. "Trust me. Now and till the end of our days. You will always be wanted."

I hope you have enjoyed *Lady for a Season*. If you have, I would really appreciate it if you would leave a rating or brief review, so that new readers can find it. I read all reviews and am always grateful for your time in writing them and touched by your kind words. There will be more books in the Regency Outsiders standalone series to come very soon, indeed, you may already have met a few of the other Outsiders in these very pages…

Have you read my other series? Explore them on my website, www.MelissaAddey.com/books

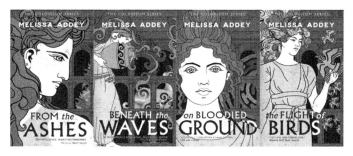

AUTHOR'S NOTE ON HISTORY

The title of Duke of Buckingham has come and gone over the years. It is currently extinct and did not exist during the time of this novel, so I have appropriated it for Edward. The Atherton family are entirely fictitious, as are all the characters.

People classed as 'lunatics' (which covered a very wide spectrum of mental health issues) from rich families were often kept privately somewhere under the care of a doctor, for fear of tarnishing the family's name and reputation. The various treatments Edward undergoes were all commonplace for the time. I have used direct quotes about treatment from practitioners of the time to replicate their style of speaking, as reported in L. Smith's very useful book, *Private Madhouses in England, 1640–1815* and S. Dickson's *Rotation therapy for maniacs, melancholics and idiots: theory, practice and perception in European medical and literary case histories* in History of Psychiatry (2017).

I first thought my storyline of a maid marrying a duke was fun, although thoroughly unlikely, but actually the second Duke of Buccleuch married his washerwoman, Sir Harry Fetherstonhaugh (a Baronet) married the dairymaid from his Uppark estate when he was seventy because he was enchanted by her singing (he sent her to Paris to be refined) and the famous Lady Emma Hamilton started life as a maid of all work and ended up married to Sir William Hamilton (she was also mistress to Sir Harry at Uppark in his younger days) before becoming the mistress of Admiral Nelson, who was made 1st Duke of Bronte. So not as unlikely as it might at first seem!

Ivy Cottage exists in Harbury, near Leamington Spa in Warwickshire, which was originally Leamington Priors before it became a spa town like Bath catering to rich invalids. In 1813 it was already well on the way to this status. I saw it during a book festival and chose it for the opening of the book, although the stream at the end of the garden is fictitious.

The illustration of Atherton Park is based on Castle Ashby in Northamptonshire, with a few building modifications of my own.

Silent Worship is the song that Maggie and Edward sing. The music is by Handel, although the lyrics were set to it in 1928, but it is so pretty that I wanted to use it (it also appears in one of the film versions of Jane Austen's *Emma*). I listened to a lot of Handel's music while writing *Lady for a Season*, as he was a committed benefactor of the Foundling Hospital from 1749, putting on benefit performances to raise money and interest. The two pieces of his music most associated with the Hospital are the *Foundling Hospital Anthem* and his oratorio *Messiah*.

My father Peter Lindley was a foundling and has written a memoir, *Looking for Billy,* about this experience and the effect it had on his life.

THANKS

Thank you to Ilina Simeonova for her beautiful photography and to Streetlight Graphics, who always have my back and make my life so easy.

Thank you to my beta readers for this book: Helen, Etain, Martin, Bernie, Susanne Dunlap (look out for her Regency novel coming soon!). Your comments and ideas are always insightful. Also, to the Regency Cook aka Paul Couchman for his help with dinner parties!

Thank you to my editor Debi Alper for patiently continuing to improve my craft.

Enormous thanks to the community and teachers at Regency Fiction Writers, who generously share their knowledge and made my research so much easier.

Andrew Macnair does beautiful digital drawings of old maps. I am grateful to him for the replica of the 1799 Horwood map of London. richardhorwoodmapoflondon.co.uk

My Regency makeover for Maggie was helped along the way by the wonderful Patrick at Lock & Co., who used a special measuring device on my head while telling me all about their history and Ben who very helpfully checked my historical details, as well as visits to perfume shop Floris, London's oldest pharmacy D.R. Harris, the shop fronts in Burlington Arcade and many other beautiful old shopping haunts still in existence in London.

Details about the Foundling Hospital and the letter given to foundlings when they left which I have quoted in full come from the fascinating book by Marthe Jocelyn, *A Home for Foundlings*, as well as the Hospital's own guidebook. Thank you to Tabitha who checked my numbers!

All errors and fictional choices are of course mine.

CURRENT AND FORTHCOMING BOOKS INCLUDE:

Historical Fiction
China: The Forbidden City series
The Consorts (novella, free on Amazon)
The Fragrant Concubine
The Garden of Perfect Brightness
The Cold Palace

Morocco: The Moroccan Empire series
The Cup (novella, free on my website)
A String of Silver Beads
None Such as She
Do Not Awaken Love

Rome: The Colosseum series
From the Ashes
Beneath the Waves
On Bloodied Ground
The Flight of Birds

England: The Regency Outsiders series
Lady for a Season
The Viscount's Pearl

Picture Books for Children

Kameko and the Monkey-King

Non-Fiction

The Storytelling Entrepreneur

Merchandise for Authors

The Happy Commuter

100 Things to Do while Breastfeeding

BIOGRAPHY

I mainly write historical fiction and have completed three series: *The Moroccan Empire*, set in 11th century Morocco and Spain, *The Forbidden City*, set in 18th century China and *The Colosseum*, set in Ancient Rome. For more information on me and my books, visit my website www.melissaaddey.com

    I have been the Leverhulme Trust Writer in Residence at the British Library and won the inaugural Novel London and Page to Podcast awards. I have a PhD in Creative Writing from the University of Surrey, run regular workshops at the British Library and speak at various writing festivals during the year. I live in London with my husband and two children.

Printed in Great Britain
by Amazon

55021187R00202